EVERYMAN, I will go with thee,

and be thy guide,

In thy most need to go by thy side

EDGAR ALLAN POE

Born in Boston, U.S.A., on 19th January 1809.
Brought up as an adopted child; educated in
England and Virginia. Abandoned a business
career; was dismissed for neglect of duty from
West Point Academy (1831), and thereafter
supported himself by writing. Most of his life
was spent in poverty, and he died on 8th
October 1849 in Baltimore.

EDGAR ALLAN POE

Poems and Essays

INTRODUCTION BY
ANDREW LANG

DENT: LONDON, MELBOURNE AND TORONTO
EVERYMAN'S LIBRARY
DUTTON : NEW YORK

All rights reserved
Printed in Great Britain
by Billing & Sons Ltd, Guildford, Surrey
for
J. M. DENT & SONS LTD
Aldine House · Welbeck Street · London
This edition was first published in
Everyman's Library in 1927
Last reprinted 1979

Published in the U.S.A. by arrangement
with J. M. Dent & Sons Ltd

No. 791   Hardback ISBN 0 460 00791 2
No. 1791   Paperback ISBN 0 460 01791 8

INTRODUCTION

THE life of Edgar Allan Poe is, fortunately, a subject
that but little concerns readers of his poetry. As far
as the events of his career illustrate the enigmatic
character of his genius, we have, perhaps, a right
to inquire about them. We may imagine that from
parents of semi-Celtic stock and artistic profession
he inherited his genius, and that his pride and per-
versity came from his training by a wealthy inju-
dicious foster-father. But the legend or myth of his
errors and misfortunes, so often told and retold
by posthumous malice or by too fond indulgence, is
really no affair of ours. Poe's career is still a topic
that excites controversy in America. The spite of
his first biographer, Griswold, was begetting a natural
reaction when Mr. Ingram published his *Edgar
Allan Poe* [1] and unwittingly stirred up the hatred
of surviving scandalmongers. Men are alive who
knew Poe, and who suffered from his scornful criti-
cism. To find their dead enemy defended by an
Englishman excited their spleen, and, for other
reasons, fairer American critics were not conciliated.
The defence of this luckless man of genius is not,
and cannot be, a wholly successful one. The viler
charges and insinuations of Griswold may be refuted,
but no skill can make Poe seem an amiable or an
ascetic human being. It is natural that admirers
of a poet's genius should wish to think well of the
man, should wish to see him among the honourable,
gentle, kindly, and wise. But Poe wanted as a man
what his poetry also lacks ; he wanted humanity.
Among the passions, he was familiar with pride, and
with the intolerable regret, the life-long *desiderium*

[1] London, 1880.

which, having lost the solitary object of its love, can find among living men and women no more than the objects of passing sentiment and affectionate caprice. Love, as the poets have known it, from Catullus to Coventry Patmore, love, whether wild and feverish or stable and domestic, appears to have been to him unknown. And by this it is not meant that Poe was not an affectionate husband of his wife, but that the stronger part of his affections, the better element of his heart, had burned away before he was a man. He knew what he calls " that sorrow which the living love to cherish for the dead, and which, in some minds, resembles the delirium of opium." His spirit was always beating against the gate of the grave, and the chief praise he could confer on a woman in his maturity was to compare her to one whom he had lost while he was still a boy. " For months after her decease," says Mr. Ingram, " Poe . . . would go nightly to visit the tomb of his revered friend, and when the nights were very drear and cold, when the autumnal rains fell, and the winds wailed mournfully over the graves, he lingered longest and came away most regretfully."

The truth of this anecdote would be more important for our purpose than a world of controversies as to whether Poe was expelled from school, or gambled, or tippled, or why he gave up the editorship of this or that journal. We see him preoccupied, even in his boyhood, with the thought of death and of the condition of the dead. In his prose romances his imagination is always morbidly busy with the secrets of the sepulchre. His dead men speak, his corpses hold long colloquies with themselves, his characters are prematurely buried and explore the veiled things of corruption, his lovers are led wandering among the *hic jacets* of the dead. This is the dominant note of all his poetry, this wistful regret, almost hopeless of any reunion of departed souls in " the distant Aidenn," and almost fearful that the sleep of the dead is not dreamless.

The lady sleeps ! Oh may her sleep,
Which is enduring, so be deep !
. . . .
I pray to God that she may lie
Forever with unopened eye,
While the dim sheeted ghosts go by !

Thus Poe's verse is so far from being a " criticism of life," that it is often, in literal earnest, a criticism of death ; and even when his thoughts are not busy with death, even when his heart is not following some Lenore or Annabel Lee or Ulalume, his fancy does not deal with solid realities, with human passions. He dwells in a world more vaporous than that of Shelley's *Witch of Atlas*, in a region where dreaming cities crumble into fathomless seas, in a fairyland with " dim vales and shadowy woods," in haunted palaces, or in a lost and wandering star.

Not only was Poe's practice thus limited, but his theory of poetry was scarcely more extensive. He avowed that " melancholy is the most legitimate of all the poetical tones." This preference was, doubt-less, caused by Poe's feeling that melancholy is the emotion most devoid of actual human stuff, the most etherealized, so to speak, the least likely to result in action. Poetry he defined as " the rhythmical creation of beauty," and beauty was in his eyes most beautiful when it was least alloyed with matter. Thus such topics as war, patriotism, prosperous love, religion, duty, were absolutely alien to the genius of Poe. He carried his theory to the absurd length of preferring Fouqué's *Undine* to the works of " fifty Molières." There is no poet more full of humanity than Molière, and no creature of fancy so empty as Undine, a sprite who is no more substantial than a morning shower, a vapour more evanescent than a solar myth. Poe, who liked the melancholy moods of this waste-watery sprite better than all the mirth and tenderness and passion of the Mascarilles and Alcestes, the Don Juans and Tartuffes, was also of opinion that no poem could be long. The Iliad and the Odyssey, he thought, were mistakes; they carried too heavy a weight of words and matter. When examined, this theory or paradox of Poe's shrinks into the commonplace observations that Poe preferred lyric poetry and that lyrics are essentially brief. In considering Poe's theory and practice, we must not forget that both were, in part, the result of reaction. American literature then intended to be extremely moral, and respectable, and didactic, and much of it was excessively uninspired. Poetry was expected, as she so often is expected, to teach morality as her main duty. We have always plenty of critics who cry out that poetry should be " palpitating with actuality," should struggle with " the living facts of the hour," should dignify industrialism, and indite pæans, perhaps, to sewing-machines and patent electric lights. Poe's nature was essentially rebellious, scornful, and aristocratic. If democratic ecstasies are a tissue of historical errors and self-complacent content with the commonplace, no one saw that more clearly than Poe. Thus he was the more encouraged by his rebellious instinct to take up what was then a singular and heterodox critical position. He has lately been called immoral in America for writing these words : " Beyond the limits of beauty the province of poetry does not extend. Its sole arbiter is taste. With the intellect or the conscience it has only collateral relations. It has no dependence, unless incidentally, upon either duty or truth."

To anyone who believes that the best, the immortal poetry, is nobly busied with great actions and great passions, Poe's theory seems fatally narrow. Without the conceptions of duty and truth we can have no *Antigone* and no *Prometheus*. These great and paramount ideas have always been the inspirers of honourable actions, and by following them men and women are led into the dramatic situations which are the materials of Shakespeare, Æschylus, and Homer. There is an immortal strength in the stories of great actions; but Poe in theory and practice disdains all action and rejects this root of immortality. He deliberately discards *sanity*, he deliberately chooses *fantasy* for his portion. Now, while it is not the business of poetry to go about distributing tracts, she can never neglect actions and situations which, under her spell, become unconscious lessons of morality. But, as we have said, Poe's natural bent, and his reaction against the cheap didactic criticism of his country and his time, made him neglect all actions and most passions, both in his practice and his theory. When he spoke of Keats as the most flawless of English poets, and of Mr. Tennyson as "the noblest poet that ever lived," he was attracted by that in them which is most magical, most intangible, and most undefinable— the inimitable and inexpressible charm of their music, by the delicious languor of the *Ode to the Nightingale* and of the *Lotus-Eaters*. These poems are, indeed, examples of the "rhythmical creation of beauty," which, to Poe's mind, was the essence and function of poetry.

As to the nature of Poe's secret and the *technique* by which he produced his melodies, much may be attributed to the singular musical appropriateness of his words and epithets, much to his elaborate care for the details of his art. George Sand, in *Un Hiver à Majorque*, describes a rainy night which Chopin passed in the half-ruinous monastery where they lived. She tells us how the melodies of the wind and rain seemed to be magically transmuted into his music, so that, without any puerile attempt at direct imitation of sounds, his compositions were alive with the air of the tempest. "Son génie était plein des mystérieuses harmonies de la nature traduites par des équivalents sublimes dans sa pensée musicale, et non par une répétition servile des sons extérieurs." In Poe's genius, too, there was a kind of pre-established harmony between musical words and melancholy thoughts. As Mr. Saintsbury points out to

me, though " his language not unfrequently passes
from vagueness into mere unmeaningness in the
literal and grammatical sense of it, yet it never
fails to convey the proper suggestion in sound if not
in sense. Take the lines in *Ulalume* :—

> *It was night in the lonesome October*
> *Of my most immemorial year.*

Here it would puzzle the most adroit student of
words to attach a distinct usual sense, authenticated
by lexicons, to ' immemorial.' And yet no one with
an ear can fail to see that it is emphatically the right
word, and supplies the necessary note of suggestion."
As to Poe's management of his metres, one cannot
do better than quote Mr. Saintsbury's criticism
again. " The same indefinite but intensely poetic
effect is produced still more obviously by Poe's
management of his metres. Everyone who is
acquainted with his critical work knows the care (a
care that brought on him the ridicule of sciolists
and poetasters) which he bestowed on metrical sub-
jects. *The Raven, Ulalume, The Haunted Palace,
Annabel Lee, For Annie,* are, each in its own way,
metrical marvels, and it is not till long after we have
enjoyed and admired the beauty of each as a sym-
phony that we discern the exquisite selection and
skilful juxtaposition of the parts and constituent
elements of each. Every one of these remains un-
approached and uncopied as a concerted piece.
In *The Haunted Palace,* the metre, stately at the
beginning, slackens and dies towards the close. In
Annabel Lee and *For Annie,* on the contrary, there
is a steady crescendo from first to last, while, in
the two other pieces the metre ebbs and flows at
uncertain but skilfully arranged intervals. Poe
stands almost alone in this arrangement of his lyric
works as a whole. With most poets the line or the
stanza is the unit, and the length of the poem is
determined rather by the sense than by the sound.
But with Poe the music as well as the sense (even

more than the sense perhaps) is arranged and pro-
jected as a whole, nor would it be possible to curtail
or omit a stanza without injuring the metrical as
well as the intelligible effect."

To a critic who himself feels that the incommuni-
cable and inexpressible charm of melodious words is
of the essense of song, Poe's practice is a perpetual
warning. It is to verse like Poe's, so deficient as it
is in all merit but lyric music and vague emotion, so
devoid of human passion—a faint rhythmical echo
among stars and graves of man's laborious life—that
we are reduced if we hold the theory of Poe. A critic
of his own native land, Mr. Henry James, has spoken
of his "valueless verse," and valueless his verse
must always appear if we ask from it more than it
can give. It has nothing to give but music, and
people who want more must go to others that sell
a different ware. We shall never appreciate Poe
if we keep comparing him to men of stronger and
more human natures. We must take him as one
of the voices, almost the "shadow of a voice," that
sound in the temple of song, and fill a little hour with
music. He is not, like Homer, or Scott, or Shake-
speare, or Molière, a poet that men can live with
always, by the sea, in the hills, in the market-place.
He is the singer of rare hours of languor, when the
soul is vacant of the pride of life, and inclined to
listen, as it were, to the echo of a lyre from behind
the hills of death. He is like a Moschus or Bion who
has crossed the ferry and sings to Plutus a song that
faintly reaches the ears of mortals.

$$\text{Οὐκ ἀγέραστος}$$
$$\text{ἐσσεῖθ᾽ ἁ μολπά.}$$

"Not unrewarded" indeed is the singing, for the
verse of Poe has been prized by men with a far wider
range and healthier powers than his own.

Poe said that with him "poetry was a passion."
Yet he spoke of his own verses, in a moment of
real modesty and insight, as trifles "not of much value

to the public, or very creditable to myself." They were; for the greater part, composed in the most miserable circumstances, when poverty, when neglect, when the cruel indignation of a born man of letters, in a country where letters had not yet won their place, were torturing the poet. He was compelled to be a bookseller's hack. The hack's is indeed " a damnable life," as Goldsmith said, and was doubly or trebly damnable when *The Bells* or *Annabel Lee* were sent the round of the newspaper offices, to be disposed of for the price of a dinner and a pair of boots. Poe's time was spent in writing elaborate masterpieces for a pittance, and in reviewing and crushing, for the sake of bread, the productions of a crowd of mediocrities. Then came violent and venomous quarrels, which, with enforced hackwork, devoured the energy of the poet. It is no wonder that he produced little ; but even had he enjoyed happier fortunes, his range is so narrow that we could not have looked for many volumes from him. He declared that he could not and would not excite his muse, " with an eye to the paltry compensations or the more paltry commendations of mankind." Thus it may, at least, be said of him, that he was himself in his poetry, though, in writing prose, he often deserted his true inspiration. In his earlier verses he is very plainly the pupil of Shelley, as anyone may see who has the courage to read through *Tamerlane* and *Al Aaraaf*. His reputation does not rest on these poems, which are longer than his own canon admitted, but on pieces of verbal music like *The Haunted Palace*, *The Sleeper*, *To One in Paradise*, *Israfel*, and the lines *To Helen*, which I have placed at the beginning of this volume. Though this beautiful piece of verse did not appear in the very earliest editions of Poe's poems, he always declared that it was written in boyhood for the woman whose death caused him, in Beddoes' phrase, " with half his heart to inhabit other worlds." Poe was well aware that his *Raven*, despite its immense popularity, was not among his best works. Indeed, it is almost too clever to be poetical, and has in it a kind of echo of Mrs. Browning, whose verse, floating in the poet's mind, probably suggested the composition. *To Helen*, *The Haunted Palace*, and *The Sleeper*, are perhaps the most coherent and powerful as well as the most melodious of Poe's verses. As his life sank in poverty, bereavement, misfortune, and misery, his verse more and more approached the vagueness of music, appealing often to mere sensation rather than to any emotion which can be stated in words. *The Bells* was written in the intervals of an unnatural lethargy ; *Ulalume* scarcely pretends to remain within the limits of the poetical art, and attracts or repels by mere sounds as vacant as possible of meaning. Mr. Stedman says, truly and eloquently, that *Ulalume* " seems an improvisation, such as a violinist might play upon the instrument which had become his one thing of worth after the death of a companion who had left him alone with his own soul." The odd definition of the highest poetry as " sense swooning into nonsense " seems made for such verse as *Ulalume*. People are so constituted that, if a critic confesses his pleasure in such a thing as *Ulalume*, he is supposed to admit his inability to admire any other poetry. Thus it may require some moral courage to assert one's belief that even *Ulalume* has an excuse for its existence. It is curious and worth observing that this sort of verse is so rare. It cannot be easy to make, or the herd of imitators who approach art by its weak points would have produced quantities of this enigmatic poetry. Yet, with the exception of Poe's later verse, of Morris's *Blue Closet*, and perhaps of some pieces by Gérard de Nerval, it is difficult to name any successful lines on the further side of the border between verse and music. In this region, this " ultimate dim Thule," Poe seems to reign almost alone. The fact is that the art of hints, of fantasies, of unfinished suggestions is not an easy one, as many critics, both of poetry and painting, seem to suppose. It is not enough to be obscure, or to introduce forms unexplained and undefined. A certain very rare sort of genius is needed to make productions live which hold themselves thus independent of nature and of the rules of art. We cannot define the nature of the witchery by which the most difficult task of romantic art was achieved. Poe did succeed, as is confessed by the wide acceptance of poems that cannot be defended if anyone chooses to attack them. They teach nothing, they mean little; their melody may be triumphantly explained as the result of a metrical trick. But, *ne faict ce tour qui veut*. The trick was one that only Poe could play. Like Hawthorne in prose, Poe possessed in poetry a style as strange as it was individual, a style trebly remarkable because it was the property of a hack-writer. When all is said, Poe remains a master of fantastic and melancholy sound. Some foolish old legend tells of a musician who surpassed all his rivals. His strains were unearthly sad, and ravished the ears of those who listened with a strange melancholy. Yet his viol had but a single string and the framework was fashioned out of a dead woman's breast-bone. Poe's verse—the parallel is much in his own taste—resembles that player's minstrelsy. It is morbidly sweet and mournful, and all touched on that single string, which thrills to a dead and immortal affection.

ANDREW LANG.

SELECT BIBLIOGRAPHY

SEPARATE WORKS. *Tamerlane and other Poems*, 1827; new edition with additions, *Al Aaraaf, Tamerlane, and Minor Poems*, 1829; *Poems*, 1831; *A Manuscript found in a Bottle* (prize tale for the Baltimore *Saturday Visitor*), 1833; *Coliseum*, poem, 1833 (prize poem for same, but ruled out as being by author of prize tale); *Narrative of Arthur Gordon Pym* (partly from the *Messenger*), 1838; *Conchologist's First Book* (from Thomas Wyatt's *Manual of Conchology*), 1839; *Tales of the Grotesque and the Arabesque*, 1839; *Prediction of the Plot of "Barnaby Rudge" (Saturday Evening Post)*, 1841; *Murders in the Rue Morgue (Graham's Magazine)*, 1841; *The Gold Bug* (prize offered by the *Dollar Newspaper*), 1843; *Balloon Hoax* (in the *Sun*), 1844; *Tales*, 1845; *The Raven (Evening Mirror)*, 1845; *The Raven and other Poems*, 1845; *Eureka, a prose Poem* (elaborated from his lecture on the *Cosmogony of the Universe*), 1848.

Some of Poe's best tales and poems were first published in the *Southern Literary Messenger*, 1835, of which magazine he became editor, but resigned the post in 1837; other tales appeared in *Graham's Magazine*, of which he was for a time editor-in-chief. He was also a contributor to the *New York Review, Broadway Journal*, and and *Godev's Lady's Book*.

COLLECTED WORKS. Ed. R. W. Griswold (with memoir), three vols., 1850; four vols., 1856; ed. H. Curwen (with life from French of C. Baudelaire), 1872; R. H. Stoddard (with memoir), 1873, 1884, 1896; J. H. Ingram (with memoir), 1874–5; newly collected and edited by E. C. Stedman and G. E. Woodberry, 1895; in World's Classics, 1902, etc.

Poetical works, ed. J. Hannay, 1852, 1863; E. F. Blanchard, 1857; C. F. Briggs, 1858; Memorial edition, Poems and Essays (including memoir), by J. H. Ingram, Prof. Lowell, and Willis, 1876; Poems and Essays, with an essay on his poetry by Andrew Lang, 1881; Poems and Essays, ed. Ingram, 1884; with biographical sketch by N. H. Dole, 1895, 1905; with introduction by H. N. Williams, 1900; with critical memoir by S. Cody, 1903; with introduction by Arthur Symons, 1904; and other editions in collections of classics.

LIFE. The following is a selection of books published on Poe in England and America during the last century. The literature of the subject is now enormous, not only in English but in French, German, and Italian.

L. M. Chase, *Poe and his Poetry*, 1913; A. S. Cody, *Poe—man, poet, and creative thinker*, 1924; J. W. Krutch, *Edgar Allan Poe: A Study in Genius*, 1926; W. Hervey Allen, *Israfel*, 1927; L. C. Bell, *Poe and Chivers*, 1931; Una Pope-Hennessy, *Edgar Allan Poe*, 1934; A. H. Quinn, *Edgar Allan Poe*, 1941; A. M. Bondurant, *Poe's*

Richmond, 1942; J. R. Cooke, *Poe as a Literary Critic*, 1946; D. M. Barnes, *Edgar Allan Poe*, 1949; H. Allen, *Israfel: The Life and Times of Edgar Allan Poe*, 1949; N. B. Fagin, *The Histrionic Mr Poe*, 1949; W. Bittner, *Poe—A Biography*, 1963; E. Wagenknecht, *Edgar Allan Poe: The Man Behind the Legend*, 1963; Lettice Cooper, *Young Edgar Allan Poe*, 1964; G. Rans, *Edgar Allan Poe* (Writers and Critics Series), 1965; R. Regan, *A Collection of Critical Essays* (20th Century Views Series), 1967; David Sinclair, *Edgar Allan Poe*, 1977.

CONTENTS

ESSAYS

Contents

POEMS PUBLISHED BEFORE 1845

POEMS

TO HELEN

HELEN, thy beauty is to me
  Like those Nicéan barks of yore,
That gently, o'er a perfumed sea,
  The weary, wayworn wanderer bore
  To his own native shore.

On desperate seas long wont to roam,
  Thy hyacinth hair, thy classic face,
Thy Naiad airs have brought me home
  To the glory that was Greece,
And the grandeur that was Rome.

Lo! in yon brilliant window niche
  How statue like I see thee stand,
  The agate lamp within thy hand!
Ah, Psyche, from the regions which
  Are Holy Land!

THE RAVEN

ONCE upon a midnight dreary, while I pondered,
    weak and weary,
Over many a quaint and curious volume of forgotten
    lore,
While I nodded, nearly napping, suddenly there came
    a tapping,
As of some one gently rapping, rapping at my chamber
    door.
" 'Tis some visitor," I muttered, " tapping at my
    chamber door—
          Only this, and nothing more."

Ah, distinctly I remember it was in the bleak
    December,
And each separate dying ember wrought its ghost
    upon the floor.
Eagerly I wished the morrow ;—vainly I had sought
    to borrow
From my books surcease of sorrow—sorrow for the
    lost Lenore—
For the rare and radiant maiden whom the angels
    name Lenore—
        Nameless here for evermore.

And the silken sad uncertain rustling of each purple
    curtain
Thrilled me—filled me with fantastic terrors never
    felt before ;
So that now, to still the beating of my heart, I stood
    repeating
" 'Tis some visitor entreating entrance at my chamber
    door—
Some late visitor entreating entrance at my chamber
    door ;—
        This it is, and nothing more."

Presently my soul grew stronger ; hesitating then no
    longer,
" Sir," said I, " or Madam, truly your forgiveness I
    implore ;
But the fact is I was napping, and so gently you came
    rapping,
And so faintly you came tapping, tapping at my
    chamber door,
That I scarce was sure I heard you "—here I opened
    wide the door ;—
        Darkness there, and nothing more.

Deep into that darkness peering, long I stood there
    wondering, fearing,
Doubting, dreaming dreams no mortal ever dared to
    dream before

But the silence was unbroken, and the darkness gave
no token,
And the only word there spoken was the whispered
word, " Lenore ! "
This I whispered, and an echo murmured back the
word, " Lenore ! "
Merely this and nothing more.

Back into the chamber turning, all my soul within
me burning,
Soon again I heard a tapping somewhat louder than
before.
" Surely," said I, " surely that is something at my
window lattice ;
Let me see, then, what thereat is, and this mystery
explore—
Let my heart be still a moment and this mystery
explore ;—
'Tis the wind and nothing more ! "

Open here I flung the shutter, when, with many a
flirt and flutter,
In there stepped a stately raven of the saintly days
of yore.
Not the least obeisance made he ; not an instant
stopped or stayed he ;
But, with mien of lord or lady, perched above my
chamber door—
Perched upon a bust of Pallas just above my chamber
door—
Perched, and sat, and nothing more.

Then this ebony bird beguiling my sad fancy into
smiling,
By the grave and stern decorum of the countenance it
wore,
" Though thy crest be shorn and shaven, thou," I
said, " art sure no craven,

Ghastly grim and ancient raven wandering from the
 Nightly shore—
Tell me what thy lordly name is on the Night's
 Plutonian shore ! "
   Quoth the raven, " Nevermore."

Much I marvelled this ungainly fowl to hear discourse
 so plainly,
Though its answer little meaning—little relevancy
 bore ;
For we cannot help agreeing that no living human
 being
Ever yet was blessed with seeing bird above his
 chamber door—
Bird or beast upon the sculptured bust above his
 chamber door,
   With such name as " Nevermore."

But the raven, sitting lonely on the placid bust, spoke
 only
That one word, as if his soul in that one word he
 did outpour.
Nothing further then he uttered—not a feather then
 he fluttered—
Till I scarcely more than muttered " Other friends
 have flown before—
On the morrow *he* will leave me, as my hopes have
 flown before."
   Then the bird said, " Nevermore."

Startled at the stillness broken by reply so aptly
 spoken,
" Doubtless," said I, " what it utters is its only stock
 and store,
Caught from some unhappy master whom unmerciful
 Disaster
Followed fast and followed faster till his songs one
 burden bore—
Till the dirges of his Hope that melancholy burden
 bore
   Of ' Never—nevermore.' "

But the raven still beguiling all my sad soul into
  smiling,
Straight I wheeled a cushioned seat in front of bird
  and bust and door ;
Then, upon the velvet sinking, I betook myself to
  linking
Fancy unto fancy, thinking what this ominous bird
  of yore—
What this grim, ungainly, ghastly, gaunt, and omin-
  ous bird of yore
   Meant in croaking " Nevermore."

This I sat engaged in guessing, but no syllable ex-
  pressing
To the fowl whose fiery eyes now burned into my
  bosom's core ;
This and more I sat divining, with my head at ease
  reclining
On the cushion's velvet lining that the lamp-light
  gloated o'er,
But whose velvet violet lining with the lamp-light
  gloating o'er,
   She shall press, ah, nevermore !

Then, methought, the air grew denser, perfumed from
  an unseen censer
Swung by angels whose faint foot-falls tinkled on the
  tufted floor.
" Wretch," I cried, " thy God hath lent thee—by
  these angels he hath sent thee
Respite—respite and nepenthe from thy memories of
  Lenore !
Quaff, oh quaff this kind nepenthe, and forget this
  lost Lenore ! "
   Quoth the raven, " Nevermore."

" Prophet ! " said I, " thing of evil !—prophet still,
  if bird or devil !—
Whether Tempter sent, or whether tempest tossed
  thee here ashore,

Desolate yet all undaunted, on this desert land
    enchanted—
On this home by Horror haunted—tell me truly, I
    implore—
Is there—*is* there balm in Gilead ?—tell me—tell me,
    I implore ! "
            Quoth the raven, " Nevermore."

" Prophet ! " said I, " thing of evil—prophet still, if
    bird or devil !
By that Heaven that bends above us—by that God
    we both adore—
Tell this soul with sorrow laden if, within the distant
    Aidenn,
It shall clasp a sainted maiden whom the angels name
    Lenore—
Clasp a rare and radiant maiden whom the angels
    name Lenore ? "
            Quoth the raven, " Nevermore."

" Be that word our sign of parting, bird or fiend ! "
    I shrieked, upstarting—
" Get thee back into the tempest and the Night's
    Plutonian shore !
Leave no black plume as a token of that lie thy soul
    hath spoken !
Leave my loneliness unbroken !—quit the bust above
    my door !
Take thy beak from out my heart, and take thy
    form from off my door ! "
            Quoth the raven, " Nevermore."

And the raven, never flitting, still is sitting, still is
    sitting
On the pallid bust of Pallas just above my chamber
    door ;

And his eyes have all the seeming of a demon's that
    is dreaming,
And the lamp-light o'er him streaming throws his
    shadow on the floor ;
And my soul from out that shadow that lies floating
    on the floor
          Shall be lifted—nevermore !

THE VALLEY OF UNREST

Once it smiled a silent dell
Where the people did not dwell ;
They had gone unto the wars,
Trusting to the mild-eyed stars,
Nightly, from their azure towers,
To keep watch above the flowers,
In the midst of which all day
The red sun-light lazily lay.
Now each visitor shall confess
The sad valley's restlessness.
Nothing there is motionless—
Nothing save the airs that brood
Over the magic solitude.
Ah, by no wind are stirred those trees
That palpitate like the chill seas
Around the misty Hebrides !
Ah, by no wind those clouds are driven
That rustle through the unquiet Heaven
Uneasily, from morn till even,
Over the violets there that lie
In Myriad types of the human eye
Over the lilies there that wave
And weep above a nameless grave !
They wave :—from out their fragrant tops
Eternal dews come down in drops.
They weep :—from off their delicate stems
Perennial tears descend in gems.

BRIDAL BALLAD

THE ring is on my hand,
    And the wreath is on my brow;
Satins and jewels grand
Are all at my command,
    And I am happy now.

And my lord he loves me well;
    But, when first he breathed his vow,
I felt my bosom swell—
For the words rang as a knell,
And the voice seemed *his* who fell
In the battle down the dell,
    And who is happy now.

But he spoke to reassure me,
    And he kissed my pallid brow,
While a reverie came o'er me,
And to the churchyard bore me,
And I sighed to him before me,
Thinking him dead D'Elormie,
    "Oh, I am happy now!"

And thus the words were spoken,
    And this the plighted vow,
And, though my faith be broken,
And, though my heart be broken,
Behold the golden token
    That *proves* me happy now!

Would God I could awaken!
    For I dream I know not how,
And my soul is sorely shaken
Lest an evil step be taken,—
Lest the dead who is forsaken
    May not be happy now.

THE SLEEPER

At midnight, in the month of June,
I stand beneath the mystic moon.
An opiate vapour, dewy, dim,
Exhales from out her golden rim,
And, softly dripping, drop by drop,
Upon the quiet mountain top,
Steals drowsily and musically
Into the universal valley.
The rosemary nods upon the grave ;
The lily lolls upon the wave ;
Wrapping the fog about its breast,
The ruin moulders into rest ;
Looking like Lethe, see ! the lake
A conscious slumber seems to take,
And would not, for the world, awake.
All Beauty sleeps !—and lo ! where lies
(Her casement open to the skies)
Irene, with her Destinies !
Oh, lady bright ! can it be right—
This window open to the night ?
The wanton airs, from the tree-top,
Laughingly through the lattice drop—
The bodiless airs, a wizard rout,
Flit through thy chamber in and out,
And wave the curtain canopy
So fitfully—so fearfully—
Above the closed and fringed lid
'Neath which thy slumb'ring soul lies hid,
That, o'er the floor and down the wall,
Like ghosts the shadows rise and fall !
Oh, lady dear, hast thou no fear ?
Why and what art thou dreaming here ?
Sure thou art come o'er far-off seas,
A wonder to these garden trees !
Strange is thy pallor ! strange thy dress !
Strange, above all, thy length of tress,
And this all-solemn silentness !

The lady sleeps! Oh, may her sleep,
Which is enduring, so be deep!
Heaven have her in its sacred keep!
This chamber changed for one more holy,
This bed for one more melancholy,
I pray to God that she may lie
Forever with unopened eye,
While the dim sheeted ghosts go by!

My love, she sleeps! Oh, may her sleep,
As it is lasting, so be deep!
Soft may the worms about her creep!
Far in the forest, dim and old,
For her may some tall vault unfold—
Some vault that oft hath flung its black
And winged panels fluttering back,
Triumphant, o'er the crested palls,
Of her grand family funerals—
Some sepulchre, remote, alone,
Against whose portal she hath thrown
In childhood many an idle stone—
Some tomb from out whose sounding door
She ne'er shall force an echo more,
Thrilling to think, poor child of sin!
It was the dead who groaned within.

THE COLISEUM

TYPE of the antique Rome! Rich reliquary
Of lofty contemplation left to Time
By buried centuries of pomp and power!
At length—at length—after so many days
Of weary pilgrimage and burning thirst
(Thirst for the springs of lore that in thee lie),
I kneel, an altered and an humble man,
Amid thy shadows, and so drink within
My very soul thy grandeur, gloom, and glory!

The Coliseum

Vastness! and Age! and Memories of Eld!
Silence! and Desolation! and dim Night!
I feel ye now—I feel ye in your strength—
O spells more sure than e'er Judæan king
Taught in the gardens of Gethsemane!
O charms more potent than the rapt Chaldee
Ever drew down from out the quiet stars!

Here, where a hero fell, a column falls!
Here, where the mimic eagle glared in gold,
A midnight vigil holds the swarthy bat!
Here, where the dames of Rome their gilded hair
Waved to the wind, now wave the reed and thistle!
Here, where on golden throne the monarch lolled,
Glides, spectre-like, unto his marble home,
Lit by the wan light of the hornéd moon,
The swift and silent lizard of the stones!

But stay! these walls—these ivy-clad arcades—
These mouldering plinths—these sad and blackened
        shafts—
These vague entablatures—this crumbling frieze—
These shattered cornices—this wreck—this ruin—
These stones—alas! these grey stones—are they all—
All of the famed, and the colossal left
By the corrosive Hours to Fate and me?

"Not all"—the Echoes answer me—"not all!
Prophetic sounds and loud, arise forever
From us, and from all Ruin, unto the wise,
As melody from Memnon to the Sun.
We rule the hearts of mightiest men—we rule
With a despotic sway all giant minds.
We are not impotent—we pallid stones.
Not all our power is gone—not all our fame—
Not all the magic of our high renown—
Not all the wonder that encircles us—

Not all the mysteries that in us lie—
Not all the memories that hang upon
And cling around about us as a garment,
Clothing us in a robe of more than glory."

LENORE

Ah, broken is the golden bowl! the spirit flown for-
    ever!
Let the bell toll!—a saintly soul floats on the Stygian
    river;
And, Guy de Vere, hast *thou* no tear?—weep now or
    never more!
See! on yon drear and rigid bier low lies thy love,
    Lenore!
Come! let the burial rite be read—the funeral song
    be sung!—
An anthem for the queenliest dead that ever died so
    young—
A dirge for her the doubly dead in that she died so
    young.

" Wretches! ye loved her for her wealth and hated
    her for her pride,
And when she fell in feeble health, ye blessed her—
    that she died!
How *shall* the ritual, then, be read?—the requiem
    how be sung
By you—by yours, the evil eye,—by yours, the
    slanderous tongue
That did to death the innocent that died, and died so
    young?"

Peccavimus; but rave not thus! and let a Sabbath
    song
Go up to God so solemnly the dead may feel no
    wrong!

The sweet Lenore hath " gone before," with Hope,
    that flew beside,
Leaving thee wild for the dear child that should have
    been thy bride—
For her, the fair and *debonair*, that now so lowly lies,
The life upon her yellow hair but not within her eyes—
The life still there, upon her hair—the death upon her
    eyes.

" Avaunt ! to-night my heart is light.   No dirge will
    I upraise,
" But waft the angel on her flight with a Pæan of
    old days !
" Let *no* bell toll !—lest her sweet soul, amid its hal-
    lowed mirth,
" Should catch the note, as it doth float—up from
    the damnéd Earth.
" To friends above, from fiends below, the indignant
    ghost is riven—
" From Hell unto a high estate far up within the
    Heaven—
" From grief and groan, to a golden throne, beside
    the King of Heaven."

CATHOLIC HYMN

At morn—at noon—at twilight dim—
Maria ! thou hast heard my hymn !
In joy and wo—in good and ill—
Mother of God, be with me still !
When the Hours flew brightly by,
And not a cloud obscured the sky,
My soul, lest it should truant be,
Thy grace did guide to thine and thee ;
Now, when storms of Fate o'ercast
Darkly my Present and my Past,
Let my Future radiant shine
With sweet hopes of thee and thine !

ISRAFEL [1]

In Heaven a spirit doth dwell
　　"Whose heart-strings are a lute";
None sing so wildly well
As the angel Israfel,
And the giddy stars (so legends tell),
Ceasing their hymns, attend the spell
　　Of his voice, all mute.

Tottering above
　　In her highest noon,
　　The enamoured moon
Blushes with love,
　　While, to listen, the red levin
　　(With the rapid Pleiads, even,
　　Which were seven),
　　Pauses in heaven.

And they say (the starry choir
　　And the other listening things)
That Israfeli's fire
Is owing to that lyre
　　By which he sits and sings—
The trembling living wire
　　Of those unusual strings.

But the skies that angel trod,
　　Where deep thoughts are a duty—
Where Love's a grown-up God—
　　Where the Houri glances are
Imbued with all the beauty
　　Which we worship in a star.

Therefore, thou art not wrong,
　　Israfeli, who despisest
An unimpassioned song;

[1] And the angel Israfel, whose heart-strings are a lute, and
who has the sweetest voice of all God's creatures.—Koran.

To thee the laurels belong,
  Best bard, because the wisest!
Merrily live and long!

The ecstasies above
  With thy burning measures suit—
Thy grief, thy joy, thy hate, thy love,
  With the fervour of thy lute—
  Well may the stars be mute!

Yes, Heaven is thine; but this
  Is a world of sweets and sours;
  Our flowers are merely—flowers,
And the shadow of thy perfect bliss
  Is the sunshine of ours.

If I could dwell
Where Israfel
  Hath dwelt, and he where I,
He might not sing so wildly well
  A mortal melody,
While a bolder note than this might swell
  From my lyre within the sky.

DREAMLAND

By a route obscure and lonely,
Haunted by ill angels only,
Where an Eidolon, named NIGHT,
On a black throne reigns upright,
I have reached these lands but newly
From an ultimate dim Thule—
From a wild weird clime that lieth, sublime,
  Out of SPACE—out of TIME.

Bottomless vales and boundless floods,
And chasms, and caves, and Titan woods,
With forms that no man can discover
For the dews that drip all over;

Mountains toppling evermore
Into seas without a shore;
Seas that restlessly aspire,
Surging, unto skies of fire;
Lakes that endlessly outspread
Their lone waters—lone and dead,—
Their still waters—still and chilly
With the snows of the lolling lily.

By the lakes that thus outspread
Their lone waters, lone and dead,—
Their sad waters, sad and chilly
With the snows of the lolling lily,—
By the mountains—near the river
Murmuring lowly, murmuring ever,—
By the grey woods,—by the swamp
Where the toad and the newt encamp,—
By the dismal tarns and pools
    Where dwell the Ghouls,—
By each spot the most unholy—
In each nook most melancholy,—
There the traveller meets aghast
Sheeted Memories of the Past—
Shrouded forms that start and sigh
As they pass the wanderer by—
White-robed forms of friends long given,
In agony, to the Earth—and Heaven.

For the heart whose woes are legion
'Tis a peaceful, soothing region—
For the spirit that walks in shadow
'Tis—oh, 'tis an Eldorado!
But the traveller, travelling through it,
May not—dare not openly view it;
Never its mysteries are exposed
To the weak human eye unclosed;
So wills its king, who hath forbid
The uplifting of the fringed lid;
And thus the sad Soul that here passes
Beholds it but through darkened glasses.

By a route obscure and lonely,
Haunted by ill angels only,
Where an Eidolon, named NIGHT,
On a black throne reigns upright,
I have wandered home but newly
From this ultimate dim Thule.

SONNET: TO ZANTE

FAIR isle, that from the fairest of all flowers,
　Thy gentlest of all gentle names dost take!
How many memories of what radiant hours
　At sight of thee and thine at once awake!
How many scenes of what departed bliss!
　How many thoughts of what entombéd hopes!
How many visions of a maiden that is
　No more—no more upon thy verdant slopes!
No more! alas, that magical sad sound
　Transforming all! Thy charm shall please *no more—*
Thy memory *no more!* Accurséd ground!
　Henceforth I hold thy flower-enamelled shore,
O hyacinthine isle! O purple Zante!
　"Isola d'oro! Fior di Levante!"

THE CITY IN THE SEA

Lo! Death has reared himself a throne
In a strange city lying alone
Far down within the dim West,
Where the good and the bad and the worst
　　and the best,
Have gone to their eternal rest.
Their shrines and palaces and towers
(Time-eaten towers that tremble not!)
Resemble nothing that is ours.
Around, by lifting winds forgot,
Resignedly beneath the sky
The melancholy waters lie.

No rays from the holy heaven come down
On the long night-time of that town;
But light from out the lurid sea
Streams up the turrets silently—
Gleams up the pinnacles far and free—
Up domes—up spires—up kingly halls—
Up fanes—up Babylon-like walls—
Up shadowy long-forgotten bowers
Of sculptured ivy and stone flowers—
Up many and many a marvellous shrine
Whose wreathéd friezes intertwine
The viol, the violet, and the vine.

Resignedly beneath the sky
The melancholy waters lie,
So blend the turrets and shadows there
That all seem pendulous in air,
While from a proud tower in the town
Death looks gigantically down.

There open fanes and gaping graves
Yawn level with the luminous waves;
But not the riches there that lie
In each idol's diamond eye—
Not the gaily-jewelled dead
Tempt the waters from their bed;
For no ripples curl, alas!
Along that wilderness of glass—
No swellings tell that winds may be
Upon some far-off happier sea—
No heavings hint that winds have been
On seas less hideously serene.

But lo, a stir is in the air!
The wave—there is a movement there!
As if the towers had thrust aside,
In slightly sinking, the dull tide—
As if their tops had feebly given
A void within the filmy Heaven.

The waves have now a redder glow—
The hours are breathing faint and low—
And when, amid no earthly moans,
  Down, down that town shall settle hence,
Hell, rising from a thousand thrones,
  Shall do it reverence.

TO ONE IN PARADISE

THOU wast all that to me, love,
  For which my soul did pine—
A green isle in the sea, love,
  A fountain and a shrine,
All wreathed with fairy fruits and flowers,
  And all the flowers were mine.

Ah, dream too bright to last!
  Ah, starry Hope! that didst arise
But to be overcast!
  A voice from out the Future cries,
"On! on!"—but o'er the Past
  (Dim gulf) my spirit hovering lies
Mute, motionless, aghast!

For, alas! alas! with me
  The light of Life is o'er!
No more—no more—no more—
(Such language holds the solemn sea
  To the sands upon the shore)
Shall bloom the thunder-blasted tree,
  Or the stricken eagle soar!

And all my days are trances,
  And all my nightly dreams
Are where thy dark eye glances,
  And where thy footstep gleams—
In what ethereal dances,
  By what eternal streams.

EULALIE

I DWELT alone
In a world of moan,
And my soul was a stagnant tide,
Till the fair and gentle Eulalie became my blushing
bride—
Till the yellow-haired young Eulalie became my
smiling bride.

Ah, less—less bright
The stars of the night
Than the eyes of the radiant girl!
And never a flake
That the vapour can make
With the moon-tints of purple and pearl,
Can vie with the modest Eulalie's most unregarded
curl—
Can compare with the bright-eyed Eulalie's most
humble and careless curl.

Now Doubt—now Pain
Come never again,
For her soul gives me sigh for sigh,
And all day long
Shines, bright and strong,
Astarté within the sky,
While ever to her dear Eulalie upturns her matron
eye—
While ever to her young Eulalie upturns her violet
eye.

TO F——s S. O——D

THOU wouldst be loved?—then let thy heart
From its present pathway part not!
Being everything which now thou art,
Be nothing which thou art not.

So with the world thy gentle ways,
    Thy grace, thy more than beauty,
Shall be an endless theme of praise,
    And love—a simple duty.

TO F——

BELOVED ! amid the earnest woes
    That crowd around my earthly path—
(Drear path, alas ! where grows
Not even one lonely rose)—
    My soul at least a solace hath
In dreams of thee, and therein knows
An Eden of bland repose.

And thus thy memory is to me
    Like some enchanted far-off isle
In some tumultuous sea—
Some ocean throbbing far and free
    With storms—but where meanwhile
Serenest skies continually
    Just o'er that one bright island smile.

SONNET : SILENCE

THERE are some qualities—some incorporate things,
    That have a double life, which thus is made
A type of that twin entity which springs
    From matter and light, evinced in solid and shade,
There is a twofold *Silence*—sea and shore—
    Body and soul. One dwells in lonely places,
    Newly with grass o'ergrown ; some solemn graces,
Some human memories and tearful lore,
Render him terrorless: his name's " No More."
He is the corporate Silence : dread him not !
    No power hath he of evil in himself ;
But should some urgent fate (untimely lot !)
    Bring thee to meet his shadow (nameless elf,
That haunteth the lone regions where hath trod
No foot of man), commend thyself to God !

THE CONQUEROR WORM

Lo! 'tis a gala night
  Within the lonesome latter years!
An angel throng, bewinged, bedight
  In veils, and drowned in tears,
Sit in a theatre, to see
  A play of hopes and fears,
While the orchestra breathes fitfully
  The music of the spheres.

Mimes, in the form of God on high,
  Mutter and mumble low,
And hither and thither fly—
  Mere puppets they, who come and go
At bidding of vast formless things
  That shift the scenery to and fro,
Flapping from out their Condor wings
  Invisible Wo!

That motley drama—oh, be sure
  It shall not be forgot!
With its Phantom chased for evermore
  By a crowd that seize it not,
Through a circle that ever returneth in
  To the self-same spot,
And much of Madness, and more of Sin,
  And Horror the soul of the plot.

But see, amid the mimic rout
  A crawling shape intrude!
A blood red thing that writhes from out
  The scenic solitude!
It writhes!—it writhes!—with mortal pangs
  The mimes become its food,
And the seraphs sob at vermin fangs
  In human gore imbued.

Out—out are the lights—out all!
  And, over each quivering form,
The curtain, a funeral pall,
  Comes down with the rush of a storm,
And the angels, all pallid and wan,
  Uprising, unveiling, affirm
That the play is the tragedy "Man,"
  And its hero the Conqueror Worm.

THE HAUNTED PALACE

IN the greenest of our valleys
  By good angels tenanted,
Once a fair and stately palace—
  Radiant palace—reared its head.
In the monarch Thought's dominion—
  It stood there!
Never seraph spread a pinion
  Over fabric half so fair!

Banners yellow, glorious, golden,
  On its roof did float and flow,
(This—all this—was in the olden
  Time long ago);
And every gentle air that dallied,
  In that sweet day,
Along the ramparts plumed and pallid,
  A wingéd odour went away.

Wanderers in that happy valley,
  Through two luminous windows, saw
Spirits moving musically,
  To a lute's well-tunéd law,
Round about a throne where, sitting
  (Porphyrogene!)
In state his glory well befitting,
  The ruler of the realm was seen.

And all with pearl and ruby glowing
  Was the fair palace door,
Through which came flowing, flowing, flowing,
  And sparkling evermore,
A troop of Echoes, whose sweet duty
  Was but to sing,
In voices of surpassing beauty,
  The wit and wisdom of their king.

But evil things, in robes of sorrow,
  Assailed the monarch's high estate.
(Ah, let us mourn!—for never morrow [1]
  Shall dawn upon him desolate!)
And round about his home the glory
  That blushed and bloomed,
Is but a dim-remembered story
  Of the old time entombed.

And travellers, now, within that valley,
  Through the red-litten windows see
Vast forms, that move fantastically
  To a discordant melody,
While, like a ghastly rapid river,
  Through the pale door
A hideous throng rush out forever,
  And laugh—but smile no more.

SCENES FROM *POLITIAN*
AN UNPUBLISHED DRAMA

I

ROME.—*A Hall in a Palace.* ALESSANDRA *and*
CASTIGLIONE

ALESSANDRA

Thou art sad, Castiglione.

[1] V. l. *sorrow*, an obvious misprint.

CASTIGLIONE

                Sad !—not I.
Oh, I'm the happiest, happiest man in Rome !
A few days more, thou' knowest, my Alessandra,
Will make thee mine. Oh, I am very happy !

ALESSANDRA

Methinks thou hast a singular way of showing
Thy happiness !—what ails thee, cousin of mine ?
Why didst thou sigh so deeply ?

CASTIGLIONE

                  Did I sigh ?
I was not conscious of it. It is a fashion,
A silly—a most silly fashion I have
When I am *very* happy. Did I sigh ? (*Sighing.*)

ALESSANDRA

Thou didst. Thou art not well. Thou hast indulged
Too much of late, and I am vexed to see it.
Late hours and wine, Castiglione,—these
Will ruin thee !—thou art already altered—
Thy looks are haggard—nothing so wears away
The constitution as late hours and wine.

CASTIGLIONE (*musing*)

Nothing, fair cousin, nothing—not even deep sorrow—
Wears it away like evil hours and wine.
I will amend.

ALESSANDRA

          Do it ! I would have thee drop
Thy riotous company, too—fellows low born
Ill suit the like with old Di Broglio's heir
And Alessandra's husband.

CASTIGLIONE

                I will drop them.

ALESSANDRA

Thou wilt—thou must. Attend thou also more
To thy dress and equipage—they are over plain
For thy lofty rank and fashion—much depends
Upon appearances.

CASTIGLIONE

I'll see to it.

ALESSANDRA

Then see to it!—pay more attention, sir,
To a becoming carriage—much thou wantest
In dignity.

CASTIGLIONE

Much, much, oh, much I want
In proper dignity.

ALESSANDRA (*haughtily*)

Thou mockest me, sir!

CASTIGLIONE (*abstractedly*)

Sweet, gentle Lalage!

ALESSANDRA

Heard I aright?
I speak to him—he speaks of Lalage!
Sir Count! (*places her hand on his shoulder*) what art
thou dreaming? He's not well!
What ails thee, sir?

CASTIGLIONE (*starting*)

Cousin! fair cousin!—madam!
I crave thy pardon—indeed I am not well—
Your hand from off my shoulder, if you please.
This air is most oppressive!—Madam—the Duke!

Enter DI BROGLIO

DI BROGLIO

My son, I've news for thee!—hey?—what's the
matter? (*observing* ALESSANDRA).
I' the pouts? Kiss her, Castiglione! kiss her,

You dog ! and make it up, I say, this minute !
I've news for you both. Politian is expected
Hourly in Rome—Politian, Earl of Leicester !
We'll have him at the wedding. 'Tis his first visit
To the imperial city.

ALESSANDRA

        What ! Politian
Of Britain, Earl of Leicester ?

DI BROGLIO

            The same, my love.
We'll have him at the wedding. A man quite young
In years, but grey in fame. I have not seen him,
But rumour speaks of him as of a prodigy
Pre-eminent in arts, and arms, and wealth,
And high descent. We'll have him at the wedding.

ALESSANDRA

I have heard much of this Politian.
Gay, volatile and giddy—is he not ?
And little given to thinking.

DI BROGLIO

            Far from it, love.
No branch, they say, of all philosophy
So deep abstruse he has not mastered it.
Learned as few are learned.

ALESSANDRA

           'Tis very strange !
I have known men have seen Politian
And sought his company. They speak of him
As of one who entered madly into life,
Drinking the cup of pleasure to the dregs.

CASTIGLIONE

Ridiculous ! Now *I* have seen Politian
And know him well—nor learned nor mirthful he.
He is a dreamer, and a man shut out
From common passions.

DI BROGLIO

                Children, we disagree.
Let us go forth and taste the fragrant air
Of the garden. Did I dream, or did I hear
Politian was a *melancholy* man ?   [*Exeunt.*

II

ROME.—*A Lady's apartment, with a window open and looking into a garden.* LALAGE, *in deep mourning, reading at a table on which lie some books and a hand-mirror. In the background* JACINTA (*a servant maid*) *leans carelessly upon a chair.*

LALAGE

Jacinta ! is it thou ?

JACINTA (*pertly*)

                Yes, ma'am, I'm here.

LALAGE

I did not know, Jacinta, you were in waiting.
Sit down !—let not my presence trouble you—
Sit down !—for I am humble, most humble.

JACINTA (*aside*)

'Tis time.
      [JACINTA *seats herself in a sidelong manner upon the chair, resting her elbows upon the back, and regarding her mistress with a contemptuous look.* LALAGE *continues to read.*

LALAGE

        " It in another climate, so he said,
" Bore a bright golden flower, but not i' this soil ! "
        (*Pauses, turns over some leaves, and resumes.*)
" No lingering winters there, nor snow, nor shower—
" But Ocean ever to refresh mankind
" Breathes the shrill spirit of the western wind."

Oh, beautiful !—most beautiful !—how like
To what my fevered soul doth dream of Heaven !
O happy land ! (*Pauses.*) She died !—the maiden
    died !
O still more happy maiden who couldst die !
Jacinta !

> [JACINTA *returns no answer, and* LALAGE *presently resumes.*

        Again !—a similar tale
Told of a beauteous dame beyond the sea !
Thus speaketh one Ferdinand in the words of the
    play—
" She died full young "—one Bossola answers him—
" I think not so—her infelicity
" Seemed to have years too many "—Ah, luckless
    lady !
Jacinta ! (*Still no answer.*)
        Here's a far sterner story—
But like—oh, very like in its despair—
Of that Egyptian queen, winning so easily
A thousand hearts—losing at length her own.
She died. Thus endeth the history—and her maids
Lean over her and weep—two gentle maids
With gentle names—Eiros and Charmion !
Rainbow and Dove !—Jacinta !

JACINTA (*pettishly*)
        Madam, what *is* it ?

LALAGE

Wilt thou, my good Jacinta, be so kind
As go down in the library and bring me
The Holy Evangelists.

JACINTA
        Pshaw !   [*Exit.*

LALAGE
        If there be balm
For the wounded spirit in Gilead it is there !
Dew in the night time of my bitter trouble

Will there be found—" dew sweeter far than that
Which hangs like chains of pearl on Hermon hill."
    [*Re-enter* JACINTA, *and throws a volume on the table.*

JACINTA

There, ma'am, 's the book. Indeed she is very
    troublesome. (*Aside.*)

LALAGE (*astonished*)

What didst thou say, Jacinta ? Have I done aught
To grieve thee or to vex thee ?—I am sorry.
For thou hast served me long and ever been
Trustworthy and respectful. (*Resumes her reading.*)

JACINTA

             I can't believe
She has any more jewels—no—no—she gave me
    all. (*Aside.*)

LALAGE

What didst thou say, Jacinta ? Now I bethink me,
Thou hast not spoken lately of thy wedding.
How fares good Ugo ?—and when is it to be ?
Can I do aught ?—is there no further aid
Thou needest, Jacinta ?

JACINTA

         Is there no *further* aid !
That's meant for me. (*Aside.*) I'm sure, madam,
    you need not
Be always throwing those jewels in my teeth.

LALAGE

Jewels ! Jacinta,—now indeed, Jacinta,
I thought not of the jewels.

JACINTA

        Oh, perhaps not !
But then I might have sworn it. After all,
There's Ugo says the ring is only paste,
For he's sure the Count Castiglione never
Would have given a real diamond to such as you !

And at the best I'm certain, madam, you cannot
Have use for jewels *now*. But I might have sworn it.
           [*Exit.*
   [LALAGE *bursts into tears, and leans her head
     upon the table—after a short pause raises it.*

LALAGE

Poor Lalage!—and is it come to this?
Thy servant maid!—but courage!—'tis but a viper
Whom thou hast cherished to sting thee to the
     soul! (*Taking up the mirror.*)
Ha! here at least's a friend—too much a friend
In earlier days—a friend will not deceive thee.
Fair mirror and true! now tell me (for thou canst)
A' tale—a pretty tale—and heed thou not
Though it be rife with wo. It answers me.
It speaks of sunken eyes, and wasted cheeks,
And Beauty long deceased—remembers me
Of Joy departed—Hope, the Seraph Hope,
Inurned and entombed!—now, in a tone
Low, sad, and solemn, but most audible,
Whispers of early grave untimely yawning
For ruined maid. Fair mirror and true!—thou liest
     not!
Thou hast no end to gain—no heart to break—
Castiglione lied who said he loved—
Thou true—he false!—false!—false!
   [*While she speaks a monk enters her apartment
     and approaches unobserved.*

MONK

                   Refuge thou hast,
Sweet daughter! in Heaven. Think of eternal
     things!
Give up thy soul to penitence, and pray!

LALAGE (*arising hurriedly*)

I *cannot* pray!—My soul is at war with God!
The frightful sounds of merriment below
Disturb my senses—go! I cannot pray—
The sweet airs from the garden worry me!

Thy presence grieves me—go !—thy priestly raiment
Fills me with dread—thy ebony cruficix
With horror and awe !

MONK

Think of thy precious soul !

LALAGE

Think of my early days !—think of my father
And mother in Heaven ! think of our quiet home,
And the rivulet that ran before the door !
Think of my little sisters !—think of them !
And think of me !—think of my trusting love
And confidence—his vows—my ruin—think—think
Of my unspeakable misery !—begone !
Yet stay ! yet stay !—what was it thou saidst of
     prayer
And penitence ? Didst thou not speak of faith
And vows before the throne ?

MONK

I did.

LALAGE

'Tis well.
There *is* a vow were fitting should be made—
A sacred vow, imperative, and urgent,
A solemn vow !

MONK

Daughter, this zeal is well !

LALAGE

Father, this zeal is anything but well !
Hast thou a crucifix fit for this thing ?
A crucifix whereon to register
This sacred vow ? (*He hands her his own.*)
Not that !—Oh ! no !—no !—no ! (*Shuddering.*)
Not that ! Not that !—I tell thee, holy man.

Thy raiments and thy ebony cross affright me!
Stand back! I have a crucifix myself,—
I have a crucifix! Methinks 'twere fitting
The deed—the vow—the symbol of the deed—
And the deed's register should tally, father!

(Draws a cross-handled dagger and raises it on high.)

Behold the cross wherewith a vow like mine
Is written in Heaven!

MONK

Thy words are madness, daughter,
And speak a purpose unholy—thy lips are livid—
Thine eyes are wild—tempt not the wrath divine!
Pause ere too late!—oh, be not—be not rash!
Swear not the oath—oh, swear it not!

LALAGE

'Tis sworn!

III

An apartment in a palace. POLITIAN *and* BALDAZZAR.

BALDAZZAR

Arouse thee now, Politian!
Thou must not—nay indeed, indeed, thou shalt not
Give way unto these humours. Be thyself!
Shake off the idle fancies that beset thee,
And live, for now thou diest!

POLITIAN

Not so, Baldazzar!
Surely I live.

BALDAZZAR

Politian, it doth grieve me
To see thee thus.

POLITIAN

Baldazzar, it doth grieve me
To give thee cause for grief, my honoured friend

Command me, sir! what wouldst thou have me do?
At thy behest I will shake off that nature
Which from my forefathers I did inherit,
Which with my mother's milk I did imbibe,
And be no more Politian, but some other.
Command me, sir!

BALDAZZAR

           To the field then—to the field—
To the senate or the field.

POLITIAN

           Alas! alas!
There is an imp would follow me even there!
There is an imp *hath* followed me even there!
There is——what voice was that?

BALDAZZAR

                I heard it not.
I heard not any voice except thine own,
And the echo of thine own.

POLITIAN

               Then I but dreamed.

BALDAZZAR

Give not thy soul to dreams: the camp—the court
Befit thee—Fame awaits thee—Glory calls—
And her the trumpet-tongued thou wilt not hear
In hearkening to imaginary sounds
And phantom voices.

POLITIAN

           It *is* a phantom voice!
Didst thou not hear it *then?*

BALDAZZAR

              I heard it not.

POLITIAN

Thou heardst it not!—Baldazzar, speak no more
To me, Politian, of thy camps and courts.
Oh! I am sick, sick, sick, even unto death,
Of the hollow and high-sounding vanities
Of the populous Earth! Bear with me yet awhile!
We have been boys together—school-fellows—
And now are friends—yet shall not be so long—
For in the eternal city thou shalt do me
A kind and gentle office, and a Power—
A Power august, benignant, and supreme—
Shall then absolve thee of all further duties
Unto thy friend.

BALDAZZAR

       Thou speakest a fearful riddle
I *will* not understand.

POLITIAN

       Yet now as Fate
Approaches, and the Hours are breathing low,
The sands of time are changed to golden grains,
And dazzle me, Baldazzar. Alas! alas!
I *cannot* die, having within my heart
So keen a relish for the beautiful
As hath been kindled within it. Methinks the air
Is balmier now than it was wont to be—
Rich melodies are floating in the winds—
A rarer loveliness bedecks the earth—
And with a holier lustre the quiet moon
Sitteth in Heaven.—Hist! hist! thou canst not say
Thou hearest not *now*, Baldazzar?

BALDAZZAR

       Indeed I hear not.

POLITIAN

Not hear it!—listen now—listen!—the faintest
     sound
And yet the sweetest that ear ever heard!

A lady's voice !—and sorrow in the tone !
Baldazzar, it oppresses me like a spell !
Again !—again !—how solemnly it falls
Into my heart of hearts ! that eloquent **voice**
Surely I never heard—yet it were well
Had I *but* heard it with its thrilling tones
In earlier days !

BALDAZZAR

            I myself hear it now.
Be still !—the voice, if I mistake not greatly,
Proceeds from yonder lattice—which you may see
Very plainly through the window—it belongs,
Does it not ? unto this palace of the Duke.
The singer is undoubtedly beneath
The roof of his Excellency—and perhaps
Is even that Alessandra of whom he spoke
As the betrothed of Castiglione,
His son and heir.

POLITIAN

          Be still !—it comes again !

VOICE (very faintly)

" And is thy heart so strong
    As for to leave me thus,
Who have loved thee so long
    In wealth and wo among ?
And is thy heart so strong
    As for to leave me thus ?
         Say nay—say nay ! "

BALDAZZAR

The song is English, and I oft have heard it
In merry England—never so plaintively—
Hist ! hist ! it comes again !

VOICE (more loudly)

" Is it so strong
    As for to leave me thus,
Who have loved thee so long

> In wealth and wo among?
> And is thy heart so strong
> As for to leave me thus?
>   Say nay—say nay!"

BALDAZZAR

'Tis hushed and all is still!

POLITIAN

                 All *is not* still.

BALDAZZAR

Let us go down.

POLITIAN

           Go down, Baldazzar, go!

BALDAZZAR

The hour is growing late—the Duke awaits us,—
Thy presence is expected in the hall
Below. What ails thee, Earl Politian?

VOICE (*distinctly*)

> " Who have loved thee so long,
>   In wealth and wo among!
>   And is thy heart so strong?
>   Say nay—say nay!"

BALDAZZAR

Let us descend!—'tis time. Politian, give
These fancies to the wind. Remember, pray,
Your bearing lately savoured much of rudeness
Unto the Duke. Arouse thee! and remember!

POLITIAN

Remember? I do. Lead on! I *do* remember.
                                    (*Going.*)
Let us descend. Believe me I would give,
Freely would give the broad lands of my earldom
To look upon the face hidden by yon lattice—
" To gaze upon that veiled face, and hear
Once more that silent tongue."

BALDAZZAR

Let me beg you, sir,
Descend with me—the Duke may be offended.
Let us go down, I pray you.

VOICE (*loudly*)
Say nay ! say nay !

POLITIAN (*aside*)
'Tis strange !—'tis very strange—methought **the**
voice
Chimed in with my desires and bade me stay !
(*Approaching the window.*)
Sweet voice ! I heed thee, and will surely stay.
Now be this Fancy, by Heaven, or be it Fate,
Still will I not descend. Baldazzar, make
Apology unto the Duke for me ;
I go not down to-night.

BALDAZZAR

Your lordship's pleasure
Shall be attended to. Good-night, Politian.

POLITIAN
Good-night, my friend, good-night.

IV

The gardens of a palace—moonlight. LALAGE *ana*
POLITIAN.

LALAGE

And dost thou speak of love
To *me*, Politian ?—dost thou speak of love
To Lalage ?—ah, wo—ah, wo is me !
This mockery is most cruel—most cruel indeed !

POLITIAN
Weep not ! oh, sob not thus !—thy bitter **tears**
Will madden me. Oh, mourn not, Lalage—

Be comforted! I know—I know it all,
And *still* I speak of love. Look at me, brightest
And beautiful Lalage!—turn here thine eyes!
Thou askest me if I could speak of love,
Knowing what I know, and seeing what I have seen.
Thou askest me that—and thus I answer thee—
Thus on my bended knee I answer thee. (*Kneeling.*)
Sweet Lalage, *I love thee—love thee—love thee;*
Thro' good and ill—thro' weal and wo *I love thee.*
Not mother, with her first-born on her knee,
Thrills with intenser love than I for thee.
Not on God's altar, in any time or clime,
Burned there a holier fire than burneth now
Within my spirit for *thee.* And do I love? (*Arising.*)
Even for thy woes I love—even for thy woes—
Thy beauty and thy woes.

LALAGE
                    Alas! proud Earl,
Thou dost forget thyself, remembering me!
How, in thy father's halls. among the maidens
Pure and reproachless of thy princely line,
Could the dishonoured Lalage abide?
Thy wife, and with a tainted memory—
My seared and blighted name, how would it tally
With the ancestral honours of thy house,
And with thy glory?

POLITIAN
                    Speak not to me of glory!
I hate—I loathe the name; I do abhor
The unsatisfactory and ideal thing.
Art thou not Lalage, and I Politian?
Do I not love—art thou not beautiful—
What need we more? Ha! glory!—now speak not
    of it:
By all I hold most sacred and most solemn—
By all my wishes now—my fears hereafter—
By all I scorn on earth and hope in heaven—
There is no deed I would more glory in,

Than in thy cause to scoff at this same glory
And trample it under foot. What matters it—
What matters it, my fairest, and my best,
That we go down unhonoured and forgotten
Into the dust—so we descend together.
Descend together—and then—and then perchance—

LALAGE

Why dost thou pause, Politian?

POLITIAN

And then perchance
Arise together, Lalage, and roam
The starry and quiet dwellings of the blest,
And still——

LALAGE

Why dost thou pause, Politian?

POLITIAN

And still *together—together.*

LALAGE

Now, Earl of Leicester!
Thou *lovest* me, and in my heart of hearts
I feel thou lovest me truly.

POLITIAN

Oh, Lalage! (*Throwing himself upon his knee.*)
And lovest thou *me?*

LALAGE

Hist! hush! within the gloom
Of yonder trees methought a figure past—
A spectral figure, solemn, and slow, and noiseless—
Like the grim shadow Conscience, solemn and noise-
    less. (*Walks across and returns.*)
I was mistaken—'twas but a giant bough
Stirred by the autumn wind. Politian!

POLITIAN

My Lalage—my love! why art thou moved?
Why dost thou turn so pale? Not Conscience' self,
Far less a shadow which thou likenest to it,
Should shake the firm spirit thus. But the night
    wind
Is chilly—and these melancholy boughs
Throw over all things a gloom.

LALAGE

                Politian!
Thou speakest to me of love. Knowest thou the
    land
With which all tongues are busy—a land new found—
Miraculously found by one of Genoa—
A thousand leagues within the golden west?
A fairy land of flowers, and fruit, and sunshine,
And crystal lakes, and over-arching forests,
And mountains, around whose towering summits the
    winds
Of Heaven untrammelled flow—which air to breathe
Is Happiness now, and will be Freedom hereafter
In days that are to come?

POLITIAN

                Oh, wilt thou—wilt thou
Fly to that Paradise—my Lalage, wilt thou
Fly thither with me? There Care shall be forgotten
And Sorrow shall be no more, and Eros be all.
And life shall then be mine, for I will live
For thee, and in thine eyes—and thou shalt be
No more a mourner—but the radiant Joys
Shall wait upon thee, and the angel Hope
Attend thee ever; and I will kneel to thee
And worship thee, and call thee my beloved,
My own, my beautiful, my love, my wife,
My all;—oh, wilt thou—wilt thou, Lalage,
Fly thither with me?

LALAGE

A deed is to be done—

Castiglione lives !

POLITIAN

And he shall die !   [*Exit.*

LALAGE (*after a pause*)

And—he—shall—die !—alas !
Castiglione die ! Who spoke the words ?
Where am I ?—what was it he said ?—Politian !
Thou *art* not gone—thou are not *gone*, Politian !
I *feel* thou art not gone—yet dare not look,.
Lest I behold thee not—thou *couldst* not go
With those words upon thy lips—Oh, speak to me !
And let me hear thy voice—one word—one word,
To say thou art not gone,—one little sentence,
To say how thou dost scorn—how thou dost hate
My womanly weakness. Ha ! ha ! thou *art* not gone—
Oh, speak to me ! I *knew* thou wouldst not go !
I knew thou wouldst not, couldst not, *durst* not go.
Villain, thou *art* not gone—thou mockest me !
And thus I clutch thee—thus !—He is gone, he is
      gone—
Gone—gone. Where am I ?—'tis well—'tis very
      well !
So that the blade be keen—the blow be sure,
'Tis well, 'tis *very* well—alas ! alas !

V

The suburbs. POLITIAN *alone.*

POLITIAN

This weakness grows upon me. I am faint,
And much I fear me ill—it will not do
To die ere I have lived !—Stay—stay thy hand,
O Azrael, yet awhile !—Prince of the Powers
Of Darkness and the Tomb, Oh, pity me !

Oh, pity me ! let me not perish now,
In the budding of my Paradisal Hope !
Give me to live yet—yet a little while :
'Tis I who pray for life—I who so late
Demanded but to die—what sayeth the Count ?

Enter BALDAZZAR

BALDAZZAR

That, knowing no cause of quarrel or of feud
Between the Earl Politian and himself.
He doth decline your cartel.

POLITIAN

         What didst thou say ?
What answer was it you brought me, good Baldazzar ?
With what excessive fragrance the zephyr comes
Laden from yonder bowers !—a fairer day,
Or one more worthy Italy, methinks
No mortal eyes have seen !—*What* said the Count ?

BALDAZZAR

That he, Castiglione, not being aware
Of any feud existing, or any cause
Of quarrel between your lordship and himself,
Cannot accept the challenge.

POLITIAN

         It is most true—
All this is very true. When saw you, sir,
When saw you, now, Baldazzar, in the frigid
Ungenial Britain which we left so lately,
A heaven so calm as this—so utterly free
From the evil taint of clouds ?—And he did *say* ?

BALDAZZAR

No more, my lord, than I have told you, sir :
The Count Castiglione will not fight,
Having no cause for quarrel.

POLITIAN

                      Now this is true—
All very true. Thou art my friend, Baldazzar,
And I have not forgotten it—thou'lt do me
A piece of service ; wilt thou go back and say
Unto this man, that I, the Earl of Leicester,
Hold him a villain ?—thus much, I prythee, say
Unto the Count—it is exceeding just
He should have cause for quarrel.

BALDAZZAR

               My lord !—my friend !——

POLITIAN (*aside*)

'Tis he—he comes himself ! (*Aloud.*) Thou reason-
   est well.
I know what thou wouldst say—not send the mes-
   sage—
Well !—I will think of it—I will not send it.
Now prythee, leave me—hither doth come a person
With whom affairs of a most private nature
I would adjust.

BALDAZZAR

          I go—to-morrow we meet,
Do we not ?—at the Vatican.

POLITIAN

At the Vatican,
                    [*Exit* BALDAZZAR.

Enter CASTIGLIONE

CASTIGLIONE

The Earl of Leicester here !

POLITIAN

I *am* the Earl of Leicester, and thou seest,
Dost thou not, that I am here ?

CASTIGLIONE

            My lord, some strange,
Some singular mistake—misunderstanding—

Hath without doubt arisen : thou hast been urged
Thereby, in heat of anger, to address
Some words most unaccountable, in writing,
To me, Castiglione ; the bearer being
Baldazzar, Duke of Surrey. I am aware
Of nothing which might warrant thee in this thing,
Having given thee no offence. Ha !—am I right ?
'Twas a mistake ?—undoubtedly—we all
Do err at times.

POLITIAN
Draw, villain, and prate no more !

CASTIGLIONE
Ha !—draw ?—and villain ? have at thee then at once,
Proud Earl ! (*Draws.*)

POLITIAN (*drawing*)
Thus to the expiatory tomb,
Untimely sepulchre, I do devote thee
In the name of Lalage !

CASTIGLIONE (*letting fall his sword and recoiling to the
extremity of the stage*)
Of Lalage !
Hold off—thy sacred hand !—avaunt I say !
Avaunt—I will not fight thee—indeed I dare not.

POLITIAN
Thou wilt not fight with me, didst say, Sir Count ?
Shall I be baffled thus ?—now this is well ;
Didst say thou *darest* not ? Ha !

CASTIGLIONE
I dare not—dare not—
Hold off thy hand—with that beloved name
So fresh upon thy lips I will not fight thee—
I cannot—dare not.

POLITIAN
Now by my halidom
I do believe thee !—coward, I do believe thee !

CASTIGLIONE

Ha !—coward !—this may not be !
    [Clutches his sword and staggers towards POLITIAN,
      but his purpose is changed before reaching him,
      and he falls upon his knee at the feet of the Earl.
                       Alas ! my lord,
It is—it is—most true. In such a cause
I am the veriest coward. Oh, pity me !

POLITIAN (*greatly softened*)

Alas !—I do—indeed I pity thee.

CASTIGLIONE

                   And Lalage——

POLITIAN

Scoundrel !—arise and die !

CASTIGLIONE

It needeth not be—thus—thus—Oh, let me die
Thus on my bended knee. It were most fitting
That in this deep humiliation I perish.
For in the fight I will not raise a hand
Against thee, Earl of Leicester. Strike thou
    home— (*Baring his bosom.*)
Here is no let or hindrance to thy weapon—
Strike home. I *will not* fight thee.

POLITIAN

             Now s'Death and Hell !
Am I not—am I not sorely—grievously tempted
To take thee at thy word ? But mark me, sir !
Think not to fly me thus. Do thou prepare
For public insult in the streets—before
The eyes of the citizens. I'll follow thee—
Like an avenging spirit I'll follow thee
Even unto death. Before those whom thou lovest—

Before all Rome I'll taunt thee, villain,—I'll taunt
     thee,
Dost hear? with *cowardice*—thou *wilt not* fight me?
Thou liest! thou *shalt!*   [*Exit.*

CASTIGLIONE
                    Now this indeed is just!
Most righteous, and most just, avenging Heaven!

SONNET TO SCIENCE

SCIENCE! true daughter of Old Time thou art!
  Who alterest all things with thy peering eyes.
Why preyest thou thus upon the poet's heart,
  Vulture, whose wings are dull realities?
How should he love thee? or how deem thee wise,
  Who wouldst not leave him in his wandering
To seek for treasure in the jewelled skies,
  Albeit he soared with an undaunted wing?
Hast thou not dragged Diana from her car?
  And driven the Hamadryad from the wood
To seek a shelter in some happier star?
  Hast thou not torn the Naiad from her flood,
The Elfin from the green grass, and from me
  The summer dream beneath the tamarind tree?

AL AARAAF [1]

PART I

OH! nothing earthly save the ray
(Thrown back from flowers) of Beauty's eye,
As in those gardens where the day
Springs from the gems of Circassy—

---

[1] A star was discovered by Tycho Brahe which appeared suddenly in the heavens—attained, in a few days, a brilliancy surpassing that of Jupiter—then as suddenly disappeared, and has never been seen since.

Oh ! nothing earthly save the thrill
Of melody in woodland rill—
Or (music of the passion-hearted)
Joy's voice so peacefully departed
That, like the murmur in the shell,
Its echo dwelleth and will dwell—
Oh ! nothing of the dross of ours—
Yet all the beauty—all the flowers
That list our Love, and deck our bowers—
Adorn yon world afar, afar—
The wandering star.

'Twas a sweet time for Nesace—for there
Her world lay lolling on the golden air,
Near four bright suns—a temporary rest—
An oasis in desert of the blest.
Away—away—'mid seas of rays that roll
Empyrean splendour o'er th' unchained soul—
The soul that scarce (the billows are so dense)
Can struggle to its destined eminence—
To distant spheres, from time to time, she rode,
And late to ours, the favour'd one of God—
But, now, the ruler of an anchor'd realm,
She throws aside the sceptre—leaves the helm,
And, amid incense and high spiritual hymns,
Laves in quadruple light her angel limbs.

Now happiest, loveliest in yon lovely Earth,
Whence sprang the " Idea of Beauty " into birth.
(Falling in wreaths thro' many a startled star,
Like woman's hair 'mid pearls, until, afar,
It lit on hills Achaian, and there dwelt)
She looked into Infinity—and knelt.
Rich clouds, for canopies, about her curled—
Fit emblems of the model of her world—
Seen but in beauty—not impeding sight
Of other beauty glittering thro' the light—
A wreath that twined each starry form around,
And all the opal'd air in colour bound.

All hurriedly she knelt upon a bed
Of flowers ; of lilies such as rear'd the head
On the fair Capo Deucato,[1] and sprang
So eagerly around about to hang
Upon the flying footsteps of—deep pride—
Of her who loved a mortal—and so died.[2]
The Sephalica, budding with young bees,
Uprear'd its purple stem around her knees :
And gemmy flower, of Trebizond misnam'd [3]
Inmate of highest stars, where erst it sham'd
All other loveliness : its honied dew
(The fabled nectar that the heathen knew)
Deliriously sweet, was dropp'd from Heaven,
And fell on gardens of the unforgiven
In Trebizond—and on a sunny flower
So like its own above, that, to this hour,
It still remaineth, torturing the bee
With madness, and unwonted reverie :
In Heaven, and all its environs, the leaf
And blossom of the fairy plant, in grief
Disconsolate linger—grief that hangs her head,
Repenting follies that full love have fled,
Heaving her white breast to the balmy air,
Like guilty beauty, chasten'd, and more fair :
Nyctanthes too, as sacred as the light
She fears to perfume, perfuming the night :
And Clytia pondering between many a sun,[4]
While pettish tears adown her petals run :
And that aspiring flower that sprang on Earth—[5]

[1] On Santa Maura—olim *Deucadia*.
[2] Sappho.
[3] This flower is much noticed by Lewenhoeck and Tourne-
ford.   The bee, feeding upon its blossom, becomes intoxicated.
[4] Clytia—*The Chrysanthemum Peruvianum*, or, to employ
a better known term, the *turnsol*—which turns continually
towards the sun, covers itself, like Peru, the country from
which it comes, with dewy clouds which cool and refresh its
flowers during the most violent heat of the day.—B. DE ST.
PIERRE.
[5] There is cultivated in the king's garden at Paris a species
of serpentine aloes without prickles, whose large and beautiful
flower exhales a strong odour of the vanilla during the time

And died, ere scarce exalted into birth,
Bursting its odorous heart in spirit to wing
Its way to Heaven, from garden of a king:
And Valisnerian lotus thither flown [1]
From struggling with the waters of the Rhone:
And thy most lovely purple perfume, Zante! [2]
Isola d'oro!—Fior di Levante!
And the Nelumbo bud that floats for ever [3]
With Indian Cupid down the holy river—
Fair flowers, and fairy! to whose care is given
To bear the Goddess' song, in odours, up to Heaven: [4]

　　　" Spirit! that dwellest where,
　　　　　In the deep sky,
　　　The terrible and fair,
　　　　　In beauty vie!
　　Beyond the line of blue—
　　　　The boundary of the star
　　Which turneth at the view
　　　　Of thy barrier and thy bar—
　　Of the barrier overgone
　　　　By the comets who were cast
　　From their pride, and from their throne,
　　　　To be drudges till the last—
　　To be carriers of fire
　　　　(The red fire of their heart)
　　With speed that may not tire,
　　　　And with pain that shall not part—
　　Who livest—*that* we know—
　　　　In Eternity—we feel—

of its expansion, which is very short. It does not blow till
towards the month of July; you then perceive it gradually
open its petals—expand them—fade—and die.—ST. PIERRE.
　[1] There is found, in the Rhone, a beautiful lily of the
Valisnerian kind. Its stem will stretch to the length of
three or four feet—thus preserving its head above water in
the swellings of the river.
　[2] The Hyacinth
　[3] It is a fiction of the Indians that Cupid was first seen
floating in one of these down the river Ganges, and that he
still loves the cradle of his childhood.
　[4] And golden vials full of odours, which are the prayers
of the saints.—REV OF ST. JOHN.

Al Aaraaf

But the shadow of whose brow
   What spirit shall reveal ?
Tho' the beings whom thy Nesace,
   Thy messenger hath known
Have dream'd for thy Infinity
   A model of their own—[1]
Thy will is done, O God !
   The star hath ridden high
Thro' many a tempest, but she rode
   Beneath thy burning eye ;
And here, in thought, to thee—
   In thought that can alone
Ascend thy empire and so be
   A partner of thy throne—
By winged Fantasy,[2]
   My embassy is given,
Till secrecy shall knowledge be
   In the environs of Heaven."

[1] The Humanitarians held that God was to be understood as having really a human form.—*Vide* CLARKE'S SERMONS, vol. i. page 26, fol. edit.

The drift of Milton's argument leads him to employ language which would appear, at first sight, to verge upon their doctrine ; but it will be seen immediately that he guards himself against the charge of having adopted one of the most ignorant errors of the dark ages of the Church.—DR. SUMNER'S NOTES ON MILTON'S CHRISTIAN DOCTRINE

This opinion, in spite of many testimonies to the contrary, could never have been very general. Andeus, a Syrian of Mesopotamia, was condemned for the opinion as heretical. He lived in the beginning of the fourth century. His disciples were called Anthropomorphites.—*Vide* DU PIN.

Among Milton's minor poems are these lines :—

> Dicite sacrorum præsides nemorum Deæ, &c.
> Quis ille primus cujus ex imagine
> Natura solers finxit humanum genus ?
> Eternus, incorruptus, æquævus polo,
> Unusque et universus exemplar Dei.

And afterwards,

> Non cui profundum Cæcitas lumen dedit
> Dircæus augur vidit hunc alto sinu, &c.

[2] Seltsamen Tochter Jovis
Seinem Schosskinde
Der Phantasie.—GOETHE.

She ceased—and buried then her burning cheek,
Abashed, amid the lilies there, to seek
A shelter from the fervour of His eye ;
For the stars trembled at the Deity.
She stirred not—breathed not—for a voice was there
How solemnly pervading the calm air !
A sound of silence on the startled ear
Which dreamy poets name " the music of the sphere."
Ours is a world of words : Quiet we call
" Silence "—which is the merest word of all.
All nature speaks, and ev'n ideal things
Flap shadowy sounds from visionary wings—
But ah ! not so when, thus, in realms on high
The eternal voice of God is passing by,
And the red winds are withering in the sky !

" What tho' in worlds which sightless cycles run,[1]
Link'd to a little system, and one sun—
Where all my love is folly and the crowd
Still think my terrors but the thunder-cloud,
The storm, the earthquake, and the ocean-wrath—
(Ah ! will they cross me in my angrier path ?)
What tho' in worlds which own a single sun
The sands of Time grow dimmer as they run,
Yet thine is my resplendency, so given
To bear my secrets thro' the upper Heaven.
Leave tenantless thy crystal home, and fly,
With all thy train, athwart the moony sky—
Apart—like fireflies in Sicilian night,[2]
And wing to other worlds another light !
Divulge the secrets of thy embassy
To the proud orbs that twinkle—and so be
To ev'ry heart a barrier and a ban
Lest the stars totter in the guilt of man ! "

Up rose the maiden in the yellow night,
The single-mooned eve !—on Earth we plight

[1] Sightless—too small to be seen.—LEGGE.
[2] I have often noticed a peculiar movement of the fire-flies ;—they will collect in a body and fly off, from a common centre, into innumerable radii.

Our faith to one love—and one moon adore—
The birthplace of young Beauty had no more.
As sprang that yellow star from downy hours,
Up rose the maiden from her shrine of flowers,
And bent o'er sheeny mountain and dim plain
Her way—but left not yet her Therasæan reign.[1]

Part II

High on a mountain of enamelléd head—
Such as the drowsy shepherd on his bed
Of giant pasturage lying at his ease,
Raising his heavy eyelid, starts and sees
With many a muttered " hope to be forgiven "
What time the moon is quadrated in Heaven—
Of rosy head, that towering far away
Into the sunlit ether, caught the ray
Of sunken suns at eve—at noon of night,
While the moon danced with the fair stranger
    light—
Upreared upon such height arose a pile
Of gorgeous columns on th' unburthen'd air,
Flashing from Parian marble that twin smile
Far down upon the wave that sparkled there,
And nursled the young mountain in its lair.
Of molten stars their pavement, such as fall [2]
Thro' the ebon air, besilvering the pall
Of their own dissolution, while they die—
Adorning then the dwellings of the sky.
A dome, by linked light from Heaven let down,
Sat gently on these columns as a crown—
A window of one circular diamond, there,
Look'd out above into the purple air,
And rays from God shot down that meteor chain
And hallow'd all the beauty twice again,

---

[1] Therasæa, or Therasea, the island mentioned by Seneca,
which, in a moment, arose from the sea to the eyes of
astonished mariners.
[2] Some star which, from the ruin'd roof
Of shak'd Olympus, by mischance did fall.—Milton.

Save when, between th' Empyrean and that ring,
Some eager spirit flapp'd his dusky wing.
But on the pillars Seraph eyes have seen
The dimness of this world : that grayish green
That nature loves the best for Beauty's grave
Lurked in each cornice, round each architrave—
And every sculptured cherub thereabout
That from his marble dwelling peeréd out,
Seemed earthly in the shadow of his niche—
Achaian statues in a world so rich ?
Friezes from Tadmor and Persepolis—[1]
From Baalbec, and the stilly, clear abyss
Of beautiful Gomorrha ! O, the wave [2]
Is now upon thee—but too late to save !

Sound loves to revel in a summer night :
Witness the murmur of the gray twilight
That stole upon the ear, in Eyraco,[3]
Of many a wild star-gazer long ago—
That stealeth ever on the ear of him
Who, musing, gazeth on the distance dim,
And sees the darkness coming as a cloud—
Is not its form—its voice—most palpable and loud ? [4]

[1] Voltaire, in speaking of Persepolis, says, " Je connois
bien l'admiration qu'inspirent ces ruines—mais un palais
erigé au pied d'une chaine des rochers sterils—peut il être
un chef d'œuvre des arts ! '

[2] " O, the wave "—Ula Deguisi is the Turkish appel-
lation ; but, on its own shores, it is called Bahar, Loth, or
Almontanah. There were undoubtedly more than two cities
engulphed in the " Dead Sea." In the Valley of Siddim
were five—Admah, Zeboim, Zoar, Sodom, and Gomorrha.
Stephen of Byzantium mentions eight, and Strabo thirteen
(engulphed)—but the last is out of all reason.

It is said [Tacitus, Strabo, Josephus, Daniel of St. Saba,
Nau, Maundrell, Troilo, D'Arvieux] that after an excessive
drought, the vestiges of columns, walls, &c., are seen
above the surface. At *any* season, such remains may
be discovered by looking down into the transparent lake,
and at such distances as would argue the existence of many
settlements in the space now usurped by the " Asphaltites."

[3] Eyraco—Chaldea.

[4] I have often thought I could distinctly hear the sound
of the darkness as it stole over the horizon.

But what is this !—it cometh—and it brings
A music with it—'tis the rush of wings—
A pause—and then a sweeping, falling strain,
And Nesace is in her halls again.
From the wild energy of wanton haste
  Her cheeks were flushing, and her lips apart ;
And zone that clung around her gentle waist
  Had burst beneath the heaving of her heart.
Within the centre of that hall to breathe
She paus'd and panted, Zanthe ! all beneath
The fairy light that kiss'd her golden hair,
And long'd to rest, yet could but sparkle there !

Young flowers were whispering in melody [1]
To happy flowers that night—and tree to tree :
Fountains were gushing music as they fell
In many a star-lit grove, or moon-lit dell ;
Yet silence came upon material things—
Fair flowers, bright waterfalls and angel wings—
And sound alone that from the spirit sprang
Bore burthen to the charm the maiden sang :

    " 'Neath blue-bell or streamer—
      Or tufted wild spray
   That keeps, from the dreamer,
      The moonbeam away— [2]
   Bright beings! that ponder,
      With half closing eyes,
  On the stars which your wonder
      Hath drawn from the skies,
  Till they glance thro' the shade, and
      Come down to your brow
  Like——eyes of the maiden
      Who calls on you now—

[1] " Fairies use flowers for their charactery "—MERRY
WIVES OF WINDSOR.

[2] In Scripture is this passage—" The sun shall not smite
thee by day, nor the moon by night." It is perhaps not
generally known that the moon, in Egypt, has the effect
of producing blindness to those who sleep with the face
exposed to its rays, to which circumstance the passage
evidently alludes.

Arise! from your dreaming
　　In violet bowers,
To duty beseeming
　　These star-litten hours—
And shake from your tresses
　　Encumber'd with dew
The breath of those kisses
　　That cumber them too—
(O! how, without you, Love!
　　Could angels be blest?)
Those kisses of true love
　　That lull'd ye to rest!
Up!—shake from your wing
　　Each hindering thing:
The dew of the night—
　　It would weigh down your flight;
And true love caresses—
　　O! leave them apart!
They are light on the tresses,
　　But lead on the heart.
Ligeia! Ligeia!
　　My beautiful one!
Whose harshest idea
　　Will to melody run,
O! is it thy will
　　On the breezes to toss?
Or, capriciously still,
　　Like the lone Albatross,[1]
Incumbent on night
　　(As she on the air)
To keep watch with delight
　　On the harmony there?

Ligeia! wherever
　　Thy image may be,
No magic shall sever
　　Thy music from thee.

[1] The Albatross is said to sleep on the wing.

Thou hast bound many eyes
    In a dreamy sleep—
But the strains still arise
    Which *thy* vigilance keep—
The sound of the rain,
    Which leaps down to the flower
And dances again
    In the rhythm of the shower—
The murmur that springs [1]
    From the growing of grass—
Are the music of things—
    But are modell'd, alas !—
Away, then, my dearest,
    O ! hie thee away
To springs that lie clearest
    Beneath the moon-ray—
To lone lake that smiles,
    In its dream of deep rest,
At the many star-isles
    That enjewel its breast—
Where wild flowers, creeping,
    Have mingled their shade,
On its margin is sleeping
    Full many a maid—
Some have left the cool glade, and
    Have slept with the bee —[2]

---

[1] I met with this idea in an old English tale, which I am now unable to obtain, and quote from memory : " The verie essence, and, as it were, springeheade and origine of all musicke is the verie pleasaunte sounde which the trees of the forest do make when they growe."

[2] The wild bee will not sleep in the shade if there be moonlight.

The rhyme in this verse, as in one about sixty lines before, has an appearance of affectation. It is, however, imitated from Sir W. Scott, or rather from Claud Halcro—in whose mouth I admired its effect :—

> " O ! were there an island,
>   Tho' ever so wild,
> Where woman might smile, and
>   No man be beguiled," &c.

Arouse them, my maiden,
  On moorland and lea—
Go! breathe on their slumber,
  All softly in ear,
The musical number
  They slumber'd to hear—
For what can awaken
  An angel so soon
Whose sleep hath been taken
  Beneath the cold moon,
As the spell which no slumber
  Of witchery may test,
The rhythmical number
  Which lulled him to rest ? "

Spirits in wing, and angels to the view,
A thousand seraphs burst th' Empyrean thro',
Young dreams still hovering on their drowsy flight—
Seraphs in all but " Knowledge," the keen light
That fell, refracted thro' thy bounds, afar,
O Death! from eye of God upon that star:
Sweet was that error—sweeter still that death—
Sweet was that error—ev'n with *us* the breath
Of Science dims the mirror of our joy—
To them 'twere the Simoom, and would destroy—
For what (to them) availeth it to know
That Truth is Falsehood—or that Bliss is Woe ?
Sweet was their death—with them to die was rife
With the last ecstasy of satiate life—
Beyond that death no immortality—
But sleep that pondereth and is not " to be "—
And there—oh! may my weary spirit dwell—
Apart from Heaven's Eternity—and yet how far from
    Hell! [1]
What guilty spirit, in what shrubbery dim,
Heard not the stirring summons of that hymn ?

[1] With the Arabians there is a medium between Heaven
and Hell, where men suffer no punishment, but yet do not
attain that tranquil and even happiness which they suppose
to be characteristic of heavenly enjoyment.

But two: they fell: for Heaven no grace imparts
To those who hear not for their beating hearts.
A maiden angel and her seraph-lover—
O! where (and ye may seek the wide skies over)
Was Love, the blind, near sober Duty known?
Unguided Love hath fallen—'mid "tears of perfect
    moan." [1]

He was a goodly spirit—he who fell:
A wanderer by moss-y-mantled well—
A gazer on the lights that shine above—
A dreamer in the moonbeam by his love:
What wonder? for each star is eye-like there,
And looks so sweetly down on Beauty's hair—
And they, and ev'ry mossy spring were holy
To his love-haunted heart and melancholy.
The night had found (to him a night of wo)
Upon a mountain crag, young Angelo—
Beetling it bends athwart the solemn sky,
And scowls on starry worlds that down beneath it lie.
Here sate he with his love—his dark eye bent
With eagle gaze along the firmament:
Now turned it upon her—but ever then
It trembled to the orb of EARTH again.

"Ianthe, dearest, see! how dim that ray!
How lovely 'tis to look so far away!

    "Un no rompido sueno—
    Un dia puro—allegre—libre
    Quiera—
    Libre de amor—de zelo—
    De odio—de esperanza—de rezelo."
              —Luis Ponce de Leon.

Sorrow is not excluded from "Al Aaraaf," but is that
sorrow which the living love to cherish for the dead, and
which in some minds resembles the delirium of opium. The
passionate excitement of Love, and the buoyancy of spirit
attendant upon intoxication, are its less holy pleasures—the
price of which, to those souls who make choice of "Al Aaraaf"
as their residence after life, is final death and annihilation.

    [1] "There be tears of perfect moan
    Wept for thee in Helicon."—Milton.

She seem'd not thus upon that autumn eve
I left her gorgeous halls—nor mourn'd to leave.
That eve—that eve—I should remember well –
The sun-ray dropp'd, in Lemnos, with a spell
On th' Arabesque carving of a gilded hall
Wherein I sate, and on the draperied wall—
And on my eye-lids—O, the heavy light !
How drowsily it weighed them into night !
On flowers, before, and mist, and love they ran
With Persian Saadi in his Gulistan :
But O, that light !—I slumbered—Death, the while,
Stole o'er my senses in that lovely isle
So softly that no single silken hair
Awoke that slept—or knew that he was there.

" The last spot of Earth's orb I trod upon
Was a proud temple called the Parthenon ; [1]
More beauty clung around her columned wall
Than even thy glowing bosom beats withal,[2]
And when old Time my wing did disenthral
Thence sprang I—as the eagle from his tower,
And years I left behind me in an hour.
What time upon her airy bounds I hung
One half the garden of her globe was flung
Unrolling as a chart unto my view—
Tenantless cities of the desert too !
Ianthe, beauty crowded on me then,
And half I wished to be again of men."

" My Angelo ! and why of them to be ?
A brighter dwelling-place is here for thee—
And greener fields than in yon world above,
And woman's loveliness—and passionate love."

[1] It was entire in 1687—the most elevated spot in Athens.
[2] " Shadowing more beauty in their airy brows
      Than have the white breasts of the queen of love."
                                        —MARLOWE.

" But list, Ianthe ! when the air so soft
 Failed, as my pennon'd spirit leapt aloft,[1]
 Perhaps my brain grew dizzy—but the world
 I left so late was into chaos hurl'd,
 Sprang from her station, on the winds apart,
 And rolled a flame, the fiery Heaven athwart.
 Methought, my sweet one, then I ceased to
   soar,
 And fell—not swiftly as I rose before,
 But with a downward, tremulous motion thro'
 Light, brazen rays, this golden star unto !
 Nor long the measure of my falling hours,
 For nearest of all stars was thine to ours—
 Dread star ! that came, amid a night of mirth,
 A red Dædalion on the timid Earth."

" We came—and to thy Earth—but not to us
 Be given our lady's bidding to discuss :
 We came, my love ; around, above, below,
 Gay fire-fly of the night we come and go,
 Nor ask a reason save the angel-nod
 She grants to us as granted by her God—
 But, Angelo, than thine grey Time unfurled
 Never his fairy wing o'er fairier world !
 Dim was its little disk, and angel eyes
 Alone could see the phantom in the skies,
 When first Al Aaraaf knew her course to be
 Headlong thitherward o'er the starry sea—
 But when its glory swelled upon the sky,
 As glowing Beauty's bust beneath man's eye,
 We paused before the heritage of men,
 And thy star trembled—as doth Beauty then ! "

Thus in discourse, the lovers whiled away
The night that waned and waned and brought no
   day.
They fell : for Heaven to them no hope imparts
Who hear not for the beating of their hearts.

---

[1] Pennon, for pinion —MILTON.

TAMERLANE

KIND solace in a dying hour!
  Such, father, is not (now) my theme—
I will not madly deem that power
    Of Earth may shrive me of the sin
    Unearthly pride hath revell'd in—
I have no time to dote or dream:
You call it hope—that fire of fire!
It is but agony of desire:
If I *can* hope—O God! I can—
  Its fount is holier—more divine—
I would not call thee fool, old man,
  But such is not a gift of thine.

Know thou the secret of a spirit
  Bowed from its wild pride into shame.
O yearning heart! I did inherit
  Thy withering portion with the fame,
The searing glory which hath shone
Amid the Jewels of my throne,
Halo of Hell! and with a pain
Not Hell shall make me fear again—
O craving heart, for the lost flowers
And sunshine of my summer hours!
The undying voice of that dead time,
With its interminable chime,
Rings, in the spirit of a spell,
Upon thy emptiness—a knell.

I have not always been as now:
The fevered diadem on my brow
  I claimed and won usurpingly—
Hath not the same fierce heirdom given
  Rome to the Cæsar—this to me?
    The heritage of a kingly mind,
And a proud spirit which hath striven
    Triumphantly with human kind.

On mountain soil I first drew life :
  The mists of the Taglay have shed
  Nightly their dews upon my head,
And, I believe, the winged strife
And tumult of the headlong air
Have nestled in my very hair.

So late from Heaven—that dew—it fell
  ('Mid dreams of an unholy night)
Upon me with the touch of Hell,
  While the red flashing of the light
From clouds that hung, like banners, o'er,
  Appeared to my half-closing eye
  The pageantry of monarchy ;
And the deep trumpet-thunder's roar
  Came hurriedly upon me, telling
    Of human battle, where my voice,
  My own voice, silly child !—was swelling
    (O ! how my spirit would rejoice,
And leap within me at the cry)
The battle-cry of Victory !

The rain came down upon my head
  Unshelter'd—and the heavy wind
  Rendered me mad and deaf and blind.
It was but man, I thought, who shed
  Laurels upon me : and the rush—
The torrent of the chilly air
Gurgled within my ear the crush
  Of empires—with the captive's prayer—
The hum of suitors—and the tone
Of flattery 'round a sovereign's throne.

My passions, from that hapless hour,
  Usurped a tyranny which men
Have deemed since I have reached to power
    My innate nature—be it so :
  But, father, there lived one who, then,

Then—in my boyhood—when their fire
  Burn'd with a still intenser glow
(For passion must, with youth, expire)
  E'en *then* who knew this iron heart
  In woman's weakness had a part.

I have no words—alas!—to tell
The loveliness of loving well!
Nor would I now attempt to trace
The more than beauty of a face
Whose lineaments, upon my mind,
Are——shadows on th' unstable wind:
Thus I remember having dwelt
  Some page of early lore upon,
With loitering eye, till I have felt
The letters—with their meaning—melt
  To fantasies—with none.

O, she was worthy of all love!
  Love—as in infancy—was mine—
'Twas such an angel minds above
  Might envy: her young heart the shrine
On which my every hope and thought
  Were incense—then a goodly gift,
    For they were childish and upright—
Pure—as her young example taught;
  Why did I leave it, and, adrift,
    Trust to the fire within, for light?

We grew in age—and love—together—
Roaming the forest, and the wild;
My breast her shield in wintry weather—
  And, when the friendly sunshine smiled.
And she would mark the opening skies,
I saw no heaven—but in her eyes.
Young Love's first lesson is—the heart:
  For 'mid that sunshine and those smiles,
When, from our little cares apart,
  And laughing at her girlish wiles,

I'd throw me on her throbbing breast,
  And pour my spirit out in tears—
There was no need to speak the rest—
  No need to quiet any fears
Of her—who ask'd no reason why,
But turn'd on me her quiet eye !

Yet *more* than worthy of the love
My spirit struggled with, and strove,
When, on the mountain peak, alone,
Ambition lent it a new tone—
I had no being—but in thee :
  The world and all it did contain
In the earth—the air—the sea—
  Its joy—its little lot of pain
That was new pleasure—the ideal,
  Dim, vanities of dreams by night—
And dimmer nothings which were real—
  (Shadows—and a more shadowy light !)
Parted upon their misty wings,
    And so, confusedly, became
    Thine image and—a name—a name !
Two separate—yet most intimate things.

I was ambitious—have you known
    The passion, father ? You have not :
A cottager, I mark'd a throne
Of half the world as all my own,
    And murmur'd at such lowly lot—
But, just like any other dream,
    Upon the vapour of the dew
My own had past, did not the beam
    Of beauty which did while it thro'
The minute—the hour—the day—oppress
My mind with double loveliness.
We walk'd together on the crown
Of a high mountain which looked down
Afar from its proud natural towers
  Of rock and forest, on the hills—
The dwindled hills ! begirt with bowers
  And shouting with a thousand rills.

I spoke to her of power and pride;
  But mystically—in such guise
That she might deem it nought beside
  The moment's converse ; in her eyes
I read, perhaps too carelessly—
  A mingled feeling with my own—
The flush on her bright cheek, to me
  Seem'd to become a queenly throne
Too well that I should let it be
  Light in the wilderness alone.

I wrapp'd myself in grandeur then,
  And donn'd a visionary crown—
    Yet it was not that Fantasy
    Had thrown her mantle over me—
But that, among the rabble—men,
    Lion Ambition is chain'd down—
And crouches to a keeper's hand—
Not so in deserts where the grand—
The wild—the terrible conspire
With their own breath to fan his fire.

Look 'round thee now on Samarcand !—
  Is she not queen of Earth ? her pride
Above all cities ? in her hand
  Their destinies ? in all beside
Of glory which the world hath known
Stands she not nobly and alone ?
Falling—her veriest stepping-stone
Shall form the pedestal of a throne—
And who her sovereign ? Timour—he
  Whom the astonished people saw
Striding o'er empires haughtily
  A diadem'd outlaw !

O, human love ! thou spirit given,
On Earth, of all we hope in Heaven !
Which fall'st into the soul like rain
Upon the Siroc-withered plain,

And, failing in thy power to bless,
But leav'st the heart a wilderness!
Idea! which bindest life around
With music of so strange a sound
And beauty of so wild a birth—
Farewell! for I have won the Earth.

When Hope, that eagle that tower'd, could see
    No cliff beyond him in the sky,
His pinions were bent droopingly—
    And homeward turn'd his softened eye.
'Twas sunset: when the sun will part
There comes a sullenness of heart
To him who still would look upon
The glory of the summer sun.
That soul will hate the ev'ning mist
So often lovely, and will list
To the sound of the coming darkness (known
To those whose spirits hearken) as one
Who, in a dream of night, *would* fly,
But *cannot*, from a danger nigh.

What tho' the moon—the white moon
Shed all the splendour of her noon,
Her smile is chilly—and *her* beam,
In that time of dreariness, will seem
(So like you gather in your breath)
A portrait taken after death.
And boyhood is a summer sun
Whose waning is the dreariest one—
For all we live to know is known
And all we seek to keep hath flown—
Let life, then, as the day-flower, fall
With the noon-day beauty—which is all.
I reach'd my home—my home no more—
    For all had flown who made it so.
I passed from out its mossy door,
    And, tho' my tread was soft and low,

A voice came from the threshold stone
Of one whom I had earlier known—
    O, I defy thee, Hell, to show
    On beds of fire that burn below,
    An humbler heart—a deeper wo.

Father, I firmly do believe—
    I *know*—for Death who comes for me
    From regions of the blest afar,
Where there is nothing to deceive,
    Hath left his iron gate ajar,
    And rays of truth you cannot see
    Are flashing thro' Eternity——
I do believe that Eblis hath
A snare in every human path—
Else how, when in the holy grove
I wandered of the idol, Love,—
Who daily scents his snowy wings
With incense of burnt-offerings
From the most unpolluted things
Whose pleasant bowers are yet so riven
Above with trellis'd rays from Heaven
No mote may shun—no tiniest fly—
The light'ning of his eagle eye—
How was it that Ambition crept,
    Unseen, amid the revels there,
Till growing bold, he laughed and leapt
    In the tangles of Love's very hair?

A DREAM

In visions of the dark night
    I have dreamed of joy departed—
But a waking dream of life and light
    Hath left me broken-hearted.

Ah! what is not a dream by day
    To him whose eyes are cast
On things around him with a ray
    Turned back upon the past?

That holy dream—that holy dream,
 While all the world were chiding,
Hath cheered me as a lovely beam,
 A lonely spirit guiding.

What though that light, thro' storm and night,
 So trembled from afar—
What could there be more purely bright
 In Truth's day-star?

ROMANCE

Romance, who loves to nod and sing,
With drowsy head and folded wing,
Among the green leaves as they shake
Far down within some shadowy lake,
To me a painted paroquet
Hath been—a most familiar bird—
Taught me my alphabet to say—
To lisp my very earliest word
While in the wild wood I did lie,
A child—with a most knowing eye.
Of late, eternal Condor years
So shake the very Heaven on high
With tumult as they thunder by,
I have no time for idle cares
Through gazing on the unquiet sky.
And when an hour with calmer wings
Its down upon my spirit flings—
That little time with lyre and rhyme
To while away—forbidden things!
My heart would feel to be a crime
Unless it trembled with the strings.

FAIRYLAND

Dim vales—and shadowy floods—
And cloudy-looking woods.

Whose forms we can't discover
For the tears that drip all over
Huge moons there wax and wane—
Again—again—again—
Every moment of the night—
For ever changing places—
And they put out the star-light
With the breath from their pale faces.
About twelve by the moon-dial
One more filmy than the rest
(A kind which, upon trial,
They have found to be the best)
Comes down—still down—and down
With its centre on the crown
Of a mountain's eminence,
While its wide circumference
In easy drapery falls
Over hamlets, over halls,
Wherever they may be—
O'er the strange woods—o'er the sea—
Over spirits on the wing—
Over every drowsy thing—
And buries them up quite
In a labyrinth of light—
And then how deep !—O, deep !
Is the passion of their sleep.
In the morning they arise,
And their moony covering
Is soaring in the skies,
With the tempests as they toss,
Like——almost any thing—
Or a yellow Albatross.
They use that moon no more
For the same end as before—
Videlicet a tent—
Which I think extravagant.
Its atomies, however,
Into a shower dissever,
Of which those butterflies,
Of Earth, who seek the skies,

And so come down again
(Never-contented things !)
Have brought a specimen
Upon their quivering wings.

TO ——

THE bowers whereat, in dreams, I see
  The wantonest singing birds,
Are lips—and all thy melody
  Of lip-begotten words—

Thine eyes, in Heaven of heart enshrined
  Then desolately fall,
O God ! on my funereal mind
  Like starlight on a pall—

Thy heart—*thy* heart !—I wake and sigh,
  And sleep to dream till day
Of the truth that gold can never buy—
  Of the baubles that it may.

TO THE RIVER ——

FAIR river ! in thy bright, clear flow
  Of crystal, wandering water,
Thou art an emblem of the glow
    Of beauty—the unhidden heart—
    The playful maziness of art
In old Alberto's daughter ;

But when within thy wave she looks—
  Which glistens then, and trembles—
Why, then, the prettiest of brooks
  Her worshipper resembles ;
For in his heart, as in thy stream,
  Her image deeply lies—
His heart which trembles at the beam
  Of her soul-searching eyes.

THE LAKE. TO ——

IN spring of youth it was my lot
To haunt of the wide world a spot
The which I could not love the less—
So lovely was the loneliness
Of a wild lake, with black rock bound,
And the tall pines that towered around.

But when the Night had thrown her pall
Upon that spot, as upon all,
And the mystic wind went by
Murmuring in melody—
Then—ah, then, I would awake
To the terror of the lone lake.
Yet that terror was not fright,
But a tremulous delight—
A feeling not the jewelled mine
Could teach or bribe me to define
Nor Love—although the Love were thine.

Death was in that poisonous wave,
And in its gulf a fitting grave
For him who thence could solace bring
To his lone imagining—
Whose solitary soul could make
An Eden of that dim lake.

SONG

I SAW thee on thy bridal day—
    When a burning blush came o'er thee,
Though happiness around thee lay,
    The world all love before thee:

And in thine eye a kindling light
    (Whatever it might be)
Was all on Earth my aching sight
    Of Loveliness could see.

That blush, perhaps, was maiden shame—
   As such it well may pass—
Though its glow hath raised a fiercer flame
   In the breast of him, alas!

Who saw thee on that bridal day,
   When that deep blush *would* come o'er thee;
Though happiness around thee lay,
   The world all love before thee.

A DREAM WITHIN A DREAM

TAKE this kiss upon the brow!
And, in parting from you now,
Thus much let me avow—
You are not wrong, who deem
That my days have been a dream;
Yet if hope has flown away
In a night, or in a day,
In a vision, or in none,
Is it therefore the less *gone*?
All that we see or seem
Is but a dream within a dream.

I stand amid the roar
Of a surf-tormented shore,
And I hold within my hand
Grains of the golden sand—
How few! yet how they creep
Through my fingers to the deep,
While I weep—while I weep!
O God! can I not grasp
Them with a tighter clasp?
O God! can I not save
One from the pitiless wave?
Is *all* that we see or seem
But a dream within a dream?

THE BELLS

I

HEAR the sledges with the bells—
Silver bells!
What a world of merriment their melody foretells!
How they tinkle, tinkle, tinkle,
In the icy air of night!
While the stars, that oversprinkle
All the heavens, seem to twinkle
With a crystalline delight;
Keeping time, time, time,
In a sort of Runic rhyme,
To the tintinabulation that so musically wells
From the bells, bells, bells, bells,
Bells, bells, bells—
From the jingling and the tinkling of the bells.

II

Hear the mellow wedding bells,
Golden bells!
What a world of happiness their harmony foretells!
Through the balmy air of night
How they ring out their delight!
From the molten-golden notes,
And all in tune,
What a liquid ditty floats
To the turtle-dove that listens, while she gloats
On the moon!
Oh, from out the sounding cells,
What a gush of euphony voluminously wells!
How it swells!
How it dwells
On the Future! how it tells
Of the rapture that impels
To the swinging and the ringing
Of the bells, bells, bells,
Of the bells, bells, bells bells,
Bells, bells, bells—
To the rhyming and the chiming of the bells!

The Bells

III

Hear the loud alarum bells—
　　　　Brazen bells !
What a tale of terror, now, their turbulency tells !
　　　In the startled ear of night
　　　How they scream out their affright !
　　　　Too much horrified to speak,
　　　　They can only shriek, shriek,
　　　　　　Out of tune,
In a clamorous appealing to the mercy of the
　　　fire,
In a mad expostulation with the deaf and frantic
　　　fire,
　　　　　Leaping higher, higher, higher,
　　　　　With a desperate desire,
　　　　And a resolute endeavour
　　　　Now—now to sit or never,
　　　By the side of the pale-faced moon.
　　　　Oh, the bells, bells, bells !
　　　　What a tale their terror tells
　　　　　Of despair !
　　　How they clang, and clash, and roar !
　　　What a horror they outpour
On the bosom of the palpitating air !
　　　　Yet the ear it fully knows,
　　　　　By the twanging,
　　　　　And the clanging,
　　　　How the danger ebbs and flows ;
　　　　Yet the ear distinctly tells,
　　　　　In the jangling,
　　　　　And the wrangling,
　　　　How the danger sinks and swells,
By the sinking or the swelling in the anger of the
　　　bells—
　　　　　Of the bells—
　　　Of the bells, bells, bells, bells,
　　　　Bells, bells, bells—
In the clamour and the clangour of the bells !

IV

Hear the tolling of the bells—
Iron bells !
What a world of solemn thought their monody
compels !
In the silence of the night,
How we shiver with affright
At the melancholy menace of their tone !
For every sound that floats
From the rust within their throats
Is a groan.
And the people—ah, the people—
They that dwell up in the steeple,
All alone,
And who tolling, tolling, tolling,
In that muffled monotone,
Feel a glory in so rolling
On the human heart a stone—
They are neither man nor woman—
They are neither brute nor human—
They are Ghouls :
And their king it is who tolls ;
And he rolls, rolls, rolls,
Rolls
A pæan from the bells !
And his merry bosom swells
With the pæan of the bells !
And he dances and he yells ;
Keeping time, time, time,
In a sort of Runic rhyme,
To the pæan of the bells—
Of the bells :
Keeping time, time, time,
In a sort of Runic rhyme,
To the throbbing of the bells,
Of the bells, bells, bells—
To the sobbing of the bells ;
Keeping time, time, time,
As he knells, knells, knells,

In a happy Runic rhyme,
   To the rolling of the bells—
  Of the bells, bells, bells,—
   To the tolling of the bells,
  Of the bells, bells, bells, bells,
    Bells, bells, bells,
To the moaning and the groaning of the bells.

TO HELEN

I SAW thee once—once only—years ago!
I must not say *how* many—but *not* many.
It was a July midnight ; and from out
A full-orbed moon, that, like thine own soul, soaring,
Sought a precipitate pathway up through heaven,
There fell a silvery-silken veil of light,
With quietude, and sultriness, and slumber,
Upon the upturn'd faces of a thousand
Roses that grew in an enchanted garden,
Where no wind dared to stir, unless on tiptoe—
Fell on the upturn'd faces of these roses
That gave out, in return for the love-light,
Their odorous souls in an ecstatic death—
Fell on the upturned faces of these roses
That smiled and died in this parterre, enchanted
By thee, and by the poetry of thy presence.

Clad all in white, upon a violet bank
I saw thee half-reclining ; while the moon
Fell on the upturn'd faces of the roses,
And on thine own, upturn'd—alas ! in sorrow !

Was it not Fate, that, on this July midnight—
Was it not Fate (whose name is also Sorrow),
That bade me pause before that garden gate,
To breathe the incense of those slumbering roses ?
No footstep stirred : the hated world all slept,
Save only thee and me—(O Heaven !—O God !
How my heart beats in coupling those two words !)

Save only thee and me. I paused—I looked—
And in an instant all things disappeared.
(Ah, bear in mind this garden was enchanted !)
The pearly lustre of the moon went out :
The mossy banks and the meandering paths,
The happy flowers and the repining trees,
Were seen no more : the very roses' odours
Died in the arms of the adoring airs.
All—all expired save thee—save less than thou *
Save only the divine light in thine eyes—
Save but the soul in thine uplifted eyes.
I saw but them—they were the world to me.
I saw but them—saw only them for hours—
Saw only them until the moon went down.
What wild heart-histories seemed to lie enwritten
Upon those crystalline, celestial spheres !
How dark a wo ! yet how sublime a hope !
How silently serene a sea of pride !
How daring an ambition ! yet how deep—
How fathomless a capacity for love !

But now, at length, dear Dian sank from sight,
Into a western couch of thunder-cloud ;
And thou, a ghost, amid the entombing trees
Didst glide away. *Only thine eyes remained.*
They *would not* go—they never yet have gone.
Lighting my lonely pathway home that night,
They have not left me (as my hopes have) since.
They follow me—they lead me through the years.
They are my ministers—yet I their slave.
Their office is to illumine and enkindle—
My duty, *to be saved* by their bright light,
And purified in their electric fire,
And sanctified in their elysian fire.
They fill my soul with Beauty (which is Hope),
And are far up in Heaven—the stars I kneel to
In the sad, silent watches of my night ;
While even in the meridian glare of day
I see them still—two sweetly scintillant
Venuses, unextinguished by the sun !

A VALENTINE

FOR her this rhyme is penned, whose luminous eyes,
  Brightly expressive as the twins of Leda,
Shall find her own sweet name, that, nestling lies
  Upon the page, enwrapped from every reader.
Search narrowly the lines!—they hold a treasure
  Divine—a talisman—an amulet
That must be worn *at heart*. Search well the
  measure—
The words—the syllables! Do not forget
The trivialest point, or you may lose your labour!
  And yet there is in this no Gordian knot
Which one might not undo without a sabre,
  If one could merely comprehend the plot.
Enwritten upon the leaf where now are peering
  Eyes scintillating soul, there lie *perdus*
Three eloquent words oft uttered in the hearing
  Of poets by poets—as the name is a poet's too.
Its letters, although naturally lying
  Like the knight Pinto—Mendez Ferdinando—
Still form a synonym for Truth—Cease trying!
  You will not read the riddle, though you do the
    best you *can* do.

[To discover the names in this and the following poem,
read the first letter of the first line in connection with the
second letter of the second line, the third letter of the third
line, the fourth of the fourth, and so on to the end. It has
not been thought necessary to retain the American spelling,
Læda, for *Leda*.]

AN ENIGMA

" SELDOM we find," says Solomon Don Dunce,
  " Half an idea in the profoundest sonnet.
Through all the flimsy things we see at once
  As easily as through a Naples bonnet—
  Trash of all trash!—how *can* a lady don it?

Yet heavier far than your Petrarchan stuff—
Owl-downy nonsense that the faintest puff
    Twirls into trunk-paper the while you con it."
And, veritably, Sol is right enough.
The general tuckermanities are arrant
Bubbles—ephemeral and *so* transparent—
    But *this* is, now—you may depend upon it—
Stable, opaque, immortal—all by dint
Of the dear names that lie concealed within't.

TO —— ——

NOT long ago, the writer of these lines,
In the mad pride of intellectuality,
Maintained " the power of words "—denied that ever
A thought arose within the human brain
Beyond the utterance of the human tongue
And now, as if in mockery of that boast,
Two words—two foreign soft dissyllables—
Italian tones, made only to be murmured
By angels dreaming in the moonlit " dew
That hangs like chains of pearl on Hermon hill,"—
Have stirred from out the abysses of his heart,
Unthought-like thoughts that are the souls of thought,
Richer, far wilder, far diviner visions
Than even the seraph harper, Israfel,
(Who has " the sweetest voice of all God's creatures "),
Could hope to utter. And I ! my spells are broken.
The pen falls powerless from my shivering hand.
With thy dear name as text, though bidden by thee,
I cannot write—I cannot speak or think—
Alas, I cannot feel ; for 'tis not feeling.
This standing motionless upon the golden
Threshold of the wide-open gate of dreams,
Gazing, entranced, adown the gorgeous vista,
And thrilling as I see, upon the right,
Upon the left, and all the way along,
Amid empurpled vapours, far away
To where the prospect terminates—*thee only.*

TO MY MOTHER

BECAUSE I feel that, in the Heavens above,
  The angels, whispering to one another,
Can find, among their burning terms of love,
  None so devotional as that of " Mother,"
Therefore by that dear name I long have called you—
  You who are more than mother unto me,
And fill my heart of hearts, where Death installed you,
  In setting my Virginia's spirit free.
My mother—my own mother, who died early,
  Was but the mother of myself ; but you
Are mother to the one I loved so dearly,
  And thus are dearer than the mother I knew
By that infinity with which my wife
  Was dearer to my soul than its soul-life.

ELDORADO

GAILY bedight,
A gallant knight,
In sunshine and in shadow,
Had journeyed long,
Singing a song,
In search of Eldorado.

But he grew old—
This knight so bold—
And o'er his heart a shadow
Fell as he found
No spot of ground
That looked like Eldorado.

And as his strength
Failed him at length,
He met a pilgrim shadow—
" Shadow," said he,
" Where can it be—
This land of Eldorado ? "

" Over the Mountains
Of the Moon,
Down the Valley of the Shadow,
Ride, boldly ride,"
The shade replied,—
" If you seek for Eldorado ! "

TO ——

I HEED not that my earthly lot
Hath—little of Earth in it—
That years of love have been forgot
In the hatred of a minute :—
I mourn not that the desolate
Are happier, sweet, than I,
But that *you* sorrow for *my* fate
Who am a passer-by.

TO M. L. S——

Of all who hail thy presence as the morning—
Of all to whom thine absence is the night—
The blotting utterly from out high heaven
The sacred sun—of all who, weeping, bless thee
Hourly for hope—for life—ah ! above all,
For the resurrection of deep-buried faith
In Truth—in Virtue—in Humanity—
Of all who, on Despair's unhallowed bed
Lying down to die, have suddenly arisen
At thy soft-murmured words, " Let there be light ! "
At the soft-murmured words that were fulfilled
In the seraphic glancing of thine eyes—
Of all who owe thee most—whose gratitude
Nearest resembles worship—oh, remember
The truest—the most fervently devoted,
And think that these weak lines are written by him—
By him who, as he pens them, thrills to think
His spirit is communing with an angel's.

FOR ANNIE

THANK Heaven! the crisis—
  The danger is past,
And the lingering illness
  Is over at last—
And the fever called " Living "
  Is conquered at last.

Sadly, I know
  I am shorn of my strength;
And no muscle I move
  As I lie at full length—
But no matter!—I feel
  I am better at length.

And I rest so composedly,
  Now, in my bed,
That any beholder
  Might fancy me dead—
Might start at beholding me,
  Thinking me dead.

The moaning and groaning,
  The sighing and sobbing,
Are quieted now,
  With that horrible throbbing
At heart :—ah, that horrible,
  Horrible throbbing!

The sickness—the nausea—
  The pitiless pain—
Have ceased, with the fever
  That maddened my brain—
With the fever called " Living "
  That burned in my brain.

And oh ! of all tortures
  That torture the worst
Has abated—the terrible
  Torture of thirst,
For the naphthaline river
  Of Passion accurst :—
I have drank of a water
  That quenches all thirst :—

Of a water that flows,
  With a lullaby sound,
From a spring but a very few
  Feet under ground—
From a cavern not very far
  Down under ground.

And ah ! let it never
  Be foolishly said
That my room it is gloomy
  And narrow my bed ;
For man never slept
  In a different bed—
And, to *sleep*, you must slumber,
  In just such a bed.

My tantalised spirit
  Here blandly reposes,
Forgetting, or never
  Regretting its roses—
Its old agitations
  Of myrtles and roses :

For now, while so quietly
  Lying, it fancies
A holier odour
  About it, of pansies—
A rosemary odour,
  Commingled with pansies—
With rue and the beautiful
  Puritan pansies.

For Annie

And so it lies happily,
  Bathing in many
A dream of the truth
  And the beauty of Annie—
Drowned in a bath
  Of the tresses of Annie.

She tenderly kissed me,
  She fondly caressed,
And then I fell gently
  To sleep on her breast—
Deeply to sleep
  From the heaven of her breast.

When the light was extinguished,
  She covered me warm,
And she prayed to the angels
  To keep me from harm—
To the queen of the angels
  To shield me from harm.

And I lie so composedly,
  Now, in my bed,
(Knowing her love)
  That you fancy me dead—
And I rest so contentedly,
  Now in my bed,
(With her love at my breast)
  That you fancy me dead—
That you shudder to look at me,
  Thinking me dead :—

But my heart it is brighter
  Than all of the many
Stars in the sky,
  For it sparkles with Annie—
It glows with the light—
  Of the love of my Annie—
With the thought of the light
  Of the eyes of my Annie.

ULALUME

THE skies they were ashen and sober;
  The leaves they were crispéd and sere—
  The leaves they were withering and sere;
It was night in the lonesome October
  Of my most immemorial year;
It was hard by the dim lake of Auber,
  In the misty mid region of Weir—
It was down by the dank tarn of Auber,
  In the ghoul-haunted woodland of Weir.

Here once, through an alley Titanic,
  Of cypress, I roamed with my Soul—
  Of cypress, with Psyche, my Soul.
These were days when my heart was volcanic
  As the scoriac rivers that roll—
  As the lavas that restlessly roll
Their sulphurous currents down Yaanek
  In the ultimate climes of the pole—
That groan as they roll down Mount Yaanek
  In the realms of the boreal pole.

Our talk had been serious and sober,
  But our thoughts they were palsied and sere—
  Our memories were treacherous and sere—
For we knew not the month was October,
  And we marked not the night of the year—
  (Ah, night of all nights in the year!)
We noted not the dim lake of Auber—
  (Though once we had journeyed down here)—
Remembered not the dank tarn of Auber,
  Nor the ghoul-haunted woodland of Weir.

And now, as the night was senescent
  And star-dials pointed to morn—
  As the star-dials hinted of morn—
At the end of our path a liquescent
  And nebulous lustre was born,

Out of which a miraculous crescent
   Arose with a duplicate horn—
Astarte's bediamonded crescent
   Distinct with its duplicate horn.

And I said—" She is warmer than Dian :
   She rolls through an ether of sighs—
   She revels in a region of sighs :
She has seen that the tears are not dry on
   These cheeks, where the worm never dies,
And has come past the stars of the Lion
   To point us the path to the skies—
   To the Lethean peace of the skies—
Come up, in despite of the Lion,
   To shine on us with her bright eyes—
Come up through the lair of the Lion,
   With love in her luminous eyes."

But Psyche, uplifting her finger,
   Said—" Sadly this star I mistrust—
   Her pallor I strangely mistrust :—
Oh, hasten !—oh, let us not linger !
   Oh, fly !—let us fly !—for we must."
In terror she spoke, letting sink her
   Wings until they trailed in the dust—
In agony sobbed, letting sink her
   Plumes till they trailed in the dust—
   Till they sorrowfully trailed in the dust.

I replied—" This is nothing but dreaming :
   Let us on by this tremulous light !
   Let us bathe in this crystalline light !
Its Sibyllic splendour is beaming
   With Hope and in Beauty to-night :—
   See !—it flickers up the sky through the night !
Ah, we safely may trust to its gleaming,
   And be sure it will lead us aright—
We safely may trust to a gleaming
   That cannot but guide us aright,
   Since it flickers up to Heaven through the night."

Thus I pacified Psyche and kissed her,
   And tempted her out of her gloom—
   And conquered her scruples and gloom ;
And we passed to the end of the vista,
   But were stopped by the door of a tomb—
   By the door of a legended tomb ;
And I said—" What is written, sweet sister,
   On the door of this legended tomb ? "
   She replied—" Ulalume—Ulalume—
   'Tis the vault of thy lost Ulalume ! "

Then my heart it grew ashen and sober
   As the leaves that were crispéd and sere—
   As the leaves that were withering and sere ;
And I cried—" It was surely October
   On *this* very night of last year
   That I journeyed—I journeyed down here—
   That I brought a dread burden down here—
   On this night of all nights in the year,
   Ah! what demon has tempted me here ?
Well I know, now, this dim lake of Auber—
   This misty mid region of Weir—
Well I know, now, this dank tarn of Auber,
   This ghoul-haunted woodland of Weir."

ANNABEL LEE

IT was many and many a year ago,
   In a kingdom by the sea,
That a maiden there lived whom you may know
   By the name of ANNABEL LEE ;
And this maiden she lived with no other thought
   Than to love and be loved by me.

I was a child and *she* was a child,
   In this kingdom by the sea :
But we loved with a love that was more than love—
   I and my ANNABEL LEE ;
With a love that the winged seraphs of heaven
   Coveted her and me.

Annabel Lee

And this was the reason that, long ago,
    In this kingdom by the sea,
A wind blew out of a cloud, chilling
    My beautiful ANNABEL LEE ;
So that her highborn kinsmen came
    And bore her away from me,
To shut her up in a sepulchre
    In this kingdom by the sea.

The angels, not half so happy in heaven,
    Went envying her and me—
Yes !—that was the reason (as all men know,
    In this kingdom by the sea)
That the wind came out of the cloud by night,
    Chilling and killing my ANNABEL LEE.

But our love it was stronger by far than the love
    Of those who were older than we—
    Of many far wiser than we—
And neither the angels in heaven above,
    Nor the demons down under the sea,
Can ever dissever my soul from the soul
    Of the beautiful ANNABEL LEE !

For the moon never beams, without bringing me
      dreams
    Of the beautiful ANNABEL LEE ;
And the stars never rise, but I feel the bright eyes
    Of the beautiful ANNABEL LEE ;
And so, all the night-tide, I lie down by the side
Of my darling,—my darling,—my life and my bride,
    In her sepulchre there by the sea,
    In her tomb by the side of the sea.

ALONE

[*Scribner's Magazine*, September 1875.]

FROM childhood's hour I have not been
As others were; I have not seen
As others saw; I could not bring
My passions from a common spring.
From the same source I have not taken
My sorrow; I could not awaken
My heart to joy at the same tone;
And all I loved, *I* loved alone.
Then—in my childhood, in the dawn
Of a most stormy life—was drawn
From every depth of good and ill
The mystery which binds me still:
From the torrent, or the fountain,
From the red cliff of the mountain,
From the sun that round me rolled
In its autumn tint of gold,
From the lightning in the sky
As it passed me flying by,
From the thunder and the storm,
And the cloud that took the form
(When the rest of Heaven was blue)
Of a demon in my view.

ESSAYS

THE POETIC PRINCIPLE

IN speaking of the Poetic Principle, I have no design to be either thorough or profound. While discussing, very much at random, the essentiality of what we call Poetry, my principal purpose will be to cite for consideration, some few of those minor English or American poems which best suit my own taste, or which, upon my own fancy, have left the most definite impression. By "minor poems" I mean, of course, poems of little length. And here, in the beginning, permit me to say a few words in regard to a somewhat peculiar principle, which, whether rightfully or wrongfully, has always had its influence in my own critical estimate of the poem. I hold that a long poem does not exist. I maintain that the phrase, "a long poem" is simply a flat contradiction in terms.

I need scarcely observe that a poem deserves its title only inasmuch as it excites, by elevating the soul. The value of the poem is in the ratio of this elevating excitement. But all excitements are, through a psychal necessity, transient. That degree of excitement which would entitle a poem to be so called at all, cannot be sustained throughout a composition of any great length. After the lapse of half an hour, at the very utmost, it flags—fails—a revulsion ensues—and then the poem is, in effect, and in fact, no longer such.

There are, no doubt, many who have found difficulty in reconciling the critical dictum that the *Paradise Lost* is to be devoutly admired throughout, with the absolute impossibility of maintaining for it, during perusal, the amount of enthusiasm which that critical dictum would demand. This great work, in fact, is to be regarded as poetical, only when, losing sight of that vital requisite in all works of Art, Unity, we view it merely as a series of minor poems. If, to preserve its Unity—its totality of effect or impression—we read it (as would be necessary) at a single sitting, the result is but a constant alternation of excitement and depression. After a passage of what we feel to be true poetry, there follows, inevitably, a passage of platitude which no critical pre-judgment can force us to admire ; but if, upon completing the work, we read it again ; omitting the first book—that is to say, commencing with the second—we shall be surprised at now finding that admirable which we before condemned—that damnable which we had previously so much admired. It follows from all this that the ultimate, aggregate, or absolute effect of even the best epic under the sun, is a nullity :—and this is precisely the fact.

In regard to the Iliad, we have, if not positive proof, at least very good reason, for believing it intended as a series of lyrics ; but, granting the epic intention, I can say only that the work is based in an imperfect sense of Art. The modern epic is, of the suppositious ancient model, but an inconsiderate and blindfold imitation. But the day of these artistic anomalies is over. If, at any time, any very long poem *were* popular in reality—which I doubt—it is at least clear that no very long poem will ever be popular again.

That the extent of a poetical work is, *ceteris paribus*, the measure of its merit, seems undoubtedly, when we thus state it, a proposition sufficiently absurd— yet we are indebted for it to the quarterly Reviews. Surely there can be nothing in mere *size*, abstractly considered—there can be nothing in mere *bulk*, so far as a volume is concerned, which has so continuously elicited admiration from these saturnine pamphlets ! A mountain, to be sure, by the mere sentiment of physical magnitude which it conveys, *does* impress us with a sense of the sublime—but no man is impressed after *this* fashion by the material grandeur of even *The Columbiad*. Even the Quarterlies have not instructed us to be so impressed by it. *As yet*, they have not *insisted* on our estimating Lamartine by the cubic foot, or Pollock by the pound —but what else are we to *infer* from their continual prating about " sustained effort ? " If, by " sustained effort," any little gentleman has accomplished an epic, let us frankly commend him for the effort —if this indeed be a thing commendable—but let us forbear praising the epic on the effort's account. It is to be hoped that common sense, in the time to come, will prefer deciding upon a work of Art, rather by the impression it makes—by the effect it produces —than by the time it took to impress the effect, or by the amount of " sustained effort " which had been found necessary in effecting the impression. The fact is, that perseverance is one thing and genius quite another—nor can all the Quarterlies in Christendom confound them. By-and-by, this proposition, with many which I have been just urging, will be received as self-evident. In the meantime, by being generally condemned as falsities, they will not be essentially damaged as truths.

On the other hand, it is clear that a poem may be improperly brief. Undue brevity degenerates into mere epigrammatism. A *very* short poem, while now and then producing a brilliant or vivid, never produces a profound or enduring effect. There must be the steady pressing down of the stamp upon the wax. De Béranger has wrought innumerable things, pungent and spirit-stirring ; but, in general, they have been too imponderous to stamp themselves deeply into the public attention ; and thus, as so many feathers of fancy, have been blown aloft only to be whistled down the wind.

A remarkable instance of the effect of undue brevity in depressing a poem—in keeping it out of the popular view—is afforded by the following exquisite little Serenade :

I arise from dreams of thee
    In the first sweet sleep of night
When the winds are breathing low,
    And the stars are shining bright.
I arise from dreams of thee,
    And a spirit in my feet
Has led me—who knows how?—
    To thy chamber-window, sweet!

The wandering airs they faint
    On the dark, the silent stream—
The champak odours fail
    Like sweet thoughts in a dream;
The nightingale's complaint,
    It dies upon her heart,
As I must die on thine,
    O, beloved as thou art!

O, lift me from the grass!
    I die, I faint, I fail!
Let thy love in kisses rain
    On my lips and eyelids pale.
My cheek is cold and white, alas!
    My heart beats loud and fast:
Oh! press it close to thine again,
    Where it will break at last!

Very few, perhaps, are familiar with these lines
—yet no less a poet than Shelley is their author.
Their warm, yet delicate and ethereal imagination
will be appreciated by all—but by none so thoroughly
as by him who has himself arisen from sweet dreams
of one beloved, to bathe in the aromatic air of a
southern midsummer night.

One of the finest poems by Willis—the very best,
in my opinion, which he has ever written—has, no
doubt, through this same defect of undue brevity,
been kept back from its proper position, not less in
the critical than in the popular view.

THE shadows lay along Broadway,
    'Twas near the twilight-tide—
And slowly there a lady fair
    Was walking in her pride
Alone walk'd she; but, viewlessly,
    Walk'd spirits at her side

Peace charm'd the street beneath her feet,
  And Honour charm'd the air ;
And all astir looked kind on her,
  And call'd her good as fair—
For all God ever gave to her
  She kept with chary care.

She kept with care her beauties rare
  From lovers warm and true—
For her heart was cold to all but gold,
  And the rich came not to woo—
But honour'd well are charms to sell
  If priests the selling do.

Now walking there was one more fair—
  A slight girl, lily-pale ;
And she had unseen company
  To make the spirit quail—
'Twixt Want and Scorn she walk'd forlorn,
  And nothing could avail.

No mercy now can clear her brow
  For this world's peace to pray ;
For, as love's wild prayer dissolved in air,
  Her woman's heart gave way !—
But the sin forgiven by Christ in Heaven
  By man is cursed alway !

In this composition we find it difficult to recognize
the Willis who has written so many mere " verses
of society." The lines are not only richly ideal,
but full of energy ; while they breathe an earnest-
ness—an evident sincerity of sentiment—for which
we look in vain throughout all the other works of
this author.

While the epic mania—while the idea that, to merit
in poetry, prolixity is indispensable—has, for some
years past, been gradually dying out of the public
mind, by mere dint of its own absurdity—we find
it succeeded by a heresy too palpably false to be
long tolerated, but one which, in the brief period
it has already endured, may be said to have
accomplished more in the corruption of our Poetical
Literature than all its other enemies combined.
I allude to the heresy of *The Didactic*. It has been

assumed, tacitly and avowedly, directly and indirectly, that the ultimate object of all Poetry is Truth. Every poem, it is said, should inculcate a moral; and by this moral is the poetical merit of the work to be adjudged. We Americans especially have patronized this happy idea; and we Bostonians, very especially, have developed it in full. We have taken it into our heads that to write a poem simply for the poem's sake, and to acknowledge such to have been our design, would be to confess ourselves radically wanting in the true Poetic dignity and force:—but the simple fact is, that, would we but permit ourselves to look into our own souls, we should immediately there discover that under the sun there neither exists nor *can* exist any work more thoroughly dignified—more supremely noble than this very poem—this poem *per se*—this poem which is a poem and nothing more—this poem written solely for the poem's sake.

With as deep a reverence for the True as ever inspired the bosom of man, I would, nevertheless, limit, in some measure, its modes of inculcation. I would limit to enforce them. I would not enfeeble them by dissipation. The demands of Truth are severe. She has no sympathy with the myrtles. All *that* which is so indispensable in Song, is precisely all *that* with which *she* has nothing whatever to do. It is but making her a flaunting paradox, to wreathe her in gems and flowers. In enforcing a truth, we need severity rather than efflorescence of language. We must be simple, precise, terse. We must be cool, calm, unimpassioned. In a word, we must be in that mood which, as nearly as possible, is the exact converse of the poetical. *He* must be blind indeed who does not perceive the radical and chasmal differences between the truthful and the poetical modes of inculcation. He must be theory-mad beyond redemption who, in spite of these differences, shall still persist in attempting to reconcile the obstinate oils and waters of Poetry and Truth.

Dividing the world of mind into its three most immediately obvious distinctions, we have the Pure Intellect, Taste, and the Moral Sense. I place Taste in the middle, because it is just this position which, in the mind, it occupies. It holds intimate relations with either extreme ; but from the Moral Sense is separated by so faint a difference that Aristotle has not hesitated to place some of its operations among the virtues themselves. Nevertheless, we find the *offices* of the trio marked with a sufficient distinction. Just as the Intellect concerns itself with Truth, so Taste informs us of the Beautiful while the Moral Sense is regardful of Duty. Of this latter, while Conscience teaches the obligation, and Reason the expediency, Taste contents herself with displaying the charms :—waging war upon Vice solely on the ground of her deformity—her disproportion—her animosity to the fitting, to the appropriate, to the harmonious—in a word, to Beauty.

An immortal instinct, deep within the spirit of man, is thus, plainly, a sense of the Beautiful. This it is which administers to his delight in the manifold forms, and sounds, and odours, and sentiments amid which he exists. And just as the lily is repeated in the lake, or the eyes of Amaryllis in the mirror, so is the mere oral or written repetition of these forms, and sounds, and colours, and odours, and sentiments, a duplicate source of delight. But this mere repetition is not poetry. He who shall simply sing, with however glowing enthusiasm, or with however vivid a truth of description, of the sights, and sounds, and odours, and colours, and sentiments, which greet *him* in common with all mankind—he, I say, has yet failed to prove his divine title. There is still a something in the distance which he has been unable to attain. We have still a thirst unquenchable, to allay which he has not shown us the crystal springs. This thirst belongs to the immortality of Man. It is at once a consequence and an indication of his perennial existence. It is the desire of the moth for the star. It is no mere appreciation of the Beauty before us—but a wild effort to reach the Beauty above. Inspired by an ecstatic prescience of the glories beyond the grave, we struggle, by multiform combinations among the things and thoughts of Time, to attain a portion of that Loveliness whose very elements, perhaps, appertain to eternity alone. And thus when by Poetry—or when by Music, the most entrancing of the Poetic moods—we find ourselves melted into tears—we weep then—not as the Abbaté Gravina supposes—through excess of pleasure, but through a certain, petulant, impatient sorrow at our inability to grasp *now*, wholly, here on earth, at once and for ever, those divine and rapturous joys, of which *through* the poem, or *through* the music, we attain to but brief and indeterminate glimpses.

The struggle to apprehend the supernal Loveliness —this struggle, on the part of souls fittingly constituted—has given to the world all *that* which it (the world) has ever been enabled at once to understand and *to feel* as poetic.

The Poetic Sentiment, of course, may develop itself in various modes—in Painting, in Sculpture, in Architecture, in the Dance—very especially in Music—and very peculiarly, and with a wide field, in the composition of the Landscape Garden. Our present theme, however, has regard only to its manifestation in words. And here let me speak briefly on the topic of rhythm. Contenting myself with the certainty that Music, in its various modes of metre, rhythm, and rhyme, is of so vast a moment in Poetry as never to be wisely rejected—is so vitally important an adjunct, that he is simply silly who declines its assistance, I will not now pause to maintain its absolute essentiality. It is in Music, perhaps, that the soul most nearly attains the great end for which, when inspired by the Poetic Sentiment, it struggles—the creation of supernal Beauty. It *may* be, indeed, that here this sublime end is, now and then, attained *in fact*. We are often made to feel, with a shivering delight, that from an earthly harp are stricken notes which *cannot* have been unfamiliar to the angels. And thus there can be little doubt that in the union of Poetry with Music in its popular sense, we shall find the widest field for the Poetic development. The old Bards and Minnesingers had advantages which we do not possess—and Thomas Moore, singing his own songs, was, in the most legitimate manner, perfecting them as poems.

To recapitulate, then :—I would define, in brief, the Poetry of words as *The Rythmical Creation of Beauty*. Its sole arbiter is Taste. With the Intellect or with the Conscience, it has only collateral relations. Unless incidentally, it has no concern whatever either with Duty or with Truth.

A few words, however, in explanation. *That* pleasure which is at once the most pure, the most elevating, and the most intense, is derived, I main tain, from the contemplation of the Beautiful. In the contemplation of Beauty we alone find it possible to attain that pleasurable elevation, or excitement, *of the soul*, which we recognize as the Poetic Sentiment, and which is so easily distinguished from Truth, which is the satisfaction of the Reason, or from Passion, which is the excitement of the heart. I make Beauty, therefore—using the word as inclusive of the sublime—I make Beauty the province of the poem, simply because it is an obvious rule of Art that effects should be made to spring as directly as possible from their causes :—no one as yet having been weak enough to deny that the peculiar elevation in question is at least *most readily* attainable in the poem. It by no means follows, however, that the incitements of Passion, or the precepts of Duty, or even the lessons of Truth, may not be introduced into a poem, and with advantage ; for they may subserve, incidentally, in various ways, the general purposes of the work :—but the true artist will always contrive to tone them down in proper subjection to that *Beauty* which is the atmosphere and the real essence of the poem.

I cannot better introduce the few poems which I shall present for your consideration, than by the citation of the Pröem to Mr. Longfellow's *Waif.*

THE day is done, and the darkness
    Falls from the wings of Night,
As a feather is wafted downward
    From an Eagle in his flight.

I see the lights of the village
    Gleam through the rain and the mist,
And a feeling of sadness comes o'er me,
    That my soul cannot resist;

A feeling of sadness and longing,
    That is not akin to pain,
And resembles sorrow only
    As the mist resembles the rain:

Come, read to me some poem,
    Some simple and heartfelt lay,
That shall soothe this restless feeling,
    And banish the thoughts of day.

Not from the grand old masters,
    Not from the bards sublime,
Whose distant footsteps echo
    Through the corridors of time:

For, like strains of martial music,
    Their mighty thoughts suggest
Life's endless toil and endeavour;
    And to-night I long for rest.

Read from some humbler poet,
    Whose songs gushed from his heart,
As showers from the clouds of summer,
    Or tears from the eyelids start;

Who through long days of labour,
    And nights devoid of ease,
Still heard in his soul the music
    Of wonderful melodies.

Such songs have power to quiet
    The restless pulse of care,
And come like the benediction
    That follows after prayer.

Then read from the treasured volume
    The poem of thy choice,
And lend to the rhyme of the poet
    The beauty of thy voice.

And the night shall be filled with music,
    And the cares, that infest the day,
Shall fold their tents, like the Arabs,
    And as silently steal away.

With no great range of imagination, these lines
have been justly admired for their delicacy of ex-
pression. Some of the images are very effective.
Nothing can be better than—

—————————The bards sublime,
Whose distant footsteps echo
Down the corridors of Time.

The idea of the last quartrain is also very effective.
The poem, on the whole, however, is chiefly to be
admired for the graceful *insouciance* of its metre,
so well in accordance with the character of the senti-
ments, and especially for the *ease* of the general
manner. This "ease," or naturalness, in a literary
style, it has long been the fashion to regard as ease
in appearance alone—as a point of really difficult
attainment. But not so:—a natural manner is
difficult only to him who should never meddle with
it—to the unnatural. It is but the result of writing
with the understanding, or with the instinct, that
the tone, in composition, should always be that which
the mass of mankind would adopt—and must per-
petually vary, of course, with the occasion. The
author who, after the fashion of *The North American
Review*, should be, upon *all* occasions, merely
" quiet," must necessarily upon *many* occasions, be
simply silly, or stupid ; and has no more right to
be considered " easy," or " natural," than a Cockney

exquisite, or than the sleeping Beauty in the wax-works.

Among the minor poems of Bryant, none has so much impressed me as the one which he entitles *June*. I quote only a portion of it :

> There, through the long, long summer hours,
>   The golden light should lie,
> And thick, young herbs and groups of flowers
>   Stand in their beauty by
> The oriole should build and tell
> His love-tale, close beside my cell ;
>   The idle butterfly
> Should rest him there, and there be heard
> The housewife-bee and humming bird.
>
> And what, if cheerful shouts, at noon,
>   Come, from the village sent,
> Or songs of maids, beneath the moon,
>   With fairy laughter blent ?
> And what if, in the evening light,
> Betrothed lovers walk in sight
>   Of my low monument !
> I would the lovely scene around
> Might know no sadder sight nor sound.
>
> I know, I know I should not see
>   The season's glorious show,
> Nor would its brightness shine for me,
>   Nor its wild music flow ;
> But if, around my place of sleep,
> The friends I love should come to weep,
>   They might not haste to go
> Soft airs, and song, and light, and bloom
> Should keep them lingering by my tomb
>
> These to their soften'd hearts should bear
>   The thought of what has been,
> And speak of one who cannot share
>   The gladness of the scene .
> Whose part in all the pomp that fills
> The circuit of the summer hills,
>   Is—that his grave is green ;
> And deeply would their hearts rejoice
> To hear again his living voice.

The rhythmical flow, here, is even voluptuous—nothing could be more melodious. The poem has always affected me in a remarkable manner. The

intense melancholy which seems to well up, perforce,
to the surface of all the poet's cheerful sayings about
his grave, we find thrilling us to the soul—while
there is the truest poetic elevation in the thrill.
The impression left is one of a pleasurable sadness.
And if, in the remaining compositions which I shall
introduce to you, there be more or less of a similar
tone always apparent, let me remind you that (how
or why we know not) this certain taint of sadness
is inseparably connected with all the higher mani-
festations of true Beauty. It is, nevertheless,

> A feeling of sadness and longing
>   That is not akin to pain,
> And resembles sorrow only
>   As the mist resembles the rain.

The taint of which I speak is clearly perceptible
even in a poem so full of brilliancy and spirit as the
Health of Edward Coote Pinkney :

> I fill this cup to one made up
>   Of loveliness alone,
> A woman, of her gentle sex
>   The seeming paragon ;
> To whom the better elements
>   And kindly stars have given
> A form so fair, that, like the air,
>   'Tis less of earth than heaven.
>
> Her every tone is music's own,
>   Like those of morning birds,
> And something more than melody
>   Dwells ever in her words ;
> The coinage of her heart are they,
>   And from her lips each flows
> As one may see the burden'd bee
>   Forth issue from the rose.
>
> Affections are as thoughts to her,
>   The measures of her hours ;
> Her feelings have the fragrancy,
>   The freshness of young flowers ;
> And lovely passions, changing oft,
>   So fill her, she appears
> The image of themselves by turns,—
>   The idol of past years !

Of her bright face one glance will trace
　　A picture on the brain,
And of her voice in echoing hearts
　　A sound must long remain ;
But memory, such as mine of her,
　　So very much endears,
When death is nigh my latest sigh
　　Will not be life's, but hers.

I fill'd this cup to one made up
　　Of loveliness alone,
A woman, of her gentle sex
　　The seeming paragon—
Her health ! and would on·earth there stood,
　　Some more of such a frame,
That life might be all poetry,
　　And weariness a name.

It was the misfortune of Mr. Pinkney to have been
born too far south.　Had he been a New Englander,
it is probable that he would have been ranked as
the first of American lyrists, by that magnanimous
cabal which has so long controlled the destinies of
American Letters, in conducting the thing called
The North American Review.　The poem just cited
is especially beautiful ; but the poetic elevation
which it induces, we must refer chiefly to our sympathy
in the poet's enthusiasm.　We pardon his hyper-
boles for the evident earnestness with which they are
uttered.

It was by no means my design, however, to ex-
patiate upon the *merits* of what I should read you.
These will necessarily speak for themselves.　Boccalini,
in his *Advertisements from Parnassus,* tells us that
Zoilus once presented Apollo a very caustic criticism
upon a very admirable book :—whereupon the god
asked him for the beauties of the work.　He replied
that he only busied himself about the errors.　On
hearing this, Apollo, handing him a sack of un-
winnowed wheat, bade him pick out *all the chaff*
for his reward.

Now this fable answers very well as a hit at the
critics—but I am by no means sure that the god was

in the right. I am by no means certain that the
true limits of the critical duty are not grossly mis-
understood. Excellence, in a poem especially, may
be considered in the light of an axiom, which need
only be properly *put*, to become self-evident. It is
not excellence if it require to be demonstrated as
such :—and thus, to point out too particularly the
merits of a work of Art, is to admit that they are
not merits altogether.

Among the *Melodies* of Thomas Moore, is one
whose distinguished character as a poem proper,
seems to have been singularly left out of view. I
allude to his lines beginning—" Come rest in this
bosom." The intense energy of their expression is
not surpassed by anything in Byron. There are two
of the lines in which a sentiment is conveyed that
embodies the *all in all* of the divine passion of Love—
a sentiment which, perhaps, has found its echo in
more, and in more passionate, human hearts than
any other single sentiment ever embodied in words :

Come, rest in this bosom, my own stricken deer,
Though the herd have fled from thee, thy home is still here ;
Here still is the smile, that no cloud can o'ercast,
And a heart and a hand all thy own to the last.

Oh ! what was love made for, if 't is not the same
Through joy and through torment, through glory and shame ?
I know not, I ask not, if guilt's in that heart,
I but know that I love thee, whatever thou art.

Thou hast call'd me thy Angel in moments of bliss,
And thy Angel I'll be, 'mid the horrors of this,—
Through the furnace, unshrinking, thy steps to pursue,
And shield thee, and save thee,—or perish there too !

It has been the fashion, of late days, to deny Moore
Imagination, while granting him Fancy—a distinc-
tion originating with Coleridge—than whom no man
more fully comprehended the great powers of Moore.
The fact is, that the fancy of this poet so far pre-
dominates over all his other faculties, and over the

fancy of all other men, as to have induced, very naturally, the idea that he is fanciful *only*. But never was there a greater mistake. Never was a grosser wrong done the fame of a true poet. In the compass of the English language I can call to mind no poem more profoundly—more weirdly *imaginative*, in the best sense, than the lines commencing—" I would I were by that dim lake "—which are the composition of Thomas Moore. I regret that I am unable to remember them.

One of the noblest—and, speaking of Fancy, one of the most singularly fanciful of modern poets, was Thomas Hood. His *Fair Ines* had always, for me, an inexpressible charm I

> O saw ye not fair Ines ?
>   She's gone into the West,
> To dazzle when the sun is down,
>   And rob the world of rest
> She took our daylight with her,
>   The smiles that we love best,
> With morning blushes on her cheek,
>   And pearls upon her breast.
>
> O turn again, fair Ines,
>   Before the fall of night,
> For fear the moon should shine alone,
>   And stars unrivall'd bright
> And blessed will the lover be
>   That walks beneath their light,
> And breathes the love against thy cheek
>   I dare not even write I
>
> Would I had been, fair Ines,
>   That gallant cavalier,
> Who rode so gaily by thy side,
>   And whisper'd thee so near !
> Were there no bonny dames at home,
>   Or no true lovers here,
> That he should cross the seas to win
>   The dearest of the dear ?
>
> I saw thee, lovely Ines,
>   Descend along the shore,
> With bands of noble gentlemen,
>   And banners wav'd before ;

And gentle youth and maidens gay,
  And snowy plumes they wore ;
It would have been a beauteous dream,
  —If it had been no more !

Alas, alas, fair Ines,
  She went away with song,
With Music waiting on her steps,
  And shoutings of the throng ;
But some were sad and felt no mirth,
  But only Music's wrong
In sounds that sang Farewell, Farewell,
  To her you've loved so long.

Farewell, farewell, fair Ines,
  That vessel never bore
So fair a lady on its deck,
  Nor danced so light before,—
Alas, for pleasure on the sea,
  And sorrow on the shore !
The smile that blest one lover's heart
  Has broken many more !

The Haunted House, by the same author, is one
of the truest poems ever written—one of the *truest*
—one of the most unexceptionable—one of the
most thoroughly artistic, both in its theme and in
its execution.   It is, moreover, powerfully ideal—
imaginative.   I regret that its length renders it
unsuitable for the purposes of this Lecture.   In
place of it, permit me to offer the universally
appreciated *Bridge of Sighs*.

One more Unfortunate,
Weary of breath,
Rashly importunate,
Gone to her death !

Take her up tenderly,
Lift her with care ;—
Fashion'd so slenderly,
Young, and so fair !

Look at her garments
Clinging like cerements ;
Whilst the wave constantly
Drips from her clothing ;

Take her up instantly,
Loving, not loathing.—

Touch her not scornfully ;
Think of her mournfully,
Gently and humanly ;
Not of the stains of her,
All that remains of her
Now, is pure womanly.

Make no deep scrutiny
Into her mutiny
Rash and undutiful ;

Past all dishonour,
Death has left on her
Only the beautiful.

Still, for all slips of hers,
One of Eve's family—
Wipe those poor lips of hers
Oozing so clammily.

Loop up her tresses
Escaped from the comb,
Her fair auburn tresses;
Whilst wonderment guesses
Where was her home?

Who was her father?
Who was her mother?
Had she a sister?
Had she a brother?
Or was there a dearer one
Still, and a nearer one
Yet, than all other?

Alas! for the rarity
Of Christian charity
Under the sun!
Oh! it was pitiful!
Near a whole city full,
Home she had none.

Sisterly, brotherly,
Fatherly, motherly,
Feelings had changed:
Love, by harsh evidence,
Thrown from its eminence;
Even God's providence
Seeming estranged.

Where the lamps quiver
So far in the river,
With many a light
From window and casement
From garret to basement,
She stood, with amazement,
Houseless by night.

The bleak wind of March
Made her tremble and shiver;
But not the dark arch,
Or the black flowing river:
Mad from life's history,
Glad of death's mystery,
Swift to be hurl'd—
Anywhere, anywhere
Out of the world!

In she plunged boldly,
No matter how coldly
The rough river ran,—
Over the brink of it,
Picture it,—think of it,
Dissolute Man!
Lave in it, drink of it
Then, if you can!

Take her up tenderly,
Lift her with care;
Fashion'd so slenderly,
Young, and so fair!

Ere her limbs frigidly
Stiffen too rigidly,
Decently,—kindly,—
Smooth and compose them
And her eyes, close them,
Staring so blindly!

Dreadfully staring
Through muddy impurity,
As when with the daring
Last look of despairing
Fixed on futurity.

Perishing gloomily,
Spurred by contumely,
Cold inhumanity,
Burning insanity,
Into her rest,—
Cross her hands humbly,
As if praying dumbly,
Over her breast!
Owning her weakness,
Her evil behaviour,
And leaving, with meekness
Her sins to her Saviour!

The vigour of this poem is no less remarkable than its pathos. The versification, although carrying the fanciful to the very verge of the fantastic, is nevertheless admirably adapted to the wild insanity which is the thesis of the poem.

Among the minor poems of Lord Byron, is one which has never received from the critics the praise which it undoubtedly deserves:

> Though the day of my destiny's over,
>   And the star of my fate hath declined,
> Thy soft heart refused to discover
>   The faults which so many could find;
> Though thy soul with my grief was acquainted,
>   It shrunk not to share it with me,
> And the love which my spirit hath painted
>   It never hath found but in *thee*.
>
> Then when nature around me is smiling,
>   The last smile which answers to mine,
> I do not believe it beguiling,
>   Because it reminds me of thine;
> And when winds are at war with the ocean,
>   As the breasts I believed in with me,
> If their billows excite an emotion,
>   It is that they bear me from *thee*.
>
> Though the rock of my last hope is shivered,
>   And its fragments are sunk in the wave,
> Though I feel that my soul is delivered
>   To pain—it shall not be its slave.
> There is many a pang to pursue me:
>   They may crush, but they shall not contemn—
> They may torture, but shall not subdue me—
>   'Tis of *thee* that I think—not of them.
>
> Though human, thou didst not deceive me,
>   Though woman, thou didst not forsake,
> Though loved, thou forborest to grieve me,
>   Though slandered, thou never couldst shake,—
> Though trusted, thou didst not disclaim me,
>   Though parted, it was not to fly,
> Though watchful, 't was not to defame me,
>   Nor mute, that the world might belie.
>
> Yet I blame not the world, nor despise it,
>   Nor the war of the many with one—
> If my soul was not fitted to prize it,
>   'T was folly not sooner to shun:

> And if dearly that error hath cost me,
>   And more than I once could foresee,
> I have found that whatever it lost me,
>   It could not deprive me of *thee*.

> From the wreck of the past, which hath perished,
>   Thus much I at least may recall,
> It hath taught me that which I most cherished
>   Deserved to be dearest of all:
> In the desert a fountain is springing,
>   In the wide waste there still is a tree,
> And a bird in the solitude singing,
>   Which speaks to my spirit of *thee*.

Although the rhythm, here, is one of the most difficult, the versification could scarcely be improved. No nobler *theme* ever engaged the pen of poet. It is the soul-elevating idea, that no man can consider himself entitled to complain of Fate while, in his adversity, he still retains the unwavering love of woman.

From Alfred Tennyson—although in perfect sincerity I regard him as the noblest poet that ever lived—I have left myself time to cite only a very brief specimen. I call him, and *think* him the noblest of poets—*not* because the impressions he produces are, at *all* times, the most profound—*not* because the poetical excitement which he induces is, at *all* times, the most intense—but because it *is*, at all times, the most ethereal—in other words, the most elevating and the most pure. No poet is so little of the earth, earthy. What I am about to read is from his last long poem, *The Princess*:

> Tears, idle tears, I know not what they mean,
> Tears from the depth of some divine despair
> Rise in the heart, and gather to the eyes,
> In looking on the happy Autumn-fields,
> And thinking of the days that are no more.

> Fresh as the first beam glittering on a sail,
> That brings our friends up from the underworld,
> Sad as the last which reddens over one
> That sinks with all we love below the verge;
> So sad, so fresh, the days that are no more.

> Ah, sad and strange as in dark summer dawns
> The earliest pipe of half-awaken'd birds
> To dying ears, when unto dying eyes
> The casement slowly grows a glimmering square;
> So sad, so strange, the days that are no more.
>
> Dear as remember'd kisses after death,
> And sweet as those by hopeless fancy feign'd
> On lips that are for others; deep as love,
> Deep as first love, and wild with all regret;
> O death in Life, the days that are no more.

Thus, although in a very cursory and imperfect manner, I have endeavoured to convey to you my conception of the Poetic Principle. It has been my purpose to suggest that, while this Principle itself is, strictly and simply, the Human Aspiration for Supernal Beauty, the manifestation of the Principle is always found in *an elevating excitement of the Soul* —quite independent of that passion which is the intoxication of the Heart—or of that Truth which is the satisfaction of the Reason. For, in regard to Passion, alas! its tendency is to degrade, rather than to elevate the Soul. Love, on the contrary —Love—the true, the divine Eros—the Uranian, as distinguished from the Dionæan Venus—is unquestionably the purest and truest of all poetical themes. And in regard to Truth—if, to be sure, through the attainment of a truth, we are led to perceive a harmony where none was apparent before, we experience, at once, the true poetical effect— but this effect is referable to the harmony alone, and not in the least degree to the truth which merely served to render the harmony manifest.

We shall reach, however, more immediately a distinct conception of what the true Poetry is, by mere reference to a few of the simple elements which induce in the Poet himself the true poetical effect. He recognizes the ambrosia which nourishes his soul, in the bright orbs that shine in Heaven—in the volutes of the flower—in the clustering of low shrubberies—in the waving of the grain-fields—in the slanting of tall, Eastern trees—in the blue distance of mountains—in the grouping of clouds—in the twinkling of half-hidden brooks—in the gleaming of silver rivers—in the repose of sequestered lakes—in the star-mirroring depths of lonely wells. He perceives it in the songs of birds—in the harp of Æolus—in the sighing of the night-wind—in the repining voice of the forest—in the surf that complains to the shore—in the fresh breath of the woods—in the scent of the violet—in the voluptuous perfume of the hyacinth—in the suggestive odour that comes to him, at eventide, from far-distant, undiscovered islands, over dim oceans, illimitable and unexplored. He owns it in all noble thoughts—in all unworldly motives—in all holy impulses—in all chivalrous, generous, and self-sacrificing deeds. He feels it in the beauty of woman—in the grace of her step—in the lustre of her eye—in the melody of her voice—in her soft laughter—in her sigh—in the harmony of the rustling of her robes. He deeply feels it in her winning endearments—in her burning enthusiasms—in her gentle charities—in her meek and devotional endurances—but above all—ah, far above all—he kneels to it—he worships it in the faith, in the purity, in the strength, in the altogether divine majesty—of her *love*.

Let me conclude—by the recitation of yet another brief poem—one very different in character from any that I have before quoted. It is by Motherwell, and is called *The Song of the Cavalier*. With our modern and altogether rational ideas of the absurdity and impiety of warfare, we are not precisely in that frame of mind best adapted to sympathize with the sentiments, and thus to appreciate the real excellence of the poem. To do this fully, we must identify ourselves, in fancy, with the soul of the old cavalier.

> Then mounte! then mounte, brave gallants, all
>   And don your helmes amaine:
> Deathe's couriers, Fame and Honour, call
>   Us to the field againe.

No shrewish tear's shall fill our eye
  When the sword-hilt's in our hand,—
Heart-whole we'll part, and no whit sighe
  For the fayrest of the land ;
Let piping swaine, and craven wight,
  Thus weepe and puling crye,
Our business is like men to fight,
  And hero-like to die !

THE RATIONALE OF VERSE

THE word " Verse " is here used not in its strict
or primitive sense, but as the term most convenient
for expressing generally and without pedantry all
that is involved in the consideration of rhythm,
rhyme, metre, and versification.

There is, perhaps, no topic in polite literature
which has been more pertinaciously discussed, and
there is certainly not one about which so much
inaccuracy, confusion, misconception, misrepresen-
tation, mystification, and downright ignorance on
all sides, can be fairly said to exist. Were the topic
really difficult, or did it lie, even, in the cloud-land
of metaphysics, where the doubt-vapours may be
made to assume any and every shape at the will
or at the fancy of the gazer, we should have less
reason to wonder at all this contradiction and per-
plexity ; but in fact the subject is exceedingly simple ;
one-tenth of it, possibly, may be called ethical ;
nine-tenths, however, appertain to the mathematics ;
and the whole is included within the limits of the
commonest common sense.

" But, if this is the case, how," it will be asked,
" can so much misunderstanding have arisen ?·
Is it conceivable that a thousand profound scholars,
investigating so very simple a matter for centuries,
have not been able to place it in the fullest light,
at least, of which it is susceptible ? " These queries
I confess, are not easily answered :—at all events
a satisfactory reply to them might cost more trouble

than would, if properly considered, the whole *vexata quæstio* to which they have reference. Nevertheless, there is little difficulty or danger in suggesting that the " thousand profound scholars " *may* have failed, first, because they were scholars, secondly, because they were profound, and thirdly, because they were a thousand—the impotency of the scholarship and profundity having been thus multiplied a thousand fold. I am serious in these suggestions ; for, first again, there is something in " scholarship " which seduces us into blind worship of Bacon's Idol of the Theatre—into irrational deference to antiquity ; secondly, the proper " profundity " is rarely profound—it is the nature of Truth in general, as of some ores in particular, to be richest when most superficial ; thirdly, the clearest subject may be overclouded by mere superabundance of talk. In chemistry, the best way of separating two bodies is to add a third ; in speculation, fact often agrees with fact and argument with argument, until an additional well-meaning fact or argument sets every thing by the ears. In one case out of a hundred a point is excessively discussed because it is obscure ; in the ninety-nine remaining it is obscure because excessively discussed. When a topic is thus circumstanced, the readiest mode of investigating it is to forget that any previous investigation has been attempted.

But, in fact, while much has been written on the Greek and Latin rhythms, and even on the Hebrew, little effort has been made at examining that of any of the modern tongues. As regards the English, comparatively nothing has been done. It may be said, indeed, that we are without a treatise on our own verse. In our ordinary grammars and in our works on rhetoric or prosody in general, may be found occasional chapters, it is true, which have the heading, " Versification," but these are, in all instances, exceedingly meagre. They pretend to no analysis ; they propose nothing like system ; they make no attempt at even rule ; everything depends upon "authority." They are confined, in fact, to mere exemplification of the supposed varieties of English feet and English lines ;—although in no work with which I am acquainted are these feet correctly given or these lines detailed in anything like their full extent. Yet what has been mentioned is all—if we except the occasional introduction of some pedagogue-ism, such as this, borrowed from the Greek Prosodies : "When a syllable is wanting, the verse is said to be catalectic ; when the measure is exact, the line is acatalectic ; when there is a redundant syllable it forms hypermeter." Now whether a line be termed catalectic or acatalectic is, perhaps, a point of no vital importance ;—it is even possible that the student may be able to decide, promptly, when the *a* should be employed and when omitted, yet be incognizant, at the same time, of *all* that is worth knowing in regard to the structure of verse.

A leading defect in each of our treaties, (if treatises they can be called,) is the confining the subject to mere *Versification*, while *Verse* in general, with the understanding given to the term in the heading of this paper, is the real question at issue. Nor am I aware of even one of our Grammars which so much as properly defines the word versification itself. "Versification," says a work now before me, of which the accuracy is far more than usual—the *English Grammer* of Goold Brown—"Versification is the art of arranging words into lines of correspondent length, so as to produce harmony by the regular alternation of syllables differing in quantity." The commencement of this definition might apply, indeed, to the *art* of versification, but not versification itself. Versification is not the art of arranging, etc., but the actual arranging—a distinction too obvious to need comment. The error here is identical with one which has been too long permitted to disgrace the initial page of every one of our school grammars.

I allude to the definitions of English Grammar itself. " English Grammar," it is said, " is the art of speaking and writing the English language correctly." This phraseology, or something essentially similar, is employed, I believe, by Bacon, Miller, Fisk, Greenleaf, Ingersoll, Kirkland, Cooper, Flint, Pue, Comly and many others. These gentlemen, it is presumed, adopted it without examination from Murray, who derived it from Lily, (whose work was " *quam solam Regia Majestas in omnibus scholis docendam præcipit,*") and who appropriated it without acknowledgment, but with some unimportant modification, from the Latin Grammar of Leonicenus. It may be shown, however, that this definition, so complacently received, is not, and cannot be, a proper definition of English Grammar. A definition is that which so describes its object as to distinguish it from all others :—it is no definition of any one thing if its terms are applicable to any one other. But if it be asked—" What is the design—the end—the aim of English Grammar ? " our obvious answer is, " The art of speaking and writing the English language correctly : "—that is to say, we must use the precise words employed as the definition of English Grammar itself. But the object to be obtained by any means is, assuredly, not the means. English Grammar and the end contemplated by English Grammar, are two matters sufficiently distinct ; nor can the one be more reasonably regarded as the other than a fishing-hook as a fish. The definition, therefore, which is applicable in the latter instance, *cannot*, in the former, be true. Grammar in general is the analysis of language ; English Grammar of the English.

But to return to Versification as defined in our extract above. " It is the art," says the extract, " of arranging words into lines *of correspondent length.*" Not so :—a correspondence in the length of lines is by no means essential. Pindaric odes are, surely, instances of versification, yet these compositions are noted for extreme diversity in the length of their lines.

The arrangement is moreover said to be for the purpose of producing " *harmony* by the regular alternation," etc. But *harmony* is not the sole aim—not even the principal one. In the construction of verse, *melody* should never be left out of view; yet this is a point which all our Prosodies have most unaccountably forborne to touch. Reasoned rules on this topic should form a portion of all systems of rhythm.

" So as to produce harmony," says the definition, " by the *regular alternation*," etc. A *regular* alternation, as described, forms no part of any prinicple of versification. The arrangement of spondees and dactyls, for example, in the Greek hexameter, is an arrangement which may be termed *at random*. At least it is arbitrary. Without interference with the line as a whole, a dactyl may be substituted for a spondee, or the converse, at any point other than the ultimate and penultimate feet, of which the former is always a spondee, the latter nearly always a dactyl. Here, it is clear, we have no " *regular* alternation of syllables differing in quantity."

" So as to produce harmony," proceeds the definition, " by the regular alternation of *syllables differing in quantity*,"—in other words by the alternation of long and short syllables ; for in rhythm all syllables are necessarily either short or long. But not only do I deny the necessity of any *regularity* in the succession of feet and, by consequence, of syllables, but dispute the essentiality of any *alternation*, regular or irregular, of syllables long and short. Our author, observe, is now engaged in a definition of versification in general, not of English versification in particular. But the Greek and Latin metres abound in the spondee and pyrrhic—the former consisting of two long syllables ; the latter of two short ; and there are innumerable instances of the immediate succession of many spondees and many pyrrhics.

Here is a passage from Silius Italicus ı

Fallis te mensas inter quod credis inermem
Tot bellis quæsita viro, tot cædibus armat
Majestas eterna ducem : si admoveris ora
Cannas et Trebium ante oculos Trasymenaque busta,
Et Pauli stare ingentem miraberis umbram.

Making the elisions demanded by the classic Prosodies, we should scan these Hexameters thus :

Fāllĭs | tē mēn—sās ĭn | tēr qŭod | crēdĭs ĭn | ērmēn |
Tōt bēl | lĭs quæ | sĭtā vĭ | rō tōt—cædĭbŭs | ārmāt |
Mājĕs | tās ē | tērnă dŭ | cēm s'ād | mōvĕrĭs | ōrā |
Cānnās | ēt Trĕbĭ' | ānt'ŏcŭ | lōs Trāsy | mēnăqŭe | būstā
ēt Pāu | lĭ stā | r'īngēn | tēm mĭ | rābĕrĭs | ūmbrām |

It will be seen that, in the first and last of these lines, we have only two short syllables in thirteen, with an uninterrupted succession of no less than *nine* long syllables. But how are we to reconcile all this with a definition of versification which describes it as " the art of arranging words into lines of correspondent length so as to produce harmony by the *regular alternation of syllables differing in quantity ?* "

It may be urged, however, that our prosodist's *intention* was to speak of the English metres alone, and that, by omitting all mention of the spondee and pyrrhic, he has virtually avowed their exclusion from our rhythms. A grammarian is never excusable on the ground of good intentions. We demand from him, if from any one, rigorous precision of style. But grant the design. Let us admit that our author, following the example of all authors on English Prosody, has, in defining versification at large, in-tended a definition merely of the English. All these prosodists, we will say, reject the spondee and pyrrhic. Still all admit the iambus, which consists of a short syllable followed by a long ; the trochee, which is the converse of the iambus ; the dactyl, formed of one long syllable followed by two short ; and the anapæst—two short succeeded by a long. The

spondee is improperly rejected, as I shall presently
show. The pyrrhic is rightfully dismissed. Its
existence in either ancient or modern rhythm is
purely chimerical, and the insisting on so perplexing
a nonentity as a foot of *two short* syllables, affords,
perhaps, the best evidence of the gross irrationality
and subservience to authority which characterize
our Prosody. In the meantime the acknowledged
dactyl and anapæst are enough to sustain my pro-
position about the " alternation," etc., without
reference to feet which are assumed to exist in the
Greek and Latin metres alone : for an anapæst
and a dactyl may meet in the same line ; when of
course we shall have an uninterrupted succession of
four short syllables. The meeting of these two
feet, to be sure, is an accident not contemplated in
the definition now discussed ; for this definition, in
demanding a " regular alternation of syllables differing
in quantity," insists on a regular succession of similar
feet. But here is an example :

Sīng tŏ mĕ | Isăbĕlle.

This is the opening line of a little ballad now before
me, which proceeds in the same rhythm—a peculiarly
beautiful one. More than all this :—English lines
are often well composed, entirely, of a regular
succession of syllables *all the same quantity :* —
the first lines, for instance, of the following quatrain
by Arthur C. Coxe :

> *March ! march ! march !*
> Making sounds as they tread,
> Ho ! ho ! how they step,
> Going down to the dead !

The line italicized is formed of three cæsuras. The
cæsura, of which I have much to say hereafter,
is rejected by the English Prosodies and grossly
misrepresented in the classic. It is a perfect foot
—the most important in all verse—and consists of

a single *long* syllable; *but the length of this syllable varies.*

It has thus been made evident that there is *not one* point of the definition in question which does not involve an error. And for anything more satisfactory or more intelligible we shall look in vain to any published treatise on the topic.

So general and so total a failure can be referred only to radical misconception. In fact the English Prosodists have blindly followed the pedants. These latter, like *les moutons de Panurge*, have been occupied in incessant tumbling into ditches, for the excellent reason that their leaders have so tumbled before. The Iliad, being taken as a starting point, was made to stand instead of Nature and common sense. Upon this poem, in place of facts and deduction from fact, or from natural law, were built systems of feet, metres, rhythms, rules,—rules that contradict each other every five minutes, and for nearly all of which there may be found twice as many exceptions as examples. If any one has a fancy to be thoroughly confounded—to see how far the infatuation of what is termed "classical scholarship" can lead a bookworm in the manufacture of darkness out of sunshine, let him turn over, for a few moments, any of the German Greek Prosodies. The only thing clearly made out in them is a very magnificent contempt for Liebnitz's principle of "a sufficient reason."

To divert attention from the real matter in hand by any further reference to these works, is unnecessary, and would be weak. I cannot call to mind, at this moment, one essential particular of information that is to be gleaned from them; and I will drop them here with merely this one observation: that, employing from among the numerous "*ancient*" feet the spondee, the trochee, the iambus, the anapæst, the dactyl, and the cæsura alone, I will engage to scan *correctly* any of the Horatian rhythms, or any true rhythm that human ingenuity can conceive. And this excess of chimerical feet is, perhaps, the very least of the scholastic supererogations. *Ex uno disce omnia*. The fact is that *Quantity* is a point in whose investigation the lumber of mere learning may be dispensed with, if ever in any. Its appreciation is universal. It appertains to no region, nor race, nor æra in especial. To melody and to harmony the Greeks hearkened with ears precisely similar to those which we employ for similar purposes at present ; and I should not be condemned for heresy in asserting that a pendulum at Athens would have vibrated much after the same fashion as does a pendulum in the city of Penn.

Verse originates in the human enjoyment of equality, fitness. To this enjoyment, also, all the moods of verse—rhythm, metre, stanza, rhyme, alliteration, the *refrain*, and other analogous effects —are to be referred. As there are some readers who habitually confound rhythm and metre, it may be as well here to say that the former concerns the *character* of feet (that is, the arrangements of syllables) while the latter has to do with the *number* of these feet. Thus by " a dactylic *rhythm* " we express a sequence of dactyls. By " a dactylic hexa*meter* " we imply a line or measure consisting of six of these dactyls.

To return to *equality*. Its idea embraces those of similarity, proportion, identity, repetition, and adaptation or fitness. It might not be very difficult to go even behind the idea of equality, and show both how and why it is that the human nature takes pleasure in it, but such an investigation would, for any purpose now in view, be supererogatory. It is sufficient that the *fact* is undeniable—the fact that man derives enjoyment from his perception of equality. Let us examine a crystal. We are at once interested by the equality between the sides and between the angles of one of its faces : the equality of the sides pleases us ; that of the angles doubles the pleasure. . On bringing to view a second face in all respects similar to the first, this pleasure

seems to be squared ; on bringing to view a third
it appears to be cubed, and so on. I have no doubt,
indeed, that the delight experienced, if measurable,
would be found to have exact mathematical relations
such as I suggest ; that is to say, as far as a certain
point, beyond which there would be a decrease in
similar relations.

The perception of pleasure in the equality of *sounds*
is the principle of *Music*. Unpractised ears can
appreciate only simple equalities, such as are found
in ballad airs. While comparing one simple sound
with another they are too much occupied to be
capable of comparing the equality subsisting between
these two simple sounds, taken conjointly, and two
other similar simple sounds taken conjointly.
Practised ears, on the other hand, appreciate both
equalities at the same instant—although it is absurd
to suppose that both are *heard* at the same instant.
One is heard and appreciated from itself : the other
is heard by the memory ; and the instant glides
into and is confounded with the secondary, apprecia-
tion. Highly cultivated musical taste in this manner
enjoys not only these double equalities, all appreciated
at once, but takes pleasurable cognizance, through
memory, of equalities the members of which occur
at intervals so great that the uncultivated taste
loses them altogether. That this latter can properly
estimate or decide on the merits of what is called
scientific music, is of course impossible. But scientific
music has no claim to intrinsic excellence—it is fit
for scientific ears alone. In its excess it is the triumph
of the *physique* over the *morale* of music. The
sentiment is overwhelmed by the sense. On the
whole, the advocates of the simpler melody and
harmony have infinitely the best of the argument ;
athough there has been very little of real argument
on the subject.

In *verse*, which cannot be better designated than
as inferior or less capable Music, there is, happily,
little chance for complexity. Its rigidly simple

character not even Science—not even Pedantry can greatly pervert.

The rudiment of verse may, possibly, be found in the *spondee*. The very germ of a thought seeking satisfaction in equality of sound, would result in the construction of words of two syllables, equally accented. In corroboration of this idea we find that spondees most abound in the most ancient tongues. The second step we can easily suppose to be the comparison, that is to say, the collocation, of two spondees—of two words composed each of a spondee. The third step would be the juxtaposition of three of these words. By this time the perception of monotone would induce further consideration : and thus arises what Leigh Hunt so flounders in discussing under the title of "The *Principle* of Variety in Uniformity." Of course there is no principle in the case —nor in maintaining it. The "Uniformity" is the principle :—the "Variety" is but the principle's natural safeguard from self-destruction by excess of self. "Uniformity," besides, is the very worst word that could have been chosen for the expression of the *general* idea at which it aims.

The perception of monotone having given rise to an attempt at its relief, the first thought in this new direction would be that of collating two or more words formed each of two syllables differently accented (that is to say, short and long) but having the same order in each word :—in other terms, of collating two or more iambuses, or two or more trochees. And here let me pause to assert that more pitiable nonsense has been written on the topic of *long* and *short* syllables than on any other subject under the sun. In general, a syllable is long or short, just as it is difficult or easy of enunciation. The *natural* long syllables are those encumbered—the *natural* short syllables are those *un*encumbered, with consonants ; all the rest is mere artificiality and jargon. The Latin Prosodies have a rule that "a vowel before two consonants is long." This rule is deduced from "authority"—that is, from the observation that vowels so circumstanced, in the ancient poems, are always in syllables long by the laws of scansion. The philosophy of the rule is untouched, and lies simply in the physical difficulty of giving voice to such syllables—of performing the lingual evolutions necessary for their utterance. Of course, it is not the *vowel* that is long, (although the rule says so) but the syllable of which the vowel is a part. It will be seen that the length of a syllable, depending on the facility or difficulty of its enunciation, must have great variation in various syllables ; but for the purposes of verse we suppose a long syllable equal to two short ones :—and the natural deviation from this relativeness we correct in perusal. The more closely our long syllables approach this relation with our short ones, the better, *ceteris paribus*, will be our verse ; but if the relation does not exist of itself, we force it by emphasis, which can, of course, make any syllable as long as desired ;—or, by an effort we can pronounce with unnatural brevity a syllable that is naturally too long. *Accented* syllables are of course always long—but, where *un*encumbered with consonants, must be classed among the *unnaturally* long. Mere custom has declared that we shall accent them—that is to say, dwell upon them ; but no inevitable lingual difficulty forces us to do so. In fine, every long syllable must of its own accord occupy in its utterance, or must be *made* to occupy, precisely the time demanded for two short ones. The only exception to this rule is found in the cæsura—of which more anon.

The success of the experiment with the trochees or iambuses (the one would have suggested the other) must have led to a trial of dactyls or anapæsts— natural dactyls or anapæsts—dactylic or anapæstic *words*. And now some degree of complexity has been attained. There is an appreciation, first, of the equality between the several dactyls, or anapæsts, and, secondly, of that between the long syllable and the two short conjointly. But here it may be said, that step after step would have been taken, in continuation of this routine, until all the feet of the Greek Prosodies became exhausted. Not so :—these remaining feet have no existence except in the brains of the scholiasts. It is needless to imagine men inventing these things, and folly to explain how and why they invented them, until it shall first show that they are actually invented. All other " feet " than those which I have specified, are, if not impossible at first view, merely combinations of the specified ; and, although this assertion is rigidly true, I will, to avoid misunderstanding, put it in a somewhat different shape. I will say, then, that at present I am aware of no *rhythm*—nor do I believe that any one can be constructed—which, in its last analysis, will not be found to consist altogether of the feet I have mentioned, either existing in their individual and obvious condition, or interwoven with each other in accordance with simple natural laws which I will endeavour to point out hereafter.

We have now gone so far as to suppose men constructing indefinite sequences of spondaic, iambic, trochaic, dactylic, or anapæstic words. In *extending* these sequences, they would be again arrested by the sense of monotone. A succession of spondees would *immediately* have displeased ; one of iambuses or of trochees, on account of the variety included within the foot itself, would have taken longer to displease ; one of dactyls or anapæsts, still longer ; but even the last, if extended very far, must have become wearisome. The idea, first, of curtailing, and secondly, of defining the length of, a sequence, would thus at once have arisen. Here then is the *line*, or verse proper.[1] The principle of equality

[1] Verse, from the Latin *vertere*, to turn, is so called on account of the turning or re-commencement of the series of feet. Thus a verse, strictly speaking, is a line. In this sense, however, I have preferred using the latter word alone ; employing the former in the general acceptation given it in the heading of this paper.

being constantly at the bottom of the whole process, lines would naturally be made, in the first instance, equal in the number of their feet ; in the second instance, there would be variation in the mere number ; one line would be twice as long as another ; then one would be some less obvious multiple of another ; then still less obvious proportions would be adopted :—nevertheless there would be *proportion*, that is to say, a phase of equality, still.

Lines being once introduced, the necessity of distinctly defining these lines *to the ear*, (as yet written verse does not exist,) would lead to a scrutiny of their capabilities *at their terminations :*—and now would spring up the idea of equality in sound between the final syllables—in other words, of *rhyme*. First, it would be used only in the iambic, anapæstic, and spondaic rhythms, (granting that the latter had not been thrown aside, long since, on account of its tameness ;) because in these rhythms, the concluding syllable being long, could best sustain the necessary protraction of the voice. No great while could elapse, however, before the effect, found pleasant as well as useful, would be applied to the two remaining rhythms. But as the chief force of rhyme must lie in the accented syllable, the attempt to create rhyme at all in these two remaining rhythms, the trochaic and dactylic, would necessarily result in double and triple rhymes, such as *beauty* with *duty* (trochaic,) and *beautiful* with *dutiful* (dactylic).

It must be observed, that in suggesting these processes, I assign them no date ; nor do I even insist upon their order. Rhyme is supposed to be of modern origin, and were this proved, my positions remain untouched. I may say, however, in passing, that several instances of rhyme occur in the *Clouds* of Aristophanes, and that the Roman poets occasionally employ it. There is an effective species of ancient rhyming which has never descended to the moderns : that in which the ultimate and penultimate syllables rhyme with each other. For example :

> Parturiunt montes et nascitur ridicu*lus* *mus*.

And again :

> Litoreis ingens inventa sub ilici*bus* *sus*.

The terminations of Hebrew verse, (as far as understood,) show no signs of rhyme ; but what thinking person can doubt that it did actually exist ? That men have so obstinately and blindly insisted, *in general*, even up to the present day, in confining rhyme to the *ends* of lines, when its effect is even better applicable elsewhere, intimates, in my opinion, the sense of some *necessity* in the connexion of the end with the rhyme—hints that the origin of rhyme lay in a necessity which connected it with the end —shows that neither mere accident nor mere fancy gave rise to the connexion—points, in a word, at the very necessity which I have suggested, (that of some mode of defining lines *to the ear*,) as the true origin of rhyme. Admit this, and we throw the origin far back in the night of Time—beyond the origin of written verse.

But, to resume. The amount of complexity I have now supposed to be attained is very considerable. Various systems of equalization are appreciated at once (or nearly so) in their respective values and in the value of each system with reference to all the others. As our present *ultimatum* of complexity, we have arrived at triple-rhymed, natural-dactylic lines, existing proportionally as well as equally with regard to other triple-rhymed, natural-dactylic lines. For example :

> Virginal Lilian, rigidly humblily dutiful ;
>> Saintlily, lowlily,
>> Thrillingly, holily
> Beautiful !

Here we appreciate, first, the absolute equality between the long syllable of each dactyl and the two

short conjointly; secondly, the absolute equality
between each dactyl and any other dactyl—in other
words, among all the dactyls; thirdly, the absolute
equality between the two middle lines; fourthly, the
absolute equality between the first line and the
three others taken conjointly; fifthly, the absolute
equality between the last two syllables of the re-
spective words " dutiful " and " beautiful "; sixthly,
the absolute equality between the two last syllables
of the respective words " lowlily " and " holily ";
seventhly, the proximate equality between the first
syllable of " dutiful " and the first syllable of " beau-
tiful "; eighthly, the proximate equality between
the first syllable of " lowlily " and that of " holily ";
ninthly, the proportional equality (that of five to
one,) between the first line and each of its members,
the dactyls; tenthly, the proportional equality (that
of two to one,) between each of the middle lines and
its members, the dactyls; eleventhly, the pro-
portional equality between the first line and each
of the two middle—that of five to two; twelfthly,
the proportional equality between the first line and
the last—that of five to one; thirteenthly, the
proportional equality between each of the middle
lines and the last—that of two to one; lastly, the
proportional equality, as concerns number, between
all the lines, taken collectively and any individual
line—that of four to one.

The consideration of this last equality would give
birth immediately to the idea of *stanza* [1]—that is
to say, the insulation of lines into equal or obviously
proportional masses. In its primitive (which was
also its best) form, the stanza would most probably
have had absolute unity. In other words, the removal
of any one of its lines would have rendered it imper-
fect; as in the case above, where, if the last line,
for example, be taken away, there is left no rhyme
to the " dutiful " of the first. Modern stanza is

[1] A stanza is often vulgarly, and with gross impropriety
called a *verse*.

excessively loose—and where so, ineffective, as a matter of course.

Now, although in the deliberate written statement which I have here given of these various systems of equalities, there seems to be an infinity of complexity—so much that it is hard to conceive the mind taking cognizance of them all in the brief period occupied by the perusal or recital of the stanza— yet the difficulty is in fact apparent only when we will it to become so. Anyone fond of mental experiment may satisfy himself, by trial, that, in listening to the lines, he does actually (although with a seeming unconsciousness, on account of the rapid evolutions of sensation,) recognize and instantaneously appreciate (more or less intensely as his ear is cultivated,) each and all of the equalizations detailed. The pleasure received, or receivable, has very much such progressive increase, and in very nearly such mathematical relations, as those which I have suggested in the case of the crystal.

It will be observed that I speak of merely a proximate equality between the first syllable of " dutiful " and that of " beautiful "; and it may be asked why we cannot imagine the earliest rhymes to have had absolute instead of proximate equality of sound. But absolute equality would have involved the use of identical words; and it is the duplicate sameness or monotony—that of sense as well as that of sound— which would have caused these rhymes to be rejected in the very first instance.

The narrowness of the limits within which verse composed of natural feet alone, must necessarily have been confined, would have led, after a *very* brief interval, to the trial and immediate adoption of artificial feet—that is to say, of feet *not* constituted each of a single word, but two or even three words; or of parts of words. These feet would be intermingled with natural ones. For example :

ă brēath | căn māke | thĕm ās | ă breāth | hăs māde.

This is an iambic line in which each iambus is formed of two words. Again :

Thĕ ūn | ĭmā | gĭnā | blĕ mĭght | ŏf Jōve

This is an iambic line in which the first foot is formed of a word and a part of a word ; the second and third, of parts taken from the body or interior of a word ; the fourth, of a part and a whole ; the fifth, of two complete words. There are no *natural* feet in either line. Again :

Cān ĭt bĕ | fāncĭĕd thăt | Dēĭty | ĕvĕr vĭn | dĭctĭvely
Māde ĭn hĭs | ĭmăge ă | mānnĭkĭn | mĕrely tŏ | māddĕn ĭt ?

These are two dactylic lines in which we find natural feet, (" Deity," " mannikin " ;) feet composed of two words (" fancied that," " image a," " merely to," " madden it " ;) feet composed of three words (" can it be," " made in his " ;) a foot composed of a part of a word (" dictively " ;) and a foot composed of a word and a part of a word (" ever vin ").

And now, in our supposititious progress, we have gone so far as to exhaust all the *essentialities* of verse. What follows may, strictly speaking, be regarded as embellishment merely—but even in this embellishment, the rudimental sense of *equality* would have been the never-ceasing impulse. It would, for example, be simply in seeking further administration to this sense that men would come, in time, to think of the *refrain*, or burden, where, at the closes of the several stanzas of a poem, one word or phrase is *repeated* ; and of alliteration, in whose simplest form a consonant is *repeated* in the commencements of various words. This effect would be extended so as to embrace repetitions both of vowels and of consonants, in the bodies as well as in the beginnings of words ; and, at a later period, would be made to infringe on the province of rhyme, by the introduction of general similarity of sound between whole feet occurring in the body of a line :—

all of which modifications I have exemplified in the line above,

Made in his image a *mannikin* merely to *madden it*.

Further cultivation would improve also the *refrain* by relieving its monotone in slightly varying the phrase at each repetition, or, (as I have attempted to do in *The Raven*,) in retaining the phrase and varying its application—although this latter point is not strictly a rhythmical effect *alone*. Finally, poets when fairly wearied with following precedent —following it the more closely the less they perceived it in company with Reason—would adventure so far as to indulge in positive rhyme at other points than the ends of lines. First, they would put it in the middle of the line ; then at some point where the multiple would be less obvious ; then, alarmed at their own audacity, they would undo all their work by cutting these lines in two. And here is the fruitful source of the infinity of " short metre," by which modern poetry, if not distinguished, is at least disgraced. It would require a high degree, indeed, both of cultivation and of courage, on the part of any versifier, to enable him to place his rhymes —and let them remain—at unquestionably their best position, that of unusual and *unanticipated* intervals.

On account of the stupidity of some people, or, (if talent be a more respectable word,) on account of their talent for misconception—I think it necessary to add here, first, that I believe the " processes " above detailed to be nearly if not accurately those which *did* occur in the gradual creation of what we now call verse ; secondly, that, although I so believe, I yet urge neither the assumed fact nor my belief in it, as a part of the true propositions of this paper ; thirdly, that in regard to the aim of this paper, it is of no consequence whether these processes did occur either in the order I have assigned them, or at all ; my design being simply, in presenting a general type of what such processes *might* have been and *must* have resembled, to help *them,* the "some people," to an easy understanding of what I have further to say on the topic of Verse.

There is one point which, in my summary of the processes, I have purposely forborne to touch ; because this point, being the most important of all, on account of the immensity of error usually involved in its consideration, would have led me into a series of detail inconsistent with the object of a summary.

Every reader of verse must have observed how seldom it happens that even any one line proceeds uniformly with a succession, such as I have supposed, of absolutely equal feet ; that is to say, with a succession of iambuses only, or of trochees only, or of dactyls only, or of anapæsts only, or of spondees only. Even in the most musical lines we find the succession interrupted. The iambic pentameters of Pope, for example, will be found, on examination, frequently varied by trochees in the beginning, or by (what seem to be) anapæsts in the body, of the line.

> ŏh thŏu | whătē | vĕr tĭ | tlĕ | pleāse | thĭne eār |
> Dĕan Drā | piĕr Bĭck | ĕrstāff | ŏr Gŭl | ĭvĕr |
> Whēthĕr ˌ thŏu choōse | Cĕrvān | tĕs' sĕ | rĭoŭs āir |
> ŏr laūgh ˌ ănd shāke | ĭn Rāb | ĕlaĭs' eā | sy chaĭr. |

Were any one weak enough to refer to the Prosodies for the solution of the difficulty here, he would find it *solved* as usual by a *rule,* stating the fact, (or what it, the rule, supposes to be the fact,) but without the slightest attempt at the *rationale.* "By a *synæresis* of the two short syllables," say the books, "an anapæst may sometimes be employed for an iambus, or a dactyl for a trochee. . . . In the beginning of a line a trochee is often used for an iambus."

Blending is the plain English for *synæresis*—but there should be *no* blending ; neither is an anapæst *ever* employed for an iambus, or a dactyl for a trochee. These feet differ in time ; and *no* feet so differing can ever be legitimately used in the same line. An anapæst is equal to four short syllables—an iambus only to three. Dactyls and trochees hold the same relation. The principle of *equality*, in verse, admits, it is true, of variation at certain points, for the relief of monotone, as I have already shown, but the point of *time* is that point which, being the rudimental one, must never be tampered with at all.

To explain :—In further efforts for the relief of monotone than those to which I have alluded in the summary, men soon came to see that there was no absolute necessity for adhering to the precise number of syllables, provided the time required for the whole foot was preserved inviolate. They saw, for instance, that in such a line as

ŏr lāugh | ănd shāke | ĭn Rāb | ĕlaĭs' ĕa | sy chāir,

the equalization of the three syllables *elais ea* with the two syllables composing any of the other feet, could be readily effected by pronouncing the two syllables *elais* in double quick time. By pronouncing each of the syllables *e* and *lais* twice as rapidly as the syllable *sy*, or the syllable *in*, or any other short syllable, they could bring the two of them, taken together, to the length, that is to say to the time, of any one short syllable. This consideration enabled them to effect the agreeable variation of three syllables in place of the uniform two. And variation was the object—variation to the ear. What sense is there, then, in supposing this object rendered null by the *blending* of the two syllables so as to render them, in absolute effect, one ? Of course, there must be *no* blending. Each syllable must be pronounced as distinctly as possible, (or the variation is lost,) but with twice the rapidity in which the ordinary short syllable is enunciated. That the syllables *elais ea* do not compose an *anapæst* is evident, and the signs (ăăă) of their accentuation are erroneous. The foot might be written thus (ɕɕɕ) the inverted crescents expressing double quick time ; and might be called a bastard iambus.

Here is a trochaic line :

Sēe thĕ dēlĭcăte | fōotĕd | rēin-deĕr. |

The prosodies—that is to say the most considerate of them—would here decide that "*delicate*" is a dactyl used in place of a trochee, and would refer to what they call their "rule," for justification. Others, varying the stupidity, would insist upon a Procrustean adjustment thus (del'cate)—an adjustment recommended to all such words as *silvery*, *murmuring*, etc., which, it is said, should be not only pronounced, but written *silv'ry*, *murm'ring*, and so on, whenever they find themselves in trochaic predicament. I have only to say that "delicate," when circumstanced as above, is neither a dactyl nor a dactyl's equivalent ; that I would suggest for it this (͝ ͝ ͝) accentuation ; that I think it as well to call it a bastard trochee ; and that all words, at all events, should be written and pronounced *in full*, and as nearly as possible as nature intended them.

About eleven years ago, there appeared in *The American Monthly Magazine*, (then edited, I believe, by Mess. Hoffman and Benjamin,) a review of Mr. Willis' Poems ; the critic putting forth his strength, or his weakness, in an endeavour to show that the poet was either absurdly affected, or grossly ignorant of the laws of verse ; the accusation being based altogether on the fact that Mr. W. made occasional use of this very word "delicate," and other similar words, in "the Heroic measure which every one knew consisted of feet of two syllables." Mr. W. has often, for example, such lines as

> That binds him to a woman's *delicate* love—
> In the gay sunshine, *reverent* in the storm—
> With its *invisible* fingers my loose hair.

Here, of course, the feet *licate love*, *verent in*, and *sible fin*, are bastard iambuses ; are *not* anapæsts ; and are *not* improperly used. Their employment, on the contrary, by Mr. Willis, is but one of the innumerable instances he has given of keen sensibility in all those matters of taste which may be classed under the general head of *fanciful embellishment.*

It is also about eleven years ago, if I am not mistaken, since Mr. Horne, (of England), the author of *Orion,* one of the noblest epics in any language, thought it necessary to preface his *Chaucer Modernized* by a very long and evidently a very elaborate essay, of which the greater portion was occupied in a discussion of the seemingly anomalous foot of which we have been speaking. Mr. Horne upholds Chaucer in its frequent use ; maintains his superiority, *on account* of his so frequently using it, over all English versifiers ; and, indignantly repelling the common idea of those who make verse on their fingers—that the superfluous syllable is a roughness and an error—very chivalrously makes battle for it as " a grace." That a grace it *is,* there can be no doubt ; and what I complain of is, that the author of the most happily versified long poem in existence, should have been under the necessity of discussing this grace merely *as* a grace, through forty or fifty vague pages, solely because of his inability to show *how* and *why* it is a grace—by which showing the question would have been settled in an instant.

About the trochee used for an iambus, as we see in the beginning of the line,

Whĕthĕr thou choose Cervantes' serious air,

there is little that need be said. It brings me to the general proposition that, in all rhythms, the prevalent or distinctive feet may be varied at will, and nearly at random, by the *occasional* introduction of equivalent feet—that is to say, feet the sum of whose syllabic times is equal to the sum of the syllabic times of the distinctive feet. Thus the trochee, *whĕthĕr,* is equal, in the sum of the times of its syllables, to the iambus, *thŏu choōse,* in the sum of the times of *its* syllables ; each foot being, in time, equal to three short syllables. Good versifiers who happen to be, also, good poets, contrive to relieve the monotone of a series of feet, by the use of equivalent feet only at rare intervals, and at such points of their subject as seem in accordance with the *startling* character of the variation. Nothing of this care is seen in the line quoted above—although Pope has some fine instances of the duplicate effect. Where vehemence is to be strongly expressed, I am not sure that we should be wrong in venturing on *two consecutive* equivalent feet—although I cannot say that I have ever known the adventure made, except in the following passage, which occurs in *Al Aaraaf*, a boyish poem, written by myself when a boy. I am referring to the sudden and rapid advent of a star.

> Dim was its little disk, and angel eyes
> Alone could see the phantom in the skies,
> Whĕn fīrst thē phāntŏm's cōurse wăs fōund tŏ bē
> *Hēadlŏng hĭthĕr*ward o'er the starry sea.

In the " general proposition " above, I speak of the *occasional* introduction of equivalent feet. It sometimes happens that unskilful versifiers, without knowing what they do, or why they do it, introduce so many " variations " as to exceed in number the " distinctive " feet ; when the ear becomes at once balked by the *bouleversement* of the rhythm. Too many trochees, for example, inserted in an iambic rhythm, would convert the latter to a trochaic. I may note here, that, in all cases, the rhythm designed should be commenced and continued, *without* variation, until the ear has had full time to comprehend what *is* the rhythm. In violation of a rule so obviously founded in common sense, many even of our best poets do not scruple to begin an iambic rhythm with a trochee, or the converse ; or a dactylic with an anapæst, or the converse ; and so on.

A somewhat less objectionable error, although still

a decided one, is that of commencing a rhythm, not with a different equivalent foot, but with a " bastard " foot of the rhythm intended.   For example :

Mānў ă | thoŭght wĭll | cōme tŏ | mĕmŏrў. |

Here *many a* is what I have explained to be a bastard trochee, and to be understood should be accented with inverted crescents.   It is objectionable solely on account of its position as the *opening* foot of a trochaic rhythm.   *Memory*, similarly accented, is also a bastard trochee, but *un*objectionable, although by no means demanded.

The further illustration of this point will enable me to take an important step.

One of our finest poets, Mr. Christopher Pease Cranch, begins a very beautiful poem thus :

> Many are the thoughts that come to me
>   In my lonely musing ;
> And they drift so strange and swift
>   There's no time for choosing
> Which to follow ; for to leave
>   Any, seems a losing.

" A losing " to Mr. Cranch, of course—but this *en passant*. It will be seen here that the intention is trochaic ;—although we do *not* see this intention by the opening foot, as we should do—or even by the opening line.   Reading the whole stanza, however, we perceive the trochaic rhythm as the general design, and so, after some reflection, we divide the first line thus :

Many are the | thōŭghts thăt | cōme tŏ | mē. |

Thus scanned, the line will seem musical.   It *is* highly so.   And it is because there is no end to instances of just such lines of apparently incomprehensible music, that Coleridge thought proper to invent his nonsensical *system* of what he calls " scanning by accents "—as if " scanning by accents " were anything more than a phrase.   Whenever *Christabel* is really *not rough*, it can be as readily scanned by the true *laws* (not the supposititious *rules*) of verse, as can the simplest pentameter of Pope ; and where it *is* rough (*passim*) these same laws will enable any one of common sense to show *why* it is rough and to point out, instantaneously, the remedy for the roughness.

A reads and re-reads a certain line, and pronounces it false in rhythm—unmusical. *B*, however, reads it to *A*, and *A* is at once struck with the perfection of the rhythm, and wonders at his dullness in not "catching" it before. Henceforward he admits the line to be musical. *B*, triumphant, asserts that, to be sure, the line is musical—for it is the work of Coleridge—and that it is *A* who is *not*; the fault being in *A*'s false reading. Now here *A* is right and *B* wrong. *That* rhythm is erroneous, (at some point or other more or less obvious,) which *any* ordinary reader *can*, without design, read improperly. It is the business of the poet so to construct his line that the intention *must* be caught *at once*. Even when these men have precisely the same understanding of a sentence, they differ, and often widely, in their modes of enunciating it. Anyone who has taken the trouble to examine the topic of emphasis, (by which I here mean not *accent* of particular syllables, but the dwelling on entire words,) must have seen that men emphasize in the most singularly arbitrary manner. There are certain large classes of people, for example, who persist in emphasizing their monosyllables. Little uniformity of emphasis prevails ; because the thing itself—the idea, emphasis—is referable to no natural—at least, to no well comprehended and therefore uniform law. Beyond a very narrow and vague limit, the whole matter is conventionality. And if we differ in emphasis even when we agree in comprehension, how much more so in the former when in the latter too ! Apart, however, from the consideration of natural disagreement, is it not clear that, by tripping here and mouthing there, any sequence of words may be twisted into any species of rhythm? But are we thence to deduce that all sequences of words are rhythmical in a rational understanding of the term?— for this is the deduction, precisely to which the *reductio ad absurdum* will, in the end, bring all the propositions of Coleridge. Out of a hundred readers of *Christabel*, fifty will be able to make nothing of its rhythm, while forty-nine of the remaining fifty will, with some ado, fancy they comprehend it, after the fourth or fifth perusal. The one out of the whole hundred who shall both comprehend and admire it at first sight—must be an unaccountably clever person —and I am by far too modest to assume, for a moment, that that very clever person is myself.

In illustration of what is here advanced I cannot do better than quote a poem :

> Pease porridge hot—pease porridge cold—
> Pease porridge in the pot—nine days old.

Now those of my readers who have never *heard* this poem pronounced according to the nursery conventionality, will find its rhythm as obscure as an explanatory note ; while those who *have* heard it, will divide it thus, declare it musical, and wonder how there can be any doubt about it.

> Pease | porridge | hot | pease | porridge | cold |
> Pease | porridge | in the | pot | nine | days | old. |

The chief thing in the way of this species of rhythm, is the necessity which it imposes upon the poet of travelling in constant company with his compositions, so as to be ready at a moment's notice to avail himself of a well understood poetical licence—that of reading aloud one's own doggrel.

In Mr. Cranch's line,

> Many are the | thoughts that | come to | me, |

the general error of which I speak is, of course, very partially exemplified, and the purpose for which, chiefly, I cite it, lies yet further on in our topic.

The two divisions (*thoughts that*) and (*come to*) are ordinary trochees. Of the last division (*me*) we will talk hereafter. The first division (many are the) would be thus accented by the Greek Prosodies (mãny ăre thĕ) and would be called by them αστρολογος. The Latin books would style the foot *Pæon Primus*, and both Greek and Latin would swear that it was composed of a trochee and what they term a pyrrhic —that is to say, a foot of two *short* syllables—a thing that *cannot be*, as I shall presently show.

But now, there is an obvious difficulty. The *astrologos*, according to the Prosodies' own showing, is equal to *five* short syllables, and the trochee to *three*—yet, in the line quoted, these two feet are equal. They occupy *precisely* the same time. In fact, the whole music of the line depends upon their being *made* to occupy the same time. The Prosodies, then, have demonstrated what all mathematicians have stupidly failed in demonstrating—that three and five are one and the same thing.

After what I have already said, however, about the bastard trochee and the bastard iambus, no one can have any trouble in understanding that *many are the* is of similar character. It is merely a bolder variation than usual from the routine of trochees, and introduces to the bastard trochee one additional syllable. But this syllable is not *short*. That is, it is not short in the sense of " *short* " as applied to the final syllable of the ordinary trochee, where the word means merely *the half of long*.

In this case, (that of the additional syllable) " short," if used at all, must be used in the sense of *the sixth of long*. And all the three final syllables can be called *short* only with the same understanding of the term. The three together are equal only to the one short syllable (whose place they supply) of the ordinary trochee. It follows that there is no sense in thus (˘) accenting these syllables. We must devise for them some new character which shall denote the sixth of long. Let it be (c)—the crescent placed with the curve to the left. The whole foot (māny are thĕ) might be called a *quick trochee*.

We come now to the final division (*me*) of Mr. Cranch's line. It is clear that this foot, short as it appears, is fully equal in time to each of the preceding. It is in fact the cæsura—the foot which, in the beginning of this paper, I called the most important in all verse. Its chief office is that of pause or termination ; and here—at the end of a line—its use is easy, because there is no danger of misapprehending its value. We pause on it, by a seeming necessity, just so long as it has taken us to pronounce the preceding feet, whether iambusses, trochees, dactyls, or anapæsts. It is thus a *variable foot*, and, with some care, may be well introduced into the body of a line, as in a little poem of great beauty by Mrs. Welby :

I have | a lit | tle step | sŏn | of on | ly three | years old. |

Here we dwell on the cæsura, *son*, just as long as it requires us to pronounce either of the preceding or succeeding iambusses. Its value, therefore, in this line, is that of three short syllables. In the following dactylic line its value is that of four short syllables.

Pale as a | lily was | Emily | Gray.

I have accented the cæsara with a (⏜) by way of expressing this variability of value.

I observed, just now, that there could be no such foot as one of two short syllables. What we start from in the very beginning of all idea on the topic of verse, is quantity, *length*. Thus when we enunciate an independent syllable it is long, as a matter of course. If we enunciate two, dwelling on both equally, we express equality in the enumeration, or length, and have a right to call them two long syllables. If we dwell on one more than the other, we have also a right to call one short, because it is short in relation to the other. But if we dwell on both equally and with a tripping voice, saying to ourselves here are two short syllables, the query might well be asked of us—' in relation to what are they short ? ' Shortness is but the negation of length. To say, then, that two syllables, placed independently of any other syllable, are short, is merely to say that they have no positive length, or enunciation—in other words that they are no syllables—that they do not exist at all. And if, persisting, we add anything about their equality, we are merely floundering in the idea of an identical equation, where x being equal to x, nothing is shown to be equal to zero. In a word, we can form no conception of a pyrrhic as of an independent foot. It is a mere chimera bred in the mad fancy of a pedant.

From what I have said about the equalization of the several feet of a *line*, it must not be deduced that any *necessity* for equality in time exists between the rhythm of *several* lines. A poem, or even a stanza, may begin with iambusses, in the first line, and proceed with anapæsts in the second, or even with the less accordant dactyls, as in the opening of quite a pretty specimen of verse by Miss Mary A. S. Aldrich :

> The wa | ter li | ly sleeps | in pride |
> Dŏwn ĭn thĕ | dĕpths ŏf thĕ | āzūre | lāke. |

Here *azure* is a spondee, equivalent to a dactyl ; *lake* a cæsura.

I shall now best proceed in quoting the initial lines of Byron's *Bride of Abydos* :

> Know ye the land where the cypress and myrtle
> Are emblems of deeds that are done in their clime—
> Where the rage of the vulture, the love of the turtle
> Now melt into softness, now madden to crime ?
> Know ye the land of the cedar and vine,
> Where the flowers ever blossom, the beams ever shine,
> And the light wings of Zephyr, oppressed with perfume,
> Wax faint o'er the gardens of Gul in their bloom ?
> Where the citron and olive are fairest of fruit
> And the voice of the nightingale never is mute—
> Where the virgins are soft as the roses they twine,
> And all save the spirit of man is divine ?

'Tis the land of the East—'tis the clime of the Sun—
Can he smile on such deeds as his children have done ?
Oh, wild as the accents of lovers' farewell
Are the hearts that they bear and the tales that they tell.

Now the flow of these lines, (as times go,) is very
sweet and musical. They have been often admired
and justly—as times go—that is to say, it is a rare
thing to find better versification of its kind.   And
where verse is pleasant to the ear, it is silly to find
fault with it because it refuses to be scanned.   Yet
I have heard men, professing to be scholars, who
made no scruple of abusing these lines of Byron's
on the ground that they were musical in spite of
all law. Other gentlemen, *not* scholars, abused
" all law " for the same reason :—and it occurred
neither to the one party nor to the other that the
law about which they were disputing might possibly
be no law at all—an ass of a law in the skin of a lion.

The Grammars said something about dactylic
lines, and it was easily seen that *these* lines were
at least meant for dactylic. The first one was,
therefore, thus divided :

Knŏw yĕ thĕ | lānd whĕre thĕ | cyprĕss ănd | myrtlĕ. |

The concluding foot was a mystery ; but the Prosodies
said something about the dactylic " measure "
calling now and then for a double rhyme ; and the
court of inquiry were content to rest in the double
rhyme, without exactly perceiving what a double
rhyme had to do with the question of an irregular
foot.   Quitting the first line, the second was thus
scanned :

Arē ĕmblĕms | ŏf deĕds thăt | āre dŏne ĭn | thēir clĭme. |

It was immediately seen, however, that *this* would
not do :—it was at war with the whole emphasis
of the reading.   It could not be supposed that Byron,
or anyone in his senses, intended to place stress upon
such monosyllables as " are," " of," and " their,"
nor could " their clime," collated with " to crime,"

in the corresponding line below, be fairly twisted into anything like a " double rhyme," so as to bring everything within the category of the Grammars. But further these Grammars spoke not. The inquirers, therefore, in spite of their sense of harmony in the lines, when considered without reference to scansion, fell back upon the idea that the " Are " was a blunder—an excess for which the poet should be sent to Coventry—and, striking it out, they scanned the remainder of the line as follows :

——ĕmblĕms ŏf | deĕds thăt ăre | dŏne ĭn thĕir clīme. |

This answered pretty well ; but the Grammars admitted no such foot as a foot of one syllable ; and besides the rhythm was dactylic. In despair, the books are well searched, however, and at last the investigators are gratified by a full solution of the riddle in the profound " Observation " quoted in the beginning of this article :—" When a syllable is wanting, the verse is said to be catalectic ; when the measure is exact, the line is acatalectic ; when there is a redundant syllable it forms hypermeter." This is enough. The anomalous line is pronounced to be catalectic at the head and to form hypermeter at the tail :—and so on, and so on ; it being soon discovered that nearly all the remaining lines are in a similar predicament, and that what flows so smoothly to the ear, although so roughly to the eye, is, after all, a mere jumble of catalecticism, acatalecticism, and hypermeter—not to say worse.

Now, had this court of inquiry been in possession of even the shadow of the *philosophy* of Verse, they would have had no trouble in reconciling this oil and water of the eye and ear, by merely scanning the passage without reference to lines, and, continuously, thus :

Know ye the | land where the | cypress and | myrtle Are emblems of | deeds that are | done in their | clime Where the rage of the | vulture the | love of the | turtle Now melt into | softness now | madden to | *crime* | Know ye the | land

of the | cedar and | vine Where the flowers ever | blossom
the | beams ever | shine Where the | light wings of | Zephyr
op | pressed by per | *fume Wax* | faint o'er the | gardens of |
Gul in their | bloom Where the citron and | olive are fairest
of fruit And the | voice of the | nightingale | never is | mute
Where the | virgins are | soft as the | roses they | *twine And* |
all save the | spirit of | man is di | vine 'Tis the | land of
the | East 'tis the | clime of the | Sun Can he | smile on
such | deeds as his | children have | *done Oh* | wild as the |
accents of | lovers' fare | well Are the | hearts that they | bear
and the | tales that they | *tell.*

Here " crime " and " tell " (italicised) are cæsuras,
each having the value of a dactyl, four short syllables ;
while " fume Wax," " twine and," and " done Oh,"
are spondees which, of course, being composed of
two long syllables, are also equal to four short,
and are the dactyl's natural equivalent. The nicety
of Byron's ear has led him into a succession of feet
which, with two trivial exceptions as regards melody,
are absolutely accurate—a very rare occurrence this
in dactylic or anapæstic rhythms. The exceptions
are found in the spondee " *twine And*," and the
dactyl, " *smile on such.*" Both feet are false in
point of melody. In " *twine And*," to make out
the rhythm, we must force " *And* " into a length
which it will not naturally bear. We are called on
to sacrifice either the proper length of the syllable
as demanded by its position as a member of a spondee,
or the customary accentuation of the word in con-
versation. There is no hesitation, and should be
none. We at once give up the sound for the sense ;
and the rhythm is imperfect. In this instance it
is *very* slightly so ;—not one person in ten thousand
could, by ear, detect the inaccuracy. But the *per-
fection* of verse, as regards melody, consists in its
never demanding any such sacrifice as is here
demanded. The rhythmical must agree, *thoroughly*,
with the reading, flow. This perfection has in no
instance been attained—but is unquestionably attain-
able. " *Smile on such*," the dactyl, is incorrect,
because " *such*," from the character of the two

consonants *ch*, cannot *easily* be enunciated in the ordinary time of a short syllable, which its position declares that it is. Almost every reader will be able to appreciate the slight difficulty here ; and yet the error is by no means so important as that of the " *And* " in the spondee. By dexterity we *may* pronounce " *such* " in the true time ; but the attempt to remedy the rhythmical deficiency of the *And* by drawing it out, merely aggravates the offence against natural enunciation, by directing attention to the offence.

My main object, however, in quoting these lines, is to show that, in spite of the Prosodies, the length of a line is entirely an arbitrary matter. We might divide the commencement of Byron's poem thus :

> Know ye the | land where the. |

or thus :

> Know ye the | land where the | cypress and. |

or thus :

> Know ye the | land where the | cypress and | myrtle are.

or thus :

> Know ye the | land where the | cypress and | myrtle are emblems of. |

In short, we may give it any division we please, and the lines will be good—provided we have at least *two* feet in a line. As in mathematics two units are required to form number, so rhythm, (from the Greek αριθμος, number,) demands for its formation at least two feet. Beyond doubt, we often see such lines as

> Know ye the—
> Land where the—

lines of one foot ; and our Prosodies admit such ; but with impropriety ; for common sense would dictate that every so obvious division of a poem as is made by a line, should include within itself

all that is necessary for its own comprehension ;
but in a line of one foot we can have no appreciation
of rhythm, which depends upon the equality between
two or more pulsations. The false lines, consisting
sometimes of a single cæsura, which are seen in
mock Pindaric odes, are of course "rhythmical"
only in connection with some other line ; and it is
this want of independent rhythm which adapts
them to the purposes of burlesque alone. Their
effect is that of incongruity (the principle of mirth ;)
for they include the blankness of prose amid the
harmony of verse.

My second object in quoting Byron's lines, was
that of showing how absurd it often is to cite a single
line from amid the body of a poem, for the purpose
of instancing the perfection or imperfection of the
line's rhythm. Were we to see by itself

> Know ye the land where the cypress and myrtle,

we might justly condemn it as defective in the final
foot, which is equal to only three, instead of being
equal to four, short syllables.

In the foot (*flowers ever*) we shall find a further
exemplification of the principle of the bastard iambus,
bastard trochee, and quick trochee, as I have been
at some pains in describing these feet above. All
the Prosodies on English verse would insist upon
making an elision in "flowers," thus (flow'rs), but
this is nonsense. In the quick trochee (mānÿ ărĕ thĕ)
occurring in Mr. Cranch's *trochaic* line, we had to
equalize the time of the three syllables (*ny, are, the,*)
to that of the one *short* syllable whose position they
usurp. Accordingly each of these syllables is equal
to the third of a short syllable, that is to say, the
sixth of a long. But in Byron's *dactylic* rhythm,
we have to equalize the time of the three syllables
(*ers, ev, er*), to that of the one *long* syllable whose
position they usurp, or, (which is the same thing,)
of the *two short*. Therefore the value of each of the
syllables (*ers, ev,* and *er*) is the *third of a long*. We

enunciate them with only half the rapidity we employ in enunciating the three final syllables of the quick trochee—which latter is a rare foot. The "*flowers ever*," on the contrary, is as common in the dactylic rhythm as is the *bastard* trochee in the trochaic, or the bastard iambus in the iambic. We may as well accent it with the curve of the crescent to the right, and call it a *bastard dactyl*. A *bastard anapæst*, whose nature I now need be at no trouble in explaining, will of course occur, now and then, in an anapæstic rhythm.

In order to avoid any chance of that confusion which is apt to be introduced in an essay of this kind by too sudden and radical an alteration of the conventionalities to which the reader has been accustomed, I have thought it right to suggest for the accent marks of the bastard trochee, bastard iambus, etc., etc., certain characters which, in merely varying the direction of the ordinary short accent (˘) should imply, what is the fact, that the feet themselves are not *new* feet, in any proper sense, but simply modifications of the feet, respectively, from which they derive their names. Thus a bastard iambus is, in its essentiality, that is to say, in its time, an iambus. The variation lies only in the *distribution* of this time. The time, for example, occupied by the one short (or *half of long*) syllable, in the ordinary iambus, is, in the bastard, spread equally over two syllables, which are accordingly the *fourth of long*.

But this fact—the fact of the essentiality, or whole time, of the foot being unchanged, is now so fully before the reader, that I may venture to propose, finally, an accentuation which shall answer the real purpose—that is to say, what should be the real purpose of all accentuation—the purpose of expressing to the eye he exact relative value of every syllable employed in Verse.

I have already shown that enunciation, or *length*, is the point from which we start. In other words, we begin with a *long syllable*. This then is our unit ;

and there will be no need of accenting it at all. An unaccented syllable, in a system of accentuation, is to be regarded always as a long syllable. Thus a spondee would be without accent. In an iambus, the first syllable being " short," or the *half* of long, should be accented with a small 2, placed *beneath* the syllable; the last syllable, being long, should be unaccented;—the whole would be thus (control).

In a trochee, these accents would be merely conversed, thus (manly.) In a dactyl, each of the two

final syllables, being the half of long, should, also, be accented with a small 2 beneath the syllable; and, the first syllable left unaccented, the whole would be thus (happiness.) In an anapæst we should

converse the dactyl thus, (in the land.) In the

bastard dactyl, each of the three concluding syllables being the *third* of long, should be accented with a small 3 beneath the syllable and the whole foot would stand thus, (flowers ever.) In the bastard

anapæst we should converse the bastard dactyl thus, (in the rebound.) In the bastard iambus,

each of the two initial syllables, being the fourth of long, should be accented, below, with a small 4; the whole foot would be thus, (in the rain). In the

bastard trochee, we should converse the bastard iambus thus, (many a). In the quick trochee,

each of the three concluding syllables, being the *sixth* of long, should be accented, below, with a small 6; the whole foot would be thus, (many are the).

The quick iambus is not yet created, and most probably never will be, for it will be excessively useless, awkward, and liable to misconception—as I have already shown that even the quick trochee is:

—but, should it appear, we must accent it by conversing the quick trochee. The cæsura, being variable in length, but always *longer than "long,"* should be accented, *above*, with a number expressing the length, or value, of the distinctive foot of the rhythm in which it occurs Thus a cæsura, occurring in a spondaic rhythm, would be accented with a small 2 above the syllable, or, rather, foot. Occurring in a dactylic or anapæstic rhythm, we also accent it with the 2, above the foot. Occurring in an iambic rhythm, however, it must be accented, above, with $1\frac{1}{2}$; for this is the relative value of the iambus. Occurring in the trochaic rhythm, we give it, of course, the same accentuation. For the complex $1\frac{1}{2}$, however, it would be advisable to substitute the simpler expression $\frac{3}{2}$ which amounts to the same thing.

In this system of accentuation Mr. Cranch's lines, quoted above, would thus be written :

Many are the | thoughts that | come to | me |

In my | lonely | musing, |

And they | drift so | strange and | swift

There's no | time for | choosing |

Which to | follow | for to | leave

Any, | seems a | losing. |

In the ordinary system the accentuation would be thus :

Mãny arĕ thĕ | thōughts thăt | cōme tŏ | mē
In my | lōnely | mŭsing, |
ãnd thĕy | drīft sŏ | strānge ănd | swīft |
Th ̄erĕ's nŏ | timē fŏr | choōsīng |
Whĭch tŏ | fōllŏw, | fŏr tŏ | lēave
āny, | seēms ă | lōsĭng. |

It must be observed, here, that I do not grant this to be the " ordinary " *scansion*. On the contrary, I never yet met the man who had the faintest comprehension of the true scanning of these lines, or of such as these. But granting this to be the mode in which our Prosodies would divide the feet, they would accentuate the syllables as just above.

Now, let any reasonable person compare the two modes. The first advantage seen in my mode is that of simplicity—of time, labour, and ink saved. Counting the fractions as *two* accents, even, there will be found only *twenty-six* accents to the stanza. In the common accentuation there are *forty-one*. But admit that all this is a trifle, which it is *not*, and let us proceed to points of importance. Does the common accentuation express the truth, in particular, in general, or in any regard ? Is it consistent with itself ? Does it convey either to the ignorant or to the scholar a just conception of the rhythm of the lines ? Each of these questions must be answered in the negative. The crescents, being precisely similar, must be understood as expressing, all of them, one and the same thing : and so all Prosodies have always understood them and wished them to be understood. They express, indeed, " short "—but this word has all kinds of meanings. It serves to represent (the reader is left to guess *when*) sometimes the half, sometimes the third, sometimes the fourth, sometimes the sixth, of " long "—while " long " itself, in the books, is left undefined and undescribed. On the other hand, the horizontal accent, it may be said, expresses sufficiently well, and unvaryingly, the syllables which are meant to be long. It does nothing of the kind. This horizontal accent is placed over the cæsura (wherever, as in the Latin Prosodies, the cæsura is recognized) as well as over the ordinary long syllable, and implies anything and everything, just as the crescent. But grant that it does express the ordinary long syllables, (leaving the cæsura out of question,) have I not given the identical expression, by not employing any expression at all? In a word, while the Prosodies, with a certain number of accents, express *precisely nothing whatever*, I, with scarcely half the number, have expressed everything which, in a system of accentuation, demands expression. In glancing at my mode in the lines of Mr. Cranch, it will be seen that it conveys not only the exact relation of the syllables and feet, among themselves, in those particular lines, but their precise value in relation to any other existing or conceivable feet or syllables, in any existing or conceivable system of rhythm.

The object of what we call *scansion* is the distinct marking of the rhythmical flow. Scansion with accents or perpendicular lines between the feet— that is to say scansion *by* the voice only—is scansion *to* the ear only; and all very good in its way. The written scansion addresses the ear through the eye. In either case the object is the distinct marking of the rhythmical, musical, or reading flow. There *can* be no other object and there is none. Of course, then, the scansion and the reading flow should go hand in hand. The former must agree with the latter. The former represents and expresses the latter; and is good or bad as it truly or falsely represents and expresses it. If by the written scansion of a line we are not enabled to perceive any rhythm or music in the line, then either the line is unrhythmical or the scansion false. Apply all this to the English lines which we have quoted, at various points, in the course of this article. It will be found that the scansion exactly conveys the rhythm, and thus thoroughly fulfils the only purpose for which scansion is required.

But let the scansion *of the schools* be applied to the Greek and Latin verse, and what result do we find?—that the verse is one thing and the scansion quite another. The ancient verse, *read* aloud, is in general musical, and occasionally *very* musical.

Scanned by the Prosodial rules we can, for the most part, make nothing of it whatever. In the case of the English verse, the more emphatically we dwell on the divisions between the feet, the more distinct is our perception of the kind of rhythm intended. In the case of the Greek and Latin, the more we dwell the *less* distinct is this perception. To make this clear by an example :

> Mæcenas, atavis edite regibus,
> O, et præsidium et dulce decus meum,
> Sunt quos curriculo pulverem Olympicum
> Collegisse juvat, metaque fervidis
> Evitata rotis, palmaque nobilis
> Terrarum dominos evehit ad Deos.

Now in *reading* these lines, there is scarcely one person in a thousand who, if even ignorant of Latin, will not immediately feel and appreciate their flow— their music. A prosodist, however, informs the public that the *scansion* runs thus :

> Mæce | nas ata | vis | edite | regibus |
> O, et | præsidi' | et | dulce de | cus meum |
> Sunt quos | curricu | lo | pulver' O | lympicum |
> Colle | gisse ju | vat | metaque | fervidis |
> Evi | tata ro | tis | palmaque | nobilis |
> Terra | rum domi | nos | evehit | ad Deos. |

Now I do not deny that we get a *certain sort* of music from the lines if we read them according to this scansion, but I wish to call attention to the fact that this scansion and the certain sort of music which grows out of it, are entirely at war not only with the reading flow which any ordinary person would naturally give the lines, but with the reading flow universally given them, and never denied them, by even the most obstinate and stolid of scholars.

And now these questions are forced upon us— " Why exists this discrepancy between the modern verse with its scansion, and the ancient verse with its scansion ? "—" Why, in the former case, are there agreement and representation, while in the latter there is neither the one nor the other?" or, to come to the point,—"How are we to reconcile the ancient verse with the scholastic scansion of it?" This absolutely necessary conciliation—shall we bring it about by supposing the scholastic scansion wrong because the ancient verse is right, or by maintaining that the ancient verse is wrong because the scholastic scansion is not to be gainsaid?

Were we to adopt the latter mode of arranging the difficulty, we might, in some measure, at least simplify the expression of the arrangement by putting it thus—Because the pedants have no eyes, therefore the old poets had no ears.

"But," say the gentlemen without the eyes, "the scholastic scansion, although certainly not handed down to us in form from the old poets themselves (the gentlemen without the ears,) is nevertheless deduced from certain facts which are supplied us by careful observation of the old poems."

And let us illustrate this strong position by an example from an American poet—who must be a poet of some eminence, or he will not answer the purpose. Let us take Mr. Alfred B. Street. I remember these two lines of his:

> His sinuous path, by blazes, wound
> Among trunks grouped in myriads round.

With the *sense* of these lines I have nothing to do. When a poet is in a "fine frenzy," he may as well imagine a large forest as a small one—and "by blazes!" is *not* intended for an oath. My concern is with the rhythm, which is iambic.

Now let us suppose that, a thousand years hence, when the "American language" is dead, a learned prosodist should be deducing from "careful observation" of our best poets, a system of scansion for our poetry. And let us suppose that this prosodist had so little dependence in the generality and immutability of the laws of Nature, as to assume in the outset, that, because we lived a thousand years before his time, and made use of steam-engines instead of mesmeric balloons, we must therefore have had a *very* singular fashion of mouthing our vowels, and altogether of hudsonizing our verse. And let us suppose that with these and other fundamental propositions carefully put away in his brain, he should arrive at the line,—

Among | trunks grouped | in my | riads round.

Finding it an obviously iambic rhythm, he would divide it as above ; and observing that " trunks " made the first member of an iambus, he would call it short, as Mr. Street intended it to be. Now further :—if instead of admitting the possibility that Mr. Street, (who by that time would be called Street simply, just as we say Homer,)—that Mr. Street might have been in the habit of writing carelessly, as the poets of the prosodist's own era did, and as all poets will do (on account of being geniuses,) —instead of admitting this, suppose the learned scholar should make a " rule " and put it in a book, to the effect that, in the American verse, the vowel *u, when found imbedded among nine consonants*, was *short :* what, under such circumstances, would the sensible people of the scholar's day have a right not only to think, but to say of that scholar ?—why, that he was " a fool—by blazes ! "

I have put an extreme case, but it strikes at the root of the error. The " rules " are grounded in " authority " ; and this " authority "— can anyone tell us what it means ? or can anyone suggest anything that it may *not* mean ? Is it not clear that the " scholar " above referred to, might as readily have deduced from authority a totally false system as a partially true one ? To deduce from authority a consistent prosody of the ancient metres would indeed have been within the limits of the barest possibility ; and the task has *not* been accomplished, for the reason that it demands a species of ratiocination altogether out of keeping with the brain of a bookworm. A rigid scrutiny will show that the very few " rules " which have not as many exceptions as examples, are those which have, by accident, their true bases not in authority, but in the omniprevalent laws of syllabification ; such, for example, as the rule which declares a vowel before two consonants to be long.

In a word, the gross confusion and antagonism of the scholastic prosody, as well as its marked inapplicability to the reading flow of the rhythms it pretends to illustrate, are attributable, first, to the utter absence of natural principle as a guide in the investigations which have been undertaken by inadequate men ; and secondly, to the neglect of the obvious consideration that the ancient poems, which have been the *criteria* throughout, were the work of men who must have written as loosely, and with as little definitive system, as ourselves.

Were Horace alive to-day, he would divide for us his first Ode thus, and "make great eyes " when assured by the prosodists that he had no business to make any such division !

> Mæcenas | atavis | edite | regibus |
> 2 2   2 2   2 2   2 2
>
> O et præ | sidium et | dulce de | cus meum |
> 2 2   3 3   3   2 2   2 2
>
> Sunt quos cur | riculo | pulverem O | lympicum |
> 2   2   2 2   3 3   3   2 2
>
> Collegisse | juvat | metaque | fervidis |
> 3 3 3   2 2   2 2
>
> Evitata | rotis | palmaque | nobilis |
> 3 3 3   2   2   2 2
>
> Terrarum | dominos | evehit | ad Deos. |
> 2 2   2 2   2 2   2 2

Read by this scansion, the flow is preserved ; and the more we dwell on the divisions, the more the intended rhythm becomes apparent. Moreover, the feet have all the same time ; while, in the scholastic scansion, trochees—admitted trochees—are absurdly employed as equivalents to spondees and dactyls. The books declare, for instance, that *Colle*, which begins the fourth line, is a trochee, and seem to be gloriously unconscious that to put a trochee in opposition with a longer foot, is to violate the inviolable principle of all music, *time*.

It will be said, however, by " some people," that I have no business to make a dactyl out of such obviously long syllables as *sunt, quos, cur*. Certainly I have no business to do so. I *never* do so, And Horace should not have done so. But he did. Mr. Bryant and Mr. Longfellow do the same thing every day. And merely because these gentlemen, now and then, forget themselves in this way, it would be hard if some future prosodist should insist upon twisting the *Thanatopsis*, or the *Spanish Student*, into a jumble of trochees, spondees, and dactyls.

It may be said, also, by some other people, that in the word *decus*, I have succeeded no better than the books, in making the scansional agree with the reading flow ; and that *decus* was not pronounced de*cus*. I reply, that there can be no doubt of the word having been pronounced, in this case, de*cus*. It must be observed, that the Latin inflection, or variation of a word in its terminating syllables, caused the Romans—*must* have caused them, to pay greater attention to the termination of a word than to its commencement, or than we do to the terminations of our words. The end of the Latin word established that relation of the word with other words which we establish by prepositions or auxiliary verbs. Therefore, it would seem infinitely less odd to them than it does to us, to dwell at any time, for any slight purpose, abnormally, on a terminating syllable. In verse, this licence—scarcely a licence— would be frequently admitted. These ideas unlock the secret of such lines as the

Litoreis ingens inventa sub ili*cibus sus*,

and the

Parturiunt montes et nascitur ridicu*lus mus*,

which I quoted, some time ago, while speaking of
rhyme.

As regards the prosodial elisions, such as that of
rem before *O* in *pulverem Olympicum*, it is really diffi-
cult to understand how so dismally silly a notion
could have entered the brain even of a pedant. Were
it demanded of me why the books cut off one *vowel*
before another, I might say—It is, perhaps, because
the books think that, since a bad reader is so apt
to slide the one vowel into the other at any rate,
it is just as well to print them *ready-slided*. But in
the case of the terminating *m*, which is the most
readily pronounced of all consonants, (as the infantile
mamma will testify,) and the most impossible to
cheat the ear of by any system of sliding—in the
case of the *m*, I should be driven to reply that, to
the best of my belief, the prosodists did the thing,
because they had a fancy for doing it, and wished
to see how funny it would look after it was done.
The thinking reader will perceive that, from the great
facility with which *em* may be enunciated, it is ad-
mirably suited to form one of the rapid short syllables
in the bastard dactyl (pulverem O ;) but because
the books had no conception of a bastard dactyl,
they knocked it in the head at once—by cutting off
its tail !

Let me now give a specimen of the true scansion
of another Horatian measure—embodying an in-
stance of proper elision.

> Integer | vitæ | scelerisque | purus |
>
> Non eget | Mauri | jaculis ne | que arcu |
>
> Nec vene | natis | gravida sa | gittis,
>
>   Fusce, pha | retrâ.

Here the regular recurrence of the bastard dactyl
gives great animation to the rhythm. The *e* before
the *a* in *que arcu*, is, almost of sheer necessity, cut

off—that is to say, run into the *a* so as to preserve the spondee. But even this licence it would have been better not to take.

Had I space, nothing would afford me greater pleasure than to proceed with the scansion of *all* the ancient rhythms, and to show how easily, by the help of common sense, the intended music of each and all can be rendered instantaneously apparent. But I have already overstepped my limits, and must bring this paper to an end.

It will never do, however, to omit all mention of the heroic hexameter.

I began the " processes " by a suggestion of the spondee as the first step towards verse. But the innate monotony of the spondee has caused its disappearance, as the basis of rhythm, from all modern poetry. We *may* say, indeed, that the French heroic —the most wretchedly monotonous verse in existence—is, to all intents and purposes, spondaic. But it is not designedly spondaic—and if the French were ever to examine it at all, they would no doubt pronounce it iambic. It must be observed, that the French language is strangely peculiar in this point— *that it is without accentuation, and consequently without verse.* The genius of the people, rather than the structure of the tongue, declares that their words are, for the most part, enunciated with an uniform dwelling on each syllable. For example—*we* say, " syl*labifica*tion." A Frenchman would say, syl-la-bi-fi-ca-ti-on ; dwelling on no one of the syllables with any noticeable particularity. Here again I put an extreme case, in order to be well understood ; but the general fact is as I give it—that, comparatively, the French have *no* accentuation. And there can be nothing worth the name of verse without. Therefore, the French have no verse worth the name—which is the fact, put in sufficiently plain terms. Their iambic rhythm so superabounds in absolute spondees, as to warrant me in calling its basis spondaic ; but French is the *only* modern tongue which has any rhythm with such basis; and even in the French, it is, as I have said, unintentional.

Admitting, however, the validity of my suggestion, that the spondee was the first approach to verse, we should expect to find, first, natural spondees (words each forming just a spondee,) most abundant in the most ancient languages; and, secondly, we should expect to find spondees forming the basis of the most ancient rhythms. These expectations are in both cases confirmed.

Of the Greek hexameter, the intentional basis is spondaic. The dactyls are the *variation* of the theme. It will be observed that there is no absolute certainty about *their* points of interposition. The penultimate foot, it is true, is usually a dactyl; but not uniformly so; while the ultimate, on which the ear *lingers*, is always a spondee. Even that the penultimate is usually a dactyl may be clearly referred to the necessity of winding up with the *distinctive* spondee. In corroboration of this idea, again, we should look to find the penultimate spondee most usual in the most ancient verse; and, accordingly, we find it more frequent in the Greek than in the Latin hexameter.

But besides all this, spondees are not only more prevalent in the heroic hexameter than dactyls, but occur to such an extent as is even unpleasant to modern ears, on account of monotony. What the modern chiefly appreciates and admires in the Greek hexameter, is the *melody of the abundant vowel sounds*. The Latin hexameters *really* please very few moderns—although so many pretend to fall into ecstasies about them. In the hexameters quoted, several pages ago, from Silius Italicus, the preponderance of the spondee is strikingly manifest. Besides the natural spondees of the Greek and Latin, numerous artificial ones arise in the verse of these tongues on account of the tendency which inflection has to throw full accentuation on terminal syllables; and the preponderance of the spondee is further ensured by the comparative infrequency of the small prepositions which *we* have to serve us *instead* of case, and also the absence of the diminutive auxiliary verbs with which *we* have to eke out the expression of our primary ones. These are the monosyllables whose abundance serves to stamp the poetic genius of a language as tripping or dactylic.

Now paying no attention to these facts, Sir Philip Sidney, Professor Longfellow, and innumerable other persons more or less modern, have busied themselves in constructing what they supposed to be " English hexameters on the model of the Greek." The only difficulty was that (even leaving out of question the melodious masses of vowel,) these gentlemen never could get their English hexameters to *sound* Greek. Did they *look* Greek ?—that should have been the query ; and the reply might have led to a solution of the riddle. In placing a copy of ancient hexameters side by side with a copy (in similar type) of such hexameters as Professor Longfellow, or Professor Felton, or the Frogpondian Professors collectively, are in the shameful practice of composing " on the model of the Greek," it will be seen that the latter (hexameters, not professors) are about one third longer *to the eye*, on an average, than the former. The more abundant dactyls make the difference. And it is the greater number of spondees in the Greek than in the English—in the ancient than in the modern tongue—which has caused it to fall out that while these eminent scholars were groping about in the dark for a Greek hexameter, which is a spondaic rhythm varied now and then by dactyls, they merely stumbled, to the lasting scandal of scholarship, over something which, on account of its long-leggedness, we may as well term a Feltonian hexameter, and which is a dactylic rhythm, interrupted, rarely, by artificial spondees which are no spondees at all, and which are curiously thrown in by the heels at all kinds of improper and impertinent points.

Here is a specimen of the Longfellownian hexameter :

Also the | church with | in was a | dorned for | this was the |
    season |
In which the | young their | parents' | hope and the | loved
    ones of | Heaven. |
Should at the | foot of the | altar re | new the | vows of
    their | baptism |
Therefore each | nook and | corner was | swept and | cleaned
    and the | dust was |
Blown from the | walls and | ceiling and | from the | oil-
    painted | benches. |

Mr. Longfellow is a man of imagination—but *can*
he imagine that any individual, with a proper under-
standing of the danger of lock-jaw, would make
the attempt of twisting his mouth into the shape
necessary for the emission of such spondees as
" par*ents*," and " from the," or such dactyls as
" cleaned and the " and " loved ones of " ? " Bap-
tism " is by no means a bad spondee—perhaps
because it happens to be a dactyl ;—of all the rest,
however, I am dreadfully ashamed.

But these feet—dactyls and spondees, all together,
—should thus be put at once into their proper position :

" Also, the church within was adorned ; for this was the
season in which the young, their parents' hope, and the
loved ones of Heaven, should, at the feet of the altar, renew
the vows of their baptism. Therefore, each nook and
corner was swept and cleaned ; and the dust was blown
from the walls and ceiling, and from the oil-painted benches."

There !—That is respectable prose ; and it will
incur no danger of ever getting its character ruined
by anybody's mistaking it for verse.

But even when we let these modern hexameters
go, as Greek, and merely hold them fast in their
proper character of Longfellownian, or Feltonian, or
Frogpondian, we must still condemn them as having
been committed in a radical misconception of the
philosophy of verse. The spondee, as I observed, is
the *theme* of the Greek line. Most of the ancient

hexameters *begin* with spondees, for the reason that the spondee *is* the theme ; and the ear is filled with it as with a burden. Now the Feltonian dactylics have, in the same way, dactyls for the theme, and most of them begin with dactyls—which is all very proper if not very Greek—but, unhappily, the one point at which they *are* very Greek is that point, precisely, at which they should be nothing but Feltonian. They always *close* with what is meant for a spondee. To be consistently silly, they should die off in a dactyl.

That a truly Greek hexameter *cannot*, however, be readily composed in English, is a proposition which I am by no means inclined to admit. I think I could manage the point myself. For example :

Do tell ! | when may we | hope to make | men of sense | out
    of the | Pundits |
Born and brought | up with their | snouts deep | down in
    the | mud of the | Frog-pond ?
Why ask ? | who ever | yet saw | money made | out of a | fat
    old |
Jew, or | downright | upright | nutmegs | out of a | pine-
    knot ? |

The proper spondee predominance is here preserved. Some of the dactyls are not so good as I could wish— but, upon the whole, the rhythm is very decent— to say nothing of its excellent sense.

THE PHILOSOPHY OF COMPOSITION

CHARLES DICKENS, in a note now lying before me, alluding to an examination I once made of the mechanism of *Barnaby Rudge*, says—" By the way, are you aware that Godwin wrote his *Caleb Williams* backwards ? He first involved his hero in a web of difficulties, forming the second volume, and then, for the first, cast about him for some mode of accounting for what had been done."

I cannot think this the *precise* mode of procedure

on the part of Godwin—and indeed what he himself acknowledges, is not altogether in accordance with Mr. Dickens' idea—but the author of *Caleb Williams* was too good an artist not to perceive the advantage derivable from at least a somewhat similar process. Nothing is more clear than that every plot, worth the name, must be elaborated to its *dénouement* before anything be attempted with the pen. It is only with the *dénouement* constantly in view that we can give a plot its indispensable air of consequence, or causation, by making the incidents, and especially the tone at all points, tend to the development of the intention.

There is a radical error, I think, in the usual mode of constructing a story. Either history affords a thesis—or one is suggested by an incident of the day—or, at best, the author sets himself to work in the combination of striking events to form merely the basis of his narrative—designing, generally, to fill in with description, dialogue, or autorial comment, whatever crevices of fact, or action, may, from page to page, render themselves apparent.

I prefer commencing with the consideration of an *effect*. Keeping originality *always* in view—for he is false to himself who ventures to dispense with so obvious and so easily attainable a source of interest—I say to myself, in the first place, " Of the innumerable effects, or impressions, of which the heart, the intellect, or (more generally) the soul is susceptible, what one shall I, on the present occasion, select ? " Having chosen a novel, first, and secondly a vivid effect, I consider whether it can be best wrought by incident or tone—whether by ordinary incidents and peculiar tone, or the converse, or by peculiarity both of incident and tone—afterward looking about me (or rather within) for such combinations of event, or tone, as shall best aid me in the construction of the effect.

I have often thought how interesting a magazine paper might be written by any author who would—

that is to say, who could—detail, step by step, the processes by which any one of his compositions attained its ultimate point of completion. Why such a paper has never been given to the world, I am much at a loss to say—but, perhaps, the autorial vanity has had more to do with the omission than any one other cause. Most writers—poets in especial —prefer having it understood that they compose by a species of fine frenzy—an ecstatic intuition— and would positively shudder at letting the public take a peep behind the scenes, at the elaborate and vacillating crudities of thought—at the true purposes seized only at the last moment—at the innumerable glimpses of idea that arrived not at the maturity of full view—at the fully matured fancies discarded in despair as unmanageable—at the cautious selections and rejections—at the painful erasures and inter-polations—in a word, at the wheels and pinions— the tackle for scene-shifting—the step-ladders and demon-traps—the cock's feathers, the red paint and the black patches, which, in ninety-nine cases out of the hundred, constitute the properties of the literary *histrio*.

I am aware, on the other hand, that the case is by no means common, in which an author is at all in condition to retrace the steps by which his con-clusions have been attained. In general, suggestions, having arisen pell-mell, are pursued and forgotten in a similar manner.

For my own part, I have neither sympathy with the repugnance alluded to, nor, at any time, the least difficulty in recalling to mind the progressive steps of any of my compositions ; and, since the interest of an analysis, or reconstruction, such as I have considered a *desideratum*, is quite independent of any real or fancied interest in the thing analysed, it will not be regarded as a breach of decorum on my part to show the *modus operandi* by which some one of my own works was put together. I select *The Raven* as most generally known. It is my design to render it manifest that no one point in its composition is referable either to accident or intuition—that the work proceeded, step by step, to its completion with the precision and rigid consequence of a mathematical problem.

Let us dismiss, as irrelevant to the poem, *per se*, the circumstance—or say the necessity—which, in the first place, gave rise to the intention of composing *a* poem that should suit at once the popular and the critical taste.

We commence, then, with this intention.

The initial consideration was that of extent. If any literary work is too long to be read at one sitting, we must be content to dispense with the immensely important effect derivable from unity of impression—for, if two sittings be required, the affairs of the world interfere, and everything like totality is at once destroyed. But since, *ceteris paribus*, no poet can afford to dispense with *anything* that may advance his design, it but remains to be seen whether there is, in extent, any advantage to counterbalance the loss of unity which attends it. Here I say no, at once. What we term a long poem is, in fact, merely a succession of brief ones—that is to say, of brief poetical effects. It is needless to demonstrate that a poem is such, only inasmuch as it intensely excites, by elevating, the soul ; and all intense excitements are, through a psychal necessity, brief. For this reason, at least one half of the *Paradise Lost* is essentially prose—a succession of poetical excitements interspersed, *inevitably*, with corresponding depressions—the whole being deprived, through the extremeness of its length, of the vastly important artistic element, totality, or unity, of effect.

It appears evident, then, that there is a distinct limit, as regards length, to all works of literary art—the limit of a single sitting—and that, although in certain classes of prose composition, such as *Robinson Crusoe*, (demanding no unity,) this limit may be advantageously overpassed, it can never properly be overpassed in a poem. Within this limit, the extent of a poem may be made to bear mathematical relation to its merit—in other words, to the excitement or elevation—again, in other words, to the degree of the true poetical effect which it is capable of inducing ; for it is clear that the brevity must be in direct ratio of the intensity of the intended effect :—this, with one proviso—that a certain degree of duration is absolutely requisite for the production of any effect at all.

Holding in view these considerations, as well as that degree of excitement which I deemed not above the popular, while not below the critical, taste, I reached at once what I conceived the proper *length* for my intended poem—a length of about one hundred lines. It is, in fact, a hundred and eight.

My next thought concerned the choice of an impression, or effect, to be conveyed : and here I may as well observe that, throughout the construction, I kept steadily in view the design of rendering the work *universally* appreciable. I should be carried too far out of my immediate topic were I to demonstrate a point upon which I have repeatedly insisted, and which, with the poetical, stands not in the slightest need of demonstration—the point, I mean, that Beauty is the sole legitimate province of the poem. A few words, however, in elucidation of my real meaning, which some of my friends have evinced a disposition to misrepresent. That pleasure which is at once the most intense, the most elevating, and the most pure, is, I believe, found in the contemplation of the beautiful. When, indeed, men speak of Beauty, they mean, precisely, not a quality, as is supposed, but an effect—they refer, in short, just to that intense and pure elevation of *soul—not* of intellect, or of heart—upon which I have commented, and which is experienced in consequence of contemplating " the beautiful." Now I designate Beauty as the province of the poem, merely because it is an obvious rule of Art that effects should be made to spring from direct causes—that objects should be attained through means best adapted for their attainment—no one as yet having been weak enough to deny that the peculiar elevation alluded to, is *most readily* attained in the poem. Now the object Truth, or the satisfaction of the intellect, and the object Passion, or the excitement of the heart, are, although attainable, to a certain extent, in poetry, far more readily attainable in prose. Truth, in fact, demands a precision, and Passion a *homeliness* (the truly passionate will comprehend me) which are absolutely antagonistic to that Beauty which, I maintain, is the excitement, or pleasurable elevation, of the soul. It by no means follows from anything here said, that passion, or even truth, may not be introduced, and even profitably introduced, into a poem—for they may serve in elucidation, or aid the general effect, as do discords in music, by contrast—but the true artist will always contrive, first, to tone them into proper subservience to the predominant aim, and, secondly, to enveil them, as far as possible, in that Beauty which is the atmosphere and the essence of the poem.

Regarding, then, Beauty as my province, my next question referred to the *tone* of its highest manifestation—and all experience has shown that this tone is one of *sadness*. Beauty of whatever kind, in its supreme development, invariably excites the sensitive soul to tears. Melancholy is thus the most legi ima e of all the poetical tones.

The length, the province, and the tone, being thus determined, I betook myself to ordinary induction, with the view of obtaining some artistic piquancy which might serve me as a key-note in the construction of the poem—some pivot upon which the whole structure might turn. In carefully thinking over all the usual artistic effects—or more properly *points*, in the theatrical sense—I did not fail to perceive immediately that no one had been so universally employed as that of the *refrain*. The universality of its employment sufficed to assure me of its intrinsic value, and spared me the necessity of submitting it to analysis. I considered it, however, with regard to its susceptibility of improvement, and soon saw it to be in a primitive condition. As commonly used, the *refrain*, or burden, not only is limited to lyric verse, but depends for its impression upon the force of monotone—both in sound and thought. The pleasure is deduced solely from the sense of identity—of repetition. I resolved to diversify, and so heighten, the effect, by adhering, in general, to the monotone of sound, while I continually varied that of thought: that is to say, I determined to produce continuously novel effects, by the variation *of the application* of the *refrain*—the *refrain* itself remaining, for the most part, unvaried.

These points being settled, I next bethought me of the *nature* of my *refrain*. Since its application was to be repeatedly varied, it was clear that the *refrain* itself must be brief, for there would have been an insurmountable difficulty in frequent variations of application in any sentence of length. In proportion to the brevity of the sentence, would, of course, be the facility of the variation. This led me at once to a single word as the best *refrain*.

The question now arose as to the *character* of the word. Having made up my mind to a *refrain*, the division of the poem into stanzas was, of course, a corollary: the *refrain* forming the close to each stanza. That such a close, to have force, must be sonorous and susceptible of protracted emphasis, admitted no doubt: and these considerations inevitably led me to the long *o* as the most sonorous vowel, in connection with *r* as the most producible consonant.

The sound of the *refrain* being thus determined, it became necessary to select a word embodying this sound, and at the same time in the fullest possible keeping with that melancholy which I had predetermined as the tone of the poem. In such a search it would have been absolutely impossible to overlook the word "Nevermore." In fact, it was the very first which presented itself.

The next *desideratum* was a pretext for the continuous use of the one word "nevermore." In observing the difficulty which I at once found in inventing a sufficiently plausible reason for its continuous repetition, I did not fail to perceive that this difficulty arose solely from the pre-assumption that the word was to be so continuously or monotonously spoken by *a human* being—I did not fail to perceive, in short, that the difficulty lay in the reconciliation of this monotony with the exercise of reason on the part of the creature repeating the word. Here, then, immediately arose the idea of a *non*-reasoning creature capable of speech; and, very naturally, a parrot, in the first instance, suggested itself, but was superseded forthwith by a Raven, as equally capable of speech, and infinitely more in keeping with the intended *tone*.

I had now gone so far as the conception of a Raven—the bird of ill omen—monotonously repeating the one word, "Nevermore," at the conclusion of each stanza, in a poem of melancholy tone, and in length about one hundred lines. Now, never losing sight of the object *supremeness*, or perfection, at all points, I asked myself—"Of all melancholy topics, what, according to the *universal* understanding of mankind, is the *most* melancholy?" Death—was the obvious reply. "And when," I said, "is this most melancholy of topics most poetical?" From what I have already explained at some length, the answer, here also, is obvious—"When it most closely allies itself to *Beauty*: the death, then, of a beautiful woman is, unquestionably, the most poetical topic in the world—and equally is it beyond doubt that the lips best suited for such topic are those of a bereaved lover."

I had now to combine the two ideas, of a lover lamenting his deceased mistress and a Raven continuously repeating the word "Nevermore."—I had to combine these, bearing in mind my design of varying, at every turn, the *application* of the word repeated ; but the only intelligible mode of such combination is that of imagining the Raven employing the word in answer to the queries of the lover. And here it was that I saw at once the opportunity afforded for the effect on which I had been depending—that is to say, the effect of the *variation of application*. I saw that I could make the first query propounded by the lover—the first query to which the Raven should reply "Nevermore "—that I could make this first query a commonplace one—the second less so—the third still less, and so on—until at length the lover, startled from his original *nonchalance* by the melancholy character of the word itself—by its frequent repetition—and by a consideration of the ominous reputation of the fowl that uttered it—is at length excited to superstition, and wildly propounds queries of a far different character—queries whose solution he has passionately at heart—propounds them half in superstition and half in that species of despair which delights in self-torture—propounds them not altogether because he believes in the prophetic or demoniac character of the bird (which, reason assures him, is merely repeating a lesson learned by rote) but because he experiences a frenzied pleasure in so modelling his questions as to receive from the *expected* "Nevermore " the most delicious because the most intolerable of sorrow. Perceiving the opportunity thus afforded me—or, more strictly, thus forced upon me in the progress of the construction—I first established in mind the climax, or concluding query —that query to which "Nevermore " should be in the last place an answer—that query in reply to which this word "Nevermore " should involve the utmost conceivable amount of sorrow and despair.

Here then the poem may be said to have its beginning—at the end, where all works of art should

begin—for it was here, at this point of my precon-
siderations, that I first put pen to paper, in the
composition of the stanza :

" Prophet," said I, " thing of evil! prophet still if bird or
    devil !
By that heaven that bends above us—by that God we both
    adore,
Tell this soul with sorrow laden, if within the distant Aidenn,
It shall clasp a sainted maiden whom the angels name
    Lenore—
Clasp a rare and radiant maiden whom the angels name
    Lenore."
        Quoth the raven " Nevermore."

I composed this stanza, at this point, first that,
by establishing the climax, I might the better vary
and graduate, as regards seriousness and importance,
the preceding queries of the lover—and, secondly,
that I might definitely settle the rhythm, the metre,
and the length and general arrangement of the
stanza—as well as graduate the stanzas which were
to precede, so that none of them might surpass this
in rhythmical effect. Had I been able, in the sub-
sequent composition, to construct more vigorous
stanzas, I should, without scruple, have purposely
enfeebled them, so as not to interfere with the
climacteric effect.

And here I may as well say a few words of the
versification. My first object (as usual) was origin-
ality. The extent to which this has been neglected,
in versification, is one of the most unaccountable
things in the world. Admitting that there is little
possibility of variety in mere *rhythm*, it is still clear
that the possible varieties of metre and stanza are
absolutely infinite—and yet, *for centuries, no man,
in verse, has ever done, or ever seemed to think of
doing, an original thing*. The fact is, that originality
(unless in minds of very unusual force) is by no means
a matter, as some suppose, of impulse or intuition.
In general, to be found, it must be elaborately sought,
and although a positive merit of the highest class,

demands in its attainment less of invention than negation.

Of course, I pretend to no originality in either the rhythm or metre of the *Raven*. The former is trochaic—the latter is octameter acatalectic, alternating with heptameter catalectic repeated in the *refrain* of the fifth verse, and terminating with tetrameter catalectic. Less pedantically—the feet employed throughout (trochees) consist of a long syllable followed by a short : the first line of the stanza consists of eight of these feet—the second of seven and a half (in effect two-thirds)—the third of eight—the fourth of seven and a half—the fifth the same—the sixth three and a half. Now, each of these lines, taken individually, has been employed before, and what originality the *Raven* has, is in their *combination into stanza* ; nothing even remotely approaching this combination has ever been attempted. The effect of this originality of combination is aided by other unusual, and some altogether novel effects, arising from an extension of the application of the principles of rhyme and alliteration.

The next point to be considered was the mode of bringing together the lover and the Raven—and the first branch of this consideration was the *locale*. For this the most natural suggestion might seem to be a forest, or the fields—but it has always appeared to me that a close *circumscription of space* is absolutely necessary to the effect of insulated incident :—it has the force of a frame to a picture. It has an indisputable moral power in keeping concentrated the attention, and, of course, must not be confounded with mere unity of place.

I determined, then, to place the lover in his chamber —in a chamber rendered sacred to him by memories of her who had frequented it. The room is represented as richly furnished—this in mere pursuance of the ideas I have already explained on the subject of Beauty, as the sole true poetical thesis.

The *locale* being thus determined, I had now to

introduce the bird—and the thought of introducing him through the window was inevitable. The idea of making the lover suppose, in the first instance, that the flapping of the wings of the bird against the shutter, is a " tapping " at the door, originated in a wish to increase, by prolonging, the reader's curiosity, and in a desire to admit the incidental effect arising from the lover's throwing open the door, finding all dark, and thence adopting the half-fancy that it was the spirit of his mistress that knocked.

I made the night tempestuous, first, to account for the Raven's seeking admission, and secondly, for the effect of contrast with the (physical) serenity within the chamber.

I made the bird alight on the bust of Pallas, also for the effect of contrast between the marble and the plumage—it being understood that the bust was absolutely *suggested* by the bird—the bust of *Pallas* being chosen, first, as most in keeping with the scholarship of the lover, and, secondly, for the sonorousness of the word, Pallas, itself.

About the middle of the poem, also, I have availed myself of the force of contrast, with a view of deepening the ultimate impression. For example, an air of the fantastic—approaching as nearly to the ludicrous as was admissible—is given to the Raven's entrance. He comes in " with many a flirt and flutter."

Not the *least obeisance made he*—not a moment stopped or stayed he,
But with *mien of lord or lady*, perched above my chamber door.

In the two stanzas which follow, the design is more obviously carried out :—

Then this ebony bird beguiling my sad fancy into smiling
By the *grave and stern decorum of the countenance it wore*,
" Though thy *crest be shorn and shaven* thou," I said, " art sure no craven
Ghastly grim and ancient Raven wandering from the nightly shore—

Tell me what thy lordly name is on the Night's Plutonian
    shore ? "
             Quoth the Raven " Nevermore."

Much I marvelled *this ungainly fowl* to hear discourse so
    plainly,
Though its answer little meaning—little relevancy bore ;
For we cannot help agreeing that no living human being
Ever yet was blessed with seeing bird above his chamber door—
Bird or beast upon the sculptured bust above his chamber door,
    With such name as " Nevermore."

The effect of the *dénouement* being thus provided
for, I immediately drop the fantastic for a tone of
the most profound seriousness :—this tone com-
mencing in the stanza directly following the one last
quoted, with the line,

But the Raven, sitting lonely on that placid bust spoke only,
    etc.

From this epoch the lover no longer jests—no
longer sees anything even of the fantastic in the
Raven's demeanour. He speaks of him as a " grim,
ungainly, ghastly, gaunt, and ominous bird of yore,"
and feels the " fiery eyes " burning into his " bosom's
core." This revolution of thought, or fancy, on
the lover's part, is intended to induce a similar one
on the part of the reader—to bring the mind into
a proper frame for the *dénouement*—which is now
brought about as rapidly and as *directly* as possible.

With the *dénouement* proper—with the Raven's
reply, " Nevermore," to the lover's final demand if
he shall meet his mistress in another world—the
poem, in its obvious phase, that of a simple narrative,
may be said to have its completion. So far, every-
thing is within the limits of the accountable—of
the real. A raven, having learned by rote the single
word " Nevermore," and having escaped from the
custody of its owner, is driven at midnight, through
the violence of a storm, to seek admission at a
window from which a light still gleams—the chamber-
window of a student, occupied half in poring over
a volume, half in dreaming of a beloved mistress

deceased. The casement being thrown open at the fluttering of the bird's wings, the bird itself perches on the most convenient seat out of the immediate reach of the student, who, amused by the incident and the oddity of the visitor's demeanour, demands of it, in jest and without looking for a reply, its name. The raven addressed, answers with its customary word, " Nevermore "—a word which finds immediate echo in the melancholy heart of the student, who, giving utterance aloud to certain thoughts suggested by the occasion, is again startled by the fowl's repetition of " Nevermore." The student now guesses the state of the case, but is impelled, as I have before explained, by the human thirst for self-torture, and in part by superstition, to propound such queries to the bird as will bring him, the lover, the most of the luxury of sorrow, through the anticipated answer " Nevermore." With the indulgence, to the extreme, of this self-torture, the narration, in what I have termed its first or obvious phase, has a natural termination, and so far there has been no overstepping of the limits of the real.

But in subjects so handled, however skilfully, or with however vivid an array of incident, there is always a certain hardness or nakedness, which repels the artistical eye. Two things are invariably required—first, some amount of complexity, or more properly, adaptation ; and, secondly, some amount of suggestiveness—some under-current, however indefinite, of meaning. It is this latter, in especial, which imparts to a work of art so much of that *richness* (to borrow from colloquy a forcible term) which we are too fond of confounding with *the ideal*. It is the *excess* of the suggested meaning—it is the rendering this the upper instead of the under current of the theme—which turns into prose (and that of the very flattest kind) the so-called poetry of the so-called transcendentalists.

Holding these opinions, I added the two concluding stanzas of the poem—their suggestiveness being thus made to pervade all the narrative which has preceded them. The under-current of meaning is rendered first apparent in the lines—

"Take thy beak from out *my heart*, and take thy form from
    off my door ! "
            Quoth the Raven " Nevermore ! "

It will be observed that the words, " from out my heart," involve the first metaphorical expression in the poem. They, with the answer, " Nevermore," dispose the mind to seek a moral in all that has been previously narrated. The reader begins now to regard the Raven as emblematical—but it is not until the very last line of the very last stanza that the intention of making him emblematical of *Mournful and Never-ending Remembrance* is permitted distinctly to be seen :

And the Raven, never flitting, still is sitting, still is sitting,
On the pallid bust of Pallas just above my chamber door ;
And his eyes have all the seeming of a demon's that is
    dreaming,
And the lamplight o'er him streaming throws his shadow on
    the floor ;
And my soul *from out that shadow* that lies floating on the
    floor
            Shall be lifted—nevermore.

NATHANIEL HAWTHORNE [1]

THE reputation of the author of *Twice-Told Tales* has been confined, until very lately, to literary society ; and I have not been wrong, perhaps, in citing him as *the* example, *par excellence*, in this country, of the privately-admired and publicly-unappreciated man of genius. Within the last year

[1] *Twice-Told Tales*. By Nathaniel Hawthorne. James Munroe & Co., Boston. 1842.
Mosses from an Old Manse. By Nathaniel Hawthorne. Wiley & Putnam, New York. 1846.

or two, it is true, an occasional critic has been urged, by honest indignation, into very warm approval. Mr. Webber, for instance, (than whom no one has a keener relish for that kind of writing which Mr. Hawthorne has best illustrated,) gave us, in a late number of *The American Review*, a cordial and certainly a full tribute to his talents ; and since the issue of the *Mosses from an Old Manse*, criticisms of similar tone have been by no means infrequent in our more authoritative journals. I can call to mind few reviews of Hawthorne published *before* the *Mosses*. One I remember in *Arcturus* (edited by Matthews and Duyckinck) for May, 1841 ; another in the *American Monthly* (edited by Hoffman and Herbert) for March, 1838 ; a third in the ninety-sixth number of the *North American Review*. These criticisms, however, seemed to have little effect on the popular taste—at least, if we are to form any idea of the popular taste by reference to its expression in the newspapers, or by the sale of the author's book. It was never the fashion (until lately) to speak of him in any summary of our best authors.

The daily critics would say, on such occasions, " Is there not Irving and Cooper, and Bryant, and Paulding, and—Smith ? " or, " Have we not Halleck and Dana, and Longfellow, and—Thompson ? " or, " Can we not point triumphantly to our own Sprague, Willis, Channing, Bancroft, Prescott and—Jenkins ? " but these unanswerable queries were never wound up by the name of Hawthorne.

Beyond doubt, this inappreciation of him on the part of the public arose chiefly from the two causes to which I have referred—from the facts that he is neither a man of wealth nor a quack ; but these are insufficient to account for the whole effect. No small portion of it is attributable to the very marked idiosyncrasy of Mr. Hawthorne himself. In one sense, and in great measure, to be peculiar is to be original, and than the true originality there is no higher literary virtue. This true or commendable originality, however, implies not the uniform, but the continuous peculiarity—a peculiarity springing from ever-active vigour of fancy—better still if from ever-present force of imagination, giving its own hue, its own character to everything it touches, and, especially, *self-impelled to touch everything*.

It is often said, inconsiderately, that very original writers always fail in popularity—that such and such persons are too original to be comprehended by the mass. " Too peculiar," should be the phrase, " too idiosyncratic." It is, in fact, the excitable, undisciplined and child-like popular mind which most keenly feels the original.

The criticism of the conservatives, of the hackneys, of the cultivated old clergymen of the *North American Review*, is precisely the criticism which condemns and alone condemns it. " It becometh not a divine," saith Lord Coke, " to be of a fiery and salamandrine spirit." Their conscience allowing them to move nothing themselves, these dignitaries have a holy horror of being moved. " Give us *quietude*," they say. Opening their mouths with proper caution, they sigh forth the word " *Repose*." And this is, indeed, the one thing they should be permitted to enjoy, if only upon the Christian principle of give and take.

The fact is, that if Mr. Hawthorne were really original, he could not fail of making himself felt by the public. But the fact is, he is *not* original in any sense. Those who speak of him as original, mean nothing more than that he differs in his manner or tone, and in his choice of subjects, from any author of their acquaintance—their acquaintance not extending to the German Tieck, whose manner, in *some* of his works, is absolutely identical with that *habitual* to Hawthorne. But it is clear that the element of the literary originality is novelty. The element of its appreciation by the reader is the reader's sense of the new. Whatever gives him a new and insomuch a pleasurable emotion, he considers original, and whoever frequently gives him such emotion, he considers an original writer. In a word, it is by the sum total of these emotions that he decides upon the writer's claim to originality. I may observe here, however, that there is clearly a point at which even novelty itself would cease to produce the legitimate originality, if we judge this originality, as we should, by the effect designed : this point is that at which *novelty becomes nothing novel* ; and here the artist, *to preserve his originality*, will subside into the commonplace. No one, I think, has noticed that, merely through inattention to this matter, Moore has comparatively failed in his *Lalla Rookh*. Few readers, and indeed few critics, have commended this poem for originality— and, in fact, the effect, originality, is not produced by it—yet no work of equal size so abounds in the happiest originalities, individually considered. They are so excessive as, in the end, to deaden in the reader all capacity for their appreciation.

These points properly understood, it will be seen that the critic (unacquainted with Tieck) who reads a single tale or essay by Hawthorne, may be justified in thinking him original ; but the tone, or manner, or choice of subject, which induces in this critic the sense of the new, will—if not in a second tale, at least in a third and all subsequent ones—not only fail of inducing it, but bring about an exactly antagonistic impression. In concluding a volume, and more especially in concluding all the volumes of the author, the critic will abandon his first design of calling him " original," and content himself with styling him " peculiar."

With the vague opinion that to be original is to be unpopular, I could, indeed, agree, were I to adopt an understanding of originality which, to my surprise, I have known adopted by many who have a right to be called critical. They have limited, in a love for mere words, the literary to the metaphysical originality. They regard as original in letters, only such combinations of thought, of incident, and so forth, as are, in fact, absolutely novel. It is clear, however, not only that it is the novelty of *effect* alone which is worth consideration, but that this effect is *best* wrought, for the end of all fictitious composition, pleasure, by shunning rather than by seeking the absolute novelty of combination. Originality, thus understood, tasks and startles the intellect, and so Lrings into undue action the faculties to which, in the lighter literature, we least appeal. And thus understood, it cannot fail to prove unpopular with the masses, who, seeking in this literature amusement, are positively offended by instruction. But the true originality—true in respect of its purposes—is that which, in bringing out the half-formed, the reluctant, or the unexpressed fancies of mankind, or in exciting the more delicate pulses of the heart's passion, or in giving birth to some universal sentiment or instinct in embryo, thus combines with the pleasurable effect of *apparent* novelty, a real egotistic delight. The reader, in the case first supposed, (that of the absolute novelty,) is excited, but embarrassed, disturbed, in some degree even pained at his own want of perception, at his own folly in not having himself hit upon the idea. In the second case, his pleasure is doubled. He is filled with an intrinsic and extrinsic delight. He feels and intensely enjoys the seeming novelty of the thought, enjoys it as really novel, as absolutely original with the writer—*and* himself. They two, he fancies, have, alone of all men, thought thus. They two have, together, created this thing. Henceforward there is a bond of sympathy between them —a sympathy which irradiates every subsequent page of the book.

There is a species of writing which, with some difficulty, may be admitted as a lower degree of what I have called the true original. In its perusal, we say to ourselves, not "how original this is!" nor "here is an idea which I and the author have alone entertained," but "here is a charmingly obvious fancy," or sometimes even, "here is a thought which I am not sure has ever occurred to myself, but which, of course, has occurred to all the rest of the world." This kind of composition (which still appertains to a high order) is usually designated as "the natural." It has little external resemblance, but strong internal affinity to the true original, if, indeed, as I have suggested, it is not of this latter an inferior degree. It is best exemplified, among English writers, in Addison, Irving and *Hawthorne*. The "ease" which is so often spoken of as its distinguishing feature, it has been the fashion to regard as ease in appearance alone, as a point of really difficult attainment. This idea, however, must be received with some reservation. The natural style is difficult only to those who should never intermeddle with it—to the unnatural. It is but the result of writing with the understanding, or with the instinct, that the *tone*, in composition, should be that which, at any given point or upon any given topic, would be the tone of the great mass of humanity. The author who, after the manner of the North Americans, is merely at *all* times *quiet*, is, of course, upon *most* occasions, merely silly or stupid, and has no more right to be thought "easy" or "natural" than has a cockney exquisite, or the sleeping beauty in the waxworks.

The "peculiarity," or sameness, or monotone of Hawthorne, would, in its mere character of "peculiarity," and without reference to what *is* the peculiarity, suffice to deprive him of all chance of popular appreciation. But at his failure to be appreciated, we can, *of course*, no longer wonder, when we find him monotonous at decidedly the worst of all possible points—at that point which, having the least concern with Nature, is the farthest removed from the popular intellect, from the popular sentiment, and from the popular taste. I allude to the strain of allegory which completely overwhelms the greater number of his subjects, and which in some measure interferes with the direct conduct of absolutely all.

In defence of allegory, (however, or for whatever object employed,) there is scarcely one respectable word to be said. Its best appeals are made to the fancy—that is to say, to our sense of adaptation, not of matters proper, but of matters improper for the purpose, of the real with the unreal; having never more of intelligible connexion than has something with nothing, never half so much of effective affinity as has the substance for the shadow. The deepest emotion aroused within us by the happiest allegory, *as* allegory, is a very, very imperfectly satisfied sense of the writer's ingenuity in overcoming a difficulty we should have preferred his not having attempted to overcome. The fallacy of the idea that allegory, in any of its moods, can be made to enforce a truth—that metaphor, for example, may illustrate as well as embellish an argument—could be promptly demonstrated; the converse of the supposed fact might be shown, indeed, with very little trouble— but these are topics foreign to my present purpose. One thing is clear, that if allegory ever establishes a fact, it is by dint of overturning a fiction. Where the suggested meaning runs through the obvious one in a *very* profound under-current, so as never to interfere with the upper one without our own volition, so as never to show itself unless *called* to the surface, there only, for the proper uses of fictitious narrative, is it available at all. Under the best circumstances, it must always interfere with that unity of effect which, to the artist, is worth all the allegory in the world. Its vital injury, however, is rendered to the most vitally important point in fiction—that of earnestness or verisimilitude. That *The Pilgrim's Progress* is a ludicrously overrated book, owing its seeming popularity to one or two of those accidents in critical literature which by the critical are sufficiently well understood, is a matter upon which no two thinking people disagree ; but the pleasure derivable from it, in any sense, will be found in the direct ratio of the reader's capacity to smother its true purpose, in the direct ratio of his ability to keep the allegory out of sight, or of his *in*ability to comprehend it. Of allegory properly handled, judiciously subdued, seen only as a shadow or by suggestive glimpses, and making its nearest approach to truth in a not obtrusive and therefore not unpleasant *appositeness,* the *Undine* of De la Motte Fouqué is the best, and undoubtedly a very remarkable specimen.

The obvious causes, however, which have prevented Mr. Hawthorne's *popularity,* do not suffice to condemn him in the eyes of the few who belong properly to books, and to whom books, perhaps, do not quite so properly belong. These few estimate an author, not as do the public, altogether by what he does, but in great measure—indeed, even in the greatest measure—by what he evinces a capability of doing. In this view, Hawthorne stands among literary people in America much in the same light as did Coleridge in England. The few, also, through a certain warping of the taste, which long pondering upon books as books merely never fails to induce, are not in condition to view the errors of a scholar as errors altogether. At any time these gentlemen are prone to think the public not right rather than an educated author wrong. But the simple truth is, that the writer who aims at impressing the people, is *always* wrong when he fails in forcing that people to receive the impression. How far Mr. Hawthorne has addressed the people at all, is, of course, not a question for me to decide. His books afford strong internal evidence of having been written to himself and his particular friends alone.

There has long existed in literature a fatal and unfounded prejudice, which it will be the office of this age to overthrow—the idea that the mere bulk of a work must enter largely into our estimate of its merit. I do not suppose even the weakest of the Quarterly reviewers weak enough to maintain that in a book's size or mass, abstractly considered, there is anything which especially calls for our admiration. A mountain, simply through the sensation of physical magnitude which it conveys, does, indeed, affect us with a sense of the sublime, but we cannot admit any such influence in the contemplation even of *The Columbiad*. The Quarterlies themselves will not admit it. And yet, what else are we to understand by their continual prating about " sustained effort " ? Granted that this sustained effort has accomplished an epic—let us then admire the effort, (if this be a thing admirable,) but certainly not the epic on the effort's account. Common sense, in the time to come, may possibly insist upon measuring a work of art rather by the object it fulfils, by the impression it makes, than by the time it took to fulfil the object, or by the extent of " sustained effort " which became necessary to produce the impression. The fact is, that perseverance is one thing and genius quite another ; nor can all the transcendentalists in Heathendom confound them.

The pieces in the volumes entitled *Twice-Told Tales*, are now in their third republication, and, of course, are thrice-told. Moreover, they are by no means *all* tales, either in the ordinary or in the legitimate understanding of the term. Many of them are pure essays ; for example, *Sights from a Steeple, Sunday at Home, Little Annie's Ramble, A Rill from the Town Pump, The Toll-Gatherer's Day, The Haunted Mind, The Sister Years, Snow-Flakes, Night Sketches*, and *Foot-Prints on the Sea-Shore*. I mention these matters chiefly on account of their discrepancy with that marked precision and finish by which the body of the work is distinguished.

Of the Essays just named, I must be content to speak in brief. They are each and all beautiful, without being characterized by the polish and

adaptation so visible in the tales proper. A painter
would at once note their leading or predominant
feature, and style it *repose*. There is no attempt
at effect. All is quiet, thoughtful, subdued. Yet
this repose may exist simultaneously with high
originality of thought ; and Mr. Hawthorne has
demonstrated the fact. At every turn we meet with
novel combinations ; yet these combinations never
surpass the limits of the quiet. We are soothed as
we read ; and withal is a calm astonishment that
ideas so apparently obvious have never occurred or
been presented to us before. Herein our author
differs materially from Lamb or Hunt or Hazlitt—
who, with vivid originality of manner and expression,
have less of the true novelty of thought than is
generally supposed, and whose originality, at best,
has an uneasy and meretricious quaintness, replete
with startling effects unfounded in nature, and
inducing trains of reflection which lead to no satis-
factory result. The Essays of Hawthorne have much
of the character of Irving, with more of originality,
and less of finish ; while, compared with the
Spectator, they have a vast superiority at all points.
The *Spectator*, Mr. Irving, and Hawthorne have in
common that tranquil and subdued manner which
I have chosen to denominate *repose* ; but, in the
case of the two former, this repose is attained rather
by the absence of novel combination, or of originality,
than otherwise, and consists chiefly in the calm,
quiet, unostentatious expression of commonplace
thoughts, in an unambitious, unadulterated Saxon.
In them, by strong effort, we are made to conceive
the absence of all. In the essays before me the
absence of effort is too obvious to be mistaken, and
a strong under-current of *suggestion* runs continuously
beneath the upper stream of the tranquil thesis.
In short, these effusions of Mr. Hawthorne are the
product of a truly imaginative intellect, restrained,
and in some measure repressed, by fastidiousness of
taste, by constitutional melancholy, and by indolence.

But it is of his tales that I desire principally to speak. The tale proper, in my opinion, affords unquestionably the fairest field for the exercise of the loftiest talent, which can be afforded by the wide domains of mere prose. Were I bidden to say how the highest genius could be most advantageously employed for the best display of its own powers, I should answer, without hesitation—in the composition of a rhymed poem, not to exceed in length what might be perused in an hour. Within this limit alone can the highest order of true poetry exist. I need only here say, upon this topic, that, in almost all classes of composition, the unity of effect or impression is a point of the greatest importance. It is clear, moreover, that this unity cannot be thoroughly preserved in productions whose perusal cannot be completed at one sitting. We may continue the reading of a prose composition, from the very nature of prose itself, much longer than we can persevere, to any good purpose, in the perusal of a poem. This latter, if truly fulfilling the demands of the poetic sentiment, induces an exaltation of the soul which cannot be long sustained. All high excitements are necessarily transient. Thus a long poem is a paradox. And, without unity of impression, the deepest effects cannot be brought about. Epics were the offspring of an imperfect sense of Art, and their reign is no more. A poem *too* brief may produce a vivid, but never an intense or enduring impression. Without a certain continuity of effort—without a certain duration or repetition of purpose—the soul is never deeply moved. There must be the dropping of the water upon the rock. De Béranger has wrought brilliant things—pungent and spirit-stirring —but, like all immassive bodies, they lack *momentum*, and thus fail to satisfy the Poetic Sentiment. They sparkle and excite, but, from want of continuity, fail deeply to impress. Extreme brevity will degenerate into epigrammatism ; but the sin of extreme length is even more unpardonable. *In medio tutissimus ibis.*

Were I called upon, however, to designate that class of composition which, next to such a poem as I have suggested, should best fulfil the demands of high genius—should offer it the most advantageous field of exertion—I should unhesitatingly speak of the prose tale as Mr. Hawthorne has here exemplified it. I allude to the short prose narrative, requiring from a half-hour to one or two hours in its perusal. The ordinary novel is objectionable, from its length, for reasons already stated in substance. As it cannot be read at one sitting, it deprives itself, of course, of the immense force derivable from *totality*. Worldly interests intervening during the pauses of perusal, modify, annul, or counteract, in a greater or less degree, the impressions of the book. But simple cessation in reading would, of itself, be sufficient to destroy the true unity. In the brief tale, however, the author is enabled to carry out the fulness of his intention, be it what it may. During the hour of perusal the soul of the reader is at the writer's control. There are no external or extrinsic influences—resulting from weariness or interruption.

A skilful literary artist has constructed a tale. If wise, he has not fashioned his thoughts to accommodate his incidents ; but having conceived, with deliberate care, a certain unique or single *effect* to be wrought out, he then invents such incidents—he then combines such events as may best aid him in establishing this preconceived effect. If his very initial sentence tend not to the outbringing of this effect, then he has failed in his first step. In the whole composition there should be no word written, of which the tendency, direct or indirect, is not to the one pre-established design. And by such means, with such care and skill, a picture is at length painted which leaves in the mind of him who contemplates it with the kindred art, a sense of the fullest satisfaction. The idea of the tale has been presented unblemished, because undisturbed ; and this is an end unattainable by the novel. Undue brevity is just as exceptionable here as in the poem ; but undue length is yet more to be avoided.

We have said that the tale has a point of superiority even over the poem. In fact, while the *rhythm* of this latter is an essential aid in the development of the poem's highest idea—the idea of the Beautiful— the artificialities of this rhythm are an inseparable bar to the development of all points of thought or expression which have their basis in *Truth*. But Truth is often, and in very great degree, the aim of the tale. Some of the finest tales are tales of ratiocination. Thus the field of this species of composition, if not in so elevated a region on the mountain of Mind, is a tableland of far vaster extent than the domain of the mere poem. Its products are never so rich, but infinitely more numerous, and more appreciable by the mass of mankind. The writer of the prose tale, in short, may bring to his theme a vast variety of modes or inflections of thought and expression—(the ratio- cinative, for example, the sarcastic or the humorous) which are not only antagonistical to the nature of the poem, but absolutely forbidden by one of its most peculiar and indispensable adjuncts ; we allude, of course, to rhythm. It may be added, here, *par parenthèse*, that the author who aims at the purely beautiful in a prose tale is labouring at a great disadvantage. For Beauty can be better treated in the poem. Not so with terror, or passion, or horror, or a multitude of such other points. And here it will be seen how full of prejudice are the usual animadversions against those *tales of effect*, many fine examples of which were found in the earlier numbers of *Blackwood*. The impressions produced were wrought in a legitimate sphere of action, and constituted a legitimate although some- times an exaggerated interest. They were relished by every man of genius : although there were found many men of genius who condemned them without just ground. The true critic will but demand that the design intended be accomplished, to the fullest extent, by the means most advantageously applicable.

We have very few American tales of real merit—we may say, indeed, none, with the exception of *The Tales of a Traveller* of Washington Irving, and these *Twice-Told Tales* of Mr. Hawthorne. Some of the pieces of Mr. John Neal abound in vigour and originality ; but in general, his compositions of this class are excessively diffuse, extravagant, and indicative of an imperfect sentiment of Art. Articles at random are, now and then, met with in our periodicals which might be advantageously compared with the best effusions of the British Magazines ; but, upon the whole, we are far behind our progenitors in this department of literature.

Of Mr. Hawthorne's Tales we would say, emphatically, that they belong to the highest region of Art—an Art subservient to genius of a very lofty order. We had supposed, with good reason for so supposing, that he had been thrust into his present position by one of the impudent *cliques* which beset our literature, and whose pretensions it is our full purpose to expose at the earliest opportunity ; but we have been most agreeably mistaken. We know of few compositions which the critic can more honestly commend than these *Twice-Told Tales*. As Americans, we feel proud of the book.

Mr. Hawthorne's distinctive trait is invention, creation, imagination, originality—a trait which, in the literature of fiction, is positively worth all the rest. But the nature of the originality, so far as regards its manifestation in letters, is but imperfectly understood. The inventive or original mind as frequently displays itself in novelty of *tone* as in novelty of matter. Mr. Hawthorne is original in *all* points.

It would be a matter of some difficulty to designate the best of these tales ; we repeat that, without exception, they are beautiful. *Wakefield* is remarkable for the skill with which an old idea—

a well-known incident—is worked up or discussed.
A man of whims conceives the purpose of quitting
his wife and residing *incognito*, for twenty years, in
her immediate neighbourhood. Something of this
kind actually happened in London. The force of
Mr. Hawthorne's tale lies in the analysis of the
motives which must or might have impelled the hus-
band to such folly, in the first instance, with the
possible causes of his perseverance. Upon this thesis
a sketch of singular power has been constructed.
The Wedding Knell is full of the boldest imagination
—an imagination fully controlled by taste. The
most captious critic could find no flaw in this pro-
duction. *The Minister's Black Veil* is a masterly
composition of which the sole defect is that to the
rabble its exquisite skill will be *caviare*. The *obvious*
meaning of this article will be found to smother
its insinuated one. The *moral* put into the mouth
of the dying minister will be supposed to convey
the *true* import of the narrative ; and that a crime
of dark dye (having reference to the " young lady ")
has been committed, is a point which only minds
congenial with that of the author will perceive.
Mr. Higginbotham's Catastrophe is vividly original
and managed most dexterously. *Dr. Heidegger's Ex-
periment* is exceedingly well imagined, and executed
with surpassing ability. The artist breathes in every
line of it. *The White Old Maid* is objectionable,
even more than the *Minister's Black Veil*, on the
score of its mysticism. Even with the thoughtful
and analytic, there will be much trouble in penetrating
its entire import.

The Hollow of the Three Hills we would quote in
full, had we space ;—not as evincing higher talent
than any of the other pieces, but as affording an
excellent example of the author's peculiar ability.
The subject is commonplace. A witch subjects the
Distant and the Past to the view of a mourner. It
has been the fashion to describe, in such cases, a
mirror in which the images of the absent appear ;

or a cloud of smoke is made to arise, and thence the figures are gradually unfolded. Mr. Hawthorne has wonderfully heightened his effect by making the ear, in place of the eye, the medium by which the fantasy is conveyed. The head of the mourner is enveloped in the cloak of the witch, and within its magic folds there arise sounds which have an all-sufficient intelligence. Throughout this article also, the artist is conspicuous—not more in positive than in negative merits. Not only is all done that should be done, but (what perhaps is an end with more difficulty attained) there is nothing done which should not be. Every word *tells*, and there is not a word which does *not* tell.

In *Howe's Masquerade* we observe something which resembles a plagiarism—but which *may be* a very flattering coincidence of thought. We quote the passage in question.

With a dark flush of wrath upon his brow they saw the general *draw his sword* and *advance to meet* the figure *in the cloak* before the latter had stepped one pace upon the floor. " *Villain, unmuffle yourself,*" cried he, " you pass no farther ! " The figure, without blenching a hair's breadth from the sword which was pointed at his breast, made a solemn pause, and *lowered the cape of the cloak* from his face, yet not sufficiently for the spectators to catch a glimpse of it. But Sir William Howe had evidently seen enough. The sternness of his countenance gave place to a look of wild amazement, if not horror, while he recoiled several steps from the figure, *and let fall his sword* upon the floor.—See vol. 2, p. 20.

The idea here is, that the figure in the cloak is the phantom or reduplication of Sir William Howe ; but in an article called " William Wilson," one of the *Tales of the Grotesque and Arabesque,* we have not only the same idea, but the same idea similarly presented in several respects. We quote two paragraphs, which our readers may compare with what has been already given. We have italicized, above, the immediate particulars of resemblance.

The brief moment in which I averted my eyes had been sufficient to produce, apparently, a material change in the arrangement at the upper or farther end of the room. A large mirror, it appeared to me, now stood where none had been perceptible before : and as I stepped up to it in extremity of terror, mine own image, but with features all pale and dabbled in blood, *advanced* with a feeble and tottering gait to meet me. Thus it appeared I say, but was not. It was Wilson, who then stood before me in the agonies of dissolution. Not a line in all the marked and singular lineaments of that face which was not even identically mine own. *His mask and cloak lay where he had thrown them, upon the floor.*— Vol. ii, p. 57.

Here, it will be observed that, not only are the two general conceptions identical, but there are various *points* of similarity. In each case the figure seen is the wraith or duplication of the beholder. In each case the scene is a masquerade. In each case the figure is cloaked. In each there is a quarrel —that is to say, angry words pass between the parties. In each the beholder is enraged. In each the cloak and sword fall upon the floor. The " villain, unmuffle yourself," of Mr. H. is precisely paralleled by a passage at page 56 of *William Wilson.*

I must hasten to conclude this paper with a summary of Mr. Hawthorne's merits and demerits.

He is peculiar and *not* original—unless in those detailed fancies and detached thoughts which his want of general originality will deprive of the appreciation due to them, in preventing them for ever reaching the *public* eye. He is infinitely too fond of allegory, and can never hope for popularity so long as he persists in it. This he will not do, for allegory is at war with the whole tone of his nature, which disports itself never so well as when escaping from the mysticism of his Goodman Browns and White Old Maids into the hearty, genial, but still Indian-summer sunshine of his Wakefields and Little Annie's Rambles. Indeed, *his* spirit of " metaphor run-mad " is clearly imbibed from the phalanx and phalanstery atmosphere in which he has been so long struggling for breath. He has not half the material for the exclusiveness of authorship that he possesses for its universality. He has the purest style, the finest taste, the most available scholarship, the most delicate humour, the most touching pathos, the most radiant imagination, the most consummate ingenuity; and with these varied good qualities he has done *well* as a mystic. But is there any one of these qualities which should prevent his doing doubly as well in a career of honest, upright, sensible, prehensible and comprehensible things? Let him mend his pen, get a bottle of visible ink, come out from the Old Manse, cut Mr. Alcott, hang (if possible) the editor of *The Dial*, and throw out of the window to the pigs all his odd numbers of *The North American Review.*

CHARLES DICKENS [1]

WE often hear it said, of this or of that proposition, that it may be good in theory, but will not answer in practice; and in such assertions we find the substance of all the sneers at critical art which so gracefully curl the upper lips of a tribe which is beneath it. We mean the small geniuses—the literary Titmice—animalculæ which judge of merit solely by *result*, and boast of the solidity, tangibility, and infallibility of the test which they employ. The worth of a work is most accurately estimated, they assure us, by the number of those who peruse it; and "does a book sell?" is a query embodying, in their opinion, all that need be said or sung on the topic of its fitness for sale. We should as soon think of maintaining, in the presence of these creatures, the *dictum* of Anaxagoras, that snow is black, as of disputing, for example, the profundity of that genius which, in a run of five hundred nights, has rendered itself evident in *London Assurance.* "What," cry

[1] *Barnaby Rudge.* By Charles Dickens, (Boz). Author of *The Old Curiosity Shop, Pickwick, Oliver Twist,* etc.

they, " are critical precepts to us, or to anybody ?
Were we to observe all the critical rules in creation
we should still be unable to write a good book "—
a point, by the way, which we shall not now pause
to deny. " Give us *results*," they vociferate, " for
we are plain men of common sense. We contend
for fact instead of fancy—for practice in opposition
to theory."

The mistake into which the Titmice have been
innocently led, however, is precisely that of dividing
the practice which they would uphold from the
theory to which they would object. They should
have been told in infancy, and thus prevented from
exposing themselves in old age, that theory and
practice are in so much *one*, that the former implies
or includes the latter. A theory is only good as such,
in proportion to its reducibility to practice. If the
practice fail, it is because the theory is imperfect.
To say what they are in the daily habit of saying—
that such or such a matter may be good in theory
but is false in practice,—is to perpetrate a bull—to
commit a paradox—to state a contradiction in terms
—in plain words, to tell a lie *which is a lie at sight*
to the understanding of anything bigger than a
Titmouse.

But we have no idea, just now, of persecuting the
Tittlebats by too close a scrutiny into their little
opinions. It is not our purpose, for example, to press
them with so grave a weapon as the *argumentum ad
absurdum*, or to ask them why, if the popularity of
a book be in fact the measure of its worth, we should
not be at once in condition to admit the inferiority
of *Newton's Principia* to *Hoyle's Games ;* of *Ernest
Maltravers* to *Jack-the-Giant-Killer*, or *Jack Sheppard*,
or *Jack Brag;* and of *Dick's Christian Philosopher*
to *Charlotte Temple*, or the *Memoirs of de Grammont*,
or to one or two dozen other works which must be
nameless. Our present design is but to speak, at
some length, of a book which in so much concerns
the Titmice, that it affords them the very kind of

demonstration which they chiefly affect—*practical* demonstration—of the fallacy of one of their favourite dogmas ; we mean the dogma that no work of fiction can fully suit, at the same time, the critical and the popular taste ; in fact, that the disregarding or contravening of critical rule is absolutely essential to success, beyond a certain and very limited extent, with the public at large. And if, in the course of our random observations—for we have no space for systematic review—it should appear, incidentally, that the vast popularity of *Barnaby Rudge* must be regarded less as the measure of its value, than as the legitimate and inevitable result of certain well-understood critical propositions reduced by genius into practice, there will appear nothing more than what has before become apparent in the *Vicar of Wakefield* of Goldsmith, or in the *Robinson Crusoe* of De Foe—nothing more, in fact, than what is a truism to all but the Titmice.

Those who know us will not, from what is here premised, suppose it our intention to enter into any wholesale *laudation* of *Barnaby Rudge*. In truth, our design may appear, at a cursory glance, to be very different indeed. Boccalini, in his *Advertisements from Parnassus*, tells us that a critic once presented Apollo with a severe censure upon an excellent poem. The god asked him for the beauties of the work. He replied that he only troubled himself about the errors. Apollo presented him with a sack of un-winnowed wheat, and bade him pick out all the chaff for his pains. Now we have not fully made up our minds that the god was in the right. We are not sure that the limit of critical duty is not very generally misapprehended. *Excellence* may be considered an axiom, or a proposition which becomes self-evident just in proportion to the clearness or precision with which it is *put*. If it fairly exists, in this sense, it requires no further elucidation. It is not excellence if it need to be demonstrated as such. To point out too particularly the beauties of a work, is to admit, tacitly, that these beauties are not wholly admirable. Regarding, then, excellence as that which is capable of self-manifestation, it but remains for the critic to show when, where, and how it fails in becoming manifest ; and, in this showing, it will be the fault of the book itself if what of beauty it contains be not, at least, placed in the fairest light. In a word, we may assume, notwithstanding a vast deal of pitiable cant upon this topic, that in pointing out frankly the errors of a work, we do nearly all that is critically necessary, in displaying its merits. In teaching what perfection *is*, how, in fact, shall we more rationally proceed than in specifying what it *is not* ?

The plot of *Barnaby Rudge* runs thus : About a hundred years ago, Geoffrey Haredale and John Chester were schoolmates in England—the former being the scapegoat and drudge of the latter. Leaving school, the boys become friends, with much of the old understanding. Haredale loves ; Chester deprives him of his mistress. The one cherishes the most deadly hatred ; the other merely contemns and avoids. By routes widely different both attain mature age. Haredale, remembering his old love, and still cherishing his old hatred, remains a bachelor and is poor. Chester, among other crimes, is guilty of the seduction and heartless abandonment of a gipsy-girl, who, after the desertion of her lover, gives birth to a son, and, falling into evil courses, is finally hung at Tyburn. The son is received and taken charge of, at an inn called the Maypole, upon the borders of Epping Forest, and about twelve miles from London. This inn is kept by one John Willet, a burly-headed and very obtuse little man, who has a son, Joe, and who employs his *protégé*, under the single name of Hugh, as perpetual hostler at the inn. Hugh's father marries, in the meantime, a rich *parvenue*, who soon dies, but not before having presented Mr. Chester with a boy, Edward. The rather, (a thoroughly selfish man-of-the-world, whose model is Chesterfield,) educates this son at a distance, seeing him rarely, and calling him to the paternal residence, at London, only when he has attained the age of twenty-four or five. He, the father, has, long ere this time, spent the fortune brought him by his wife, having been living upon his wits and a small annuity for some eighteen years. The son is recalled chiefly that by marrying an heiress, on the strength of his own personal merit and the reputed wealth of old Chester, he may enable the latter to continue his gayeties in old age. But of this design, as well as of his poverty, Edward is kept in ignorance for some three or four years after his recall; when the father's discovery of what he considers an inexpedient love-entanglement on the part of the son, induces him to disclose the true state of his affairs, as well as the real tenor of his intentions.

Now the love-entanglement of which we speak, is considered inexpedient by Mr. Chester for two reasons —the first of which is, that the lady beloved is the orphan niece of his old enemy, Haredale, and the second is, that Haredale (although in circumstances which have been much and very unexpectedly improved during the preceding twenty-two years) is still insufficiently wealthy to meet the views of Mr. Chester.

We say that, about twenty-two years before the period in question, there came an unlooked-for change in the worldly circumstances of Haredale. This gentleman has an elder brother, Reuben, who has long possessed the family inheritance of the Haredales, residing at a mansion called The Warren not far from the Maypole Inn, which is itself a portion of the estate. Reuben *is a widower*, with one child, a daughter, Emma. Besides this daughter, there are living with him a gardener, a steward (whose name is Rudge) and *two* women servants, one of whom is the wife of Rudge. On the night of the nineteenth of March, 1733, Rudge murders his master for the sake of a large sum of money which he is known to have in possession. During the struggle, Mr. Haredale grasps the cord of an alarm-bell which hangs within his reach, but succeeds in sounding it only once or twice, when it is severed by the knife of the ruffian, who then, completing his bloody business, and securing the money, proceeds to quit the chamber. While doing this, however, he is disconcerted by meeting the gardener, whose pallid countenance evinces suspicion of the deed committed. The murderer is thus forced to kill his fellow-servant. Having done so, the idea strikes him of transferring the burden of the crime from himself. He dresses the corpse of the gardener in his own clothes, puts upon its finger his own ring, and in its pocket his own watch—then drags it to a pond in the grounds, and throws it in. He now returns to the house, and, disclosing all to his wife, requests her to become a partner in his flight. Horror-stricken, she falls to the ground. He attempts to raise her. She seizes his wrist, *staining her hand with blood in the attempt*. She renounces him for ever; yet promises to conceal the crime. Alone, he flees the country. The next morning, Mr. Haredale being found murdered, and the steward and gardener being both missing, both are suspected. Mrs. Rudge leaves The Warren, and retires to an obscure lodging in London (where she lives upon an annuity allowed her by Haredale), having given birth, *on the very day after the murder*, to a son, Barnaby Rudge, who proves an idiot, who bears upon his wrist a red mark, and who is born possessed with a maniacal horror of blood.

Some months since the assassination having elapsed, what appears to be the corpse of Rudge is discovered, and the outrage is attributed to the gardener. Yet not universally :—for, as Geoffrey Haredale comes into possession of the estate, there are not wanting suspicions (fomented by Chester) of his own participation in the deed. This taint of suspicion, acting upon his hereditary gloom, together with the

natural grief and horror of the atrocity, embitters
the whole life of Haredale. He secludes himself at
The Warren, and acquires a monomaniac acerbity
of temper relieved only by love of his beautiful
niece.

Time wears away. Twenty-two years pass by.
The niece has ripened into womanhood, and loves
young Chester without the knowledge of her uncle
or the youth's father. Hugh has grown a stalwart
man— the type of man *the animal*, as his father is
of man the ultra-civilized. Rudge, the murderer,
returns, urged to his undoing by Fate. He appears
at the Maypole and inquires stealthily of the cir-
cumstances which have occurred at The Warren in
his absence. He proceeds to London, discovers the
dwelling of his wife, threatens her with the betrayal
of her idiot son into vice and extorts from her the
bounty of Haredale. Revolting at such appropriation
of such means, the widow, with Barnaby, again seeks
The Warren, renounces the annuity, and, refusing to
assign any reason for her conduct, states her intention
of quitting London for ever, and of burying herself
in some obscure retreat—a retreat which she begs
Haredale not to attempt discovering. When he seeks
her in London the next day, she is gone ; and there
are no tidings, either of herself or of Barnaby ;
until the expiration of five years—which brings the
time up to that of the celebrated " No Popery "
Riots of Lord George Gordon.

In the meanwhile, and immediately subsequent
to the reappearance of Rudge, Haredale and the
elder Chester, each heartily desirous of preventing
the union of Edward and Emma, have entered into
a covenant, the result of which is that, by means
of treachery on the part of Chester, permitted on
that of Haredale, the lovers misunderstand each
other and are estranged. Joe, also, the son of the
innkeeper, Willet, having been coquetted with, to
too great an extent, by Dolly Varden, (the pretty
daughter of one Gabriel Varden, a locksmith of

Clerkenwell, London) and having been otherwise maltreated at home, enlists in his Majesty's army and is carried beyond seas, to America ; not returning until towards the close of the riots. Just before their commencement, Rudge, in a midnight prowl about the scene of his atrocity, is encountered by an individual who had been familiar with him in earlier life, while living at The Warren. This individual, terrified at what he supposes, very naturally, to be the ghost of the murdered Rudge, relates his adventure to his companions at the Maypole, and John Willet conveys the intelligence, forthwith, to Mr. Haredale. Connecting the apparition, in his own mind, with the peculiar conduct of Mrs. Rudge, this gentleman imbibes a suspicion, at once, of the true state of affairs. This suspicion (which he mentions to no one) is, moreover, very strongly confirmed by an occurrence happening to Varden, the locksmith, who, visiting the woman late one night, finds her in communion, of a nature apparently most confidential, with a ruffian whom the locksmith knows to be such, without knowing the man himself. Upon an attempt, on the part of Varden, to seize this ruffian, he is thwarted by Mrs. R. ; and upon Haredale's inquiring minutely into the personal appearance of the man, he is found to accord with Rudge. We have already shown that the ruffian was in fact Rudge himself. Acting upon the suspicion thus aroused, Haredale watches, by night, alone, in the deserted house formerly occupied by Mrs. R. in hope of her coming upon the murderer, and makes other exertions with the view of arresting him ; but all in vain.

It is, also, at the conclusion *of the five years,* that the hitherto uninvaded retreat of Mrs. Rudge is disturbed by a message from her husband, demanding money. He has discovered her abode by accident. Giving him what she has at the time, she afterwards eludes him, and hastens, with Barnaby, to bury herself in the crowd of London, until she can find opportunity again to seek retreat in some more distant region of England. But the riots have now begun. The idiot is beguiled into joining the mob, and, becoming separated from his mother (who, growing ill through grief, is borne to a hospital) meets with his old playmate Hugh, and becomes with him a ringleader in the rebellion.

The riots proceed. A conspicuous part is borne in them by one Simon Tappertit, a fantastic and conceited little apprentice of Varden's, and a sworn enemy to Joe Willet, who has rivalled him in the affection of Dolly. A hangman, Dennis, is also very busy amid the mob. Lord George Gordon, and his secretary, Gashford, with John Grueby, his servant, appear, of course, upon the scene. Old Chester, who, during the five years, has become Sir John, instigates Gashford, who has received personal insult from Haredale, (a Catholic and consequently obnoxious to the mob) instigates Gashford to procure the burning of The Warren, and to abduct Emma during the excitement ensuing. The mansion is burned, (Hugh, who also fancies himself wronged by Har dale, being chief actor in the outrage) and Miss H. carried off, in company with Dolly, who had long lived with her, and whom Tappertit abducts upon his own responsibility. Rudge, in the meantime, finding the eye of Haredale upon him, (since he has become aware of the watch kept nightly at his wife's,) goaded by the dread of solitude, and fancying that his sole chance of safety lies in joining the rioters, hurries upon their track to the doomed Warren. He arrives too late—the mob have departed. Skulking about the ruins, he is discovered by Haredale, and finally captured without a struggle, within the glowing walls of the very chamber in which the deed was committed. He is conveyed to prison, where he meets and recognizes Barnaby, who had been captured as a rioter. The mob assail and burn the jail. The father and son escape. Betrayed by Dennis, both are again retaken, and Hugh shares their fate. In Newgate, Dennis, through accident, discovers the parentage of Hugh, and an effort is made in vain to interest Chester in behalf of his son. Finally, Varden procures the pardon of Barnaby ; but Hugh, Rudge, and Dennis are hung. At the eleventh hour, Joe returns from abroad with one arm. In company with Edward Chester, he performs prodigies of valour (during the last riots) on behalf of the Government. The two, with Haredale and Varden, rescue Emma and Dolly. A double marriage, of course, takes place ; for Dolly has repented her fine airs, and the prejudices of Haredale are overcome. Having killed Chester in a duel, he quits England for ever, and ends his days in the seclusion of an Italian convent. Thus, after summary disposal of the understrappers, ends the drama of *Barnaby Rudge*.

We have given, as may well be supposed, but a very meagre outline of the story, and we have given it in the simple or natural sequence. That is to say, we have related the events, as nearly as might be, in the order of their occurrence. But this order would by no means have suited the purpose of the novelist, whose design has been to maintain the secret of the murder, and the consequent mystery which encircles Rudge, and the actions of his wife, until the catastrophe of his discovery by Haredale. The *thesis* of the novel may thus be regarded as based upon curiosity. Every point is so arranged as to perplex the reader, and whet his desire for elucidation :—for example, the first appearance of Rudge at the Maypole ; his questions ; his persecution of Mrs. R. ; the ghost seen by the frequenter of the Maypole ; and Haredale's impressive conduct in consequence. What *we* have told, in the very beginning of our digest, in regard to the shifting of the gardener's dress, is sedulously kept from the reader's knowledge until he learns it from Rudge's own confession in jail. We say sedulously ; for, *the intention once known*, the *traces* of the design can be found upon every page. There is an amusing and exceedingly ingenious instance at page 145, where Solomon Daisy describes his adventure with the ghost.

> " It was a ghost—a spirit," cried Daisy.
> " Whose ? " they all three asked together.
> In the excess of his emotion (for he fell back trembling in his chair and waved his hand as if entreating them to question him no further) *his answer was lost upon all* but old John Willet, who happened to be seated close beside him.
> " Who ! " cried Parkes and Tom Cobb—" Who was it ? "
> " Gentlemen," said Mr. Willet, after a long pause, " you needn't ask. The likeness of a murdered man. This is the nineteenth of March."
> A profound silence ensued.

The impression here skilfully conveyed is, that the ghost seen is that of Reuben Haredale ; and the mind of the not-too-acute reader is at once averted from the true state of the case—from the murderer, Rudge, living in the body.

Now there can be no question that, by such means as these, many points which are comparatively insipid in the natural sequence of our digest, and which would have been comparatively insipid even if given in full detail in a natural sequence, are endued with the interest of mystery ; but neither can it be denied that a vast many more points are at the same time deprived of all effect, and become null, through the impossibility of comprehending them without the key. The author, who, cognizant of his plot, writes with this cognizance continually operating upon him, and thus *writes to himself* in spite of himself, does not, of course, feel that much of what is effective to his own informed perception, must necessarily be lost upon his uninformed readers ; and he himself is never in condition, as regards his own work, to bring the matter to test. But the reader may easily satisfy himself of the validity of our objection. Let him *re-peruse Barnaby Rudge*, and with a pre-comprehension of the mystery, these points of which we speak break out in all directions like stars, and throw quadruple brilliance over the narrative—a brilliance which a correct taste will at once declare unprofitably sacrificed at the shrine of the keenest interest of mere mystery.

The design of *mystery*, however, being once determined upon by an author, it becomes imperative, first, that no undue or inartistical means be employed to conceal the secret of the plot ; and, secondly, that the secret be well kept. Now, when at page 16, we read that " the body of *poor Mr. Rudge, the steward, was found*" months after the outrage, etc., we see that Mr. Dickens has been guilty of no misdemeanour against Art in stating what was not the fact ; since the falsehood is put into the mouth of Solomon Daisy, and given merely as the impression of this individual and of the public. The writer has not asserted it in his own person, but ingeniously conveyed an idea (false in itself, yet a belief in which is necessary for the effect of the tale) by the mouth of one of his characters. The case is different, however, when Mrs. Rudge is repeatedly denominated " the widow." It is the author who, himself, frequently so terms her. This is disingenuous and inartistical : accidentally so, of course. We speak of the matter merely by way of illustrating our point, and as an oversight on the part of Mr. Dickens.

That the secret be well kept is obviously necessary. A failure to preserve it until the proper moment of *dénouement* throws all into confusion, so far as regards the *effect* intended. If the mystery leaks out, against the author's will, his purposes are immediately at odds and ends ; for he proceeds upon the supposition that certain impressions *do* exist, which do *not* exist in the mind of his readers. We are not prepared to say, so positively as we could wish, whether, by the public at large, the whole *mystery* of the murder committed by Rudge, with the identity of the Maypole ruffian with Rudge himself, was fathomed at any period previous to the period intended, or, if so, whether at a period so early as materially to interfere with the interest designed; but we are forced, through sheer modesty, to suppose this the case; since, by ourselves individually, the secret was distinctly understood immediately upon the perusal of the story of Solomon Daisy, which occurs at the seventh page of this volume of three hundred and twenty-three. In the number of the *Philadelphia Saturday Evening Post*, for May the first, 1841, (the tale having then only begun) will be found a *prospective notice* of some length, in which we made use of the following words:

> That Barnaby is the son of the murderer may not appear evident to our readers—but we will explain. The person murdered is Mr. Reuben Haredale. He was found assassinated in his bed-chamber. His steward, (Mr. Rudge, senior,) and his gardener (name not mentioned) are missing. At first both are suspected. "Some months afterward"—here we use the words of the story—"the steward's body, scarcely to be recognized but by his clothes, and the watch and ring he wore—was found at the bottom of a piece of water in the grounds, with a deep gash in the breast, where he had been stabbed by a knife. He was only partly dressed; and all people agreed that he had been sitting up reading in his own room, where there were many traces of blood, and was suddenly fallen upon and killed, before his master."

> Now, be it observed, it is not the author himself who asserts that *the steward's body was found*; he has put the words in the mouth of one of his characters. His design is to make it appear, in the *dénouement*, that the steward, Rudge, first murdered the gardener, then went to his master's chamber, murdered *him*, was interrupted by his (Rudge's) wife, whom he seized and held *by the wrist*, to prevent her giving the alarm—that he then, after possessing himself of the booty desired, returned to the gardener's room, exchanged clothes with him, put upon the corpse his own watch and ring, and secreted it where it was afterwards discovered at so late a period that the features could not be identified.

The differences between our pre-conceived ideas, as here stated, and the actual facts of the story, will be found immaterial. The gardener was murdered, not before but after his master; and that Rudge's wife seized *him* by the wrist, instead of his seizing *her*, has so much the air of a mistake on the part

of Mr. Dickens, that we can scarcely speak of our
own version as erroneous. The grasp of a murderer's
bloody hand on the wrist of a woman *enciente*, would
have been more likely to produce the effect described
(and this every one will allow) than the grasp of
the hand of the woman upon the wrist of the assassin.
We may therefore say of our supposition as Talley-
rand said of some cockney's bad French—*que s'il
ne soit pas Français, assurément donc il le doit être*—
that if we did not rightly prophesy, yet, at least, our
prophecy *should have been* right.

We are informed in the Preface to *Barnaby Rudge*
that " no account of the Gordon Riots having been
introduced into any work of fiction, and the sub-
ject presenting very extraordinary and remarkable
features," our author " was led to project this tale."
But for this distinct announcement (for Mr. Dickens
can scarcely have deceived himself) we should have
looked upon the riots as altogether an afterthought.
It is evident that they have no necessary connexion
with the story. In our digest, which carefully
includes all *essentials* of the plot, we have dismissed
the doings of the mob in a paragraph. The whole
event of the drama would have proceeded as well
without as with them. They have even the appear-
ance of being *forcibly* introduced. In our compendium
above, it will be seen that we emphasized several
allusions to an interval of *five years*. The action
is brought up to a certain point. The train of events
is so far uninterrupted—nor is there any apparent
need of interruption—yet all the characters are now
thrown forward for a period of *five years*. And why?
We ask in vain. It is not to bestow upon the lovers
a more decorous maturity of age—for this is the
only possible idea which suggests itself—Edward
Chester is already eight-and-twenty, and Emma
Haredale would, in America at least, be upon the
list of old maids. No—there is no such reason ;
nor does there appear to be any one more plausible
than that, as it is now the year of our Lord 1775,

an advance of five years will bring the *dramatis
personæ* up to a very remarkable period, affording
an admirable opportunity for their display—the
period, in short, of the "No Popery" riots. This
was the idea with which we were forcibly impressed
in perusal, and which nothing less than Mr. Dickens'
positive assurance to the contrary would have been
sufficient to eradicate.

It is, perhaps, but one of a thousand instances
of the disadvantages, both to the author and the
public, of the present absurd fashion of periodical
novel-writing, that our author had not sufficiently
considered or determined upon *any* particular plot
when he began the story now under review. In
fact, we see, or fancy that we see, numerous traces
of indecision—traces which a dexterous supervision
of the complete work might have enabled him to
erase. We have already spoken of the intermission
of a lustrum. The opening speeches of old Chester
are by far too *truly* gentlemanly for his subsequent
character. The wife of Varden, also, is too whole-
sale a shrew to be converted into the quiet wife—
the original design was to punish her. At page 16
we read thus—Solomon Daisy is telling his story:

"I put as good a face upon it as I could, and muffling
myself up, started out with a lighted lantern in one hand
and the key of the church in the other"—at this point of
the narrative, the dress of the strange man rustled as if he
had turned to hear more distinctly.

Here the design is to call the reader's attention
to a *point* in the tale; but no subsequent explanation
is made. Again, a few lines below—

The houses were all shut up, and the folks indoors, and
perhaps there is only one man in the world who knows how
dark it really was.

Here the intention is still more evident, but there
is no result. Again, at page 54, the idiot draws

Mr. Chester to the window, and directs his attention to the clothes hanging upon the lines in the yard—

"Look down," he said softly; "do you mark how they whisper in each other's ears, then dance and leap to make believe they are in sport? Do you see how they stop for a moment, when they think there is no one looking, and mutter among themselves again; and then how they roll and gambol, delighted with the mischief they've been plotting? Look at 'em now! See how they whirl and plunge. And now they stop again, and whisper cautiously together—little thinking, mind, how often I have lain upon the ground and watched them. I say—what is it that they plot and hatch? Do you know?"

Upon perusal of these ravings, we at once supposed them to have allusion to some *real* plotting; and even now we cannot force ourselves to believe them not so intended. They suggested the opinion that Haredale himself would be implicated in the murder, and that the counsellings alluded to might be those of that gentleman with Rudge. It is by no means impossible that some such conception wavered in the mind of the author. At page 32 we have a confirmation of our idea, when Varden endeavours to arrest the murderer in the house of his wife—

"Come back—come back!" exclaimed the woman, wrestling with and clasping him. "Do not touch him on your life. *He carries other lives beside his own.*"

The *dénouement* fails to account for this exclamation.

In the beginning of the story much emphasis is placed upon the *two* female servants of Haredale, and upon his journey to and from London, as well as upon his wife. We have merely said, in our digest, that he was a widower, italicizing the remark. All these other points are, in fact, singularly irrelevant, in the supposition that the original design has not undergone modification.

Again, at page 57, when Haredale talks of "his dismantled and beggared hearth" we cannot help fancying that the author had in view some different wrong, or series of wrongs, perpetrated by Chester, than any which appear in the end.   This gentleman, too, takes extreme and frequent pains to acquire dominion over the rough Hugh—this matter is particularly insisted upon by the novelist—we look, of course, for some important result—but the filching of a letter is nearly all that is accomplished.   That Barnaby's delight in the desperate scenes of the Rebellion, is inconsistent with his horror of blood, will strike every reader ; and this inconsistency seems to be the consequence of the *after-thought* upon which we have already commented.   In fact, the title of the work, the elaborate and pointed manner of the commencement, the impressive description of The Warren, and especially of Mrs. Rudge, go far to show that Mr. Dickens has really deceived himself—that the soul of the plot, as originally conceived, was the murder of Haredale, with the subsequent discovery of the murderer in Rudge—but that this idea was afterwards abandoned, or rather suffered to be merged in that of the Popish riots.   The result has been most unfavourable.   That which, of itself, would have proved highly effective, has been rendered nearly null by its situation.   In the multitudinous outrage and horror of the Rebellion, the *one* atrocity is utterly whelmed and extinguished.

The reasons of this deflection from the first purpose appears to us self-evident.   One of them we have already mentioned.   The other is that our author discovered, when too late, that *he had anticipated, and thus rendered valueless, his chief effect.*   This will be readily understood.   The particulars of the assassination being withheld, the strength of the narrator is put forth, in the beginning of the story, to *whet curiosity* in respect to these particulars ; and, so far, he is but in proper pursuance of his main design.   But from this intention he unwittingly passes into the error of *exaggerating anticipation.* And error though it be, it is an error wrought with consummate skill.   What, for example, could more vividly enhance our impression of the unknown horror enacted, than the deep and enduring gloom of Haredale—than the idiot's inborn awe of blood— or, especially, than the expression of countenance so imaginatively attributed to Mrs. Rudge—" the capacity for expressing terror—something only dimly seen, but never absent for a monemt—the shadow of some look to which an instant of intense and most unutterable horror only could have given rise " ?   But it is a condition of the human fancy that the promises of such words are irredeemable.   In the notice before mentioned we thus spoke upon this topic :

> This is a conception admirably adapted to whet curiosity in respect to the character of that event which is hinted at as forming the basis of the story.   But this observation should not fail to be made—that the anticipation must surpass the reality ;   that no matter how terrific be the circumstances which, in the *dénouement*, shall appear to have occasioned the expression of countenance worn habitually by Mrs. Rudge, still they will not be able to satisfy the mind of the reader. He will surely be disappointed.   The skilful intimation of horror held out by the artist, produces an effect which will deprive his conclusion of all.   These intimations—these dark hints of some uncertain evil—are often rhetorically praised as effective—but are only justly so praised where there is *no dénouement* whatever—where the 'reader's imagination is left to clear up the mystery for itself—and this is not the design of Mr. Dickens.

And, in fact, our author was not long in seeing his precipitancy.   He had placed himself in a dilemma from which even his high genius could not extricate him.   He at once shifts the main interest—and in truth we do not see what better he could have done. The reader's attention becomes absorbed in the riots, and he fails to observe that what should have been the true catastrophe of the novel is exceedingly feeble and ineffective.

A few cursory remarks :—Mr. Dickens fails peculiarly in *pure* narration.   See, for example, page 296, where the connexion of Hugh and Chester is detailed by Varden.   See also in *The Old Curiosity Shop*, where, when the result is fully known, so many words are occupied in explaining the relationship of the brothers. The effect of the present narrative might have been materially increased by confining the action within the limits of London. The *Notre-Dame* of Hugo affords a fine example of the force which can be gained by concentration, or unity of place. The unity of time is also sadly neglected, to no purpose, in *Barnaby Rudge*. That Rudge should so long and so deeply feel the sting of conscience is inconsistent with his brutality. On page 15, the interval elapsing between the murder and Rudge's return, is variously stated at twenty-two and twenty-four years. It may be asked why the inmates of The Warren failed to hear the alarm-bell which was heard by Solomon Daisy. The idea of persecution by being tracked, as by blood-hounds, from one spot of quietude to another, is a favourite one with Mr. Dickens. Its effect cannot be denied. The stain upon Barnaby's wrist, caused by fright in the mother at so late a period of gestation as one day before mature parturition, is shockingly at war with all medical experience. When Rudge, escaped from prison, unshackled, with money at command, is in agony at his wife's refusal to perjure herself for his salvation—is it not *queer* that he should demand any other salvation than lay in his heels?

Some of the conclusions of chapters—see pages 40 and 100—seem to have been written for the mere purpose of illustrating tail-pieces.

The leading idiosyncrasy of Mr. Dickens' remarkable humour is to be found in his *translating the language of gesture, or action, or tone*. For example—

The cronies nodded to each other, and Mr. Parkes remarked in an undertone, shaking his head meanwhile, *as who should say " let no man contradict me, for I won't believe him,"* that Willet was in amazing force to-night.

The riots form a series of vivid pictures never surpassed. At page 17, the road between London and the Maypole is described as a horribly rough and dangerous, and at page 97, as an uncommonly smooth and convenient one. At page 116, how comes Chester in possession of the key of Mrs. Rudge's vacated house ?

Mr. Dickens' English is usually pure. His most remarkable error is that of employing the adverb " directly " in the sense of " as soon as." For example—" Directly he arrived, Rudge said," etc. Bulwer is uniformly guilty of the same blunder.

It is observable that so original a stylist as our author should occasionally lapse into a gross imitation of what, itself, is a gross imitation. We mean the manner of Lamb—a manner based in the Latin construction. For example—

> In summer time its pumps suggest to thirsty idlers springs cooler and more sparkling and deeper than other wells; and as they trace the spillings of full pitchers on the heated ground, they snuff the freshness, and, sighing, cast sad looks towards the Thames, and think of baths and boats, and saunter on, despondent.

The wood-cut *designs* which accompany the edition before us are occasionally good. The copper engravings are pitiably ill-conceived and ill-drawn ; and not only this, but are in broad contradiction of the wood-designs and text.

There are many *coincidences* wrought into the narrative—those, for example, which relate to the nineteenth of March ; the dream of Barnaby, respecting his father, at the very period when his father is actually in the house ; and the dream of Haredale previous to his final meeting with Chester. These things are meant to *insinuate* a fatality which, very properly, is not expressed in plain terms—but it is questionable whether the story derives more in ideality from their introduction, than it might have gained of verisimilitude from their omission.

The *dramatis personæ* sustain the high fame of Mr. Dickens as a delineator of character. Miggs, the disconsolate handmaiden of Varden ; Tappertit, his chivalrous apprentice ; Mrs. Varden, herself ; and

Dennis, a hangman—may be regarded as original caricatures, of the highest merit as such. Their traits are founded in acute observation of nature, but are exaggerated to the utmost admissible extent. Miss Haredale and Edward Chester are commonplaces—no effort has been made in their behalf. Joe Willet is a naturally drawn country youth. Stagg is a mere make-weight. Gashford and Gordon are truthfully copied. Dolly Varden is truth itself. Haredale, Rudge and Mrs. Rudge, are impressive only through the circumstances which surround them. Sir John Chester, is, of course, not original, but is a vast improvement upon all his predecessors—his heartlessness is rendered somewhat too amusing, and his end too much that of a man of honour. Hugh is a noble conception. His fierce exultation in his animal powers; his subserviency to the smooth Chester; his mirthful contempt and patronage of Tappertit, and his *brutal* yet firm courage in the hour of death—form a picture to be set in diamonds. Old Willet is not surpassed by any character even among those of Dickens. He is nature itself—yet a step farther would have placed him in the class of caricatures. His combined conceit and obtusity are indescribably droll, and his peculiar misdirected energy when aroused is one of the most exquisite touches in all humorous painting. We shall never forget how heartily we laughed at his shaking Solomon Daisy and threatening to put him behind the fire, because the unfortunate little man was too much frightened to articulate. Varden is one of those free, jovial, honest fellows, at charity with all mankind, whom our author is so fond of depicting. And lastly, Barnaby, the hero of the tale—in him we have been somewhat disappointed. We have already said that his delight in the atrocities of the Rebellion is at variance with his horror of blood. But this horror of blood is *inconsequential*; and of this we complain. Strongly insisted upon in the beginning of the narrative, it produces no adequate result. And here how fine an opportunity has Mr. Dickens missed! The conviction of the assassin, after the lapse of twenty-two years, might easily have been brought about through his son's mysterious awe of blood—*an awe created in the unborn by the assassination itself*—and this would have been one of the finest possible embodiments of the idea which we are accustomed to attach to "poetical justice." The raven, too, intensely amusing as it is, might have been made, more than we now see it, a portion of the conception of the fantastic Barnaby. Its croakings might have been *prophetically* heard in the course of the drama. Its character might have performed, in regard to that of the idiot, much the same part as does, in music, the accompaniment in respect to the air. Each might have been distinct. Each might have differed remarkably from the other. Yet between them there might have been wrought an analogical resemblance, and although each might have existed apart, they might have formed together a whole which would have been imperfect in the absence of either.

From what we have here said—and, perhaps, said without due deliberation—(for alas! the hurried duties of the journalist preclude it)—there will not be wanting those who will accuse us of a mad design to detract from the pure fame of the novelist. But to such we merely say in the language of heraldry, "ye should wear a plain point sanguine in your arms." If this be understood, well; if not, well again. There lives no man feeling a deeper reverence for genius than ourself. If we have not dwelt so specially upon the high merits as upon the trivial defects of *Barnaby Rudge* we have already given our reasons for the omission, and these reasons will be sufficiently understood by all whom we care to understand them. The work before us is not, we think, equal to the tale which immediately preceded it; but there are few—very few others to which we consider it inferior. Our chief objection has not, perhaps, been so distinctly stated as we could wish. That this fiction, or indeed that any fiction written by Mr. Dickens, should be based in the excitement and maintenance of curiosity we look upon as a misconception, on the part of the writer, of his own very great yet very peculiar powers. He has done this thing well, to be sure—he would do anything well in comparison with the herd of his contemporaries—but he has not done it so thoroughly well as his high and just reputation would demand. We think that the whole book has been an effort to him—solely through the nature of its design. He has been smitten with an untimely desire for a novel path. The idiosyncrasy of his intellect would lead him, naturally, into the most fluent and simple style of narration. In tales of ordinary sequence he may and will long reign triumphant. He has a *talent* for all things, but no positive *genius* for *adaptation*, and still less for that metaphysical art in which the souls of all *mysteries* lie. *Caleb Williams* is a far less noble· work than *The Old Curiosity Shop* ; but Mr. Dickens could no more have constructed the one than Mr. Goodwin could have dreamed of the other.

ELIZABETH BARRETT BARRETT [1]

"A WELL-BRED *man*," says Sir James Puckle, in his *Gray Cap for a Green Head*, "will never give himself the liberty to speak ill of women." We emphasize the "man." Setting aside, for the present, certain rare commentators and compilers of the species ——— creatures neither precisely men, women, nor Mary Wollstonecrafts—setting these aside as unclassifiable, we may observe that the race of critics are masculine—men. With the exception, perhaps, of Mrs. Anne Royal, we can call to mind

[1] *The Drama of Exile, and other Poems :* By Elizabeth Barrett Barrett, Author of *The Seraphim*, and other Poems.

no female who has occupied, even temporarily, the Zoilus throne. And this, the Salic law, is an evil; for the inherent chivalry of the critical *man* renders it not only an unpleasant task to him "to speak ill of a woman," (and a woman and her book are identical,) but an almost impossible task not to laud her *ad nauseam*. In general, therefore, it is the unhappy lot of the authoress to be subjected, time after time, to the downright degradation of mere puffery. On her own side of the Atlantic, Miss Barrett has indeed, in one instance at least, escaped the infliction of this lamentable contumely and wrong; but if she had been really solicitous of its infliction in America, she could not have adopted a more effectual plan than that of saying a few words about "the great American people," in an American edition of her work, published under the superintendence of an American author.[1] Of the innumerable "native" notices of *The Drama of Exile*, which have come under our observation, we can call to mind *not one* in which there is anything more remarkable than the critic's dogged determination to find *nothing* barren, from Beersheba to Dan. Another in the *Democratic Review* has proceeded so far, it is true, as to venture a *very* delicate insinuation to the effect that the poetess "will not fail to speak her mind *though it bring upon her a bad rhyme*"; beyond this, nobody has proceeded: and as for the elaborate paper in the new Whig Monthly, all that anybody can say or think, and all that Miss Barrett can *feel* respecting it is, that

---

[1] We are sorry to notice, in the American edition, a multitude of typographical errors, many of which affect the sense, and should therefore be corrected in a second impression, if called for. How far they are chargeable to the London copy, we are not prepared to say. "Froze," for instance, is printed "frore"; "Foregone," throughout, is printed "forgone." "Wordless" is printed "worldless"— "worldly," "wordly"—"spilt," "split," etc., etc.,—while transpositions, false accents, and mis-punctuations abound.

it is an eulogy as well written as it is an insult well
intended. Now of all the friends of the fair author,
we doubt whether one exists, with more profound—
with more enthusiastic reverence and admiration of
her genius, than the writer of these words. And it
is for this very reason, beyond all others, that he
intends to speak of her *the truth*. Our chief regret
is, nevertheless, that the limits of this work will
preclude the possibility of our speaking this truth so
fully, and so much in detail, as we could wish. By
far the most valuable criticism that we, or that any
one could give, of the volumes now lying before us,
would be the quotation of three-fourths of their
contents. But we have this advantage—that the
work has been long published, and almost universally
read—and thus, in some measure, we may proceed,
concisely, as if the text of our context were an
understood thing.

In her preface to this, the "American edition"
of her late poems, Miss Barrett, speaking of the
Drama of Exile, says :—" I decided on publishing
it, after considerable hesitation and doubt. Its
subject rather fastened on me than was chosen ;
and the form, approaching the model of the Greek
tragedy, shaped itself under my hand rather by
force of pleasure than of design. But when the
compositional excitement had subsided, I felt afraid
of my position. My own object was the new and
strange experiment of the fallen Humanity, as it
went forth from Paradise in the Wilderness, with
a peculiar reference to Eve's allotted grief, which,
considering that self-sacrifice belonged to her woman-
hood, and the consciousness of being the organ of
the Fall to her offence, appeared to me imperfectly
apprehended hitherto, and more expressible by a
woman than by a man." In this abstract announce-
ment of the theme, it is difficult to understand the
ground of the poet's hesitation to publish ; for
the theme in itself seems admirably adapted to the
purposes of the closest drama. The poet, neverthe-

less, is, very properly, conscious of failure—a failure which occurs not in the general, but in the particular conception, and which must be placed to the account of "the model of the Greek tragedies." The Greek tragedies *had* and even *have* high merits ; but we act wisely in now substituting for the external and typified human sympathy of the antique Chorus, a direct, internal, living and moving sympathy itself ; and although Æschylus might have done service as "a model," to either Euripides or Sophocles, yet were Sophocles and Euripides in London to-day, they would, perhaps, while granting a certain form-less and shadowy grandeur, indulge a quiet smile at the shallowness and uncouthness of that Art, which, in the old amphitheatres, had beguiled them into applause of the *Œdipus at Colonos*.

It would have been better for Miss Barrett if, throwing herself independently upon her own very extraordinary resources and forgetting that a Greek had ever lived, she had involved her Eve in a series of adventures merely natural, or if not this, of adventures preternatural within the limits of at least a conceivable relation—a relation of matter to spirit and spirit to matter, that should have left room for something like palpable action and comprehensible emotion—that should not have utterly precluded the development of that womanly character which is admitted as the principal object of the poem. As the case actually stands, it is only in a few snatches of verbal intercommunication with Adam and Lucifer, that we behold her as a woman at all. For the rest, she is a mystical something or nothing, enwrapped in a fog of rhapsody about Transfigura-tion, and the Seed, and the Bruising of the Heel, and other talk of a nature that no man ever pretended to understand in plain prose, and which, when solar-microscoped into poetry "upon the model of the Greek drama," is about as convincing as the Egyptian Lectures of Mr. Silk Buckingham—about as much to any purpose under the sun as the *hi presto !*

conjurations of Signor Blitz.   What are we to make,
for example, of dramatic colloquy such as this ?—
the words are those of a Chorus of Invisible Angels
addressing Adam :

> Live, work on, O Earthy !
>   By the Actual's tension
> Speed the arrow worthy
>   Of a pure ascension.
> From the low earth round you
>   Reach the heights above you ;
> From the stripes that wound you
>   Seek the loves that love you !
> God's divinest burneth plain
> Through the crystal diaphane
>   Of our loves that love you.

Now we do not mean to assert that, by excessive
" tension " of the intellect, a reader accustomed to
the cant of the transcendentalists (or of those who
degrade an ennobling philosophy by styling them-
selves such) may not succeed in ferreting from the
passage quoted, and indeed from each of the thousand
similar ones throughout the book, something that
shall bear the aspect of an absolute idea—but we
do mean to say, first, that in nine cases out of ten,
the thought when dug out will be found very poorly
to repay the labour of the digging ;—for it is the
nature of thought in general, as it is the nature of
some ores in particular, to be richest when most
superficial.   And we do mean to say, secondly, that,
in nineteen cases out of twenty, the reader will suffer
the most valuable ore to remain unmined to all
eternity, before he will be put to the trouble of
digging for it one inch.   And we do mean to assert,
thirdly, that no reader is to be condemned for *not*
putting himself to the trouble of digging even the
one inch ; for no writer has the right to impose
any such necessity upon him.   What is worth thinking
is distinctly thought : what is distinctly thought, can
and should be distinctly expressed or should not be
expressed at all.   Nevertheless, there is no more
appropriate opportunity than the present for admit-

ting and maintaining, at once, what has never before
been either maintained or admitted—that there is
a justifiable exception to the rule for which we
contend. It is where the design is to convey the
fantastic—not the obscure. To give the idea of the
latter we need, as in general, the most precise and
definitive terms, and those who employ other terms
but confound obscurity of expression with the
expression of obscurity. The fantastic in itself,
however,—phantasm—may be materially furthered
in its development by the *quaint* in phraseology :—
a proposition which any moralist may examine at
his leisure for himself.

The *Drama of Exile* opens with a very palpable
bull :—" Scene, the outer side of the gate of Eden,
shut fast with clouds "—[a scene out of sight !]—
" from the depth of which revolves the sword of fire,
self-moved. A watch of innumerable angels, rank
above rank, slopes up from around it to the zenith ;
and the glare cast from their brightness and from
the sword, extends many miles into the wilderness.
Adam and Eve are seen in the distance, flying along
the glare. The angel Gabriel and Lucifer are beside
the gate."—These are the " stage directions " which
greet us on the threshold of the book. We complain
first of the bull : secondly, of the blue-fire melo-
dramatic aspect of the revolving sword ; thirdly,
of the duplicate nature of the sword, which, if steel,
and sufficiently inflamed to do service in burning,
would, perhaps, have been in no temper to cut ;
and on the other hand, if sufficiently cool to have
an edge, would have accomplished little in the way
of scorching a personage so well accustomed to fire
and brimstone and all that, as we have very good
reason to believe Lucifer was. We cannot help
objecting, too, to the " innumerable angels," as a
force altogether disproportioned to the one enemy
to be kept out : either the self-moving sword itself,
we think, or the angel Gabriel alone, or five or six
of the " innumerable " angels, would have sufficed

to keep the devil (or is it Adam ?) outside of the gate which, after all, he might not have been able to discover, on account of the clouds.

Far be it from us, however, to dwell irreverently on matters which have venerability in the faith or in the fancy of Miss Barrett. We allude to these *niaiseries* at all—found here in the very first paragraph of her poem,—simply by way of putting in the clearest light the mass of inconsistency and antagonism in which her *subject* has inextricably involved her. She has made allusion to Milton, and no doubt felt secure in her theme (as a theme merely) when she considered his *Paradise Lost*. But even in Milton's own day, when men had the habit of believing all things, the more nonsensical the more readily, and of worshipping, in blind acquiescence, the most preposterous of impossibilities—even *then*, there were not wanting individuals who would have read the great epic with more zest, could it have been explained to their satisfaction, how and why it was, not only that a snake quoted Aristotle's *Ethics*, and behaved otherwise pretty much as he pleased, but that bloody battles were continually being fought between bloodless " innumerable angels," that found no inconvenience in losing a wing one minute and a head the next, and if pounded up into puff-paste late in the afternoon, were as good " innumerable angels " as new the next morning, in time to be at *réveillé* roll-call. And now—at the present epoch—there are few people who do not occasionally *think*. This is emphatically the thinking age ;—indeed, it may very well be questioned whether mankind ever substantially thought before. The fact is, if the *Paradise Lost* were written to-day (assuming that it had never been written when it was,) not even its eminent, although over-estimated merits, would counterbalance, either in the public view, or in the opinion of any critic at once intelligent and honest, the multitudinous incongruities which are part and parcel of its plot.

But in the plot of the drama of Miss Barrett it is something even worse than incongruity which affronts :—a continuous mystical strain of ill-fitting and exaggerated allegory—if, indeed, allegory is not much too respectable a term for it. We are called upon, for example, to sympathize in the whimsical woes of two Spirits, who, upspringing from the bowels of the earth, set immediately to bewailing their miseries in jargon such as this :

> I am the spirit of the harmless earth ;
>   God spake me softly out among the stars,
> As softly as a blessing of much worth—
> And then his smile did follow unawares,
> That all things, fashioned, so, for use and duty,
> Might shine anointed with his chrism of beauty—
>   Yet I wail !
> I drave on with the worlds exultingly,
>   Obliquely down the Godlight's gradual fall—
> Individual aspect and complexity
>   Of gyratory orb and interval,
> Lost in the fluent motion of delight
> Toward the high ends of Being, beyond Sight—
>   Yet I wail !

Innumerable other spirits discourse successively after the same fashion, each ending every stanza of his lamentation with the " yet I wail ! " When at length they have fairly made an end, Eve touches Adam upon the elbow, and hazards, also, the profound and pathetic observation—" Lo, Adam, they wail ! "—which is nothing more than the simple truth—for they *do*—and God deliver us from any such wailing again !

It is not our purpose, however, to demonstrate what every reader of these volumes will have readily seen self-demonstrated—the utter indefensibility of *The Drama of Exile*, considered uniquely, as a work of art. We have none of us to be told that a medley of metaphysical recitatives sung out of tune, at Adam and Eve, by all manner of inconceivable abstractions, is not exactly the best material for a poem. Still it may very well happen that among

this material there shall be individual passages of
great beauty. But should anyone doubt the possi-
bility, let him be satisfied by a single extract such
as follows :

> On a mountain peak
> Half sheathed in primal woods and glittering
> In *spasms of awful sunshine*, at that hour
> A lion couched,—part raised upon his paws,
> *With his calm massive face turned full on thine,*
> *And his mane listening.* When the ended curse
> Left silence in the world, right suddenly
> He sprang up rampant, and stood straight and stiff,
> *As if the new reality of death*
> *Were dashed against his eyes,*—and roared so fierce,
> (*Such thick carnivorous passion in his throat*
> *Tearing a passage through the wrath and fear*)—
> And roared so wild, and smote from all the hills
> Such *fast keen echoes crumbling down the vales*
> *To distant silence,*—that the forest beasts,
> One after one, did mutter a response
> In savage and in sorrowful complaint
> *Which trailed along the gorges.*

There is an Homeric force here—a vivid picturesque-
ness which all men will appreciate and admire. It
is, however, the longest quotable passage in the
drama, not disfigured with blemishes of importance ;
—although there are many—very many passages of
a far loftier order of excellence, so disfigured, and
which, therefore, it would not suit our immediate
purpose to extract. The truth is,—and it may be
as well mentioned at this point as elsewhere—that
we are not to look in Miss Barrett's works for any
examples of what has been occasionally termed
" sustained effort " ; for neither are there, in any
of her poems, any long commendable paragraphs,
nor are there any individual compositions which will
bear the slightest examination as consistent Art-
products. Her wild and magnificent genius seems
to have contented itself with points—to have
exhausted itself in flashes ;—but it is the profusion
—the unparalleled number and close propinquity of

these points and flashes which render her book *one flame*, and justify us in calling her, unhesitatingly, the greatest—the most glorious of her sex.

The *Drama of Exile* calls for little more, in the way of comment, than what we have generally said. Its finest particular feature is, perhaps, the rapture of Eve—rapture bursting through despair—upon discovering that she still possesses in the unwavering love of Adam an undreamed-of and priceless treasure. The poem ends, as it commences, with a bull. The last sentence gives us to understand that "there is a sound through the silence, as of the falling tears of an angel." How there can be sound during silence, and how an audience are to distinguish by such sound, angel tears from any other species of tears, it may be as well, perhaps, not too particularly to inquire.

Next, in length, to the Drama is, *The Vision of Poets*. We object to the didacticism of its design, which the poetess thus states : " I have attempted to express here my view of the mission of the veritable poet—of the self-abnegation implied in it, of the uses of sorrow suffered in it, of the great work accomplished in it through suffering, and of the duty and glory of what Balzac has beautifully and truly called ' *la patience angélique du génie.*' " This " view " may be correct, but neither its correctness nor its falsity has anything to do with a poem. If a thesis is to be demonstrated, we need *prose* for its demonstration. In this instance, so far as the allegorical instruction and argumentation are lost sight of, in the upper current—so far as the main admitted intention of the work is kept out of view—so far only is the work a poem, and so far only is the poem worth notice, or worthy of its author. Apart from its poetical character, the composition is thoughtful, vivid, epigrammatic, and abundant in just observation—although the critical opinions introduced are not always our own. A reviewer in *Blackwood's Magazine*, quoting many of these critical portraits, takes occasion to find fault with the grammar of this tristich :

> Here Æschylus—the women swooned
> To see so awful when he frowned
> As the Gods did—he standeth crowned.

"What on earth," says the critic, "are we to make of the words 'the women swooned to see so awful'? . . . The syntax will punish future commentators as much as some of his own corrupt choruses." In general, we are happy to agree with this reviewer, whose decisions respecting the book are, upon the whole, so nearly coincident with ours, that we hesitated, through fear of repetition, to undertake a *critique* at all, until we considered that we might say a very great deal in simply supplying his omissions ; but he frequently errs through mere hurry, and never did he err more singularly than at the point now in question. He evidently supposes that "awful" has been misused as an adverb and made referable to "women." But not so ; and although the construction of the passage is unjustifiably involute, its grammar is intact. Disentangling the construction, we make this evident at once : "Here Æschylus (he) standeth crowned, (whom) the women swooned to see so awful, when he frowned as the Gods did." The "he" is excessive, and the "whom" is understood. Respecting the lines,

> Euripides, with close and mild
> Scholastic lips, that could be wild,
> And laugh or sob out like a child
> Right in the classes,

the critic observes :—"'Right in the classes' throws our intellect completely upon its beam-ends." But, if so, the fault possibly lies in the crankness of the intellect ; for the words themselves mean merely that Sophocles laughed or cried like a schoolboy— like a child right (or just) in his classes—one who had not yet left school. The phrase is affected, we grant, but quite intelligible. A still more remarkable misapprehension occurs in regard to the triplet,

> And Goethe, with that reaching eye
> His soul reached out from, far and high,
> And fell from inner entity.

The reviewer's remarks upon this are too preposterous not to be quoted in full ;—we doubt if any commentator of equal dignity ever so egregiously committed himself before. " Goethe," he says, " is a perfect enigma; what does the word ' fell ' mean ? δεινος we suppose—that is, ' not to be trifled with.' But surely it sounds very strange, although it may be true enough, to say that his ' fellness ' is occasioned by ' inner entity.' But perhaps the line has some deeper meaning which we are unable to fathom." Perhaps it has : and this is the criticism—the British criticism—the *Blackwood* criticism—to which we have so long implicitly bowed down ! As before, Miss Barrett's verses are needlessly involved, but their meaning requires no Œdipus. Their construction is thus intended :—" And Goethe, with that reaching eye from which his soul reached out, far and high, and (in so reaching) fell from inner entity." The plain prose is this :—Goethe, (the poet would say,) in involving himself too far and too profoundly in external speculations—speculations concerning the world without him—neglected, or made miscalculations concerning, his inner entity, or being,—concerning the world within. This idea is involved in the metaphor of a person leaning from a window so far that finally he falls from it—the person being the soul, the window the eye.

Of the twenty-eight *Sonnets*, which immediately succeed the *Drama of Exile*, and which receive the especial commendation of *Blackwood*, we have no very enthusiastic opinion. The *best* sonnet is objectionable from its extreme artificiality ; and, to be effective, this species of composition requires a minute management—a well-controlled dexterity of touch—compatible neither with Miss Barrett's deficient constructiveness, nor with the fervid rush and whirl of her genius. Of the particular instances here given, we prefer *The Prisoner*, of which the conclusion is particularly beautiful. In general, the themes are obtrusively metaphysical, or didactic.

The Romaunt of the Page, an imitation of the old English ballad, is neither very original in subject, nor very skilfully put together. We speak comparatively, of course :—It is not very good—for Miss Barrett :—and what we have said of this poem will apply equally to a very similar production, *The Rhyme of the Duchess May*. The *Poet and the Bird—A Child Asleep—Crowned and Wedded—Crowned and Buried—To Flush my Dog—The Four-fold Aspect— A Flower in a Letter—A Lay of the Early Rose—That Day—L. E. L.'s Questio—Catarina to Camoëns—Wine of Cyprus—The Dead Pan—Sleeping and Watching— A Portrait—The Mournful Mother*—and *A Valediction* —although all burning with divine fire, manifested only in scintillations, have nothing in them idiosyncratic. *The House of Clouds* and *The Last Bower* are superlatively lovely, and show the vast powers of the poet in the field best adapted to their legitimate display :—the *themes*, here, could not be improved. The former poem is purely imaginative ; the latter is unobjectionably because unobtrusively suggestive of a moral, and is, perhaps, upon the whole, the most admirable composition in the two volumes :—or, if it is not, then *The Lay of the Brown Rosarie* is. In this last the ballad-character is elevated—etherealized —and thus made to afford scope for an ideality at once the richest and most vigorous in the world. The peculiar foibles of the author are here, too, dropped bodily, as a mantle, in the tumultuous movement and excitement of the narrative.

Miss Barrett has need only of *real* self-interest in her subjects, to do justice to her subjects and to herself. On the other hand, *A Rhapsody of Life's Progress*, although gleaming with cold corruscations, is the least meritorious, because the most philosophical, effusion of the whole :—this, we say, in flat contradiction of the "*spoudiotaton kai philosophikotaton genos*" of Aristotle. *The Cry of the Human* is singularly effective, not more from the vigour and ghastly passion of its thought, than from the artistically-conceived *arabesquerie* of its rhythm. *The Cry of the Children*, similar, although superior in tone and handling, is full of a nervous unflinching energy—a horror sublime in its simplicity—of which a far greater than Dante might have been proud. *Bertha in the Lane*, a rich ballad, very singularly excepted from the wholesale commendation of the *Democratic Review*, as "perhaps not one of the best," and designated by *Blackwood*, on the contrary, as "decidedly the finest poem of the collection," is *not* the *very* best, we think, only because mere pathos, however exquisite, cannot be ranked with the loftiest exhibitions of the ideal. Of *Lady Geraldine's Courtship*, the magazine last quoted observes that "some pith is put forth in its passionate parts." We will not pause to examine the delicacy or lucidity of the metaphor embraced in the "*putting forth* of some pith"; but unless by "some pith" itself, is intended the utmost conceivable intensity and vigour, then the critic is merely damning with faint praise. With the exception of Tennyson's *Locksley Hall*, we have never perused a poem combining so much of the fiercest passion with so much of the most ethereal fancy, as the *Lady Geraldine's Courtship*, of Miss Barrett. We are forced to admit, however, that the latter work *is* a very palpable imitation of the former, which it surpasses in plot, or rather in thesis, as much as it falls below it in artistical management, and a certain calm energy—lustrous and indomitable—such as we might imagine in a broad river of molten gold.

It is in the *Lady Geraldine* that the critic of *Blackwood* is again put at fault in the comprehension of a couple of passages. He confesses his inability

" to make out the construction of the words, ' all
that spirits pure and ardent are cast out of love and
reverence, because chancing not to hold.' " There
are comparatively few American schoolboys who
could not parse it. The prosaic construction would
run thus :—all *that* (wealth understood) because
chancing not to hold *which,* (or on account of not
holding which) all pure and ardent spirits are cast
out of love and reverence." The " which " is involved
in the relative pronoun " that "—the second word
of the sentence. *All that we know is, that Miss
Barrett is right :*—here is a parallel phrase, meaning
—" all that (which) we know," etc. The fact is,
that the accusation of imperfect grammar would
have been more safely, if more generally, urged :
in descending to particular exceptions, the reviewer
has been doing little more than exposing himself at
all points.

Turning aside, however, from grammar, he declares
his incapacity to fathom the meaning of

She has halls and she has castles, and the resonant steam-
    eagles
  Follow far on the directing of her floating dove-like hand—
With a thunderous vapour trailing underneath the starry
    vigils,
  So to mark upon the blasted heaven the measure of her
    land.

Now it must be understood that he is profoundly
serious in his declaration—he really *does not* appre-
hend the thought designed—and he is even more
than profoundly serious, too, in intending these his
own comments upon his own stolidity, for wit :—
" We thought that steam-coaches generally followed
the directing of no hand except the stoker's, but *it,*
certainly, is always much *liker* a raven than a dove."
After this, who shall question the infallibility of
Christopher North ? We presume there are very few
of *our* readers who will not easily appreciate the
richly imaginative conception of the poetess :—The
Lady Geraldine is supposed to be standing in her

own door, (positively *not* on the top of an engine),
and thence pointing, " with her floating dove-like
hand," to the lines of vapour, from the " resonant
steam-eagles," that designate upon the " blasted
heaven," the remote boundaries of her domain.—
But, perhaps, we are guilty of a very gross absurdity
ourselves, in commenting *at all* upon the whimsicalities
of a reviewer who can deliberately *select* for special
animadversion the second of the four verses we here
copy :

Eyes, he said, now throbbing through me ! are ye eyes that
    did undo me ?
Shining eyes like antique jewels set in Parian statue-stone !
Underneath that calm white forehead are ye ever burning
    torrid
O'er the desolate sand desert of my heart and life undone ?

The ghost of the Great Frederick might, to be
sure, quote at us, in his own Latin, his favourite
adage, " De gustibus non est disputand*us* " ;—but,
when we take into consideration the moral designed,
the weirdness of effect intended, and the historical
adaptation of the fact alluded to, in the line italicized,
(a fact of which it is by no means impossible that
the critic is ignorant), we cannot refrain from
expressing our conviction—and we here *express it*
in the teeth of the whole horde of the Ambrosianians
—that from the entire range of poetical literature
there shall not, in a century, be produced a more
sonorous—a more vigorous verse—a juster—a nobler
—a more ideal—a more magnificent image—than
this very image, in this very verse, which the most
noted magazine of Europe has so especially and so
contemptuously condemned.

The Lady Geraldine is, we think, the only poem
of its author which is not deficient, considered as
an artistical whole. Her constructive ability, as we
have already suggested, is either not very remarkable,
or has never been properly brought into play :— in
truth, her genius is too impetuous for the minuter
technicalities of that elaborate *Art* so needful in

the building up of pyramids for immortality. This deficiency, then—if there be any such—is her chief weakness. Her other foibles, although some of them are, in fact, glaring, glare, nevertheless, to no very material ill purpose. There are none which she will not readily dismiss in her future works. She retains them now, perhaps, because unaware of their existence.

Her affectations are unquestionably many, and generally inexcusable. We may, perhaps, tolerate such words as " blé," " chrysm," " nympholeptic," " œnomel," and " chrysopras "—they have at least the merit either of distinct meaning, or of terse and sonorous expression ;—but what can be well said in defence of the unnecessary nonsense of " 'ware " for " aware "—of " 'bide," for " abide "—of " 'gins," for " begins "—of " 'las " for " alas "—of " oftly," " ofter," and " oftest," for " often," " more often," and " most often "—or of " erelong " in the sense of " long ago " ? That there is *authority* for the mere words proves nothing ; those who employed them in their day would not employ them if writing *now*. Although we grant, too, that the poetess is very usually Homeric in her compounds, there is no intelligibility of construction, and therefore no force of meaning in " dew-pallid," " pale-passioned," and " silver-solemn." Neither have we any partiality for " drave " or " s*u*preme," or " *la*ment " ; and while upon this topic, we may as well observe that there are few readers who do anything but laugh or stare at such phrases as " L. E. L.'s Last Questio " —" The Cry of the Human "—" Leaning from my Human "—" Heaven assist the human "—" the full sense of your mortal "—" a grave for your divine " —" falling off from our created "—" he sends this gage for thy pity's counting "—" they could not press their futures on the present of her courtesy " —or " could another fairer lack to thee, lack to thee ? " There are few, at the same time, who do not feel disposed to weep outright, when they hear of such things as " Hope withdrawing her peradven-

ture "—" spirits dealing in pathos of antithesis "—
" angels in antagonism to God and his reflex
beatitudes "—" songs of glories ruffling down door-
ways "—" God's possibles "—and " rules of Man-
dom."

We have already said, however, that mere *quaint-
ness* within reasonable limit is not only *not* to be
regarded as affectation, but has its proper artistic uses
in aiding a fantastic effect. We quote, from the lines
To my Dog Flush, a passage in exemplification :

> Leap ! thy broad tail waves a light !
> Leap ! thy slender feet are bright,
>   Canopied in fringes !
> Leap ! those tasselled ears of thine
> Flicker strangely, fair and fine,
>   *Down their golden inches !*

And again—from the song of a tree-spirit, in the
Drama of Exile :

> The Divine impulsion cleaves
> In dim movements to the leaves
> *Dropt and lifted, dropt and lifted,*
> In the sun-light greenly sifted,—
> *In the sun-light and the moon-light*
> *Greenly sifted through the trees.*
> Ever wave the Eden trees,
> *In the night-light and the moon-light,*
> With a ruffling of green branches,
> *Shaded off to resonances,*
> Never stirred by rain or breeze.

The thoughts, here, belong to the highest order of
poetry, but they could not have been wrought into
effective expression, without the instrumentality of
those repetitions—those unusual phrases—in a word,
those *quaintnesses*, which it has been too long the
fashion to censure, indiscriminately, under the one
general head of " affectation." No true poet will fail
to be enraptured with the two extracts above quoted
—but we believe there are few who would not find
a difficulty in reconciling the psychal impossibility
of refraining from admiration, with the too-hastily

attained mental conviction that, critically, there is nothing to admire.

Occasionally, we meet in Miss Barrett's poems a certain *far-fetchedness* of imagery, which is reprehensible in the extreme. What, for example, are we to think of

> Now he hears the angel voices
> Folding silence in the room ?—

undoubtedly, that it is nonsense, and no more; or of

> How the silence round you shivers
> While our voices through it go ?—

again, unquestionably, that it is nonsense, and nothing beyond.

Sometimes we are startled by knotty paradoxes; and it is not acquitting their perpetrator of all blame on their account to admit that, in some instances, they are susceptible of solution. It is really difficult to discover anything for approbation in enigmas such as

> That bright impassive, passive angel-hood,

or—

> The silence of my heart is full of sound.

At long intervals, we are annoyed by specimens of repulsive imagery, as where the children cry :

> How long, O cruel nation,
> Will you stand, to move the world, *on a child's heart—*
> *Stifle down with a mailed heel its palpitation ?* etc.

Now and then, too, we are confounded by a pure platitude, as when Eve exclaims :

> Leave us not
> In agony beyond what we can bear,
> And in abasement *below thunder-mark* !

or, when the Saviour is made to say :

> So, at last,
> He shall look round on you *with lids too straight*
> *To hold the grateful tears.*

"Strait" was, no doubt, intended, but does not materially elevate, although it slightly elucidates, the thought. A very remarkable passage is that, also, wherein Eve bids the infant voices

> Hear the steep generations, how they fall
> Adown the visionary stairs of Time,
> Like supernatural thunders—far yet near,
> Sowing their fiery echoes through the hills !

Here, saying nothing of the affectation in "adown"; not alluding to the insoluble paradox of "far yet near"; not mentioning the inconsistent metaphor involved in the "sowing of *fiery* echoes"; adverting but slightly to the misusage of "like," in place of "as," and to the impropriety of making anything fall like *thunder*, which has never been known to fall at all ; merely hinting, too, at the misapplication of "steep," to the "generations," instead of to the "stairs"—a perversion in no degree to be justified by the fact that so preposterous a figure as *synecdoche* exists in the school-books ;—letting these things pass, for the present, we shall still find it difficult to understand how Miss Barrett should have been led to think that the principal idea itself—the abstract idea—the idea of *tumbling downstairs*, in any shape, or under any circumstances—either a poetical or a decorous conception. And yet we have seen this very passage quoted as "sublime," by a critic who seems to take it for granted, as a general rule, that Nat-Leeism is the loftiest order of literary merit. That the lines very *narrowly missed* sublimity, we grant ; that they came within a step of it, we admit ; —but, unhappily, the step is that *one* step which, time out of mind, has intervened between the sublime and the ridiculous. So true is this, that any person— that even *we*—with a very partial modification of the imagery—a modification that shall not interfere with its richly spiritual *tone*—may elevate the quotation into unexceptionability. For example: and we offer it with profound deference—

> Hear the far generations—how they crash,
> From crag to crag, down the precipitous Time,
> In multitudinous thunders that upstartle,
> Aghast, the echoes from their cavernous lairs
> In the visionary hills !

We have no doubt that our version has its faults —but it has, at least, the merit of consistency. Not only is a mountain more poetical than a pair of stairs ; but echoes are more appropriately typified as wild beasts than as seeds ; and echoes and wild beasts agree better with a mountain, than does a pair of stairs with the *sowing* of seeds—even admitting that these seeds be seeds of fire, and be sown broadcast " among the hills," by a steep generation, while in the act of tumbling down the stairs—that is to say, of coming down the stairs—in too violent a hurry to be capable of sowing the seeds as accurately as all seeds should be sown ; nor is the matter rendered any better for Miss Barrett, even if the construction of her sentence is to be understood as implying that the fiery seeds were sown, not immediately by the steep generations that tumbled down the stairs, but mediately, through the intervention of the " supernatural thunders " that were *occasioned* by the " steep generations " that tumbled down the stairs.

The poetess is not unfrequently guilty of repeating herself. The " thunder cloud veined by lightning " appears, for instance, on pages 34 of the first, and 228 of the second volume. The " silver clash of wings " is heard at pages 53 of the first, and 269 of the second ; and angel tears are discovered to be falling as well at page 27, as at the conclusion of *The Drama of Exile*. Steam, too, in the shape of Death's White Horse, comes upon the ground, both at page 244 of the first, and 179 of the second volume—and there are multitudinous other repetitions both of phrase and idea—but it is the excessive reiteration of pet *words* which is, perhaps, the most obtrusive of the minor errors of the poet. " Chrys-

talline," "Apocalypse," "foregone," "evangel,"
" 'ware," "throb," "level," "loss," and the musical
term "minor," are for ever upon her lips. The chief
favourites, however, are "down" and "leaning,"
which are echoed and re-echoed not only *ad infinitum,*
but in every whimsical variation of import. As Miss
Barrett certainly cannot be aware of the extent of
this mannerism, we will venture to call her attention
to a few—comparatively a *very* few examples.

> Pealing *down* the depths of Godhead . . .
> Smiling *down*, as Venus *down* the waves . . .
> Smiling *down* the steep world very purely . . .
> *Down* the purple of this chamber . . .
> Moving *down* the hidden depths of loving . . .
> Cold the sun shines *down* the door . . .
> Which brought angels *down* our talk . . .
> Let your souls behind you *lean* gently moved . . .
> But angels *leaning* from the golden seats . . .
> And melancholy *leaning* out of heaven . . .
> And I know the heavens are *leaning* down . . .
> Then over the casement she *leaneth* . . .
> Forbear that dream, too near to heaven it *leaned* . . .
> I would *lean* my spirit o'er you . . .
> Thou, O sapient angel, *leanest o'er* . . .
> Shapes of brightness *overlean* thee . . .
> They are *leaning* their young heads . . .
> Out of heaven shall o'er you *lean* . . .
> While my spirit *leans* and reaches . . .
>   etc., etc., etc

In the matter of grammar, upon which the
Edinburgh critic insists so pertinaciously, the author
of *The Drama of Exile* seems to us even peculiarly
without fault. The nature of her studies has, no
doubt, imbued her with a very delicate instinct of
constructive accuracy. The occasional use of phrases
so questionable as "from whence" and the far-
fetchedness and involution of which we have already
spoken, are the only noticeable blemishes of an ex-
ceedingly chaste, vigorous, and comprehensive style.

In her inattention to rhythm, Miss Barrett is guilty
of an error that might have been fatal to her fame
—that *would* have been fatal to any reputation less
solidly founded than her own. We do not allude,

so particularly, to her multiplicity of inadmissible rhymes. We would wish, to be sure, that she had not thought proper to couple Eden and succeeding —glories and floorwise—burning and morning—thither and æther—enclose me and across me—misdoers and flowers—centre and winter—guerdon and pardon—conquer and anchor—desert and unmeasured —atoms and fathoms—opal and people—glory and doorway—trumpet and accompted—taming and overcame him—coming and woman—is and trees—off and sun-proof—eagles and vigils—nature and satire—poems and interflowings—certes and virtues—pardon and burden—threat and great—children and bewildering—mortal and turtle—moonshine and sunshine. It would have been better, we say, if such apologies for rhymes as these had been rejected. But deficiencies of *rhythm* are more serious. In some cases it is nearly impossible to determine what metre is intended. *The Cry of the Children* cannot be scanned : we *never saw* so poor a specimen of verse. In imitating the rhythm of *Locksley Hall,* the poetess has preserved with accuracy (so far as mere syllables are concerned) the forcible line of seven trochees with a final cæsura. The " double rhymes " have only the force of a single long syllable—a cæsura ; but the natural rhythmical division, occurring at the close of the fourth trochee, should never be forced to occur, as Miss Barrett constantly forces it, in the middle of a word, or of an indivisible phrase. If it do so occur, we must sacrifice, in perusal, either the sense or the rhythm. If she will consider, too, that this line of seven trochees and a cæsura is nothing more than two lines written in one—a line of four trochees, succeeded by one of three trochees and a cæsura—she will at once see how unwise she has been in composing her poem in quatrains of the long line with alternate rhymes, instead of immediate ones, as in the case of *Locksley Hall.* The result is, that the ear, expecting the rhymes before they occur, does not appreciate them when they do.

These points, however, will be best exemplified by transcribing one of the quatrains in its *natural* arrangement. That actually employed is addressed only to the eye.

> Oh, she fluttered like a tame bird
>   In among its forest brothers
> Far too strong for it, then, drooping,
>   Bowed her face upon her hands—
> And I spake out wildly, fiercely,
>   Brutal truths of her and others !
> I, she planted in the desert,
>   Swathed her 'wind-like, with my sands.

Here it will be seen that there is a paucity of rhyme, and that it is expected at closes where it does not occur. In fact, if we consider the eight lines as two independent quatrains (which they are,) then we find them *entirely rhymeless*. Now so unhappy are these metrical defects—of so much importance do we take them to be, that we do not hesitate in declaring the general inferiority of the poem to its prototype to be altogether chargeable to *them*. With equal rhythm *Lady Geraldine* had been far—very far the superior poem. Inefficient rhythm is inefficient poetical expression; and expression, in poetry,—what is it ?—what is it not ? No one living can better answer these queries than Miss Barrett.

We conclude our comments upon her versification by quoting (we will not say whence—from what one of her poems)—a few verses without the linear division as it appears in the book. There are many readers who would never suspect the passage to be intended for metre at all.—" Ay !—and sometimes, on the hillside, while we sat down on the gowans, with the forest green behind us, and its shadow cast before, and the river running under, and, across it from the rowens a partridge whirring near us till we felt the air it bore—there, obedient to her praying, did I read aloud the poems made by Tuscan flutes, or instruments more various of our own—read the pastoral parts of Spencer—or the subtle interflowing

found in Petrarch's sonnets ;—here's the book !—
the leaf is folded down ! "

With this extract we make an end of our fault-
finding—and *now*, shall we speak, equally in detail,
of the *beauties* of this book ? Alas ! here, indeed,
do we feel the impotence of the pen. We have
already said that the supreme excellence of the
poetess whose works we review is made up of the
multitudinous sums of a world of lofty merits. It
is the multiplicity—it is the *aggregation*—which
excites our most profound enthusiasm, and enforces
our most earnest respect. But unless we had space
to extract three-fourths of the volumes, how could
we convey this aggregation by specimens ? We might
quote, to be sure, an example of keen insight into our
psychal nature, such as this :

> I fell flooded with a Dark,
>   In the silence of a swoon—
> When I rose, still cold and stark,
>   There was night,—I saw the moon ;
> And the stars, each in its place,
> And the May-blooms on the grass,
> Seemed to wonder what I was.
> And I walked as if apart
>   From myself when I could stand—
> And I pitied my own heart,
>   As if I held it in my hand
> Somewhat coldly,—with a sense
> Of fulfilled benevolence.

Or we might copy an instance of the purest and most
radiant imagination, such as this :

> So, young muser, I sat listening
> To my Fancy's wildest word—
> On a sudden, through the glistening
> Leaves around, a little stirred,
> Came a sound, a sense of music, which was rather felt than
>   heard.
> Softly, finely, it inwound me—
> From the world it shut me in—
> Like a fountain falling round me
> Which with silver waters thin,
> Holds a little marble Naiad sitting smilingly within.

Or, again, we might extract a specimen of wild

Dantesque vigour, such as this—in combination with
a pathos never excelled :

> Ay ! be silent—let them hear each other breathing
>   For a moment, mouth to mouth—
> Let them touch each others' hands in a fresh wreathing
>   Of their tender human youth !
> Let them feel that this cold metallic motion
>   Is not all the life God fashions or reveals—
> Let them prove their inward souls against the notion
>   That they live in you, or under you, O wheels !

Or, still again, we might give a passage embodying
the most elevated sentiment, most tersely and
musically thus expressed :

> And since, Prince Albert, men have called thy spirit high
>   and rare,
> And true to truth, and brave for truth, as some at Augsburg
>   were—
> We charge thee by thy lofty thoughts and by thy poet-mind,
> Which not by glory or degree takes measure of mankind,
> Esteem that wedded hand less dear for sceptre than for ring,
> And hold her uncrowned womanhood to be the royal thing !

These passages, we say, and a hundred similar ones,
exemplifying particular excellences, might be dis-
played, and we should still fail, as lamentably as
the *skolastikos* with his brick, in conveying an idea
of the vast *totality*. By no individual stars can we
present the constellatory radiance of the book. *To
the book*, then, with implicit confidence we appeal.

That Miss Barrett has done more, in poetry, than
any woman living or dead, will scarcely be ques-
tioned :—that she has surpassed all her poetical
contemporaries of either sex (with a single exception,)
is our deliberate opinion—not idly entertained, we
think, nor founded on any visionary basis. It may
not be uninteresting, therefore, in closing this
examination of her claims, to determine in what
manner she holds poetical relation with these con-
temporaries, or with her immediate predecessors, and
especially with the great exception to which we have
alluded—if at all.

If ever mortal " wreaked his thoughts upon

expression," it was Shelley. If ever poet sang (as a bird sings)—impulsively—earnestly—with utter abandonment—to himself solely—and for the mere joy of his own song—that poet was the author of *The Sensitive Plant*. Of Art—beyond that which is the inalienable instinct of Genius—he either had little or disdained all. He *really* disdained that Rule which is the emanation from Law, because his own soul was law in itself. His rhapsodies are but the rough notes—the stenographic memoranda of poems—memoranda which, because they were all-sufficient for his own intelligence, he cared not to be at the trouble of transcribing in full for mankind. In his whole life he wrought not thoroughly out a single conception. For this reason it is that he is the most fatiguing of poets. Yet he wearies in having done too little, rather than too much; what seems in him the diffuseness of one idea, is the conglomerate concision of many;—and this concision it is which renders him obscure. With such a man, to imitate was out of the question; it would have answered no purpose—for he spoke to his own spirit alone, which would have comprehended no alien tongue;—he was, therefore, profoundly original. His quaintness arose from intuitive perception of that truth to which Lord Verulam alone has given distinct voice :—" There is no exquisite beauty which has not some strangeness in its proportion." But whether obscure, original, or quaint, he was at all times sincere. He had no *affectations*.

From the ruins of Shelley there sprang into existence, affronting the Heavens, a tottering and fantastic pagoda, in which the salient angles, tipped with mad jangling bells, were the idiosyncratic *faults* of the great original—faults which cannot be called such in view of his purposes, but which are monstrous when we regard his works as addressed to mankind. A " school " arose—if that absurd term must still be employed—a school—a system of rules—upon the basis of the Shelley who had none. Young men innumerable, dazzled with the glare and bewildered with the *bizarrerie* of the divine lightning that flickered through the clouds of the *Prometheus*, had no trouble whatever in heaping up imitative vapours, but, for the lightning, were content, perforce, with its *spectrum*, in which the *bizarrerie* appeared without the fire. Nor were great and mature minds unimpressed by the contemplation of a greater and more mature ; and thus gradually were interwoven into this school of all Lawlessness—of obscurity, quaintness, exaggeration—the misplaced didacticism of Wordsworth, and the even more preposterously anomalous metaphysicianism of Coleridge. Matters were now fast verging to their worst, and at length, in Tennyson, poetic inconsistency attained its extreme. But it was precisely this extreme (for the greatest error and the greatest truth are scarcely two points in a circle)—it was this extreme which, following the law of all extremes, wrought in him—in Tennyson—a natural and inevitable revulsion, leading him first to contemn and secondly to investigate his early manner, and, finally, to winnow from its magnificent elements the truest and purest of all poetical styles. But not even yet is the process complete ; and for this reason in part, but chiefly on account of the mere fortuitousness of that mental and moral combination which shall unite in one person (if *ever* it shall) the Shelleyan *abandon*, the Tennysonian poetic sense, the most profound instinct of Art, and the sternest Will properly to blend and vigorously to control all ;—chiefly, we say, because such combination of antagonisms must be purely fortuitous, has the world never yet seen the noblest of the poems of which it is *possible* that it may be put in possession.

And yet Miss Barrett has narrowly missed the fulfilment of these conditions. Her poetic inspiration is the highest—we can conceive nothing more august. Her sense of Art is pure in itself, but has been contaminated by pedantic study of false models—a

study which has the more easily led her astray,
because she placed an undue value upon it as rare
—as alien to her character of woman. The accident
of having been long secluded by ill health from the
world has effected, moreover, in her behalf, what an
innate recklessness did for Shelley—has imparted to
her, if not precisely that *abandon* to which I have
referred, at least a something that stands well in its
stead—a comparative independence of men and
opinions with which she did not come personally
in contact—a happy audacity of thought and ex-
pression never before known in one of her sex. It
is, however, this same accident of ill health, perhaps,
which has invalidated her original Will—diverted her
from proper individuality of purpose—and seduced
her into the sin of imitation. Thus, what she might
have done, we cannot altogether determine. What
she has actually accomplished is before us. With
Tennyson's works beside her, and a keen appreciation
of them in her soul—appreciation too keen to be
discriminative ;—with an imagination even more
vigorous than his, although somewhat less ethereally
delicate ; with inferior art and more feeble volition ;
she has written poems such as he *could not write*,
but such as he, under *her* conditions of ill health
and seclusion, *would have written* during the epoch
of his pupildom in that school which arose out of
Shelley, and from which, over a disgustful gulf of
utter incongruity and absurdity, lit only by miasmatic
flashes, into the broad open meadows of Natural
Art and Divine Genius, he—Tennyson—is at once
the bridge and the transition.

R. H. HORNE [1]

MR. R. H. HORNE, the author of the *Orion*, has,
of late years, acquired a high and extensive *home*

[1] *Orion : an Epic Poem in Three Books.* By R. H. Horne.
Fourth Edition. London : Published by J. Miller.

reputation, although, as yet, he is only partially known in America. He will be remembered, however, as the author of a very well-written Introduction to Black's Translation of Schlegel's *Lectures on Dramatic Art and Literature*, and as a contributor with Wordsworth, Hunt, Miss Barrett, and others, to *Chaucer Modernized*. He is the author, also, of *Cosmo de Medici*, of *The Death of Marlowe*, and, especially, of *Gregory the Seventh*, a fine tragedy, prefaced with an *Essay on Tragic Influence*. *Orion* was originally advertised to be sold for a *farthing*; and, at this price, three large editions were actually sold. The fourth edition (a specimen of which now lies before us) was issued at a shilling, and also *sold*. A fifth is promised at half a crown; this likewise, with even a sixth at a crown, may be disposed of —partly through the intrinsic merit of the work itself—but chiefly through the ingenious novelty of the original price.

We have been among the earliest readers of Mr. Horne—among the most earnest admirers of his high genius;—for a man of high, of the highest genius, he unquestionably is. With an eager wish to do justice to his *Gregory the Seventh*, we have never yet found exactly that opportunity we desired. Meantime, we looked, with curiosity, for what the British critics would say of a work which, in the boldness of its conception, and in the fresh originality of its management, would necessarily fall beyond the *routine* of their customary verbiage. We saw nothing, however, that either could or should be understood— nothing, certainly, that was worth understanding. The tragedy itself was, unhappily, not devoid of the ruling cant of the day, and its critics (that cant incarnate) took their cue from some of its infected passages, and proceeded forthwith to rhapsody and æsthetics, by way of giving a common-sense public an intelligible idea of the book. By the "cant of the day" we mean the disgusting practice of putting on the airs of an owl, and endeavouring to look

miraculously wise ;—the affectation of second sight—
of a species of ecstatic prescience—of an intensely
bathetic penetration into all sorts of mysteries,
psychological ones in especial ;—an Orphic—an
ostrich affectation, which buries its head in balderdash,
and, seeing nothing itself, fancies, therefore, that its
preposterous carcass is not a visible object of derision
for the world at large.

Of *Orion* itself, we have, as yet, seen few notices
in the British periodicals, and these few are merely
repetitions of the old jargon. All that has been said,
for example, might be summed up in some such
paragraph as this :

"*Orion* is the *earnest* outpouring of the oneness
of the psychological MAN. It has the individuality
of the true SINGLENESS. It is not to be regarded as
a Poem, but as a WORK—as a multiple THEOGONY
—as a manifestation of the WORKS and the DAYS.
It is a pinion in the PROGRESS—a wheel in the
MOVEMENT that moveth ever and goeth always—a
mirror of SELF-INSPECTION, held up by the SEER of
the Age essential—of the Age *in esse*—for the SEERS
of the Ages possible—*in posse*. We hail a brother
in the work."

Of the mere opinions of the donkeys who bray
thus—of their mere dogmas and doctrines, literary,
æsthetical, or what not—we know little, and, upon
our honour, we wish to know less. Occupied,
Laputically, in their great work of a progress that
never progresses, we take it for granted, also, that
they care as little about ours. But whatever the
opinions of these people may be—however portentous
the " IDEA " which they have been so long threatening
to " evolve "—we still think it clear that they take
a very roundabout way of evolving it. The use of
Language is in the promulgation of Thought. If a
man—if an Orphicist—or a SEER—or whatever else
he may choose to call himself, while the rest of the
world calls him an ass if this gentleman have an
idea which he does not understand himself, the best

thing he can do is to say nothing about it ; for, of course, he can entertain no hope that what he, the SEER, cannot comprehend, should be comprehended by the mass of common humanity ; but if he have an idea which is actually intelligible to himself, and if he sincerely wishes to render it intelligible to others, we then hold it as indisputable that he should employ those forms of speech which are the best adapted to further his object. He should speak to the people in that people's ordinary tongue. He should arrange words, such as are habitually employed for the several preliminary and introductory ideas to be conveyed—he should arrange them in collocations such as those in which we are accustomed to see those words arranged.

But to all this the Orphicist thus replies : " I am a SEER. My IDEA—the idea which by providence I am especially commissioned to evolve—is one so vast—so novel—that ordinary words, in ordinary collocations, will be insufficient for its comfortable evolution." Very true. We grant the vastness of the IDEA—it is manifested in the sucking of the thumb—but, then, if *ordinary* language be insufficient—ordinary language which men understand—*a fortiori* will be insufficient that inordinate language which no man has *ever* understood, and which any well-educated baboon would blush in being accused of understanding. The " SEER," therefore, has no resource but to oblige mankind by holding his tongue, and suffering his IDEA to remain quietly " unevolved," until some Mesmeric mode of intercommunication shall be invented, whereby the antipodal brains of the SEER and of the man of Common Sense shall be brought into the necessary *rapport*. Meantime we earnestly ask if *bread-and-butter* be the vast IDEA in question—if *bread-and-butter* be any portion of this vast IDEA ; for we have often observed that when a SEER has to speak of even so usual a thing as bread-and-butter, he can never be induced to mention it outright. He will, if you choose, say anything and everything *but* bread-and-butter. He will consent to hint at buckwheat cake. He may even accommodate you so far as to insinuate oatmeal porridge—but, if bread-and-butter be really the matter intended, we never yet met the Orphicist who could get out the three individual words " bread-and-butter."

We have already said that " Gregory the Seventh " was unhappily infected with the customary cant of the day—the cant of the muddle-pates who dishonour a profound and ennobling philosophy by styling themselves transcendentalists. In fact, there are few highly sensitive or imaginative intellects for which the vortex of *mysticism*, in any shape, has not an almost irresistible influence, on account of the shadowy confines which separate the Unknown from the Sublime. Mr. Horne, then, is in some measure, infected. The success of his previous works has led him to attempt, zealously, the production of a poem which should be worthy his high powers. We have no doubt that he revolved carefully in mind a variety of august conceptions, and from these thoughtfully selected what his judgment, rather than what his impulses, designated as the noblest and the best. In a word, he has weakly yielded his own poetic sentiment of the poetic—yielded it, in some degree, to the pertinacious opinion, and *talk*, of a certain junto by which he is surrounded—a junto of dreamers whose absolute intellect may, perhaps, compare with his own very much after the fashion of an ant-hill with the Andes. By this talk—by its continuity rather than by any other quality it possessed—he has been badgered into the attempt at commingling the obstinate oils and waters of Poetry and of Truth. He has been so far blinded as to permit himself to imagine that a maudlin philosophy (granting it to be worth enforcing) could be enforced by poetic imagery, and illustrated by the jingling of rhythm ; or, more unpardonably, he has been induced to believe that a poem, whose single object is the creation of Beauty—the novel collocation of old forms of the Beautiful and of the Sublime—could be advanced by the abstractions of a maudlin philosophy.

But the question is not even this. It is not whether it be not possible to introduce didacticism, with effect, into a poem, or possible to introduce poetical images and measures, with effect, into a didactic essay. To do either the one or the other, would be merely to surmount a difficulty—would be simply a feat of literary sleight of hand. But the true question is, whether the author who shall attempt either feat, will not be labouring at a disadvantage—will not be guilty of a fruitless and wasteful expenditure of energy. In minor poetical efforts, we may not so imperatively demand an adherence to the true poetical thesis. We permit *trifling* to some extent, in a work which we consider a trifle at best. Although we agree, for example, with Coleridge, that poetry and *passion* are discordant, yet we are willing to permit Tennyson to bring, to the intense *passion* which prompted his *Locksley Hall*, the aid of that terseness and pungency which are derivable from rhythm and from rhyme. The effect he produces, however, is a purely passionate, and not, unless in detached passages of this magnificent philippic, a properly poetic effect. His *Œnone*, on the other hand, exalts the soul not into passion, but into a conception of pure *beauty*, which in its elevation—its calm and intense rapture—has in it a foreshadowing of the future and spiritual life, and as far transcends earthly passion as the holy radiance of the sun does the glimmering and feeble phosphorescence of the glow-worm. His *Morte D'Arthur* is in the same majestic vein. The *Sensitive Plant* of Shelley is in the same sublime spirit. Nor, if the passionate poems of Byron excite more intensely a greater number of readers than either the *Œnone* or the *Sensitive Plant*—does this indisputable fact prove anything more than that the majority of mankind are more susceptible of the impulses of passion than of the impressions of beauty. Readers do exist, however, and always will exist, who, to hearts of maddening fervour, unite, in perfection, the sentiment of the beautiful—that divine sixth sense which is yet so faintly understood —that sense which phrenology has attempted to embody in its organ of *ideality*—that sense which is the basis of all Cousin's dreams—that sense which speaks of GOD through his purest, if not his *sole* attribute—which proves, and which alone proves his existence.

To readers such as these—and only to such as these—must be left the decision of what the true Poesy is. And these—with *no* hesitation—will decide that the origin of Poetry lies in a thirst for a wilder Beauty than Earth supplies—that Poetry itself is the imperfect effort to quench this immortal thirst by novel combinations of beautiful forms (collocations of forms) physical or spiritual, and that this thirst when even partially allayed—this sentiment when even feebly meeting response—produces emotion to which all other human emotions are vapid and insignificant.

We shall now be fully understood. If, with Coleridge, who, however erring at times, was precisely the mind fitted to decide a question such as this—if, with him, we reject *passion* from the true—from the pure poetry—if we reject even passion—if we discard as feeble, as unworthy the high spirituality of the theme, (which has its origin in a sense of the Godhead,) if we dismiss even the nearly divine emotion of human *love*—that emotion which, merely to name, causes the pen to tremble—with how much greater reason shall we dismiss all else? And yet there are men who would mingle with the august theme the merest questions of expediency—the cant topics of the day—the doggerel æsthetics of the time—who would trammel the soul in its flight to an ideal Helusion, by the quirks and quibbles of chopped logic. There are men who do this—lately there are a set of men who make a practice of doing this—and who defend it on the score of the advancement of what they suppose to be *truth*. Truth is, in its own essence, sublime—but her loftiest sublimity, as derived from man's clouded and erratic reason, is valueless—is pulseless—is utterly ineffective when brought into comparison with the unerring *sense* of which we speak ; yet grant this *truth* to be all which its seekers and worshippers pretend—they forget that it is not truth, *per se*, which is made their thesis, but an *argumentation*, often maudlin and pedantic, always shallow and unsatisfactory (as from the mere inadaptation of the vehicle it *must* be) by which this *truth*, in casual and indeterminate glimpses, is—*or is not*—rendered manifest.

We have said that, in minor poetical efforts, we may tolerate some deflection from the true poetical thesis ; but when a man of the highest powers sets himself seriously to the task of constructing what shall be most worthy those powers, we expect that he shall so choose his theme as to render it certain that he labour not at disadvantage. We regret to see any trivial or partial imperfection of detail ; but we grieve deeply when we detect any radical error of conception.

In setting about *Orion*, Mr. Horne proposed to himself, (in accordance with the views of his junto) to " elaborate a morality "—he ostensibly proposed this to himself—for, in the depths of his heart, we *know* that he wished all juntos and all moralities in Erebus. In accordance with the notions of his *set*, however, he felt a species of shamefacedness in not making the enforcement of some certain dogmas or doctrines (questionable or unquestionable) about PROGRESS, the obvious or apparent object of his poem. This shamefacedness is the cue to the concluding sentence of the Preface. " Meantime, the design of this poem of *Orion* is far from being intended as a mere echo or reflection of the past, and is, in itself, and in other respects, a novel experiment upon the mind of a nation." Mr. Horne conceived, in fact, that to compose a poem merely for that poem's sake—and to acknowledge such to be his purpose— would be to subject himself to the charge of imbecility —of triviality—of deficiency in the true dignity and force ; but, had he listened to the dictates of his own soul, he could not have failed to perceive, at once, that under the sun there exists no work more intrinsically noble, than this very poem *written solely for the poem's sake.*

But let us regard *Orion* as it is. It has an under and an upper current of meaning ; in other words, it is an allegory. But the poet's sense of fitness (which, under no circumstances of mere conventional opinion, could be more than half subdued) has so far softened this allegory as to keep it, generally, well subject to the ostensible narrative. The purport of the moral conveyed is by no means clear—showing conclusively that the heart of the poet was not with it. It vacillates. At one time a certain set of opinions predominate—then another. We may generalize the subject, however, by calling it a homily against supineness or apathy in the cause of human PROGRESS, and in favour of energetic action for the good of the race. This is precisely *the* IDEA of the present school of canters. How feebly the case is made out in the poem—how insufficient has been all Mr. Horne's poetical rhetoric in convincing even himself—may be gleaned from the unusual bombast, rigmarole, and mystification of the con- cluding paragraph, in which he has thought it necessary to say something *very* profound, by way of putting the sting to his epigram,—the point to his moral. The words put us much in mind of the " nonsense verses " of Du Bartas.

> And thus, in the end each soul may to itself,
> With truth before it as its polar guide,
> Become both Time and Nature, whose fixt paths
> Are spiral, and when lost will find new stars,
> And in the universal MOVEMENT join.

The upper current of the theme is based upon the various Greek fables about Orion. The author, in his brief preface, speaks about "writing from an old Greek fable"—but his story is, more properly, a very judicious selection and modification of a great variety of Greek and Roman fables concerning Orion and other personages with whom these fables bring Orion in collision. And here we have only to object that the really magnificent abilities of Mr. Horne might have been better employed in an entirely original conception. The story he tells is beautiful indeed,—and *nil tetigit*, certainly, *quod non ornavit*—but our memories—our classic recollections are continually at war with his claims to regard, and we too often find ourselves rather speculating upon what he might have done, than admiring what he has really accomplished.

The narrative, as our poet has arranged it, runs nearly thus : Orion, hunting on foot amid the mountains of Chios, encounters Artemis (Diana) with her train. The goddess, at first indignant at the giant's intrusion upon her grounds, becomes, in the second place, enamoured. Her pure love spiritualizes the merely animal nature of Orion, but does not render him happy. He is filled with vague aspirations and desires. He buries himself in sensual pleasures. In the mad dreams of intoxication, he beholds a vision of Merope, the daughter of Œnopion, king of Chios. She is the type of physical beauty. She cries in his ear, " Depart from Artemis ! She loves thee not—thou art too full of earth." Awaking, he seeks the love of Merope. It is returned. Œnopion, dreading the giant and his brethren, yet scorning his pretensions, temporizes. He consents to bestow upon Orion the hand of Merope, on condition of the island being cleared, within six days, of its savage beasts and serpents. Orion, seeking the aid of his brethren, accomplishes the task. Œnopion again hesitates. Enraged, the giants make war upon him, and carry off the princess. In a

remote grove Orion lives, in bliss, with his earthly
love. From this delirium of happiness, he is aroused
by the vengeance of Œnopion, who causes him to
be surprised while asleep, and deprived of sight.
The princess, being retaken, immediately forgets and
deserts her lover, who, in his wretchedness, seeks,
at the suggestion of a shepherd, the aid of Eos
(Aurora), who, also becoming enamoured of him,
restores his sight. The love of Eos, less earthly
than that of Merope, less cold than that of Artemis,
fully satisfies his soul. He is at length happy. But
the jealousy of Artemis destroys him. She pierces
him with her arrows while in the very act of grate-
fully renovating her temple at Delos. In despair,
Eos flies to Artemis, reproves her, represents to her
the baseness of her jealousy and revenge, softens
her, and obtains her consent to unite with herself—
with Eos—in a prayer to Zeus (Jupiter) for the
restoration of the giant to life. The prayer is heard.
Orion is not only restored to life, but rendered
immortal, and placed among the constellations, where
he enjoys for ever the pure affection of Eos, and
becomes extinguished, each morning, in her rays.

In ancient mythology, the giants are meant to
typify various energies of Nature. Pursuing, we
suppose, this idea, Mr. Horne has made his own
giants represent certain principles of human action
or passion. Thus Orion himself is the Worker or
Builder, and is the type of Action or Movement
itself—but, in various portions of the poem, this
allegorical character is left out of sight, and that
of speculative philosophy takes its place ; a mere
consequence of the general uncertainty of purpose,
which is the chief defect of the work. Sometimes
we even find Orion a Destroyer in place of a Builder
—as, for example, when he destroys the grove about
the temple of Artemis, at Delos. Here he usurps
the proper allegorical attribute of Rhexergon, (the
second of the seven giants named,) who is the
Breaker-down, typifying the Revolutionary Principle.

Autarces, the third, represents the Mob, or, more strictly, Waywardness—Capricious Action. Harpax, the fourth, serves for Rapine—Briastor, the fifth, for Brute Force—Encolyon, the sixth, the "Chainer of the Wheel," for Conservatism—and Akinetos, the seventh, and most elaborated, for Apathy. He is termed "The Great Unmoved," and in his mouth is put all the "worldly wisdom," or selfishness, of the tale. The philosophy of Akinetos is, that no merely human exertion has any appreciable effect upon the *Movement*; and it is amusing to perceive how this great *Truth* (for most sincerely do we hold it to be such) speaks out from the real heart of the poet, through his Akinetos, in spite of all endeavour to overthrow it by the example of the brighter fate of Orion.

The death of Akinetos is a singularly forcible and poetic conception, and will serve to show how the giants are made to perish, generally, during the story, in agreement with their allegorical natures. The "Great Unmoved" quietly seats himself in a cave after the death of all his brethren, except Orion.

Thus Akinetos sat from day to day,
Absorbed in indolent sublimity,
Reviewing thoughts and knowledge o'er and o'er;
And now he spake, now sang unto himself,
Now sank to brooding silence. From above,
While passing, Time the rock touch'd, and it oozed
Petrific drops—gently at first and slow.
Reclining lonely in his fixed repose,
The Great Unmoved unconsciously became
Attached to that he pressed; and soon a part
Of the rock. *There clung th' excrescence, till strong hands,*
Descended from Orion, made large roads,
And built steep walls, squaring down rocks for use.

The italicized conclusion of this fine passage affords an instance, however, of a very blameable concision, too much affected throughout the poem.

In the deaths of Autarces, Harpax, and Encolyon, we recognize the same exceeding vigour of conception. These giants conspire against Orion, who

seeks the aid of Artemis, who, in her turn, seeks the
assistance of Phoibos (Phœbus). The conspirators
are in a cave, with Orion.

> Now Phoibos thro' the cave
> Sent a broad ray! and lo! the solar beam
> Filled the great cave with radiance equable
> And not a cranny held one speck of shade.
> A moony halo round Orion came,
> As of some pure protecting influence,
> While with intense light glared the walls and roof,
> The heat increasing. The three giants stood
> With glazing eyes, fixed. Terribly the light
> Beat on the dazzled stone, and the cave hummed
> With reddening heat, till the red hair and beard
> Of Harpax showed no difference from the rest,
> Which once were iron-black. The sullen walls
> Then smouldered down to steady oven heat,
> Like that with care attain'd when bread has ceased
> Its streaming and displays an angry tan.
> The appalled faces of the giants showed
> Full consciousness of their immediate doom.
> And soon the cave a potter's furnace glow'd
> Or kiln for largest bricks, and thus remained
> The while Orion, in his halo clasped
> By some invisible power, beheld the clay
> Of these his early friends change. Life was gone,
> Now sank the heat—the cave-walls lost their glare,
> The red lights faded, and the halo pale
> Around him into chilly air expanded.
> There stood the three great images, in hue
> Of chalky white and red, like those strange shapes
> In Egypt's ancient tombs; but presently
> Each visage and each form with cracks and flaws
> Was seamed, and the lost countenance brake up,
> As, with brief toppling, forward prone they fell.

The deaths of Rhexergon and Biastor seem to
discard (and this we regret not) the allegorical
meaning altogether, but are related with even more
exquisite richness and delicacy of imagination, than
those of the other giants. Upon this occasion it is
the *jealousy* of Artemis which destroys.

> —— But with the eve
> Fatigue o'ercame the giants, and they slept.
> Dense were the rolling clouds, starless the glooms;
> But o'er a narrow rift, once drawn apart,
> Showing a field remote of violet hue,

R. H. Horne 257

The high Moon floated, and her downward gleam
Shone on the upturned giant faces. Rigid
Each upper feature, loose the nether jaw ;
Their arms cast wide with open palms ; their chests
Heaving like some large engine Near them lay
Their bloody clubs, with dust and hair begrimed,
Their spears and girdles, and the long-noosed thongs.
Artemis vanished ; all again was dark.
With day's first streak Orion rose, and loudly
To his companions called. But still they slept.
Again he shouted ; yet no limb they stirred,
Tho' scarcely seven strides distant. He approached,
And found the spot, so sweet with clover flower
When they had cast them down, was now arrayed
With many-headed poppies, like a crowd
Of dusky Ethiops in a magic cirque
Which had sprung up beneath them in the night,
And all entranced the air.

There are several minor defects in *Orion*, and we may as well mention them here. We sometimes meet with an instance of bad taste in a revolting picture or image ; for example, at page 59, of this edition :

Naught fearing, swift, brimful of raging life,
Stiffning they lay in pools of jellied gore.

Sometimes—indeed very often—we encounter an altogether purposeless oddness or foreignness of speech. For example, at page 78 :

As in Dodona once, ere driven thence
By Zeus *for that* Rhexergon burnt some oaks.

Mr. Horne will find it impossible to assign a good reason for not here using " because."

Pure *vaguenesses* of speech abound. For example, page 89 :

—— once central heart wherein
Time beats twin pulses with Humanity.

Now and then sentences are rendered needlessly obscure through mere involution—as at page 103 :

Star-rays that first played o'er my blinded orbs,
E'en as they glance above the lids of sleep,
Who else had never known surprise, nor hope,
Nor useful action.

Here the "who" has no grammatical antecedent, and would naturally be referred to sleep; whereas it is intended for "me," understood, or involved, in the pronoun "my"; as if the sentence were written thus—"rays that first played o'er the blinded orbs of me, who, etc." It is useless to dwell upon so pure an affectation.

The versification throughout is, generally, of a very remarkable excellence. At times, however, it is rough, to no purpose; as at page 44:

> And ever tended to some central point
> *In some place—nought more could I understand.*

And here, at page 81:

> The shadow of a stag stoops to the stream
> *Swift rolling toward the cataract, and drinks deeply.*

The above is an unintentional and false Alexandrine —including a foot too much, and that a trochee in place of an iambus. But here, at page 106, we have the utterly unjustifiable anomaly of half a foot too little:

> *And Eos ever rises circling*
> The varied regions of mankind, etc.

All these are mere inadvertences, of course; for the general handling of the rhythm shows the profound metrical sense of the poet. He is, perhaps, somewhat too fond of "making the sound an echo to the sense." *Orion* embodies some of the most remarkable instances of this on record; but if smoothness—if the true rhythm of a verse be sacrificed, the sacrifice is an error. The effect is only a beauty, we think, where *no* sacrifice is made in its behalf. It will be found possible to reconcile *all* the objects in view. Nothing can justify such lines as this, at page 69:

> As snake-songs midst stone hollows thus has taught me.

We might urge, as another minor objection, that all the giants are made to speak in the same manner

—with the same phraseology. Their characters are broadly distinctive, while their words are identical in spirit. There is sufficient individuality of sentiment, but little, or none, of language.

We *must* object, too, to the personal and political allusions—to the Corn-Law question, for example—to Wellington's statue, etc. These things, *of course*, have no business in a poem.

We will conclude our fault-finding with the remark that, as a consequence of the one radical error of conception upon which we have commented at length, the reader's attention, throughout, is painfully *diverted*. He is always pausing, amid poetical beauties, in the expectation of detecting among them some philosophical, allegorical moral. Of course, he does not fully, because he cannot uniquely, appreciate the beauties. The absolute necessity of re-perusing the poem, in order thoroughly to comprehend it, is also, most surely, to be regretted, and arises, likewise, from the one radical sin.

But of the *beauties* of this most remarkable poem, what shall we say? And here we find it a difficult task to be calm. And yet we have never been accused of enthusiastic encomium. It is our deliberate opinion that, in all that regards the loftiest and holiest attributes of the true Poetry, *Orion* has *never* been excelled. Indeed, we feel strongly inclined to say that it has never been *equalled*. Its imagination —that quality which is all in all—is of the most refined—the most elevating—the most august character. And here we deeply regret that the necessary limits of this review will prevent us from entering, at length, into specification. In reading the poem, we marked passage after passage for extract—but, in the end, we found that we had marked nearly every passage in the book. We can now do nothing more than select a few. This, from page 3, introduces Orion himself, and we quote it, not only as an instance of refined and picturesque imagination, but as evincing the high artistical skill

with which a scholar in spirit can paint an elaborate
picture by a few brief touches.

> The scene in front two sloping mountains' sides
> Displayed ; in shadow one and one in light.
> The loftiest on its summit now sustained
> The sun-beams, raying like a mighty wheel
> Half seen, which left the forward surface dark
> In its full breadth of shade ; the coming sun
> Hidden as yet behind ; the other mount,
> Slanting transverse, swept with an eastward face,
> Catching the golden light. Now while the peal
> Of the ascending chase told that the rout
> Still midway rent the thickets, suddenly
> Along the broad and sunny slope appeared
> *The shadow of a stag that fled across*
> *Followed by a giant's shadow with a spear.*

These shadows are those of the coming Orion and
his game. But who can fail to appreciate the intense
beauty of the heralding shadows ? Nor is this all.
This " Hunter of shadows, he himself a shade," is
made symbolical, or suggestive, throughout the
poem, of the speculative character of Orion ; and occa-
sionally, of his pursuit of visionary happiness. For
example, at page 81, Orion, possessed of Merope,
dwells with her in a remote and dense grove of
cedars. Instead of directly describing his attained
happiness—his perfected bliss—the poet, with an
exalted sense of Art, *for which we look utterly in vain
in any other poem*, merely introduces the image of
the tamed or subdued *shadow-stag*, quietly browsing
and drinking beneath the cedars.

> There, underneath the boughs, mark where the gleam
> Of sunrise thro' the roofing's chasm is thrown
> Upon a grassy plot below, whereon
> The shadow of a stag stoops to the stream,
> Swift rolling toward the cataract, and drinks.
> Throughout the day unceasingly it drinks,
> While ever and anon the nightingale,
> Not waiting for the evening, swells his hymn—
> His one sustained and heaven-aspiring tone—
> And when the sun hath vanished utterly,
> Arm over arm the cedars spread their shade,

With arching wrist and long extended hands,
And grave-ward fingers lengthening in the moon,
Above that shadowy stag whose antlers still
Hung o'er the stream.

There is nothing more richly—more weirdly—more chastely—more sublimely imaginative—in the wide realm of poetical literature. It will be seen that we *have* enthusiasm—but we reserve it for pictures such as this

At page 62, Orion, his brethren dead, is engaged alone in extirpating the beasts from Chios. In the passages we quote, observe, in the beginning, the singular *lucidness* of detail ; the arrangement of the barriers, etc., by which the hunter accomplishes his purpose, is given in a dozen lines of verse, with far more perspicuity than ordinary writers could give it in as many pages of prose. In this species of narration Mr. Horne is approached only by Moore in his *Alciphron*. In the latter portions of our extract, observe the vivid picturesqueness of the description.

Four days remain. Fresh trees he felled and wove
More barriers and fences ; inaccessible
To fiercest charge of droves, and to o'erleap
Impossible. These walls he so arranged
That to a common centre each should force
The flight of those pursued ; and from that centre
Diverged three outlets. One, the wide expanse
Which from the rocks and inland forests led ;
One was the clear-skyed windy gap above
A precipice ; the third, a long ravine
Which through steep slopes, down to the seashore ran
Winding, and then direct into the sea.

Two days remain. Orion, in each hand
Waving a torch, his course at night began,
Through wildest haunts and lairs of savage beasts.
With long-drawn howl, before him trooped the wolves—
The panthers, terror-stricken, and the bears
With wonder and gruff rage ; from desolate crags,
Leering hyenas, griffin, hippogrif,
Skulked, or sprang madly, as the tossing brands
Flashed through the midnight nooks and hollows cold,
Sudden as fire from flint ; o'er crashing thickets,
With crouched head and curled fangs dashed the wild boar,

Gnashing forth on with reckless impulses,
While the clear-purposed fox crept closely down
Into the underwood, to let the storm,
Whate'er its cause, pass over.   Through dark fens,
Marshes, green rushy swamps, and margins reedy,
Orion held his way—and rolling shapes
Of serpent and of dragon moved before him
With high-reared crests, swan-like yet terrible,
And often looking back with gem-like eyes.

All night Orion urged his rapid course
In the vex'd rear of the swift-droving din,
And when the dawn had peered, the monsters all
Were hemmed in barriers.   These he now o'erheaped
With fuel through the day, and when again
Night darkened, and the sea a gulf-like voice
Sent forth, the barriers at all points he fired,
Mid prayers to Hephæstos and his Ocean-Sire.
Soon as the flames had eaten out a gap
In the great barrier fronting the ravine
That ran down to the sea, Orion grasped
Two blazing boughs; one high in air he raised,
The other, *with its roaring foliage trailed*
Behind him as he sped.   Onward the droves
Of frantic creatures with one impulse rolled
Before this night-devouring thing of flames,
With multitudinous voice and downward sweep
Into the sea, which now first knew a tide,
And, ere they made one effort to regain
The shore, had caught them in its flowing arms,
And bore them past all hope.   The living mass,
Dark heaving o'er the waves resistlessly,
At length, in distance, seemed a circle small,
Midst which one creature in the centre rose,
Conspicuous in the long, red quivering gleams
That from the dying brands streamed o'er the waves.
It was the oldest dragon of the fens,
Whose forky flag-wings and horn-crested head
O'er crags and marshes regal sway had held:
And now he rose up like an embodied curse,
From all the doomed, fast sinking—some just sunk—
Looked landward o'er the sea, and flapped his vans,
Until Poseidon drew them swirling down.

Poseidon (Neptune) is Orion's father, and lends
him his aid.   The first line italicized is an example
of sound made echo to sense.   The rest we have
merely emphasized as peculiarly imaginative.

At page 9 Orion thus describes a palace built by him for Hephæstos (Vulcan).

> But, ere a shadow-hunter I became—
> A dreamer of strange dreams by day and night—
> For him I built a palace underground,
> Of iron, black and rough as his own hands.
> Deep in the groaning disemboweled earth,
> The tower-broad pillars and huge stanchions,
> And slant supporting wedges I set up,
> Aided by the Cyclops who obeyed my voice,
> *Which through the metal fabric rang and pealed*
> *In orders echoing far, like thunder-dreams.*
> With arches, galleries and domes all carved—
> *So that great figures started from the roof*
> *And lofty coignes, or sat and downward gazed*
> *On those who stood below and gazed above—*
> I filled it; in the centre framed a hall;
> Central in that, a throne; *and for the light,*
> *Forged mighty hammers that should rise and fall*
> *On slanted rocks of granite and of flint,*
> *Worked by a torrent, for whose passage down*
> *A chasm I hewed. And here the God could take,*
> *Midst showery sparks and swathes of broad gold fire,*
> *His lone repose, lulled by the sounds he loved :*
> *Or, casting back the hammer-heads till they choked*
> *The water's course, enjoy, if so he wished,*
> *Midnight tremendous, silence, and iron sleep.*

The description of the Hell in *Paradise Lost* is *altogether inferior* in graphic effect, in originality, in expression, in the true imagination—to these magnificent—to these unparalleled passages. For this assertion there are tens of thousands who will condemn us as heretical ; but there are a " chosen few " who will feel, in their inmost souls, the simple truth of the assertion. The former class would at least be silent, could they form even a remote conception of *that* contempt with which we hearken to their conventional jargon.

We have room for no further extracts of length ; but we refer the reader who shall be so fortunate as to procure a copy of *Orion*, to a passage at page 22, commencing

> One day at noontide, when the chase was done.

It is descriptive of a group of lolling hounds, intermingled with sylvans, fawns, nymphs, and oceanides. We refer him also to page 25, where Orion, enamoured of the naked beauty of Artemis, is repulsed and *frozen* by her dignity. These lines end thus:

> And ere the last collected shape he saw
> Of Artemis, dispersing fast amid
> Dense vapoury clouds, the aching wintriness
> Had risen to his teeth, and fixed his eyes,
> Like glistening stones in the congealing air.

We refer, especially, too, to the description of *Love*, at page 29; to that of a Bacchanalian orgie, at page 34; to that of drought succeeded by rain, at page 70; and to that of the palace of Eos, at page 104.

Mr. Horne has a very peculiar and very delightful faculty of enforcing, or giving vitality to a picture, by some one vivid and intensely characteristic point or touch. He seizes the most salient feature of his theme, and makes this feature convey the whole. The combined *naïveté* and picturesqueness of some of the passages thus enforced cannot be sufficiently admired. For example:

> The archers soon
> *With bow-arm forward thrust*, on all sides twanged
> Around, above, below.

Now, it is this thrusting forward of the bow-arm which is the idiosyncrasy of the action of a mass of archers. Again: Rhexergon and his friends endeavour to persuade Akinetos to be king. Observe the silent refusal of Akinetos—the peculiar *passiveness* of his action—if we may be permitted the paradox.

> " Rise, therefore, Akinetos, thou art king."
> So saying, in his hand he placed a spear.
> *As though against a wall 'twere sent aslant,*
> *Flatly the long spear fell upon the ground.*

Here again: Merope departs from Chios in a ship.

And, as it sped along, she closely pressed
The rich globes of her bosom on the side
O'er which she bent with those black eyes, and gazed
Into the sea *that fled beneath her face.*

The fleeing of the sea beneath the face of one who gazes into it from a ship's side is the idiosyncrasy of action—of the subject. It is that which chiefly impresses the gazer.

We conclude with some brief quotations at random, which we shall not pause to classify. Their merits need no demonstration. They *gleam* with the purest imagination. They abound in picturesqueness—force—happily chosen epithets, each in itself a picture. They are redolent of all for which a poet will value a poem.

—— her silver sandals glanc'd i' the rays,
As doth a lizard playing on a hill,
And on the spot where she that instant stood
Naught but the bent and quivering grass was seen.

Above the Isle of Chios, night by night,
The clear moon lingered ever on her course
Covering the forest foliage, where it swept
In its unbroken breadth along the slopes,
With placid silver ; edging leaf and trunk
Where gloom clung deep around ; but chiefly sought
With melancholy splendour to illume
The dark-mouthed caverns where Orion lay,
Dreaming among his kinsmen.

The ocean realm below, and all its caves
And bristling vegetation, plant and flower,
And forests in their dense petrific shade
Where the tides moan for sleep that never comes.

A fawn, who on a quiet green knoll sat
Somewhat apart, sang a melodious ode,
Made rich by harmonies of hidden strings.

Autarces seized a satyr, with intent,
Despite his writhing freaks and furious face,
To dash him on a gong, but that amidst
The struggling mass Encolyon thrust a pine,
Heavy and black as Charon's ferrying pole,
O'er which they, *like a bursting billow,* fell. . . .

—— then round the blaze,
Their shadows brandishing afar and athwart,
Over the level space and up the hills,
Six giants held portentous dance. . . .

his safe return
To corporal sense, by shaking off these nets
Of moonbeams from his soul. . . .

—— old memories
Slumbrously hung above the purple line
Of distance, to the East, while odorously
Glistened the tear-drops of a new-fall'n shower. . . .

Sing on !
Sing on, great tempest ! in the darkness sing !
Thy madness is a music that brings calm
Into my central soul ; and from its waves
That now with joy begin to heave and gush,
The burning image of all life's desire,
Like an absorbing, fire breathed, phantom god,
Rises and floats ! here touching on the foam,
There hovering o'er it ; *ascending swift*
Starward, then swooping down the hemisphere
Upon the lengthening javelins of the blast ! . . .

Now a sound we heard,
Like to some well-known voice in prayer ; and next
An iron clang *that* seemed to break great bonds
Beneath the earth, shook us to conscious life. . . .

It is Oblivion ! In his hand—though naught
Knows he of this—a dusky purple flower
Droops over its tall stem. Again ! ah see !
He wanders into mist and now is lost !—
Within his brain what lovely realms of death
Are pictured, *and what knowledge through the doors*
Of his forgetfulness of all the earth
A path may gain ?

But we are positively forced to conclude. It was
our design to give *Orion* a careful and methodical
analysis—thus to bring clearly forth its multitudinous
beauties to the eye of the American public. Our
limits have constrained us to treat it in an imper-
fect and cursory manner. We have had to content
ourselves chiefly with assertion, where our original
purpose was to demonstrate. We have left unsaid

a hundred things which a well-grounded enthusiasm would have prompted us to say. One thing, however, we must and will say, in conclusion. *Orion* will be admitted, by every man of genius, to be one of the noblest, if not the very noblest poetical work of the age. Its defects are trivial and conventional—its beauties intrinsic and *supreme*.

LONGFELLOW'S BALLADS [1]

"*Il y à parier,*" says Chamfort, "*que toute idée publique, toute convention reçue, est une sottise, car elle a convenue au plus grand nombre.*"—One would be safe in wagering that any given public idea is erroneous, for it has been yielded to the clamour of the majority ;—and this strictly philosophical, although somewhat French assertion, has especial bearing upon the whole race of what are termed maxims and popular proverbs ; nine-tenths of which are the quintessence of folly. One of the most deplorably false of them is the antique adage, *De gustibus non est disputandum*—there should be no disputing about taste. Here the idea designed to be conveyed is that any one person has as just right to consider his own taste *the true*, as has any one other—that taste itself, in short, is an arbitrary something, amenable to no law, and measurable by no definite rules. It must be confessed, however, that the exceedingly vague and impotent treatises which are alone extant, have much to answer for as regards confirming the general error. Not the least important service which, hereafter, mankind will owe to *Phrenology*, may, perhaps, be recognized in an analysis of the real principles, and a digest of the resulting laws of taste. These principles,

---

[1] *Ballads and other Poems.* By Henry Wadsworth Longfellow, Author of *Voices of the Night, Hyperion*, etc. Second Edition. John Owen : Cambridge.

in fact, are as clearly traceable, and these laws as readily susceptible of system, as are any whatever.

In the meantime, the insane adage above mentioned is in no respect more generally, more stupidly, and more pertinaciously quoted than by the admirers of what is termed the "good old Pope," or the "good old Goldsmith school" of poetry, in reference to the bolder, more natural, and *more ideal* compositions of such authors as Coëtlogon and Lamartine [1] in France; Herder, Körner, and Uhland in Germany; Brun and Baggesen in Denmark; Bellman, Tegnér, and Nyberg [2] in Sweden; Keats, Shelley, Coleridge, and Tennyson in England; Lowell and Longfellow in America. "*De gustibus non,*" say these "good-old-school" fellows; and we have no doubt that their mental translation of the phrase is—"We pity your taste—we pity everybody's taste but our own."

It is our purpose to controvert the popular idea that the poets just mentioned owe to novelty, to trickeries of expression, and to other meretricious effects, their appreciation by certain readers :—to demonstrate (for the matter is susceptible of demonstration) that such poetry and *such alone* has fulfilled the legitimate office of the muse; has thoroughly satisfied an earnest and unquenchable desire existing in the heart of man.

This volume of Ballads and Tales includes, with several brief original pieces, a translation from the Swedish of Tegnér. In attempting (what never should be attempted) a literal version of both the words and the metre of this poem, Professor Longfellow has failed to do justice either to his author or himself. He has striven to do what no man ever did well, and what, from the nature of language itself, never *can* be well done. Unless, for example, we shall come to have an influx of *spondees* in our English tongue, it will always be impossible to

[1] We allude here chiefly to the *David* of Coëtlogon, and *only* to the *Chute d'un Ange* of Lamartine.

[2] C. Julia Nyberg, author of the *Dikter von Euphrosyne.*

construct an English hexameter. Our spondees, or, we should say, our spondaic words, are rare. In the Swedish they are nearly as abundant as in the Latin and Greek. We have only " *compound,*" " *context,*" " *footfall,*" and a few other similar ones. This is the difficulty ; and that it *is* so will become evident upon reading *The Children of the Lord's Supper,* where the sole *readable* verses are those in which we meet with the rare spondaic dissyllables. We mean to say *readable as hexameters ;* for many of them will read very well as mere English dactylics with certain irregularities.

Much as we admire the genius of Mr. Longfellow, we are fully sensible of his many errors of affectation and imitation. His artistical skill is great, and his ideality high. But his conception of the *aims* of poesy *is all wrong* ; and this we shall prove at some future day—to our own satisfaction, at least. His didactics are all *out of place.* He has written brilliant poems—by accident ; that is to say when permitting his genius to get the better of his conventional habit of thinking—a habit deduced from German study. We do not mean to say that a didactic moral may not be well made the *under-current* of a poetical thesis ; but that it can never be well put so obtrusively forth, as in the majority of his compositions. . . .

We have said that Mr. Longfellow's conception of the *aims* of poesy is erroneous ; and that thus, labouring at a disadvantage, he does violent wrong to his own high powers ; and now the question is, what *are* his ideas of the aims of the Muse, as we gather these ideas from the *general* tendency of his poems ? It will be at once evident that, imbued with the peculiar spirit of German song (in pure conventionality) he regards the inculcation of a *moral* as essential. Here we find it necessary to repeat that we have reference only to the *general* tendency of his compositions`; for there are some magnificent exceptions, where, as if by accident, he has permitted his genius to get the better of his conventional prejudice. But didacticism is the prevalent *tone* of his song. His invention, his imagery, his all, is made subservient to the elucidation of some one or more points (but rarely of more than one) which he looks upon as *truth*. And that this mode of procedure will find stern defenders should never excite surprise, so long as the world is full to overflowing with cant and conventicles. There are men who will scramble on all fours through the muddiest sloughs of vice to pick up a single apple of virtue. There are things called men who, so long as the sun rolls, will greet with snuffling huzzas every figure that takes upon itself the semblance of truth, even although the figure, in itself only a " stuffed Paddy," be as much out of place as a toga on the statue of Washington, or out of season as rabbits in the days of the dog-star. . . .

We say this with little fear of contradiction. Yet the spirit of our assertion must be more heeded than the letter. Mankind have *seemed* to define Poesy in a thousand, and in a thousand conflicting definitions. But the war is one only of words. Induction is as well applicable to this subject as to the most palpable and utilitarian ; and by its sober processes we find that, in respect to compositions which have been really received as poems, the *imaginative*, or, more popularly, the creative portions *alone* have ensured them to be so received. Yet these works, on account of these portions, having once been so received and so named, it has happened, naturally and inevitably, that other portions totally unpoetic have not only come to be regarded by the popular voice as poetic, but have been made to serve as false standards of perfection, in the adjustment of other poetical claims. Whatever has been found in whatever has been received as a poem has been blindly regarded as *ex statû* poetic. And this is a species of gross error which scarcely could have made its way into any less intangible topic. In fact that licence which appertains to the Muse herself, it has been thought decorous, if not sagacious to indulge, in all examination of her character. . . .

Poesy is a response—unsatisfactory it is true—but still in some measure a response, to a natural and irrepressible demand. Man being what he is, the time could never have been in which Poesy was not. Its first element is the thirst for supernal BEAUTY —a beauty which is not afforded the soul by any existing collocation of earth's forms—a beauty which, perhaps, *no possible* combination of these forms would fully produce. Its second element is the attempt to satisfy this thirst by *novel* combinations among those forms of beauty which already exist—or by novel combinations *of those combinations which our predecessors, toiling in chase of the same phantom, have already set in order*. We thus clearly deduce the *novelty*, the *originality*, the *invention*, the *imagination*, or lastly the *creation* of BEAUTY, (for the terms as here employed are synonymous,) as the essence of all Poesy. Nor is this idea so much at variance with ordinary opinion as, at first sight, it may appear. A multitude of antique dogmas on this topic will be found, when divested of extrinsic speculation, to be easily resoluble into the definition now proposed. We do nothing more than present tangibly the vague clouds of the world's idea. We recognize the idea itself floating, unsettled, indefinite, in every attempt which has yet been made to circumscribe the conception of " Poesy " in words. A striking instance of this is observable in the fact that no definition exists, in which either " the beautiful," or some one of those qualities which we have above designated synonymously with " creation," has not been pointed out as the *chief* attribute of the Muse. " Invention," however, or " imagination," is by far more commonly insisted upon. The word ποιησις itself (creation) speaks volumes upon this point. Neither will it be amiss here to mention Count Bielfeld's definition of poetry as " *L'art d'exprimer les pensées par la fiction.*" With this definition (of which the philosophy is

profound to a certain extent) the German terms
Dichthunst, the art of fiction, and *Dichten*, to feign,
which are used for " *poetry* " and " *to make verses*,"
are in full and remarkable accordance. It is, never-
theless, in the *combination* of the two omni-prevalent
ideas that the novelty, and, we believe, the force of
our own proposition is to be found. . . .

The elements of that beauty, which is felt in sound,
may be the mutual or common heritage of Earth and
Heaven. Contenting ourselves with the firm con-
viction, that music (in its modifications of rhythm
and rhyme) is of so vast a moment to Poesy, as
never to be neglected by him who is truly poetical—
is of so mighty a force in furthering the great aim
intended, that he is mad who rejects its assistance—
content with this idea we shall not pause to maintain
its absolute essentiality, for the mere sake of round-
ing a definition. That our definition of poetry will
necessarily exclude much of what, through a supine
toleration, has been hitherto ranked as poetical, is
a matter which affords us not even momentary
concern. We address but the thoughtful, and heed
only their approval—with our own. If our sug-
gestions are truthful, then " after many days " shall
they be understood as truth, even though found in
contradiction of *all* that has been hitherto so under-
stood. If false, shall we not be the first to bid
them die ?

We would reject, of course, all such matters as
Armstrong on Health, a revolting production ; Pope's
Essay on Man, which may well be content with the
title of an " Essay in Rhyme " ; *Hudibras* and other
merely humorous pieces. We do not gainsay the
peculiar merits of either of these latter compositions
—but deny them the position held. In a notice of
Brainard's Poems, we took occasion to show that the
common use of a certain instrument, (rhythm,) had
tended, more than aught else, to confound humorous
verse with poetry. The observation is now recalled
to corroborate what we have just said in respect to

the vast effect or force of melody in itself—an effect which could elevate into even momentary confusion with the highest efforts of mind, compositions such as are the greater number of satires or burlesques. . . .

We have shown our ground of objection to the general *themes* of Professor Longfellow. In common with all who claim the sacred title of poet, he should limit his endeavours to the creation of novel moods of beauty, in form, in colour, in sound, in sentiment; for over all this wide range has the poetry of words dominion. To what the world terms *prose* may be safely and properly left all else. The artist who doubts of his thesis may always resolve his doubt by the single question—" might not this matter be as well or better handled in *prose?*" If it *may*, then is it no subject for the Muse. In the general acceptation of the term *Beauty* we are content to rest; being careful only to suggest that, in our peculiar views, it must be understood as inclusive of *the sublime*.

Of the pieces which constitute the present volume, there are not more than one or two thoroughly fulfilling the ideas we have proposed; although the volume, as a whole, is by no means so chargeable with didacticism as Mr. Longfellow's previous book. We would mention as poems *nearly true, The Village Blacksmith; The Wreck of the Hesperus*, and especially *The Skeleton in Armour*. In the first-mentioned we have the *beauty* of simple-mindedness as a genuine thesis; and this thesis is inimitably handled until the concluding stanza, where the spirit of legitimate poesy is aggrieved in the pointed antithetical deduction of a *moral* from what has gone before. In *The Wreck of the Hesperus* we have the *beauty* of child-like confidence and innocence, with that of the father's stern courage and affection. But, with slight exception, those particulars of the storm here detailed are not poetic subjects. Their thrilling *horror* belongs to prose, in which it could be far more effectively discussed, as Professor Longfellow may assure himself

at any moment by experiment. There *are* points of
a tempest which afford the loftiest and truest poetical
themes— points in which pure beauty is found, or,
better still, beauty heightened into the sublime, by
terror. But when we read, among other similar
things, that

> The salt sea was frozen on her breast,
> The salt tears in her eyes,

we feel, if not positive disgust, at least a chilling sense
of the inappropriate. In the *Skeleton in Armour*
we find a pure and perfect thesis artistically treated.
We find the beauty of bold courage and self-confidence,
of love and maiden devotion, of reckless adventure,
and finally of life-contemning grief. Combined with
all this, we have numerous *points* of beauty apparently
insulated, but all aiding the main effect or impression.
The heart is stirred, and the mind does not lament
its mal-instruction. The metre is simple, sonorous,
well-balanced, and fully adapted to the subject.
Upon the whole, there are few truer poems than
this. It has but one defect—an important one.
The prose remarks prefacing the narrative are really
necessary. But every work of art should contain
within itself all that is requisite for its own com-
prehension. And this remark is especially true of
the ballad. In poems of magnitude the mind of
the reader is not, at all times, enabled to include,
in one comprehensive survey, the proportions and
proper adjustment of the whole. He is pleased, if
at all, with particular passages ; and the sum of
his pleasure is compounded of the sums of the
pleasurable sentiments inspired by these individual
passages in the progress of perusal. But, in pieces
of less extent, the pleasure is *unique*, in the proper
acceptation of this term—the understanding is
employed, without difficulty, in the contemplation
of the picture *as a whole* ; and thus its effect will
depend, in great measure, upon the perfection of
its finish, upon the nice adaptation of its constituent

parts, and especially, upon what is rightly termed by Schlegel *the unity or totality of interest*. But the practice of prefixing explanatory passages is utterly at variance with such unity. By the prefix, we are either put in possession of the subject of the poem, or some hint, historic fact, or suggestion, is thereby afforded, not included in the body of the piece, which, without the hint, is incomprehensible. In the latter case, while perusing the poem, the reader must revert, in mind at least, to the prefix, for the necessary explanation. In the former, the poem being a mere paraphrase of the prefix, the interest is divided between the prefix and the paraphrase. In either instance the totality of effect is destroyed.

Of the other original poems in the volume before us, there is none in which the aim of instruction, or *truth*, has not been too obviously substituted for the legitimate aim, *beauty*. We have heretofore taken occasion to say that a didactic moral might be happily made the *under-current* of a poetical theme, and we have treated this point at length, in a review of Moore's *Alciphron* ; but the moral thus conveyed is invariably an ill effect when obtruding beyond the upper-current of the thesis itself. Perhaps the worst specimen of this obtrusion is given us by our poet in *Blind Bartimeus* and *The Goblet of Life*, where it will be observed that the *sole* interest of the upper-current of meaning depends upon its relation or reference to the under. What we read upon the surface would be *vox et preterea nihil* in default of the moral beneath. The Greek *finales* of *Blind Bartimeus* are an affectation altogether inexcusable. What the small, second-hand, Gibbonish pedantry of Byron introduced, is unworthy the imitation of Longfellow.

Of the translations we scarcely think it necessary to speak at all. We regret that our poet will persist in busying himself about such matters. *His* time might be better employed in original conception. Most of these versions are marked with the error upon which we have commented. This error is in fact essentially Germanic. *The Luck of Edenhall*, however, is a truly beautiful poem ; and we say this with all that deference which the opinion of the *Democratic Review* demands. This composition appears to us *one of the very finest*. It has all the free, hearty, *obvious* movement of the true ballad-legend. The greatest force of language is combined in it with the richest imagination, acting in its most legitimate province. Upon the whole, we prefer it even to the *Sword-Song* of Körner. The pointed moral with which it terminates is so exceedingly natural—so perfectly fluent from the incidents—that we have hardly heart to pronounce it in ill taste. We may observe of this ballad, in conclusion, that its subject is more *physical* than is usual in Germany. Its images are rich rather in physical than in moral beauty. And this tendency, in Song, is the true one. It is chiefly, if we are not mistaken—it is chiefly amid forms of physical loveliness (we use the word *forms* in its widest sense as embracing modifications of sound and colour) that the soul seeks the realization of its dreams of BEAUTY. It is to her demand in this sense especially that the poet, who is wise, will most frequently and most earnestly respond.

The Children of the Lord's Supper is, beyond doubt, a true and most beautiful poem in great part, while, in some particulars, it is too metaphysical to have any pretension to the name. We have already objected, briefly, to its metre—the ordinary Latin or Greek Hexameter—dactyls and spondees at random, with a spondee in conclusion. We maintain that the hexameter can never be introduced into our language, from the nature of that language itself. This rhythm d mands, *for English ears*, a preponderance of natural spondees. Our tongue has few. Not only does the Latin and Greek, with the Swedish, and some others, abound in them ; but the Greek and Roman ear had become reconciled (why or how

is unknown) to the reception of artificial spondees—
that is to say, spondaic words formed partly of one
word and partly of another, or from an excised part
of one word. In short, the ancients were content
to read *as they scanned*, or nearly so. It may be
safely prophesied that we shall never do this ; and
thus we shall never admit English hexameters. The
attempt to introduce them, after the repeated failures
of Sir Philip Sidney, and others, is perhaps, some-
what discreditable to the scholarship of Professor
Longfellow. The *Democratic Review,* in saying that
he has triumphed over difficulties in this rhythm,
has been deceived, it is evident, by the facility with
which some of these verses may be read.   In glancing
over the poems, we do not observe a single verse
which can be read, *to English ears, as a Greek hexa-
meter.* There are many, however, which can be well
read as mere English dactylic verses ; such, for
example, as the well-known lines of Byron, com-
mencing

Know ye the | land where the | cypress and | myrtle.

These lines (although full of irregularities) are, in
their perfection, formed of three dactyls and a cæsura
—just as if we should cut short the initial verse of
the *Bucolics* thus—

Tityre | tu patu | læ recu | bans—

The " myrtle," at the close of Byron's line, is a
double rhyme, and must be understood as one
syllable.

Now a great number of Professor Longfellow's
hexameters are merely these dactylic lines, *continued
for two feet.* For example—

Whispered the | race of the | flowers and | merry on |
    balancing | branches.

In this example, also " branches," which is a
double ending, must be regarded as the cæsura, or
one syllable, of which alone it has the force.

As we have already alluded, in one or two regards, to a notice of these poems which appeared in the *Democratic Review*, we may as well here proceed with some few further comments upon the article in question —with whose general tenor we are happy to agree.

The *Review* speaks of *Maidenhood* as a poem, " not to be understood but at the expense of more time and trouble than a song can justly claim." We are scarcely less surprised at this opinion from Mr. Langtree than we were at the condemnation of *The Luck of Edenhall.*

Maidenhood is faulty, it appears to us, only on the score of its theme, which is somewhat didactic. Its *meaning* seems simplicity itself. A maiden on the verge of womanhood, hesitating to enjoy life (for which she has a strong appetite) through a false idea of duty, is bidden to fear nothing, having purity of heart as her lion of Una.

What Mr. Langtree styles " an unfortunate peculiarity " in Mr. Longfellow, resulting from " adherence to a false system," has really been always regarded by us as one of his idiosyncratic merits. " In each poem," says the critic, " he has but *one* idea, which, in the progress of his song, is gradually unfolded, and at last reaches its full development in the concluding lines ; this singleness of thought might lead a harsh critic to suspect intellectual barrenness." It leads *us*, individually, only to a full sense of the artistical power and knowledge of the poet. We confess that now, for the first time, we hear unity of conception objected to as a defect. But Mr. Langtree seems to have fallen into the singular error of supposing the poet to have absolutely *but one idea* in each of his ballads. Yet how " one idea " can be " gradually unfolded " without other ideas, is, to us, a mystery of mysteries. Mr. Longfellow, very properly, has but one *leading* idea which forms the basis of his poem ; but to the aid and development of this one there are innumerable others, of which the rare excellence is, that all are in keeping, that none could be well omitted, that each tends to the one general effect. It is unnecessary to say another word upon this topic.

In speaking of *Excelsior*, Mr. Langtree (are we wrong in attributing the notice to his very forcible pen ?) seems to labour under some similar misconception. " It carries along with it," says he, " a false moral which greatly diminishes its merit in our eyes. The great merit of a picture, whether made with the pencil or pen, is its *truth* ; and this merit does not belong to Mr. Longfellow's sketch. Men of genius may, and probably do, meet with greater difficulties in their struggles with the world than their fellow-men who are less highly gifted ; but their power of overcoming obstacles is proportionately greater, and the result of their laborious suffering is not death but immortality."

That the chief merit of a picture is its *truth*, is an assertion deplorably erroneous. Even in Painting, which is, more essentially than Poetry, a mimetic art, the proposition cannot be sustained. Truth is not even *the aim*. Indeed, it is curious to observe how very slight a degree of truth is sufficient to satisfy the mind, which acquiesces in the absence of numerous essentials in the thing depicted. An outline frequently stirs the spirit more pleasantly than the most elaborate picture. We need only refer to the compositions of Flaxman and of Retzch. Here all details are omitted—nothing can be farther from *truth*. Without even colour the most thrilling effects are produced. In statues we are rather pleased than disgusted with *the want of the eyeball*. The hair of the Venus de Medicis *was gilded*. Truth indeed! The grapes of Zeuxis as well as the curtain of Parrhasius were received as indisputable evidence of the truthful ability of these artists—but they were not even *classed among their pictures*. If truth is the highest aim of either Painting or Poesy, then Jan Steen was a greater artist than Angelo, and Crabbe is a more noble poet than Milton.

But we have not quoted the observation of Mr. Langtree to deny its philosophy; our design was simply to show that he has misunderstood the poet. *Excelsior* has not even a remote tendency to the interpretation assigned it by the critic. It depicts the *earnest upward impulse of the soul*—an impulse not to be subdued even in Death. Despising danger, resisting pleasure, the youth, bearing the banner inscribed "*Excelsior !*" (higher still!), struggles through all difficulties to an Alpine summit. Warned to be content with the elevation attained, his cry is still "*Excelsior !*" and, even in falling dead on the highest pinnacle, his cry is *still "Excelsior !"* There is yet an immortal height to be surmounted —an ascent in Eternity. The poet holds in view the idea of never-ending *progress*. That he is misunderstood is rather the misfortune of Mr. Langtree than the fault of Mr. Longfellow. There is an old adage about the difficulty of one's furnishing an auditor both with matter to be comprehended and brains for its comprehension.

FANCY AND IMAGINATION

DRAKE'S "CULPRIT FAY" AND MOORE'S "ALCIPHRON" [1]

AMID the vague mythology of Egypt, the voluptuous scenery of her Nile, and the gigantic mysteries of her pyramids, Anacreon Moore has found all of that striking *matériel* which he so much delights in working up, and which he has embodied in the poem before us. The design of the story (for plot it has none) has been a less consideration than its facilities, and is made subservient to its execution. The subject is comprised in five epistles. In the first, Alciphron, the head of the Epicurean sect at Athens, writes,

[1] *Alciphron, a Poem.* By Thomas Moore, Esq., author of *Lalla Rookh*, etc., etc. Carey and Hart, Philadelphia.

from Alexandria, to his friend Cleon, in the former
city. He tells him (assigning a reason for quitting
Athens and her pleasures) that, having fallen asleep
one night after protracted festivity, he beholds, in
a dream, a spectre, who tells him that, beside the
sacred Nile, he, the Epicurean, shall find that Eternal
Life for which he had so long been sighing. In the
second, from the same to the same, the traveller
speaks, at large and in rapturous terms, of the
scenery of Egypt; of the beauty of her maidens;
of an approaching Festival of the Moon; and of
a wild hope entertained that amid the subterranean
chambers of some huge pyramid lies the secret which
he covets, the secret of Life Eternal. In the third
letter he relates a love adventure at the Festival.
Fascinated by the charms of one of the nymphs of
a procession, he is first in despair at losing sight of
her, then overjoyed at again seeing her in Necropolis,
and finally traces her steps until they are lost near
one of the smaller pyramids. In epistle the fourth,
(still from the same to the same,) he enters and
explores the pyramid, and, passing through a com-
plete series of Eleusinian mysteries, is at length
successfully initiated into the secrets of Memphian
priestcraft; we learning this latter point from letter
the fifth, which concludes the poem, and is addressed
by Orcus, high priest of Memphis, to Decius, a præ-
torian prefect.

A new poem from Moore calls to mind that critical
opinion respecting him which had its origin, we
believe, in the dogmatism of Coleridge—we mean
the opinion that he is essentially the poet of *fancy*—
the term being employed in contradistinction to
imagination. "The Fancy," says the author of the
Ancient Mariner, in his *Biographia Literaria*, "the
fancy combines, the imagination creates." And this
was intended, and has been received, as a distinction.
If so at all, it is one without a difference; without
even a difference of *degree.* The fancy as nearly
creates as the imagination; and neither creates in

any respect. All novel conceptions are merely un-usual combinations. The mind of man can *imagine* nothing which has not really existed ; and this point is susceptible of the most positive demonstration— see the Baron de Bielfeld, in his *Premiers Traits de L'Érudition Universelle*, 1767. It will be said, per-haps, that we can imagine a *griffin*, and that a griffin does not exist. Not the griffin certainly, but its component parts. It is a mere compendium of known limbs and features—of known qualities. Thus with all which seems to be *new*—which appears to be a *creation* of intellect. It is re-soluble into the old. The wildest and most vigorous effort of mind cannot stand the test of this analysis.

We might make a distinction, *of degree*, between the fancy and the imagination, in saying that the latter is the former *loftily employed*. But experience proves this distinction to be unsatisfactory. What we *feel* and *know* to be fancy, will be found still only *fanciful*, whatever be the theme which engages it. It retains its idiosyncrasy under all circumstances. No *subject* exalts it into the ideal. We might exemplify this by reference to the writings of one whom our patriotism, rather than our judgment, has elevated to a niche in the Poetic Temple which he does not becomingly fill, and which he cannot long uninterruptedly hold. We allude to the late Dr. Rodman Drake, whose puerile abortion, *The Culprit Fay*, we examined, at some length, in a *critique* elsewhere ; proving it, we think, beyond all question, to belong to that class of the pseudo-ideal, in dealing with which we find ourselves embarrassed between a kind of half-consciousness that we ought to admire, and the certainty that we do not. Dr. Drake was employed upon a good subject—at least it is a subject precisely identical with those which Shakespeare was wont so happily to treat, and in which, especially, the author of *Lilian* has so wonder-fully succeeded. But the American has brought to his task a mere *fancy*, and has grossly failed in doing what many suppose him to have done—in writing an ideal or imaginative poem. There is not one particle of the true ποιησις about *The Culprit Fay.* We say that the subject, even at its best points, did not aid Dr. Drake in the slightest degree. He was never more than *fanciful.* The passage, for example, chiefly cited by his admirers, is the account of the "Sylphid Queen"; and to show the difference between the false and true ideal, we collated, in the review just alluded to, this, the most admired passage, with one upon a similar topic by Shelley. We shall be pardoned for repeating here, as nearly as we remember them, some words of what we then said.

The description of the Sylphid Queen runs thus :

> But oh, how fair the shape that lay
>   Beneath a rainbow bending bright;
> She seemed to the entranced Fay,
>   The loveliest of the forms of light;
> Her mantle was the purple rolled
>   At twilight in the west afar ;
> 'Twas tied with threads of dawning gold,
>   And buttoned with a sparkling star.
> Her face was like the lily roon
>   That veils the vestal planet's hue ;
> Her eyes two beamlets from the moon
>   Set floating in the welkin blue.
> Her hair is like the sunny beam,
> And the diamond gems which round it gleam
> Are the pure drops of dewy even
> That ne'er have left their native heaven.

In the *Queen Mab* of Shelley, a Fairy is thus introduced :

> Those who had looked upon the sight,
> Passing all human glory,
> Saw not the yellow moon,
> Saw not the mortal scene,
> Heard not the night-wind's rush,
> Heard not an earthly sound,
> Saw but the fairy pageant,
> Heard but the heavenly strains
> That filled the lonely dwelling—

And thus described—

> The Fairy's frame was slight; yon fibrous cloud
> That catches but the palest tinge of even,
> And which the straining eye can hardly seize
> When melting into eastern twilight's shadow,
> Were scarce so thin, so slight; but the fair star
> That gems the glittering coronet of morn,
> *Sheds not a light so mild, so powerful,*
> *As that which, bursting from the Fairy's form,*
> *Spread a purpureal halo round the scene,*
> *Yet with an undulating motion,*
> *Swayed to her outline gracefully.*

In these exquisite lines the faculty of mere comparison is but little exercised—that of ideality in a wonderful degree. It is probable that in a similar case Dr. Drake would have formed the face of the fairy of the " fibrous cloud," her arms of the " pale tinge of even," her eyes of the " fair stars," and her body of the " twilight shadow." Having so done, his admirers would have congratulated him upon his *imagination*, not taking the trouble to think that they themselves could at any moment *imagine* a fairy of materials equally as good, and conveying an equally distinct idea. Their mistake would be precisely analogous to that of many a schoolboy who admires the imagination displayed in *Jack the Giant-Killer*, and is finally rejoiced at discovering his own imagination to surpass that of the author, since the monsters destroyed by Jack are only about forty feet in height, and he himself has no trouble in imagining some of one hundred and forty. It will be seen that the fairy of Shelley is not a mere compound of incongruous natural objects, inartificially put together, and unaccompanied by any *moral* sentiment—but a being, in the illustration of whose nature some physical elements are used collaterally as adjuncts, while the main conception springs immediately, *or thus apparently springs*, from the brain of the poet, enveloped in the moral sentiments of grace, of colour, of motion—of the beautiful, of the *mystical*, of the august—in short, of the ideal.

The truth is, that the just distinction between the fancy and the imagination (and which is still but a distinction *of degree*) is involved in the consideration of the *mystic*. We give this as an idea of our own altogether. We have no authority for our opinion—but do not the less firmly hold it. The term *mystic* is here employed in the sense of Augustis William Schlegel, and of most other German critics. It is applied by them to that class of composition in which there lies beneath the transparent upper-current of meaning, an under or *suggestive* one. What we vaguely term the *moral* of any sentiment is its mystic or secondary expression. It has the vast force of an accompaniment in music. This vivifies the air ; that spiritualizes the *fanciful* conception, and lifts it into the *ideal*.

This theory will bear, we think, the most rigorous test which can be made applicable to it, and will be acknowledged as tenable by all who are themselves imaginative. If we carefully examine those poems, or portions of poems, or those prose romances, which mankind have been accustomed to designate as *imaginative*, (for an instinctive feeling leads us to employ properly the term whose full import we have still never been able to define,) it will be seen that all so designated are remarkable for the *suggestive* character which we have discussed. They are strongly *mystic*—in the proper sense of the word. We will here only call to the reader's mind the *Prometheus Vinctus* of Æschylus ; the *Inferno* of Dante ; the *Destruction of Numantia* by Cervantes ; the *Comus* of Milton ; the *Ancient Mariner*, the *Christabel*, and the *Kubla Khan*, of Coleridge ; the *Nightingale* of Keats ; and, most especially, the *Sensitive Plant* of Shelley, and the *Undine* of De la Motte Fouqué. These two latter poems (for we call them both such) are the finest possible examples of the purely *ideal*. There is little of fancy here, and everything of imagination. With each note of the lyre is heard a ghostly, and not always a distinct, but an august and soul-exalting *echo*.   In every glimpse of beauty presented, we catch, through long and wild vistas, dim bewildering visions of a far more ethereal beauty *beyond*.   But not so in poems which the world has always persisted in terming *fanciful*.   Here the upper-current is often exceedingly brilliant and beautiful ; but then men *feel* that this upper-current *is all*.   No Naiad voice addresses them *from below*.   The notes of the air of the song do not tremble with the according tones of the accompaniment.

It is the failure to perceive these truths which has occasioned the embarrassment experienced by our critics while discussing the topic of Moore's station in the poetic world—that hesitation with which we are obliged to refuse him the loftiest rank among the most noble.   The popular voice, and the popular heart, have denied him that happiest quality, imagination—and here the popular voice (*because* for once it is gone with the popular heart) is right —but yet only relatively so.   Imagination is not the leading feature of the poetry of Moore ; but he possesses it in no little degree.

We will quote a few instances from the poem now before us—instances which will serve to exemplify the distinctive feature which we have attributed to ideality.

It is the *suggestive* force which exalts and etherealizes the passages we copy.

> Or is it that there lurks, indeed,
> Some truth in man's prevailing creed,
> And that our guardians from on high,
>   Come, in that pause from toil and sin,
> To put the senses' curtain by,
>   And on the wakeful soul look in !

Again—

> The eternal pyramids of Memphis burst
> Awfully on my sight—standing sublime
> 'Twixt earth and heaven, the watch-towers of time,
> From whose lone summit, when his reign hath past,
> From earth forever, he will look his last.

And again—

> Is there for man no hope—but this which dooms
> His only lasting trophies to be tombs !
> But 'tis not so—earth, heaven, all nature shows
> He *may* become immortal, *may* unclose
> The wings within him wrapt, and proudly rise
> Redeemed from earth a creature of the skies !

And here—

> The pyramid shadows, stretching from the light,
> Look like the first colossal steps of night,
> Stalking across the valley to invade
> The distant hills of porphyry with their shade !

And once more—

> There Silence, thoughtful God, who loves
> The neighbourhood of Death, in groves
> Of asphodel lies hid, and weaves
> His hushing spell among the leaves.

Such lines as these, we must admit, however, are not of frequent occurrence in the poem—the sum of whose great beauty is composed of the several sums of a world of minor excellences.

Moore has always been renowned for the number and appositeness, as well as novelty, of his similes ; and the renown thus acquired is strongly indicial of his deficiency in that nobler merit—the noblest of them all. No poet thus distinguished was ever richly ideal. Pope and Cowper are remarkable instances in point. Similes (so much insisted upon by the critics of the reign of Queen Anne) are never, in our opinion, strictly in good taste, whatever may be said to the contrary, and certainly can never be made to accord with other high qualities, except when naturally arising from the subject in the way of illustration—and, when thus arising, they have seldom the merit of novelty. To be novel, they must fail in essential particulars. The higher minds will avoid their frequent use. They form no portion of the ideal, and appertain to the fancy alone.

We proceed with a few random observations upon

Alciphron. The poem is distinguished throughout by a very happy facility which has never been mentioned in connexion with its author, but which has much to do with the reputation he has obtained. We allude to the facility with which he recounts a poetical story in a *prosaic* way. By this is meant that he preserves the tone and method of arrangement of a prose relation, and thus obtains great advantages over his more stilted compeers. His is no poetical *style*, (such, for example, as the French have—a distinct style for a distinct purpose,) but an easy and ordinary prose manner, *ornamented into poetry*. By means of this he is enabled to enter, with ease, into details which would baffle any other versifier of the age, and at which Lamartine would stand aghast. For anything that we see to the contrary, Moore might solve a cubic equation in verse. His facility in this respect is truly admirable, and is, no doubt, the result of long practice after mature deliberation. We refer the reader to page 50 of the pamphlet now reviewed; where the minute and conflicting incidents of the descent into the pyramid are detailed with absolutely *more* precision than we have ever known a similar relation detailed with in prose.

In general dexterity and melody of versification the author of *Lalla Rookh* is unrivalled ; but he is by no means at all times accurate, falling occasionally into the common foible of throwing accent upon syllables too unimportant to sustain it. Thus, in the lines which follow, where we have italicized the weak syllables :

> And mark 'tis nigh ; already *the* sun bids. . . .
> While hark from all the temples *a* rich swell. . . .
> I rushed in*to* the cool night air.

He also too frequently draws out the word Heaven into two syllables—a protraction which it *never* will support.

His English is now and then objectionable, as, at page 26, where he speaks of

> lighted barks
> That down Syene's cataract *shoots*

making *shoots* rhyme with flutes, below; also, at page 6, and elsewhere, where the word *none* has improperly a singular, instead of a plural force. But such criticism as this is somewhat captious, for in general he is most highly polished.

At page 27, he has stolen his " woven snow " from the *ventum textilem* of Apuleius.

At page 8, he either himself has misunderstood the tenets of Epicurus, or wilfully misrepresents them through the voice of Alciphron. We incline to the former idea, however; as the philosophy of that most noble of the sophists is habitually perverted by the moderns. Nothing could be more spiritual and less sensual than the doctrines we so torture into wrong. But we have drawn out this notice at somewhat too great length, and must conclude. In truth the exceeding beauty of *Alciphron* has bewildered and detained us. We could not point out a poem in any language which, as a whole, greatly excels it. It is far superior to *Lalla Rookh*. While Moore does not reach, except in rare snatches, the height of the loftiest qualities of some whom we have named, yet he has written finer poems than any, of equal length, by the greatest of his rivals. His radiance, not always as bright as some flashes from other pens, is yet a radiance of equable glow, whose total amount of light exceeds, by very much, we think, that total amount in the case of any cotemporary writer whatsoever. A vivid fancy; an epigrammatic spirit; a fine taste; vivacity, dexterity, and a musical ear; have made him very easily what he is, the most popular poet now living—if not the most popular that ever lived—and perhaps, a slight modification at birth of that which phrenologists have agreed to term *temperament*, might have made him the truest and noblest votary of the muse of any age or clime. As it is, we have only casual glimpses of that *mens divinior* which is assuredly enshrined within him.

MESMERIC REVELATION

WHATEVER doubt may still envelop the *rationale* of mesmerism, its startling *facts* are now almost universally admitted. Of these latter, those who doubt, are your mere doubters by profession—an unprofitable and disreputable tribe. There can be no more absolute waste of time than the attempt to *prove*, at the present day, that man, by mere exercise of will, can so impress his fellow, as to cast him into an abnormal condition, of which the phenomena resemble very closely those of *death*, or at least resemble them more nearly than they do the phenomena of any other normal condition within our cognizance ; that, while in this state, the person so impressed employs only with effort, and then feebly, the external organs of sense, yet perceives, with keenly refined perception, and through channels supposed unknown, matters beyond the scope of the physical organs ; that, moreover, his intellectual faculties are wonderfully exalted and invigorated ; that his sympathies with the person so impressing him are profound ; and, finally, that his susceptibility to the impression increases with its frequency, while, in the same proportion, the peculiar phenomena elicited are more extended and more *pronounced*.

I say that these—which are the laws of mesmerism in its general features—it would be supererogation to demonstrate ; nor shall I inflict upon my readers so needless a demonstration to-day. My purpose at present is a very different one indeed. I am impelled, even in the teeth of a world of prejudice, to detail without comment the very remarkable substance of a colloquy, occurring between a sleep-waker and myself.

I had been long in the habit of mesmerizing the person in question (Mr. Vankirk,) and the usual acute susceptibility and exaltation of the mesmeric perception had supervened. For many months he had been labouring under confirmed phthisis, the more distressing effects of which had been relieved by my manipulations ; and on the night of Wednesday, the fifteenth instant, I was summoned to his bedside.

The invalid was suffering with acute pain in the region of the heart, and breathed with great difficulty, having all the ordinary symptoms of asthma. In spasms such as these he had usually found relief from the application of mustard to the nervous centres, but to-night this had been attempted in vain.

As I entered his room he greeted me with a cheerful smile, and although evidently in much bodily pain, appeared to be, mentally, quite at ease.

" I sent for you to-night," he said, " not so much to administer to my bodily ailment, as to satisfy me concerning certain psychal impressions which, of late, have occasioned me much anxiety and surprise. I need not tell you how sceptical I have hitherto been on the topic of the soul's immortality. I cannot deny that there has always existed, as if in that very soul which I have been denying, a vague half-sentiment of its own existence. But this half-sentiment at no time amounted to conviction. With it my reason had nothing to do. All attempts at logical inquiry resulted, indeed, in leaving me more sceptical than before. I had been advised to study Cousin. I studied him in his own works as well as in those of his European and American echoes. The *Charles Elwood* of Mr. Brownson, for example, was placed in my hands. I read it with profound attention. Throughout I found it logical, but the portions which were not *merely* logical were unhappily the initial arguments of the disbelieving hero of the book. In his summing up it seemed evident to me that the reasoner had not even succeeded in convincing himself. His end had plainly forgotten his beginning, like the government of Trinculo. In short, I was not long in perceiving that if man is to be intellectually convinced of his own immortality, he will never be so convinced by the mere abstractions which have been so long the fashion of the moralists of England, of France, and of Germany. Abstractions may amuse and exercise, but take no hold on the mind. Here upon earth, at least, philosophy, I am persuaded, will always in vain call upon us to look upon qualities as things. The will may assent—the soul—the intellect, never.

"I repeat, then, that I only half felt, and never intellectually believed. But latterly there has been a certain deepening of the feeling, until it has come so nearly to resemble the acquiescence of reason, that I find it difficult to distinguish between the two. I am enabled, too, plainly to trace this effect to the mesmeric influence. I cannot better explain my meaning than by the hypothesis that the mesmeric exaltation enables me to perceive a train of ratiocination which, in my abnormal existence, convinces, but which, in full accordance with the mesmeric phenomena, does not extend, except through its *effect*, into my normal condition. In sleep-waking, the reasoning and its conclusion—the cause and its effect—are present together. In my natural state, the cause vanishing, the effect only, and perhaps only partially, remains.

"These considerations have led me to think that some good results might ensue from a series of well-directed questions propounded to me while mesmerized. You have often observed the profound self-cognizance evinced by the sleep-waker—the extensive knowledge he displays upon all points relating to the mesmeric condition itself; and from this self-cognizance may be deduced hints for the proper conduct of a catechism."

I consented of course to make this experiment. A

few passes threw Mr. Vankirk into the mesmeric sleep. His breathing became immediately more easy, and he seemed to suffer no physical uneasiness. The following conversation then ensued :—V. in the dialogue representing the patient, and P. myself.

P. Are you asleep ?

V. Yes—no ; I would rather sleep more soundly.

P. (*After a few more passes.*) Do you sleep now ?

V. Yes.

P. How do you think your present illness will result ?

V. (*After a long hesitation and speaking as if with effort.*) I must die.

P. Does the idea of death afflict you ?

V. (*Very quickly.*) No—no !

P. Are you pleased with the prospect ?

V. If I were awake I should like to die, but now it is no matter. The mesmeric condition is so near death as to content me.

P. I wish you would explain yourself, Mr. Vankirk.

V. I am willing to do so, but it requires more effort than I feel able to make. You do not question me properly.

P. What then shall I ask ?

V. You must begin at the beginning.

P. The beginning ! but where is the beginning ?

V. You know that the beginning is GOD. (*This was said in a low, fluctuating tone, and with every sign of the most profound veneration.*)

P. What then is God ?

V. (*Hesitating for many minutes.*) I cannot tell.

P. Is not God spirit ?

V. While I was awake I knew what you meant by "spirit," but now it seems only a word—such for instance as truth, beauty—a quality, I mean.

P. Is not God immaterial ?

V. There is no immateriality—it is a mere word. That which is not matter, is not at all—unless qualities are things.

P. Is God, then, material ?

V. No. (*This reply startled me very much.*)

P. What then is he ?

V. (*After a long pause, and mutteringly.*) I see—but it is a thing difficult to tell. (*Another long pause.*) He is not spirit, for he exists. Nor is he matter, *as you understand it.* But there are *gradations* of matter of which man knows nothing ; the grosser impelling the finer, the finer pervading the grosser. The atmosphere, for example, impels the electric principle, while the electric principle permeates the atmosphere. These gradations of matter increase in rarity or fineness, until we arrive at a matter *unparticled*—without particles—indivisible—*one ;* and here the law of impulsion and permeation is modified. The ultimate, or unparticled matter, not only permeates all things but impels all things—and thus *is* all things within itself. This matter is God. What men attempt to embody in the word " thought," is this matter in motion.

P. The metaphysicians maintain that all action is reducible to motion and thinking, and that the latter is the origin of the former.

V. Yes ; and I now see the confusion of idea. Motion is the action of *mind*—not of *thinking*. The unparticled matter, or God, in quiescence, is (as nearly as we can conceive it) what men call mind. And the power of self-movement (equivalent in effect to human volition) is, in the unparticled matter, the result of its unity and omniprevalence ; *how* I know not, and now clearly see that I shall never know. But the unparticled matter, set in motion by a law, or quality, existing within itself, is thinking.

P. Can you give me no more precise idea of what you term the unparticled matter ?

V. The matters of which man is cognizant, escape the senses in gradation. We have, for example, a metal, a piece of wood, a drop of water, the atmosphere, a gas, caloric, electricity, the luminiferous ether. Now we call all these things matter, and embrace all matter in one general definition ; but in spite of this, there can be no two ideas more essentially distinct than that which we attach to a metal, and that which we attach to the luminiferous ether. When we reach the latter, we feel an almost irresistible inclination to class it with spirit, or with nihility. The only consideration which restrains us is our conception of its atomic constitution; and here, even, we have to seek aid from our notion of an atom, as something possessing in infinite minuteness, solidity, palpability, weight. Destroy the idea of the atomic constitution and we should no longer be able to regard the ether as an entity, or at least as matter. For want of a better word we might term it spirit. Take, now, a step beyond the luminiferous ether—conceive a matter as much more rare than the ether, as this ether is more rare than the metal, and we arrive at once (in spite of all the school dogmas) at a unique mass—an unparticled matter. For although we may admit infinite littleness in the atoms themselves, the infinitude of littleness in the spaces between them is an absurdity. There will be a point—there will be a degree of rarity, at which, if the atoms are sufficiently numerous, the interspaces must vanish, and the mass absolutely coalesce. But the consideration of the atomic constitution being now taken away, the nature of the mass inevitably glides into what we conceive of spirit. It is clear, however, that it is as fully matter as before. The truth is, it is impossible to conceive spirit, since it is impossible to imagine what is not. When we flatter ourselves that we have formed its conception, we have merely deceived our understanding by the consideration of infinitely rarified matter.

P. There seems to me an insurmountable objection to the idea of absolute coalescence;—and that is the very slight resistance experienced by the heavenly bodies in their revolutions through space—a resistance now ascertained, it is true, to exist in *some* degree, but which is, nevertheless, so slight as to have been quite overlooked by the sagacity even of Newton. We know that the resistance of bodies is, chiefly, in proportion to their density. Absolute coalescence is absolute density. Where there are no interspaces, there can be no yielding. An ether, absolutely dense, would put an infinitely more effectual stop to the progress of a star than would an ether of adamant or of iron.

V. Your objection is answered with an ease which is nearly in the ratio of its apparent unanswerability. —As regards the progress of the star, it can make no difference whether the star passes through the ether *or the ether through it.* There is no astronomical error more unaccountable than that which reconciles the known retardation of the comets with the idea of their passage through an ether : for, however rare this ether be supposed, it would put a stop to all sidereal revolution in a very far briefer period than has been admitted by those astronomers who have endeavoured to slur over a point which they found it impossible to comprehend. The retardation actually experienced is, on the other hand, about that which might be expected from the *friction* of the ether in the instantaneous passage through the orb. In the one case, the retarding force is momentary and complete within itself—in the other it is endlessly accumulative.

P. But in all this—in this identification of mere matter with God—is there nothing of irreverence ? (*I was forced to repeat this question before the sleep-waker fully comprehended my meaning.*)

V. Can you say *why* matter should be less reverenced than mind ? But you forget that the matter of which I speak is, in all respects, the very " mind " or " spirit " of the schools, so far as regards its high capacities, and is, moreover, the " matter " of these schools at the same time. God, with all the powers attributed to spirit, is but the perfection of matter.

P. You assert, then, that the unparticled matter, in motion, is thought ?

V. In general, this motion is the universal thought of the universal mind. This thought creates. All created things are but the thoughts of God.

P. You say, " in general."

V. Yes. The universal mind is God. For new individualities, *matter* is necessary.

P. But you now speak of " mind " and " matter " as do the metaphysicians.

V. Yes—to avoid confusion. When I say " mind," I mean the unparticled or ultimate matter ; by " matter," I intend all else.

P. You were saying that " for new individualities matter is necessary."

V. Yes ; for mind, existing unincorporate, is merely God. To create individual, thinking beings, it was necessary to incarnate portions of the divine mind. Thus man is individualized. Divested of corporate investiture, he were God. Now, the particular motion of the incarnated portions of the unparticled matter is the thought of man ; as the motion of the whole is that of God.

P. You say that divested of the body man will be God ?

V. (*After much hesitation.*) I could not have said this ; it is an absurdity.

P. (*Referring to my notes.*) You *did* say that " divested of corporate investiture man were God."

V. And this is true. Man thus divested *would* be God—would be unindividualized. But he can never be thus divested—at least never *will be*—else we must imagine an action of God returning upon itself—a purposeless and futile action. Man is a creature. Creatures are thoughts of God. It is the nature of thought to be irrevocable.

P. I do not comprehend. You say that man will never put off the body ?

V. I say that he will never be bodiless.

P. Explain.

V. There are two bodies—the rudimental and the complete ; corresponding with the two conditions of

the worm and the butterfly. What we call " death,"
is but the painful metamorphosis. Our present incar-
nation is progressive, preparatory, temporary. Our
future is perfected, ultimate, immortal. The ultimate
life is the full design.

P. But of the worm's metamorphosis we are
palpably cognizant.

V. We, certainly—but not the worm. The matter
of which our rudimental body is composed, is within
the ken of the organs of that body ; or, more dis-
tinctly, our rudimental organs are adapted to the
matter of which is formed the rudimental body ;
but not to that of which the ultimate is composed.
The ultimate body thus escapes our rudimental
senses, and we perceive only the shell which falls, in
decaying, from the inner form ; not that inner form
itself ; but this inner form, as well as the shell, is
appreciable by those who have already acquired the
ultimate life.

P. You have often said that the mesmeric state
very nearly resembles death. How is this ?

V. When I say that it resembles death, I mean
that it resembles the ultimate life ; for when I am
entranced the senses of my rudimental life are in
abeyance, and I perceive external things directly,
without organs, through a medium which I shall
employ in the ultimate, unorganized life.

P. Unorganized ?

V. Yes ; organs are contrivances by which the
individual is brought into sensible relation with
particular classes and forms of matter, to the exclu-
sion of other classes and forms. The organs of man
are adapted to his rudimental condition, and to that
only ; his ultimate condition, being unorganized, is
of unlimited comprehension in all points but one—
the nature of the volition of God—that is to say, the
motion of the unparticled matter. You will have a
distinct idea of the ultimate body by conceiving it to
be entire brain. This it is *not ;* but a conception of
this nature will bring you near a comprehension of

what it *is*. A luminous body imparts vibration to the luminiferous ether. The vibrations generate similar ones within the retina ; these again communicate similar ones to the optic nerve. The nerve conveys similar ones to the brain ; the brain, also, similar ones to the unparticled matter which permeates it. The motion of this latter is thought, of which perception is the first undulation. This is the mode by which the mind of the rudimental life communicates with the external world ; and this external world is, to the rudimental life, limited, through the idiosyncrasy of its organs. But in the ultimate, unorganized life, the external world reaches the whole body (which is of a substance having affinity to brain, as I have said), with no other intervention than that of an infinitely rarer ether than even the luminiferous ; and to this ether—in unison with it—the whole body vibrates, setting in motion the unparticled matter which permeates it. It is to the absence of idiosyncratic organs, therefore, that we must attribute the nearly unlimited perception of the ultimate life. To rudimental beings, organs are the cages necessary to confine them until fledged.

P. You speak of rudimental " beings." Are there other rudimental thinking beings than man ?

V. The multitudinous conglomeration of rare matter into nebulæ, planets, suns, and other bodies which are neither nebulæ, suns, nor planets, is for the sole purpose of supplying *pabulum* for the idiosyncrasy of the organs of an infinity of rudimental beings. But for the necessity of the rudimental, prior to the ultimate life, there would have been no bodies such as these. Each of these is tenanted by a distinct variety of organic, rudimental, thinking creatures. In all, the organs vary with the features of the place tenanted. At death, or metamorphosis, these creatures, enjoying the ultimate life—immortality—and cognizant of all secrets but *the one*, act all things and pass everywhere by mere volition :— indwelling, not the stars, which to us seem the sole

palpabilities, and for the accommodation of which we
blindly deem space created—but that SPACE itself—
that infinity of which the truly substantive vastness
swallows up the star-shadows—blotting them out as
non-entities from the perception of the angels.

P. You say that "but for the *necessity* of the
rudimental life" there would have been no stars.
But why this necessity ?

V. In the inorganic life, as well as in the inorganic
matter generally, there is nothing to impede the
action of one simple *unique* law—the Divine Volition.
With the view of producing impediment, the organic
life and matter (complex, substantial, and law-en-
cumbered), were contrived.

P. But again—why need this impediment have
been produced ?

V. The result of law inviolate is perfection—right
—negative happiness. The result of law violate is
imperfection, wrong, positive pain. Through the
impediments afforded by the number, complexity,
and substantiality of the laws of organic life and
matter, the violation of law is rendered, to a certain
extent, practicable. Thus pain, which in the inorganic
life is impossible, is possible in the organic.

P. But to what good end is pain thus rendered
possible ?

V. All things are either good or bad by com-
parison. A sufficient analysis will show that pleasure,
in all cases, is but the contrast of pain. *Positive*
pleasure is a mere idea. To be happy at any one
point we must have suffered at the same. Never to
suffer would have been never to have been blessed.
But it has been shown that, in the inorganic life, pain
cannot be ; thus the necessity for the organic. The
pain of the primitive life of Earth is the sole basis of
the bliss of the ultimate life in Heaven.

P. Still, there is one of your expressions which I
find it impossible to comprehend—" the truly *sub-
stantive* vastness of infinity."

V. This, probably, is because you have no sufficiently generic conception of the term "*substance*" itself. We must not regard it as a quality, but as a sentiment :—it is the perception, in thinking beings, of the adaptation of matter to their organization. There are many things on the Earth which would be nihility to the inhabitants of Venus—many things visible and tangible in Venus which we could not be brought to appreciate as existing at all. But to the inorganic beings—to the angels—the whole of the unparticled matter is substance ; that is to say, the whole of what we term " space " is to them the truest substantiality ;—the stars, meantime, through what we consider their materiality, escaping the angelic sense, just in proportion as the unparticled matter, through what we consider its immateriality, eludes the organic.

As the sleep-waker pronounced these latter words, in a feeble tone, I observed on his countenance a singular expression, which somewhat alarmed me, and induced me to awake him at once. No sooner had I done this, than, with a bright smile irradiating all his features, he fell back upon his pillow and expired. I noticed that in less than a minute afterward his corpse had all the stern rigidity of stone. His brow was of the coldness of ice. Thus, ordinarily, should it have appeared, only after long pressure from Azrael's hand. Had the sleep-waker, indeed, during the latter portion of his discourse, been addressing me from out the region of the shadows ?

MARGINALIA

INTRODUCTION

In getting my books, I have been always solicitous of an ample margin ; this not so much through any love of the thing in itself, however agreeable, as for the facility it affords me of pencilling suggested thoughts, agreements, and differences of opinion, or brief critical comments in general. Where what I have to note is too much to be included within the narrow limits of a margin, I commit it to a slip of paper, and deposit it between the leaves ; taking care to secure it by an imperceptible portion of gum tragacanth paste.

All this may be whim ; it may be not only a very hackneyed, but a very idle practice ;—yet I persist in it still ; and it affords me pleasure ; which is profit, in despite of Mr. Bentham with Mr. Mill on his back.

This making of notes, however, is by no means the making of mere *memoranda*—a custom which has its disadvantages, beyond doubt. " *Ce que je mets sur papier*," says Bernardin de St. Pierre, " *je remets de ma mémoire, et par conséquence je l'oublie* " ; —and, in fact, if you wish to forget anything on the spot, make a note that this thing is to be remembered.

But the purely marginal jottings, done with no eye to the Memorandum Book, have a distinct complexion, and not only a distinct purpose, but none at all ; this it is which imparts to them a value. They have a rank somewhat above the chance and desultory comments of literary chit-chat—for these latter are not unfrequently " talk for talk's sake," hurried out of the mouth ; while the *marginalia* are deliberately pencilled, because the mind of the reader wishes to unburthen itself of a *thought*—however flippant—however silly—however trivial—still a thought indeed, not merely a thing that might have been a thought in time, and under more favourable circumstances. In the *marginalia*, too, we talk only to ourselves ; we therefore talk freshly—boldly— originally—with *abandonnément*—without conceit— much after the fashion of Jeremy Taylor, and Sir Thomas Browne, and Sir William Temple, and the anatomical Burton, and that most logical analogist, Butler, and some other people of the old day, who were too full of their matter to have any room for their manner, which being thus left out of question, was a capital manner, indeed—a model of manners, with a richly marginalic air.

The circumscription of space, too, in these pen-
cillings, has in it something more of advantage than
inconvenience. It compels us (whatever diffuseness
of idea we may clandestinely entertain) into Mon-
tesquieu-ism, into Tacitus-ism, (here I leave out of
view the concluding portion of the *Annals*,)—or
even into Carlyle-ism—a thing which, I have been
told, is not to be confounded with your ordinary
affectation and bad grammar. I say "bad grammar,"
through sheer obstinacy, because the grammarians
(who should know better) insist upon it that I should
not. But then grammar is not what these gram-
marians will have it ; and, being merely the analysis
of language, with the result of this analysis, must
be good or bad just as the analyst is sage or silly—
just as he is a Horne Tooke or a Cobbett.

But to our sheep. During a rainy afternoon, not
long ago, being in a mood too listless for continuous
study, I sought relief from *ennui* in dipping here
and there, at random, among the volumes of my
library—no very large one, certainly, but sufficiently
miscellaneous ; and, I flatter myself, not a little
recherché.

Perhaps it was what the Germans call the "brain-
scattering" humour of the moment ; but, while the
picturesqueness of the numerous pencil-scratches
arrested my attention, their helter-skelteriness of
commentary amused me. I found myself, at length,
forming a wish that it had been some other hand
than my own which had so bedevilled the books,
and fancying that, in such case, I might have derived
no inconsiderable pleasure from turning them over.
From this the transition-thought (as Mr. Lyell, or
Mr. Murchison, or Mr. Featherstonhaugh would have
it) was natural enough :—there might be something
even in *my* scribblings which, for the mere sake of
scribbling, would have interest for others.

The main difficulty respected the mode of trans-
ferring the notes from the volumes—the context
from the text—without detriment to that exceedingly

frail fabric of intelligibility in which the context was imbedded. With all appliances to boot, with the printed pages at their back, the commentaries were too often like Dodona's oracles—or those of Lycophron Tenebrosus—or the essays of the pedant's pupils, in Quintillian, which were "necessarily excellent, since even he (the pedant) found it impossible to comprehend them" :—what, then, would become of it—this context—if transferred ?—if translated ? Would it not rather be *traduit* (traduced), which is the French synonym, or *overzezet* (turned topsy-turvy), which is the Dutch one ?

I concluded, at length. to put extensive faith in the acumen and imagination of the reader :—this as a general rule. But, in some instances, where even faith would not remove mountains, there seemed no safer plan than so to remodel the note as to convey at least a ghost of a conception as to what it was all about. Where, for such conception, the text itself was absolutely necessary, I could quote it ; where the title of the book commented upon was indispensable, I could name it. In short, like a novel hero dilemma'd, I made up my mind "to be guided by circumstances," in default of more satisfactory rules of conduct.

As for the multitudinous opinion expressed in the subjoined *farrago*—as for my present assent to all, or dissent from any portion of it—as to the possibility of my having, in some instances, altered my mind—or as to the impossibility of my not having altered it often—these are points upon which I say nothing, because upon these there can be nothing cleverly said. It may be as well to observe, however, that just as the goodness of your true pun is in the direct ratio of its intolerability, so is nonsense the essential sense of the Marginal Note.

A SOMNAMBULE

ONE of the happiest examples, in a small way, of the carrying-one's-self-in-a-hand-basket logic, is to be found in a London weekly paper, called *The Popular Record of Modern Science ; a Journal of Philosophy and General Information.* This work has a vast circulation, and is respected by eminent men. Sometime in November, 1845, it copied from the *Columbian Magazine*, of New York, a rather adventurous article of mine, called "Mesmeric Revelation." It had the impudence, also, to spoil the title by improving it to "The Last Conversation of a Somnambule"—a phrase that is nothing at all to the purpose, since the person who "converses" is *not* a somnambule. He is a sleep-waker—*not* a sleep-walker ; but I presume that the *Record* thought it was only the difference of an *l*. What I chiefly complain of, however, is that the London editor prefaced my paper with these words :—" The following is an article communicated to the *Columbian Magazine*, a journal of respectability and influence in the United States, by Mr. Edgar A. Poe. *It bears internal evidence of authenticity.*" ! There is no subject under heaven about which funnier ideas are, in general, entertained than about this subject of internal evidence. It is by "internal evidence," observe, that we decide upon the mind. But to the *Record* :—On the issue of my " Valdemar Case," this journal copies it as a matter of course, and (also as a matter of course) improves the title, as in the previous instance. But the editorial comments may as well be called profound. Here they are :

The following narrative appears in a recent number of the *American Magazine*, a respectable periodical in the United States. It comes, it will be observed, from the narrator of the " Last Conversation of a Somnambule," published in the *Record* of the 29th of November. In extracting this case the *Morning Post*, of Monday last, takes what it considers the safe side, by remarking—" For our own parts we do not believe it ; and there are several statements made, more especially with regard to the disease of which the patient died, which at once prove the case to be either a fabrication, or the work of one little acquainted with consumption. The story, however, is wonderful, and we therefore give it." The editor, however, does not point out the especial statements which are inconsistent with what we know of the progress of consumption, and as few scientific persons would be willing to take their pathology any more than their logic from the *Morning Post*, his caution, it is to be feared, will not have much weight. The reason assigned by the *Post* for publishing the account is quaint, and would apply equally to an adventure from *Baron Munchausen* :—" it is wonderful and we therefore give it." . . The above case is obviously one that cannot be received except on the strongest testimony, and it is equally clear that the testimony by which it is at present accompanied, is not of that character. The most favourable circumstances in support of it, consist in the fact that credence is understood to be given to it at New York, within a few miles of which city the affair took place, and where consequently the most ready means must be found for its authentication or disproval. The initials of the medical men and of the young medical student must be sufficient in the immediate locality, to establish their identity, especially as M. Valdemar was well known, and had been so long ill as to render it out of the question that there should be any difficulty in ascertaining the names of the physicians by whom he had been attended. In the same way the nurses and servants under whose cognizance the case must have come during the seven months which it occupied, are of course accessible to all sorts of inquiries. It will, therefore, appear that there must have been too many parties concerned to render prolonged deception practicable. The angry excitement and various rumours which have at length rendered a public statement necessary, are also sufficient to show that *something* extraordinary must have taken place. On the other hand there is no strong point for disbelief. The circumstances are, as the *Post* says, " wonderful " ; but so are all circumstances that come to our knowledge for the first time—and in Mesmerism everything is new. An objection may be made that the article has rather a Magazinish air ; Mr. Poe having evidently written with a view to effect, and so as to excite rather than to subdue the vague appetite for the mysterious and the horrible which such a case, under any circumstances, is sure to awaken—but apart from this there is nothing to deter a philosophic mind from further inquiries regarding it. It is a matter entirely for testimony. [So it is.] Under this view we shall take steps to procure from some of the most intelligent and influential citizens of New York all the evidence that can be had upon the subject. No steamer will leave England for America till the 3rd of February, but within a few weeks of that time we doubt not it will be possible to lay before the readers of the *Record* information which will enable them to come to a pretty accurate conclusion.

Yes ; and no doubt they came to one accurate enough, in the end. But all this rigmarole is what people call testing a thing by " internal evidence." The *Record* insists upon the truth of the story because of certain facts—because " the initials of the young men *must* be sufficient to establish their identity " —because " the nurses *must* be accessible to all sorts of inquiries "—and because the " angry excitement and various rumours which at length rendered a public statement necessary, are sufficient to show that *something* extraordinary *must* have taken place." To be sure ! The story is proved by these facts— the facts about the students, the nurses, the excitement, the credence given the tale at New York. And now all we have to do is to prove these facts. Ah !—*they* are proved *by the story*. As for the *Morning Post*, it evinces more weakness in its disbelief than the *Record* in its credulity. What the former says about doubting on account of inaccuracy in the detail of the phthisical symptoms, is a mere *fetch*, as the Cockneys have it, in order to make a very few little children believe that it, the *Post*, is not quite so stupid as a post proverbially is. It knows nearly as much about pathology as it does about English grammar—and I really hope it will not feel called upon to blush at the compliment. I represented the symptoms of M. Valdemar as " severe," to be sure. I put an extreme case ; for it was necessary that I should leave on the reader's mind no doubt as to the certainty of death without the aid of the Mesmerist—but such symptoms *might* have appeared—the identical symptoms *have appeared*, and will be presented again and again. Had the *Post* been only half as honest as ignorant, it would have owned that it disbelieved for no reason more profound than that which influences all dunces in disbelieving—it would have owned that it doubted the thing merely because the thing was a " wonderful " thing, and had never yet been printed in a book.

PUNCTUATION

THAT punctuation is important all agree; but how few comprehend the extent of its importance! The writer who neglects punctuation, or mispunctuates, is liable to be misunderstood—this, according to the popular idea, is the sum of the evils arising from heedlessness or ignorance. It does not seem to be known that, even where the sense is perfectly clear, a sentence may be deprived of half its force—its spirit—its point—by improper punctuations. For the want of merely a comma, it often occurs that an axiom appears a paradox, or that a sarcasm is converted into a sermonoid. There is *no* treatise on the topic—and there is no topic on which a treatise is more needed. There seems to exist a vulgar notion that the subject is one of pure conventionality, and cannot be brought within the limits of intelligible and consistent *rule*. And yet, if fairly looked in the face, the whole matter is so plain that its *rationale* may be read as we run. If not anticipated, I shall hereafter, make an attempt at a magazine paper on "The Philosophy of Point." In the meantime let me say a word or two of *the dash*. Every writer for the press, who has any sense of the accurate, must have been frequently mortified and vexed at the distortion of his sentences by the printer's now general substitution of a semicolon, or comma, for the dash of the MS. The total or nearly total disuse of the latter point, has been brought about by the revulsion consequent upon its excessive employment about twenty years ago. The Byronic poets were *all* dash. John Neal, in his earlier novels, exaggerated its use into the grossest abuse—although his very error arose from the philosophical and self-dependent spirit which has always distinguished him, and which will even yet lead him, if I am not greatly mistaken in the man, to do something for the literature of the country which the country "will not willingly," and cannot

possibly " let die." Without entering now into the
why, let me observe that the printer may always
ascertain when the dash of the MS. is properly and
when improperly employed, by bearing in mind that
this point represents *a second thought—an emendation*.
In using it just above I have exemplified its use.
The words " an emendation " are, speaking with
reference to grammatical construction, put in
*ap*position with the words " a second thought."
Having written these latter words, I reflected whether
it would not be possible to render their meaning
more distinct by certain other words. Now, instead
of erasing the phrase " a second thought," which is
of *some* use—which *partially* conveys the idea intended
—which advances me *a step toward* my full purpose—
I suffer it to remain, and merely put a dash between
it and the phrase " an emendation." The dash gives
the reader a choice between two, or among three or
more expressions, one of which may be more forcible
than another, but all of which help out the idea.
It stands, in general, for these words—*or, to make
my meaning more distinct*. This force *it has*—and
this force no other point can have ; since all other
points have well-understood uses quite different from
this. Therefore, the dash *cannot* be dispensed with.
It has its phases—its variation of the force described ;
but the one principle—that of second thought or
emendation—will be found at the bottom of all.

RHYME

THE effect derivable from well-managed rhyme
is very imperfectly understood. Conventionally
" rhyme " implies merely close similarity of sound
at the ends of verse, and it is really curious to
observe how long mankind have been content with
their limitation of the idea. What, in rhyme, first
and principally pleases, may be referred to the human
sense or appreciation of *equality*—the common
element, as might be easily shown, of all the grati-
fication we derive from music in its most extended

sense—very especially in its modifications of metre and rhythm. We see, for example, a crystal, and are immediately interested by the equality between the sides and angles of one of its faces—but, on bringing to view a second face, in all respects similar to the first, our pleasure seems to be *squared*—on bringing to view a third, it appears to be *cubed*, and so on : I have no doubt, indeed, that the delight experienced, if measurable, would be found to have exact mathematical relations, such, or nearly such, as I suggest—that is to say, as far as a certain point, beyond which there would be a decrease, in similar relations. Now here, as the ultimate result of analysis, we reach the sense of mere *equality*, or rather the human delight in this sense ; and it was an instinct, rather than a clear comprehension of this delight as a principle, which, in the first instance, led the poet to attempt an increase of the effect arising from the mere similarity (that is to say equality) between two sounds—led him, I say, to attempt increasing this effect by making a secondary equalization, in placing the rhymes at equal distances —that is, at the ends of lines of equal length. In this manner, rhyme and the termination of the line grew connected in men's thoughts—grew into a conventionalism—the principle being lost sight of altogether. And it was simply because Pindaric verses had, before this epoch, existed—*i.e.* verses of unequal length—that rhymes were subsequently found at unequal distances. It was for this reason solely, I say—for none more profound. Rhyme had come to be regarded as of right appertaining to the *end* of verse—and here we complain that the matter has finally rested. But it is clear that there was much more to be considered. So far, the sense of *equality* alone, entered the effect ; or if this equality was slightly varied, it was varied only through an accident—the accident of the existence of Pindaric metres. It will be seen that the rhymes were always *anticipated.* The eye, catching the end of a verse,

whether long or short, expected, for the ear, a rhyme.
The great element of unexpectedness was not dreamed
of—that is to say, of novelty—of originality. " But,'
says Lord Bacon, (how justly !) " there is no exquisite
beauty without some *strangeness* in the proportions."
Take away this element of strangeness—of unex-
pectedness—of novelty—of originality—call it what
we will—and all that is *ethereal* in loveliness is lost
at once. We lose—we miss the *unknown*—the vague
—the uncomprehended because offered before we
have time to examine and comprehend. We lose,
in short, all that assimilates the beauty of earth
with what we dream of the beauty of Heaven.
Perfection of rhyme is attainable only in the com-
bination of the two elements, Equality and Unex-
pectedness. But as evil cannot exist without good,
so unexpectedness must arise from expectedness.
We do not contend for mere *arbitrariness* of rhyme.
In the first place, we must have equi-distant or
regularly recurring rhymes, to form the basis,
expectedness, out of which arises the element,
unexpectedness, by the introduction of rhymes, not
arbitrarily, but with an eye to the greatest amount
of unexpectedness. We should not introduce them,
for example, at such points that the entire line is
a multiple of the syllables preceding the points.
When, for instance, I write—

And the silken, sad, uncertain rustling of each purple curtain,

I produce more, to be sure, but not remarkably more
than the ordinary effect of rhymes regularly recurring
at the ends of lines ; for the number of syllables in
the whole verse is merely a multiple of the number
of syllables preceding the rhyme introduced at the
middle, and there is still left, therefore, a certain
degree of expectedness. What there is of the element,
unexpectedness, is addressed, in fact, to the eye
only—for the ear divides the verse into two ordinary
lines, thus :

> And the silken, sad, uncertain
> Rustling of each purple curtain

I obtain, however, the whole effect of unexpectedness, when I write—

Thrilled me, *filled* me with fantastic terrors never felt before.

N.B.—It is very commonly supposed that rhyme, as it now ordinarily exists, is of modern invention—but see the *Clouds* of Aristophanes. Hebrew verse, however, did *not* include it—the terminations of the lines, where most distinct, never showing anything of the kind.

SCHWARMEREI

THE German " *Schwarmerei* "—not exactly " humbug," but " sky-rocketing "—seems to be the only term by which we can conveniently designate that peculiar style of criticism which has lately come into fashion, through the influence of certain members of the *Fabian* family—people who live (upon beans) about Boston.

THOUGHTS AND WORDS

SOME Frenchman—possibly Montaigne—says : "People talk about thinking, but for my part I never think, except when I sit down to write." It is this never thinking, unless when we sit down to write, which is the cause of so much indifferent composition. But perhaps there is something more involved in the Frenchman's observation than meets the eye. It is certain that the mere act of inditing, tends, in a great degree, to the logicalization of thought. Whenever, on account of its vagueness, I am dissatisfied with a conception of the brain, I resort forthwith to the pen, for the purpose of obtaining, through its aid, the necessary form, consequence and precision.

How very commonly we hear it remarked, that such and such thoughts are beyond the compass of words ! I do not believe that any thought, properly so called, is out of the reach of language. I fancy, rather, that where difficulty in expression is experienced, there is, in the intellect which experiences it, a want either of deliberateness or of method. For my own part, I have never had a thought which I could not set down in words, with even more distinctness than that with which I conceived it :—as I have before observed, the thought is logicalized by the effort at (written) expression. There is, however, a class of fancies, of exquisite delicacy, which are *not* thoughts, and to which, *as yet*, I have found it absolutely impossible to adapt language. I use the word *fancies* at random, and merely because I must use *some* word ; but the idea commonly attached to the term is not even remotely applicable to the shadows of shadows in question. They seem to me rather psychal than intellectual. They arise in the soul (alas, how rarely !) only at its epochs of most intense tranquillity—when the bodily and mental health are in perfection—and at those mere points of time where the confines of the waking world blend with those of the world of dreams. I am aware of these " fancies " only when I am upon the very brink of sleep, with the consciousness that I am so. I have satisfied myself that this condition exists but for an inappreciable *point* of time—yet it is crowded with these " shadows of shadows " ; and for absolute *thought* there is demanded time's *endurance*. These " fancies " have in them a pleasurable ecstasy, as far beyond the most pleasurable of the world of wakefulness, or of dreams, as the heaven of the Northman theology is beyond its hell. I regard the visions, even as they arise, with an awe which, in some measure, moderates or tranquillizes the ecstasy—I so regard them, through a conviction (which seems a portion of the ecstasy itself) that this ecstasy, in itself, is of a character supernal to the human nature—is a glimpse of the spirit's outer world ; and I arrive at this conclusion if this term is at all applicable to instantaneous intuition by a perception that the delight experienced has, as its element, but *the absoluteness of novelty*.

I say the absoluteness—for in these fancies—let me now term them psychal impressions—there is really nothing even approximate in character to impressions ordinarily received. It is as if the five senses were supplanted by five myriad others alien to mortality.

Now, so entire is my faith in the *power of words*, that, at times, I have believed it possible to embody even the evanescence of fancies such as I have attempted to describe. In experiments with this end in view, I have proceeded so far as, first, to control (when the bodily and mental health are good) the existence of the condition :—that is to say, I can now (unless when ill) be sure that the condition will supervene, if I so wish it, at the point of time already described :—of its supervention, until lately, I could never be certain, even under the most favourable circumstances. I mean to say, merely, that now I can be sure, when all circumstances are favourable, of the supervention of the condition, and feel even the capacity of inducing or compelling it :— the favourable circumstances, however, are not the less rare—else had I compelled, already, the heaven into the earth.

I have proceeded so far, secondly, as to prevent the lapse from *the point* of which I speak—the point of blending between wakefulness and sleep—as to prevent at will, I say, the lapse from this border-ground into the dominion of sleep. Not that I can *continue* the condition—not that I can render the point more than a point—but that I can startle myself from the point into wakefulness ; *and thus transfer the point itself into the realm of Memory ;* convey its impressions, or more properly their recollections, to a situation where (although still for a very brief period) I can survey them with the eye of analysis. For these reasons—that is to say, because I have been enabled to accomplish thus much—I do not altogether despair of embodying in words at least enough of the fancies in question to convey, to certain classes of intellect, a shadowy

conception of their character. In saying this I am
not to be understood as supposing that the fancies,
or psychal impressions, to which I allude, are con-
fined to my individual self—are not, in a word,
common to all mankind—for on this point it is quite
impossible that I should form an opinion—but nothing
can be more certain than that even a partial record
of the impressions would startle the universal intel-
lect of mankind, by the *supremeness of the novelty*
of the material employed, and of its consequent sug-
gestions. In a word—should I ever write a paper on
this topic, the world will be compelled to acknowledge
that, at last, I have done an original thing.

MAGAZINES

WHATEVER may be the merits or demerits, generally,
of the Magazine Literature in America, there can be
no question as to its extent or influence. The Topic
—Magazine Literature—is therefore an important
one. In a few years its importance will be found
to have increased in geometrical ratio. The whole
tendency of the age is Magazine-ward. The Quarterly
Reviews have *never* been popular. Not only are
they too stilted, (by way of keeping up a due dignity,)
but they make a point, with the same end in view,
of discussing only topics which are *caviare* to the
many, and which, for the most part, have only a
conventional interest even with the few. Their issues,
also, are at too long intervals ; their subjects get
cold before being served up. In a word, their
ponderosity is quite out of keeping with the *rush*
of the age. We now demand the light artillery of
the intellect ; we need the curt, the condensed, the
pointed, the readily diffused—in place of the verbose,
the detailed, the voluminous, the inaccessible. On
the other hand, the lightness of the artillery should
not degenerate into popgunnery—by which term we
may designate the character of the greater portion
of the newspaper press—their sole legitimate object
being the discussion of ephemeral matters in an

ephemeral manner. Whatever talent may be brought to bear upon our daily journals, and in many cases this talent is very great, still the imperative necessity of catching, *currente calamo*, each topic as it flits before the eye of the public, must of course materially narrow the limits of their power. The bulk and the period of issue of the monthly magazines, seem to be precisely adapted, if not to all the literary wants of the day, at least to the largest and most imperative, as well as the most consequential portion of them.

IMAGINATION

THE *pure Imagination* chooses, from *either Beauty or Deformity*, only the most combinable things hitherto uncombined; the compound, as a general rule, partaking, in character, of beauty, or sublimity, in the ratio of the respective beauty or sublimity of the things combined—which are themselves still to be considered as atomic—that is to say, as previous combinations. But, as often analogously happens in physical chemistry, so not unfrequently does it occur in this chemistry of the intellect, that the admixture of two elements results in a something that has nothing of the qualities of one of them, or even nothing of the qualities of either. . . . Thus, the range of Imagination is unlimited. Its materials extend throughout the universe. Even out of deformities it fabricates that *Beauty* which is at once its sole object and its inevitable test. But, in general, the richness of force of the matters combined; the facility of discovering combinable novelties worth combining; and, especially, the absolute "chemical combination" of the completed mass—are the particulars to be regarded in our estimate of Imagination. It is this thorough harmony of an imaginative work which so often causes it to be undervalued by the thoughtless, through the character of *obviousness* which is superinduced. We are apt to find ourselves asking *why* it is that these combinations have never been imagined before.

EMERSON

WHEN I consider the true talent—the real force
of Mr. Emerson, I am lost in amazement at finding
in him little more than a respectful imitation of
Carlyle. Is it possible that Mr. E. has ever seen a
copy of Seneca ? Scarcely—or he would long ago
have abandoned his model in utter confusion at the
parallel between his own worship of the author of
Sartor Resartus and the aping of Sallust by Aruntius,
as described in the 114th Epistle. In the writer
of the *History of the Punic Wars* Emerson is por-
trayed to the life. The parallel is close ; for not
only is the imitation of the same character, but the
things imitated are identical. Undoubtedly it is to
be said of Sallust, far more plausibly than of Carlyle,
that his obscurity, his unusuality of expression, and
his Laconism (which had the effect of diffuseness,
since the time gained in the mere perusal of his
pithinesses is trebly lost in the necessity of cogitating
them out)—that these qualities bore the impress of
his genius, and were but a portion of his unaffected
thought. If there is any difference between Aruntius
and Emerson, this difference is clearly in favour of the
former, who was in some measure excusable, on the
ground that he was as great a fool as the latter *is not.*

" UNDINE "

How radically has *Undine* been misunderstood !
Beneath its obvious meaning there runs an under-
current, simple, quite intelligible, artistically managed,
and richly philosophical.

From internal evidence afforded by the book itself,
I gather that the author suffered from the ills of a
mal-arranged marriage—the bitter reflections thus
engendered, inducing the fable.

In the contrast between the artless, thoughtless,
and careless character of Undine before possessing
a soul, and her serious, enwrapt, and anxious yet
happy condition after possessing it,—a condition
which, with all its multiform disquietudes, she still

feels to be preferable to her original state,—Fouqué has beautifully painted the difference between the heart unused to *love*, and the heart which has received its inspiration.

The jealousies which follow the marriage, arising from the conduct of Bertalda, are but the natural troubles of love ; but the persecutions of Kuhleborn and the other water-spirits who take umbrage at Huldbrand's treatment of his wife, are meant to picture certain difficulties from the interference of relations in conjugal matters—difficulties which the author has himself experienced. The warning of Undine to Huldbrand—" Reproach me not upon the waters, or we part forever "—is intended to embody the truth that quarrels between man and wife are seldom or never irremediable unless when taking place in the presence of third parties. The second wedding of the knight with his gradual forgetfulness of Undine, and Undine's intense grief beneath the waters—are dwelt upon so pathetically—so passionately—that there can be no doubt of the author's personal opinions on the subject of second marriages—no doubt of his deep personal interest in the question. How thrillingly are these few and simple words made to convey his belief that the mere death of a beloved wife does not imply a separation so final or so complete as to justify an union with another !

The fisherman had loved Undine with exceeding tenderness, and it was a doubtful conclusion to his mind that the mere disappearance of his beloved child could be properly viewed as her death.

This is where the old man is endeavouring to dissuade the knight from wedding Bertalda.

I cannot say whether the novelty of the conception of *Undine*, or the loftiness and purity of its ideality, or the intensity of its pathos, or the rigour of its simplicity, or the high artistical ability with which all are combined into a well-kept, well-*motivirt* whole of absolute unity of effect—is the particular chiefly to be admired.

How delicate and graceful are the transitions from subject to subject !—a point severely testing the autorial power—as, when, for the purposes of the story, it becomes necessary that the knight, with Undine and Bertalda, shall proceed down the Danube. An ordinary novelist would have here tormented both himself and his readers, in his search for a sufficient motive for the voyage. But, in a fable such as *Undine*, how all-sufficient—how well in keeping—appears the simple motive assigned !—

In this grateful union of friendship and affection, winter came and passed away; and spring, with its foliage of tender green, and its heaven of softest blue, succeeded to gladden the hearts of the three inmates of the castle. *What wonder, then, that its storks and swallows inspired them also with a disposition to travel ?*

SUE'S "MYSTERIES OF PARIS"

I HAVE just finished the *Mysteries of Paris*—a work of unquestionable power—a museum of novel and ingenious incident—a paradox of childish folly and consummate skill. It has this point in common with all the " convulsive " fictions—that the incidents are *consequential* from the premises, while the premises themselves are laughably incredible. Admitting, for instance, the possibility of such a man as Rodolphe, and of such a state of society as would tolerate his perpetual interference, we have no difficulty in agreeing to admit the possibility of his accomplishing all that is accomplished. Another point which distinguishes the Sue school, is the total want of the *ars celare artem*. In effect the writer is always saying to the reader, " Now—in one moment—you shall see what you shall see. I am about to produce on you a remarkable impression. Prepare to have your imagination, or your pity, greatly excited." The wires are not only not concealed, but displayed as things to be admired, equally with the puppets they set in motion. The result is, that in perusing, for example, a pathetic chapter in the *Mysteries of Paris* we say to ourselves, without shedding a tear—" Now, here is something which will be sure to move every reader to tears." The philosophical motives attributed to Sue are absurd in the extreme. His first, and in fact his sole object, is to make an exciting, and therefore saleable book. The cant (implied or direct) about the amelioration of society, etc., is but a very usual trick among authors, whereby they hope to add such a tone of dignity or utilitarianism to their pages as shall gild the pill of their licentiousness. The *ruse* is even more generally employed by way of engrafting a meaning upon the otherwise unintelligible. In the latter case, however, this *ruse* is an after-thought, manifested in the shape of a moral, either appended (as in Æsop) or dovetailed into the body of the work, piece by piece, with great care, but never without leaving evidence of its after-insertion.

SHELLEY

IF ever mortal " wreaked his thoughts upon expression," it was *Shelley*. If ever poet sang—as a bird sings—earnestly—impulsively—with utter abandonment—to himself solely—and for the mere joy of his own song—that poet was the author of *The Sensitive Plant*. Of art—beyond that which is instinctive with genius—he either had little or disdained all. He *really* disdained that Rule which is an emanation from Law, because his own soul was Law in itself. His rhapsodies are but the rough notes—the stenographic memoranda of poems—memoranda which, because they were all sufficient for his own intelligence, he cared not to be at the trouble of writing out in full for mankind. In all his works we find no conception thoroughly wrought. For this reason he is the most fatiguing of poets. Yet he wearies in saying too little rather than too much. What in him, seems the diffuseness of one idea, is the conglomerate concision of many : and this species of concision it is which renders him

obscure. With such a man, to imitate was out of
the question. It would have served no purpose ;
for he spoke to his own spirit alone, which would
have comprehended no alien tongue. Thus he was
profoundly original. His quaintness arose from
intuitive perception of that truth to which Bacon
alone has given distinct utterance :—" There is no
exquisite Beauty which has not some strangeness in
its proportions." But whether obscure, original, or
quaint, Shelley had no *affectations*. He was at all
times sincere.

From his *ruins*, there sprang into existence,
affronting the heavens, a tottering and fantastic
pagoda, in which the salient angles, tipped with mad
jangling bells, were the idiosyncratic *faults* of the
original—faults which cannot be considered such in
view of his purposes, but which are monstrous when
we regard his works as addressed to mankind. A
" school " arose—if that absurd term must still be
employed—a school—a system of *rules* upon the
basis of the Shelley who had none. Young men
innumerable, dazzled with the glare and bewildered
by the *bizarrerie* of the lightning that flickered through
the clouds of *Alastor*, had no trouble whatever in
heaping up imitative vapours, but, for the lightning,
were forced to be content with its *spectrum*, in which
the *bizarrerie* appeared without the fire. Nor were
mature minds unimpressed by the contemplation
of a greater and more mature ; and thus, gradually,
into this school of all Lawlessness—of obscurity,
quaintness and exaggeration—were interwoven the
out-of-place didacticism of Wordsworth, and the
more anomalous metaphysicianism of Coleridge.
Matters were now fast verging to their worst ; and
at length, in *Tennyson* poetic inconsistency attained
its extreme. But it was precisely this extreme (for
the greatest truth and the greatest error are scarcely
two points in a circle) which, following the law of
all extremes, wrought in him (Tennyson) a natural
and inevitable revulsion ; leading him first to con-

temn, and secondly to investigate, his early manner, and finally to winnow, from its magnificent elements, the truest and purest of all poetical styles. But not even yet is the process complete; and for this reason in part, but chiefly on account of the mere fortuitousness of that mental and moral combination which shall unite in one person (if *ever* it shall) the Shelleyan *abandon* and the Tennysonian poetic sense, with the most profound Art (based both in Instinct and *Analysis*) and the sternest Will properly to blend and rigorously to control all—chiefly, I say, because such combination of seeming antagonisms will be only a " happy chance "—the world has never yet seen the noblest poem which, possibly, *can* be composed.

AMERICA AND THE CRITICS

No doubt, the association of idea is somewhat singular—but I never can hear a crowd of people singing and gesticulating, all together, at an Italian opera, without fancying myself at Athens, listening to that particular tragedy, by Sophocles, in which he introduces a full chorus of turkeys, who set about bewailing the death of Meleager. It is noticeable in this connexion, by the way, that there is not a goose in the world who, in point of sagacity, would not feel itself insulted in being compared with a turkey. The French seem to feel this. In Paris, I am sure, no one would think of saying to Mr. F——, " What a goose you are ! "—" Quel *dindon* tu es ! " would be the phrase employed as equivalent.

Alas ! how many American critics neglect the happy suggestion of M. Timon—" *que le ministre de L'Instruction Publique doit lui-même savoir parler Français.*"

It is folly to assert, as some at present are fond of asserting, that the Literature of any nation or age was ever injured by plain speaking on the part of the Critics. As for American Letters, plain-speaking about *them* is, simply, the one thing needed.

They are in a condition of absolute quagmire—a quagmire, to use the words of Victor Hugo, *d'où on ne peut se tirer par des périphrases—par des quemadmodums et des verumenimveros.*

AMERICAN NATIONALITY IN LITERATURE

MUCH has been said, of late, about the necessity of maintaining a proper *nationality* in American Letters; but what this nationality *is*, or what is to be gained by it, has never been distinctly understood. That an American should confine himself to American themes, or even prefer them, is rather a political than a literary idea—and at best is a questionable point. We would do well to bear in mind that "distance lends enchantment to the view." *Ceteris paribus*, a foreign theme is, in a strictly literary sense, to be preferred. After all, the world at large is the only legitimate stage for the autorial *histrio*.

But of the need of *that* nationality which defends our own literature, sustains our own men of letters, upholds our own dignity, and depends upon our own resources, there cannot be the shadow of a doubt. Yet here is the very point at which we are most supine. We complain of our want of an International Copyright, on the ground that this want justifies our publishers in inundating us with British opinion in British books; and yet when these very publishers, at their own obvious risk, and even obvious loss, do publish an American book, we turn up our noses at it with supreme contempt (this as a general thing) until it (the American book) has been dubbed "readable" by some illiterate Cockney critic. Is it too much to say that, with us, the opinion of Washington Irving—of Prescott—of Bryant—is a mere nullity in comparison with that of any anonymous sub-sub-editor of the *Spectator*, the *Athenæum*, or the London *Punch*? It is *not* saying too much, to say this. It is a solemn—an absolutely awful fact. Every publisher in the country will admit it to be a fact. There is not a more disgusting spectacle under the sun than our subserviency to British criticism. It is disgusting, first, because it is truckling, servile, pusillanimous—secondly, because of its gross irrationality. We *know* the British to bear us little but ill will—we know that, in no case do they utter unbiased opinions of American books —we know that in the few instances in which our writers have been treated with common decency in England, these writers have either openly paid homage to English institutions, or have had lurking at the bottom of their hearts a secret principle at war with Democracy :—we *know* all this, and yet, day after day, submit our necks to the degrading yoke of the crudest opinion that emanates from the fatherland. Now if we *must* have nationality, let it be a nationality that will throw off this yoke.

The chief of the rhapsodists who have ridden us to death like the Old Man of the Mountain, is the ignorant and egotistical Wilson. We use the term rhapsodists with perfect deliberation ; for, Macaulay, and Dilke, and one or two others, excepted, there is not in Great Britain a critic who can be fairly considered worthy the name. The Germans, and even the French, are infinitely superior. As regards Wilson, no man ever penned worse criticism or better rodomontade. That he is " egotistical " his works show to all men, running as they read. That he is " ignorant " let his absurd and continuous schoolboy blunders about Homer bear witness. Not long ago we ourselves pointed out a series of similar inanities in his review of Miss Barrett's poems—a series, we say, of gross blunders, arising from sheer ignorance—and we defy him or anyone to answer a single syllable of what we then advanced.

And yet this is the man whose simple *dictum* (to our shame be it spoken) has the power to make or to mar any American reputation ! In the last number of *Blackwood,* he has a continuation of the dull "Specimens of the British Critics," and makes

occasion wantonly to insult one of the noblest of
our poets, Mr. Lowell. The point of the whole
attack consists in the use of slang epithets and
phrases of the most ineffably vulgar description.
" Squabashes " is a pet term. " Faugh ! " is another.
"We are Scotsmen to *the spine !*" says Sawney—as if
the thing were not more than self-evident. Mr.
Lowell is called " a magpie," an " ape," a " Yankee
cockney," and his name is intentionally miswritten
John Russell Lowell. Now were these indecencies
perpetrated by an American critic, that critic would
be sent to Coventry by the whole press of the country,
but since it is Wilson who insults, we, as in duty
bound, not only submit to the insult, but echo it,
as an excellent jest, throughout the length and
breadth of the land. *Quamdiu Catilina ?* We do
indeed demand the nationality of self-respect. In
Letters as in Government we require a Declaration
of Independence. A better thing still would be a
Declaration of War—and that war should be carried
forthwith " into Africa."

THE ELDER POETS

IT cannot, we think, be a matter of doubt with
any reflecting mind, that at least one-third of the
reverence, or of the *affection*, with which we regard
the elder poets of Great Britain, should be credited
to what is, in itself, a thing apart from poetry—we
mean to the simple love of the antique—and that
again a third and even the proper *poetic sentiment*
inspired by these writings should be ascribed to a
fact which, while it has a strict connexion with
poetry in the abstract, and also with the particular
poems in question, must not be looked upon as a
merit appertaining to the writers of the poems.
Almost every devout reader of the old English bards,
if demanded his opinion of their productions, would
mention vaguely, yet with perfect sincerity, a sense
of dreamy, wild, indefinite, and, he would perhaps
say, undefinable delight. Upon being required to

point out the source of this so shadowy pleasure, he would be apt to speak of the quaint in phraseology and of the grotesque in rhythm. And this quaintness and grotesqueness are, as we have elsewhere endeavoured to show, very powerful, and, if well managed, very admissible adjuncts to ideality. But in the present instance they arise independently of the author's will, and are matters altogether apart from his intention.

MEN OF GENIUS

MEN of genius are far more abundant than is supposed. In fact, to appreciate thoroughly the work of what we call genius, is to possess all the genius by which the work was produced. But the person appreciating may be utterly incompetent to reproduce the work, or anything similar, and this solely through lack of what may be termed the constructive ability—a matter quite independent of what we agree to understand in the term "genius" itself. This ability is based, to be sure, in great part, upon the faculty of analysis, enabling the artist to get full view of the machinery of his proposed effect, and thus work it and regulate it at will; but a great deal depends also upon properties strictly moral—for example, upon patience, upon concentrativeness, or the power of holding the attention steadily to the one purpose, upon self-dependence and contempt for all opinion which is opinion and no more—in especial, upon energy or industry. So vitally important is this last, that it may well be doubted if anything to which we have been accustomed to give the title of a "work of genius" was ever accomplished without it, and it is chiefly because this quality and genius are nearly incompatible, that "works of genius" are few, while mere men of genius are, as I say, abundant. The Romans, who excelled us in acuteness of *observation*, while falling below us in induction from facts observed, seem to have been so fully aware of the inseparable connexion between industry and a "work of genius," as to have adopted the error that industry, in great measure, was genius itself. The highest compliment is intended by a Roman, when, of an epic, or anything similar, he says that it is written *industriâ mirabili* or *incredibili industriâ*.

BULWER LYTTON

WE have long learned to reverence the fine intellect of Bulwer. We take up any production of his pen with a positive certainty that, in reading it, the wildest passions of our nature, the most profound of our thoughts, the brightest visions of our fancy, and the most ennobling and lofty of our aspirations will, in due turn, be enkindled within us. We feel sure of rising from the perusal a wiser if not a better man. In no instance are we deceived. From the brief tale—from the *Monos and Daimonos* of the author—to his most ponderous and laboured novels —all is richly, and glowingly intellectual—all is energetic, or astute, or brilliant, or profound. There *may* be men now living who possess the power of Bulwer—but it is quite evident that very few have made that power so palpably manifest. Indeed we know of *none*. Viewing him as a novelist—a point of view exceedingly unfavourable (if we hold to the common acceptation of " the novel ") for a proper contemplation of his genius—he is unsurpassed by any writer living or dead. Why should we hesitate to say this, feeling, as we do, thoroughly persuaded of its truth ? Scott has excelled him in *many* points and *The Bride of Lammermoor* is a better book than any individual work by the author of *Pelham—Ivanhoe* is, perhaps, equal to any. Descending to particulars, D'Israeli has a more brilliant, a more lofty, and a more delicate (we do not say a *wilder*) imagination. Lady Dacre has written *Ellen Wareham*, a more forcible tale of passion. In some species of wit Theodore Hook rivals, and in broad humour our own Paulding surpasses him. The writer of

Godolphin equals him in energy. Banim is a better sketcher of character. Hope is a richer colourist. Captain Trelawney is as original—Moore is as fanciful, and Horace Smith is as learned. But who is there, uniting in one person the imagination, the passion, the humour, the energy, the knowledge of the heart, the artist-like eye, the originality, the fancy, and the learning of Edward Lytton Bulwer? In a vivid wit—in profundity and a Gothic massiveness of thought—in style—in a calm certainty and definitiveness of purpose—in industry—and above all, in the power of controlling and regulating by volition his illimitable faculties of mind, he is unequalled—he is unapproached.

TOM HOOD

"FREQUENTLY since his recent death," says the American editor of Hood, "he has been called a great author—a phrase used not inconsiderately or in vain." Yet, if we adopt the conventional idea of "a great author," there has lived, perhaps, no writer of the last half century who, with equal notoriety, was less entitled than Hood to be so called. In fact, he was a literary merchant, whose main stock in trade was *littleness*; for, during the larger portion of his life, he seemed to breathe only for the purpose of perpetrating puns—things of so despicable a platitude that the man who is capable of habitually committing them, is seldom found capable of anything else. Whatever merit *may* be discovered in a pun, arises altogether from *unexpectedness*. This is the pun's element and is twofold. First, we demand that the *combination* of the pun be unexpected; and, secondly, we require the most entire unexpectedness in the pun *per se*. A rare pun, rarely appearing, is, to a certain extent, a pleasurable effect; but to no mind, however debased in taste, is a continuous effort at punning otherwise than unendurable. The man who maintains that he derives gratification from any such chapters of punnage as Hood was in the daily practice of committing to paper, should not be credited upon oath.

The puns of the author of *Fair Inez*, however, are to be regarded as the weak points of the man. Independently of their ill effect, in a literary view, as mere puns, they leave upon us a painful impression ; for too evidently they are the hypochondriac's struggles at mirth—the grinnings of the death's-head. No one can read his *Literary Reminiscences* without being convinced of his habitual despondency :—and the species of false wit in question is precisely of that character which would be adopted by an author of Hood's temperament and cast of intellect, when compelled to write at an emergency. That his heart had no interest in these *niaiseries*, is clear. I allude, of course, to his *mere* puns for the pun's sake—a class of letters by which he attained his widest renown. That he did *more* in this way than in any other, is but a corollary from what I have already said, for, generally, he was unhappy, and almost continually he wrote *invitâ Minerva*. But his true province was a very rare and ethereal *humour*, in which the mere pun was left out of sight, or took the character of the richest *grotesquerie* ; impressing the imaginative reader with remarkable force, as if by a new phase of the ideal. It is in this species of brilliant, or, rather, *glowing* grotesquerie, uttered with a rushing *abandon* vastly heightening its effect, that Hood's marked originality mainly consisted :—and it is this which entitles him, at times, to the epithet " great " :—for *that* undeniably may be considered great (of whatever seeming littleness in itself) which is capable of inducing intense emotion in the minds or hearts of those who are themselves undeniably great.

The field in which Hood is *distinctive* is a borderland between Fancy and Fantasy. In this region he reigns supreme. Nevertheless, he has made successful and frequent incursions, although vacillatingly, into the domain of the true Imagination.

I mean to say that he is never truly or purely imaginative for more than a paragraph at a time. In a word, his peculiar genius was the result of vivid *Fancy* impelled by Hypochondriasis.

LORD BYRON AND MARY CHAWORTH

" *Les anges*," says Madame Dudevant, a woman who intersperses many an admirable sentiment amid a chaos of the most shapeless and altogether objectionable fiction—" *Les anges ne sont plus pures que le cœur d'un jeune homme qui aimé en vérité.*" The angels are not more pure than the heart of a young man who loves with fervour. The hyperbole is scarcely less than true. It would be truth itself were it averred of the love of him who is at the same time young and a poet. The boyish poet-love is indisputably that one of the human sentiments which most nearly realizes our dreams of the chastened voluptuousness of heaven.

In every allusion made by the author of *Childe Harold* to his passion for Mary Chaworth, there runs a vein of almost spiritual tenderness and purity, strongly in contrast with the gross earthliness pervading and disfiguring his ordinary love-poems. *The Dream*, in which the incidents of his parting with her when about to travel, are said to be delineated, or at least paralleled, has never been excelled (certainly never excelled by him) in the blended fervour, delicacy, truthfulness and ethereality which sublimate and adorn it. For this reason, it may well be doubted if he has written anything so universally popular. That his attachment for this " Mary " (in whose very name there indeed seemed to exist for him an " enchantment ") was earnest, and long-abiding, we have every reason to believe. There are a hundred evidences of this fact, scattered not only through his own poems and letters, but in the memoirs of his relatives, and cotemporaries in general. But that it *was* thus earnest and enduring, does not controvert, in any degree, the opinion that it was a passion (if passion it can properly be termed) of the most thoroughly romantic, shadowy and imaginative character. It was born of the hour, and of the youthful necessity to love, while it was nurtured by the waters and the hills, and the flowers, and the stars. It had no peculiar regard to the person, or to the character, or to the reciprocating affection of Mary Chaworth. Any maiden, not immediately and positively repulsive, he would have loved, under the same circumstances of hourly and unrestricted communion, such as the engravings of the subject shadow forth. They met without restraint and without reserve. As mere children they sported together ; in boyhood and girlhood they read from the same books, sang the same songs, or roamed hand in hand through the grounds of the conjoining estates. The result was not merely natural or merely probable, it was as inevitable as destiny itself.

In view of a passion thus engendered, Miss Chaworth, (who is represented as possessed of no little personal beauty and some accomplishments,) could not have failed to serve sufficiently well as the incarnation of the ideal that haunted the fancy of the poet. It is perhaps better, nevertheless, for the mere romance of the love-passages between the two, that their intercourse was broken up in early life and never uninterruptedly resumed in after years. Whatever of warmth, whatever of soul-passion, whatever of the truer nare and essentiality of romance was elicited during the youthful association is to be attributed altogether to the poet. If *she* felt at all, it was only while the magnetism of *his* actual presence compelled her to feel. If *she* responded at all, it was merely because the necromancy of *his* words of fire could not do otherwise than exhort a response. In absence, the bard bore easily with him all the fancies which were the basis of his flame—a flame which absence itself but served to keep in vigour—while the less ideal but at the same time the less really substantial affection of his lady-love, perished utterly and forthwith, through simple lack of the element which had fanned it into being. He to her, in brief, was a not unhandsome, and not ignoble, but somewhat portionless, somewhat eccentric and rather lame young man. She to him was the Egeria of his dreams—the Venus Aphrodite that sprang, in full and supernal loveliness, from the bright foam upon the storm-tormented ocean of his thoughts.

"THE LADY OF LYONS"

A HUNDRED criticisms to the contrary notwithstanding, I must regard *The Lady of Lyons* as one of the most successful dramatic efforts of modern times. It is popular, and justly so. It could not fail to be popular so long as the people have a heart. It abounds in sentiments which stir the soul as the sound of a trumpet. It proceeds rapidly and consequentially ; the interest not for one moment being permitted to flag. Its incidents are admirably conceived and skilfully wrought into execution. Its *dramatis personæ*, throughout, have the high merit of being natural, although, except in the case of Pauline, there is no marked individuality. She is a creation which would have done no dishonour to Shakespeare. She excites profound emotion. It has been sillily objected to her, that she is weak, mercenary, and at points ignoble. She is ; and what then ? We are not dealing with Clarissa Harlowe. Bulwer has painted a woman. The chief defect of the play lies in the heroine's consenting to wed Beauseant, while aware of the existence and even the continued love of Claude. As the plot runs, there is a question in Pauline's soul between a comparatively trivial (because merely worldly) injury to her father, and utter ruin and despair inflicted upon her husband. Here there should not have been an instant's hesitation. The audience have no sympathy with any. Nothing on earth should have induced the wife to give up the living Melnotte.

Only the assurance of his death could have justified her in sacrificing herself to Beauseant. As it is, we hate her for the sacrifice. The effect is repulsive—but I must be understood as calling this effect objectionable solely on the ground of its being at war with the whole genius of the play.

WHAT IS POETRY?

If need were, I should have little difficulty, perhaps, in defending a certain apparent dogmatism to which I am prone, on the topic of versification.

"What is Poetry?" notwithstanding Leigh Hunt's rigmarolic attempt at answering it, is a query that, with great care and deliberate agreement beforehand on the exact value of certain leading words, *may*, possibly, be settled to the partial satisfaction of a few analytical intellects, but which, in the existing condition of metaphysics, never *can* be settled to the satisfaction of the majority; for the question is purely metaphysical, and the whole science of metaphysics is at present a chaos, through the impossibility of fixing the meanings of the words which its very nature compels it to employ. But as regards versification, this difficulty is only partial; for although one-third of the topic may be considered metaphysical, and thus may be mooted at the fancy of this individual or of that, still the remaining two-thirds belong, undeniably, to the mathematics. The questions ordinarily discussed with so much gravity in regard to rhythm, metre, etc., are susceptible of positive adjustment by demonstration. Their laws are merely a portion of the Median laws of form and quantity—of relation. In respect, then, to any of these ordinary questions—these sillily moot points which so often arise in common criticism—the prosodist would speak as weakly in saying "this or that proposition is *probably* so and so, or *possibly* so and so," as would the mathematician in admitting that, in his humble opinion, or if he were not greatly mistaken, any two sides of a triangle were, together, greater than the third side. I must add, however, as some palliation of the discussions referred to, and of the objections so often urged with a sneer to "particular theories of versification binding no one but their inventor"—that there is really extant no such work as a Prosody *Raisonnée*. The Prosodies of the schools are merely collections of vague *laws*, with their more vague exceptions, based upon no principles whatever, but extorted in the most speculative manner from the usages of the ancients, who had *no* laws beyond those of their ears and fingers. "And these were sufficient," it will be said, "since the Iliad is melodious and harmonious beyond anything of modern times." Admit this :—but neither do we write in Greek, nor has the invention of modern times been as yet exhausted. An analysis based on the natural laws of which the bard of Scios was ignorant, would suggest multitudinous improvements to the best passages of even the Iliad—nor does it in any manner follow from the supposititious fact that Homer found in his ears and fingers a satisfactory system of rules (the point which I have just denied)—nor does it follow, I say, from this, that the rules which *we* deduce from the Homeric *effects* are to supersede those immutable principles of time, quantity, etc.—the mathematics, in short, of music— which must have stood to these Homeric effects in the relation of *causes*—the *mediate* causes of which these "ears and fingers" are simply the *intermedia*.

"THE OLD CURIOSITY SHOP"

THE great feature of the *Curiosity Shop* is its chaste, vigorous, and glorious *imagination*. This is the one charm, all potent, which alone would suffice to compensate for a world more of error than Mr. Dickens ever committed. It is not only seen in the conception, and general handling of the story, or in the invention of character ; but it pervades every sentence of the book. We recognize its prodigious influence in every inspired word. It is this which induces the reader who is at all ideal, to pause frequently, to re-read the occasionally quaint phrases, to muse in uncontrollable delight over thoughts which, while he wonders he has never hit upon them before, he yet admits that he never has encountered. In fact, it is the wand of the enchanter.

Had we room to particularise, we would mention as points evincing most distinctly the ideality of the *Curiosity Shop*—the picture of the shop itself—the newly-born desire of the worldly old man for the peace of green fields—his whole character and conduct, in short—the schoolmaster, with his desolate fortunes, seeking affection in little children—the haunts of Quilp among the wharf-rats—the tinkering of the Punch-men among the tombs—the glorious scene where the man of the forge sits poring, at deep midnight, into that dread fire—again the whole conception of this character ; and, last and greatest, the stealthy approach of Nell to her death—her gradual sinking away on the journey to the village, so skilfully indicated rather than described—her pensive and prescient meditation—the fit of strange musing which came over her when the house *in which she was to die* first broke upon her sight—the description of this house, of the old church, and of the churchyard—everything in rigid consonance with the one impression to be conveyed—that deep meaningless well—the comments of the Sexton upon death, and upon his own secure life—this whole world of mournful yet peaceful idea merging, at length, into the decease of the child Nelly, and the uncomprehending despair of the grandfather. These concluding scenes are so drawn that human language, urged by human thought, could go no farther in the excitement of human feelings. And the pathos is of that best order which is relieved, in great measure, by ideality. Here the book has never been equalled, —never approached except in one instance, and that is in the case of the *Undine* of De la Motte Fouqué. The imagination is perhaps as great in this latter work, but the pathos, although truly beautiful and deep, fails of much of its effect through the material from which it is wrought. The chief character, being endowed with purely fanciful attributes, cannot command our full sympathies, as can a simple denizen of earth. In saying, a page or so above, that the death of the child left too painful an impression, and should therefore have been avoided, we must, of course, be understood as referring to the work as a whole, and in respect to its general appreciation and popularity. The death, as recorded, is, we repeat, of the highest order of literary excellence —yet while none can deny this fact, there are few who will be willing to read the concluding passages a second time.

Upon the whole we think the *Curiosity Shop* very much the best of the works of Mr. Dickens. It is scarcely possible to speak of it too well. It is in all respects a tale which will secure for its author the enthusiastic admiration of every man of genius.

TENNYSON

I AM not sure that Tennyson is not the greatest of poets. The uncertainty attending the public conception of the term " poet " alone prevents me from demonstrating that he *is*. Other bards produce effects which are, now and then, otherwise produced than by what we call poems ; but Tennyson an effect which only a poem does. His alone are idiosyncratic poems. By the enjoyment or non-enjoyment of the *Morte d'Arthur*, or of the *Œnone*, I would test any one's ideal sense. There are passages in his works which rivet a conviction I had long entertained, that the *indefinite* is an element in the true $\pi o \iota \eta \sigma \iota \varsigma$. Why do some persons fatigue themselves in attempts to unravel such fantasy-pieces as the *Lady of Shalott* ? As well unweave the " *ventum textilem.*" If the author did not deliberately propose to himself a suggestive indefinitiveness of meaning, with the view of bringing about a definitiveness of vague and

therefore of spiritual *effect*—this, at least, arose from
the silent analytical promptings of that poetic genius
which, in its supreme development, embodies all
orders of intellectual capacity. I *know* that indefini-
tiveness is an element of the true music—I mean
of the true musical expression. Give to it any
undue decision—imbue it with any very determinate
tone—and you deprive it, at once, of its ethereal,
its ideal, its intrinsic and essential character. You
dispel its luxury of dream. You dissolve the atmo-
sphere of the mystic upon which it floats. You exhaust
it of its breath of faery. It now becomes a tangible
and easily appreciable idea—a thing of the earth,
earthy. It has not, indeed, lost its power to please,
but all which I consider the distinctiveness of that
power. And to the uncultivated talent, or to the
unimaginative apprehension, this deprivation of its
most delicate nare will be, not unfrequently, a
recommendation. A determinateness of expression
is sought—and often by composers who should know
better—is sought as a beauty rather than rejected
as a blemish. Thus we have, even from high
authorities, attempts at absolute *imitation* in music.
Who can forget the silliness of the *Battle of Prague* ?
What man of taste but must laugh at the intermin-
able drums, trumpets, blunderbuses, and thunder ?
" *Vocal* music," says l'Abbate Gravina, who would
have said the same thing of instrumental, " ought
to imitate the natural language of the human
feelings and passions, rather than the warblings of
Canary birds, which our sin ers, nowadays, affect
so vastly to mimic with their quaverings and boasted
caden es." This is true only so far as the " rather "
is concerned. If any music must imitate anything,
it were assuredly better to limit the imitation as
Gravina suggests. Tennyson's shorter pieces abound
in minute rhythmical lapses sufficient to assure me
that—in common with all poets living or dead—he
has neglected to make precise investigation of the

perfect is his rhythmical instinct in general, that, like the present Viscount Canterbury, he seems *to see with his ear.*

DEFOE

WHILE Defoe would have been fairly entitled to immortality had he never written *Robinson Crusoe,* yet his many other very excellent writings have nearly faded from our attention, in the superior lustre of the Adventures of the Mariner of York. What better possible species of reputation could the author have desired for that book than the species which it has so long enjoyed? It has become a household thing in nearly every family in Christendom. Yet never was admiration of any work—universal admiration—more indiscriminately or more inappropriately bestowed. Not one person in ten—nay, not one person in five hundred, has, during the perusal of *Robinson Crusoe,* the most remote conception that any particle of genius, or even of common talent, has been employed in its creation! Men do not look upon it in the light of a literary performance. Defoe has none of their thoughts—Robinson all. The powers which have wrought the wonder have been thrown into obscurity by the very stupendousness of the wonder they have wrought! We read, and become perfect abstractions in the intensity of our interest—we close the book, and are quite satisfied that we could have written as well ourselves. All this is effected by the potent magic of verisimilitude. Indeed, the author of *Crusoe* must have possessed, above all other faculties, what has been termed the faculty of *identification*—that dominion exercised by volition over imagination which enables the mind to lose its own, in a fictitious, individuality. This includes, in a very great degree, the power of abstraction; and with these keys we may partially unlock the mystery of that spell which has so long invested the volume before us. But a complete analysis of our interest in it cannot be thus afforded. Defoe is largely indebted to his subject. The idea of man in a state of perfect isolation, although often entertained, was never before so comprehensively carried out. Indeed, the frequency of its occurrence to the thoughts of mankind argued the extent of its influence on their sympathies, while the fact of no attempt having been made to give an embodied form to the conception, went to prove the difficulty of the undertaking. But the true narrative of Selkirk in 1711, with the powerful impression it then made upon the public mind, sufficed to inspire Defoe with both the necessary courage for his work and entire confidence in its success. How wonderful has been the result !

MAGAZINE LITERATURE

THE increase, within a few years, of the magazine literature, is by no means to be regarded as indicating what some critics would suppose it to indicate—a downward tendency in American taste or in American letters. It is but a sign of the times—an indication of an era in which men are forced upon the curt, the condensed, the well-digested—in place of the voluminous—in a word, upon journalism in lieu of dissertation. We need now the light artillery rather than the Peace-makers of the intellect. I will not be sure that men at present think more profoundly than half a century ago, but beyond question they think with more rapidity, with more skill, with more tact, with more of method and less of excrescence in the thought. Besides all this, they have a vast increase in the thinking material'; they have more facts, more to think about. For this reason, they are disposed to put the greatest amount of thought in the smallest compass and disperse it with the utmost attainable rapidity. Hence the journalism of the age ; hence, in especial, magazines. Too many we cannot have, as a general proposition ; but we demand that they have sufficient merit to render them noticeable in the beginning, and that they continue in existence sufficiently long to permit us a fair estimation of their value.

LISTENERS' LURE

ONE half the pleasure experienced at a theatre arises from the spectator's sympathy with the rest of the audience, and, especially, from his belief in their sympathy with him. The eccentric gentleman who not long ago, at the Park, found himself the solitary occupant of box, pit, and gallery, would have derived but little enjoyment from his visit, had he been suffered to remain. It was an act of mercy to turn him out. The present absurd rage for lecturing is founded in the feeling in question. Essays which we would not be hired to read—so trite is their subject—so feeble is their execution—so much easier is it to get better information on similar themes out of any encyclopædia in Christendom—we are brought to tolerate, and alas, even to applaud in their tenth and twentieth repetition, through the sole force of our sympathy with the throng. In the same way we listen to a story with greater zest when there are others present at its narration beside ourselves. Aware of this, authors without due reflection hav erepeatedly attempted, by supposing a circle of listeners, to imbue their narratives with the interest of sympathy. At a cursory glance the idea seems plausible enough. But, in the one case, there is an actual, personal, and palpable sympathy, conveyed in looks, gestures and brief comments—a sympathy of real individuals, all with the matters discussed to be sure, but then especially, *each with each*. In the other instance, we, alone in our closet, are required to sympathise *with* the sympathy of fictitious listeners, who, so far from being present in body, are often studiously kept out of sight and out of mind for two or three hundred pages at a time. This is sympathy double-diluted—the shadow of a shade. It is unnecessary to say that the design invariably fails of its effect.

POEMS PUBLISHED
BEFORE 1845

THE HAPPIEST DAY, THE HAPPIEST HOUR

[Tamerlane and other Poems, 1827.]

THE happiest day—the happiest hour
  My sear'd and blighted heart hath known,
The highest hope of pride and power,
  I feel hath flown.

Of power! said I? yes! such I ween;
  But they have vanish'd long, alas!
The visions of my youth have been—
  But let them pass.

And, pride, what have I now with thee?
  Another brow may even inherit
The venom thou hast pour'd on me—
  Be still, my spirit!

The happiest day—the happiest hour
  Mine eyes shall see—have ever seen,
The brightest glance of pride and power,
  I feel—have been:

But were that hope of pride and power
  Now offer'd, with the pain
Even *then* I felt—that brightest hour
  I would not live again:

For on its wing was dark alloy,
  And, as it flutter'd—fell
An essence—powerful to destroy
  A soul that knew it well.

343

STANZAS

[Tamerlane and other Poems, 1827.]

How often we forget all time, when lone
Admiring Nature's universal throne;
Her woods—her wilds—her mountains—the intense
Reply of HERS to OUR intelligence!

[BYRON, *The Island.*]

I

IN youth have I known one with whom the Earth
In secret communing held—as he with it,
In daylight, and in beauty from his birth:
Whose fervid, flickering torch of life was lit
From the sun and stars, whence he had drawn forth
A passionate light—such for his spirit was fit—
And yet the spirit knew not, in the hour
Of its own fervour, what had o'er it power.

2

Perhaps it may be that my mind is wrought
To a fever by the moonbeams that hangs o'er,
But I will half believe that wild light fraught
With more of sovreignty than ancient lore
Hath ever told—or is it of a thought
The unembodied essence, and no more,
That with a quickening spell doth o'er us pass
As dew of the night-time o'er the summer grass?

3

Doth o'er us pass, when, as th' expanding eye
To the loved object—so the tear to the lid
Will start, which lately slept in apathy?
And yet it need not be—(that object) hid
From us in life—but common—which doth lie
Each hour before us—but *then* only, bid
With a strange sound, as of a harp-string broken,
To awake us—'Tis a symbol and a token

4

Of what in other worlds shall be—and given
In beauty by our God, to those alone
Who otherwise would fall from life and Heaven
Drawn by their heart's passion, and that tone,
That high tone of the spirit which hath striven
Tho' not with Faith—with godliness—whose throne
With desperate energy 't hath beaten down;
Wearing its own deep feeling as a crown.

EVENING STAR

[Tamerlane and other Poems, 1827.]

'TWAS noontide of summer
    And mid-time of night;
And stars, in their orbits,
    Shone pale, thro' the light
Of the brighter, cold moon,
    'Mid planets her slaves,
Herself in the Heavens,
    Her beam on the waves.
        I gazed awhile
        On her cold smile;
Too cold—too cold for me—
    There pass'd, as a shroud,
    A fleecy cloud,
And I turn'd away to thee,
    Proud Evening Star,
    In thy glory afar,
And dearer thy beam shall be;
    For joy to my heart
    Is the proud part
Thou bearest in Heaven at night,
    And more I admire
    Thy distant fire,
Than that colder, lowly light.

DREAMS

[Tamerlane and other Poems, 1827.]

OH! that my young life were a lasting dream!
My spirit not awakening, till the beam
Of an Eternity should bring the morrow.
Yes! tho' that long dream were of hopeless sorrow,
'Twere better than the cold reality
Of waking life, to him whose heart must be,
And hath been still, upon the lovely earth,
A chaos of deep passion, from his birth.
But should it be—that dream eternally
Continuing—as dreams have been to me
In my young boyhood—should it thus be given,
'Twere folly still to hope for higher Heaven.
For I have revell'd, when the sun was bright
I' the summer sky, in dreams of living light
And loveliness,—have left my very heart
In climes of my imagining, apart
From mine own home, with beings that have been
Of mine own thought—what more could I have seen?
'Twas once—and only once—and the wild hour
From my remembrance shall not pass—some power
Or spell had bound me—'twas the chilly wind
Came o'er me in the night, and left behind
Its image on my spirit—or the moon
Shone on my slumbers in her lofty noon
Too coldly—or the stars—howe'er it was
That dream was as that night-wind—let it pass.
I *have been* happy, tho' in a dream.
I have been happy—and I love the theme:
Dreams! in their vivid colouring of life,
As in that fleeting, shadowy, misty strife
Of semblance with reality, which brings
To the delirious eye, more lovely things
Of Paradise and Love—and all our own!
Than young Hope in his sunniest hour hath known.

SPIRITS OF THE DEAD

[Al Aaraaf, Tamerlane, and Minor Poems, 1829.]

THY soul shall find itself alone
'Mid dark thoughts of the grey tomb-stone;
Not one, of all the crowd, to pry
Into thine hour of secrecy.

Be silent in that solitude,
    Which is not loneliness—for then
The spirits of the dead, who stood
    In life before thee, are again
In death around thee, and their will
Shall overshadow thee; be still.

The night, though clear, shall frown,
And the stars shall not look down
From their high thrones in the Heaven
With light like hope to mortals given,
But their red orbs, without beam,
To thy weariness shall seem
As a burning and a fever
Which would cling to thee for ever.

Now are thoughts thou shalt not banish,
Now are visions ne'er to vanish;
From thy spirit shall they pass
No more, like dew-drops from the grass.

The breeze, the breath of God, is still,
And the mist upon the hill
Shadowy, shadowy, yet unbroken,
Is a symbol and a token.
How it hangs upon the trees,
A mystery of mysteries!

TO M——

[*Al Aaraaf, Tamerlane, and Minor Poems,* 1829.]

O! I care not that my earthly lot
 Hath little of Earth in it,
That years of love have been forgot
 In the fever of a minute:

I heed not that the desolate
 Are happier, sweet, than I,
But that you meddle with my fate
 Who am a passer by.

It *is* not that my founts of bliss
 Are gushing—strange! with tears—
Or that the thrill of a single kiss
 Hath palsied many years—

'Tis not that the flowers of twenty springs
 Which have wither'd as they rose
Lie dead on my heart-strings
 With the weight of an age of snows.

Not that the grass—O! may it thrive!
 On my grave is growing or grown—
But that, while I am dead yet alive
 I cannot be, lady, alone.